# THE FORESIGHT WAR

*An alternative history of World War 2*

by

Anthony G Williams

Visit us online at www.authorsonline.co.uk

An AuthorsOnLine Book

Copyright © Authors OnLine Ltd 2004

Text Copyright © Anthony G Williams

Cover design by Tim O'Brien and James Fitt

All rights reserved. No part of this publication may be reproduced, stored in a retrieval system, or transmitted in any form or by any means, electronic, mechanical, photocopy, recording or otherwise, without prior written permission of the copyright owner. Nor can it be circulated in any form of binding or cover other than that in which it is published and without similar condition including this condition being imposed on a subsequent purchaser.

ISBN 0 7552 0156 6

Authors OnLine Ltd
40 Castle Street
Hertford SG14 1HR
England

This book is also available in e-book format, details of which are available at
www.authorsonline.co.uk

Anthony G Williams is a military technology historian. He is the author of 'Rapid Fire: The Development of Automatic Cannon, Heavy Machine Guns and their Ammunition for Armies, Navies and Air Forces', and the co-author of 'Assault Rifle: the Development of the Modern Military Rifle and its Ammunition' (with Maxim Popenker) and the three-volume series 'Flying Guns: Development of Aircraft Guns, Ammunition and Installations' (with Emmanuel Gustin). 'The Foresight War' is his first novel. He maintains a website at:

http://www.quarry.nildram.co.uk

# CHAPTER 1 - THROWBACK

He woke, and instantly wished that he hadn't. The throbbing headache which consumed him seemed to extend beyond his head into every part of his body. He began to moan, but stopped abruptly as the ache intensified. He lay unmoving, gritting his teeth, enduring in silent desperation.

After an indeterminate period, the pain subsided enough to risk an attempt at coherent thought. What on earth had he done last night? He was not a heavy drinker, and besides, the worst hangover he could recall was a pale shadow of this suffering. Had he been in an accident? Fallen ill? He gingerly searched his memory, but could find nothing to account for such appalling agony. The pain gradually dimmed further. Slowly, he opened his eyes to the dull light of early morning.

He was lying on his back, staring at a ceiling. The ceiling was plain, with an old-fashioned frilly lampshade surrounding the single bulb. The lampshade stayed steady and his head remained intact. Adventurously, he turned his head sideways and immediately shut his eyes to ward off the surge of nausea. Time passed. Slowly, he opened his eyes again. No reaction. He took stock of what he could see.

The wallpaper was dull and also old-fashioned. So was the varnished wooden door and the brown Bakelite light switch next to it. Puzzlement began to grow. He was certainly not in his bedroom, nor in anyone else's that he recognised. Curiosity overcoming the gradually receding pain, he raised his head. A thin, brass curtain rail, suspending thin, drab curtains, framed a sash window. A further effort brought a pair of discoloured brass taps into view, followed by a porcelain washbasin on a metal stand, framed and partly obscured by the foot of a brass bedstead. A pair of brown leather shoes completed his field of view. He wiggled his feet and the shoes moved in sympathy. Turning his head to the other side, he saw a large wardrobe in dark wood. There was nothing else in the room, apart from a wooden chair on which sat his holdall.

Experimentally he tried moving his legs. They obeyed orders promptly. The pain was fading rapidly now, and he swung his legs over the side of the bed with more confidence. Slowly sitting upright, he took stock.

He appeared to be uninjured, and although weak and shaky, did not feel ill. He was fully dressed, still possessed a full wallet and his keys, and he confirmed (after a careful stretch to the chair) that his holdall retained its usual contents. Not a robbery, then. A careful shuffle to the end of the bed gave him a limited view of rooftops with a larger structure some distance beyond. At first, the rooftops caught his attention. There was something odd about them. The wisps of smoke rising from the chimneys was an unusual sight, but he suddenly realised that what puzzled him wasn't anything he could see, but something he couldn't see: there were no aerials; not a satellite dish, not even the most humble antenna.

Something else nagged at him. He looked at the structure in the distance. It appeared to be an enormous, barrel-roofed greenhouse with towers at each end. He stared at it blankly, until he gradually realised that his memory was telling him what it was, but his mind was refusing to accept the data. He was looking at the Crystal Palace.

For a long time he sat unmoving, his mind jammed by the utter impossibility of the evidence of his eyes. Slowly, his thoughts unfroze. He could not deny what he was seeing: the pride of the Great Exhibition of 1851, moved from Hyde Park to a permanent home at Sydenham Hill, destroyed by fire in the 1930s.

Destroyed by fire in the 1930s – nearly seventy years ago! His mind locked again and he fought desperately to regain some equilibrium. He tried to think logically, to build on small steps. How did he know this was the Crystal Palace? Because he had seen pictures a hundred times, there was nothing of this size remotely like it. How did he know when it was destroyed? Because he was a historian, it was his business to know. So which year did he think he was in? 2004, at the end of the summer. How did he know that? Because he was a lecturer at London University, preparing for the next academic year. Knowledge flooded back into him as if a dam had burst.

His name was Don, Dr Don Erlang. He repeated this out loud, to make sure it sounded right. The sound of his own voice in the quiet room startled him. He was forty years old, divorced five years ago, living alone in a flat in Kennington. He couldn't possibly be seeing the view out of the window, and as he never took hallucinogens he must be experiencing an extremely vivid dream. Feeling very self-conscious, he pinched himself hard. It hurt. The Crystal Palace floated serene and unperturbed in the distance. He tottered to the washbasin, poured some cold water, splashed it into his face, then looked up. Still there. This close to the window, he could see more.

The street was cobbled; near by was a junction with a larger road. Ancient cars crossed the narrow field of view. A couple pushed a pram across the junction, the woman in a long dress and coat, the man wearing a trilby. The pram had huge overlapping wheels. His mind dived for cover again and he forced it to work with an effort of will. There had to be a rational explanation.

The simplest was that he was suffering from an intense delusion. How this came to be, he had no idea. Certainly life was much less rewarding these days, with steady increases in class sizes, pressures to research and publish, the obtrusive quality assessments. Still, it wasn't so bad that he was likely to have cracked under the pressure. His discipline was his all-consuming interest, indeed a contributory cause of the failure of his marriage. He knew more about the military history of the Twentieth Century than all but a handful of other academics and his life was in its study.

Suppose he had lost his sanity? What should he, could he, do about it? How should he behave? Most immediately, what should he do now?

He realised that he would have to leave this room, and instantly felt a strong reluctance to do so. The room was a little old-fashioned, but it was known, safe, explicable. The outside world was another matter. He forced himself to straighten up from the sink, walk to the chair, pick up his bag and walk to the door. It felt like a journey towards unknown terrors. He braced himself, opened the door and walked out.

**Autumn 1934**

Afterwards, Don remembered little of the building he walked through. It appeared to be some sort of low-cost boarding house but he met no-one to ask. The street was equally deserted, so he walked to the junction with the main road. The light breeze did not entirely dispel the smell of smoke.

Across the road there were some shops, one of them a newsagent. He walked over, feeling an icy chill of apprehension. A looming shape and the blare of a horn caused him to jump quickly to the pavement. He entered the shop and approached the piles of newspapers. The nearest had the headline 'THOUSANDS OFF THE MEANS TEST'. He noted vaguely that it was the *Daily Mirror*, and that the lead story was about Government efforts to help the workless. It took a real effort to force his eyes to the date. Monday 3rd September 1934. His vision spun in front of him, and he grasped at the counter to stay on his feet.

'Are you all right mate?' He barely heard the concerned voice, but nodded and staggered out into the street. He began thinking again some time later, when he was already a distance from the shop. He looked at his digital watch, which informed him that the time was 9.37 a.m., and the date Friday 3rd September 2004. Exactly seventy years. He was only a few yards further down the road when the significance of the date struck him. It was precisely five years before the British Prime Minister, Neville Chamberlain, would announce that the German refusal to withdraw from their invasion of Poland meant that Britain was at war with Germany; five years before the start of the Second World War.

He kept on walking blindly and after a while realised that he was beginning to feel calmer, more relaxed. There must be a limit to the amount of stress a mind could take before it began adjusting, accepting the current appearance of reality, no matter how absurd. At least this particular delusion was remarkably consistent as well as detailed, with no obvious anachronisms. Of course, that could simply reflect his knowledge of the times. That being so, he reflected that he might as well behave accordingly: as if the delusion were reality.

What to do next? He was already beginning to feel hungry and it was clear that this delusion required him to go through the motions of eating if he were not to become uncomfortable. He had enough money to buy food, but when he stopped to check his wallet he found that it still held twenty-first century currency, useless in this context. He would need to find someone to help him. He noticed from the position of the sun that he had been instinctively walking north, towards the centre of London. He had a long way to walk, but although it had evidently rained earlier, it was becoming warm and sunny. As he walked, he considered who he might contact. It occurred to him that he was not without resources. Some of the gadgets he possessed would be of great interest, and above all he had knowledge. The thought struck him with such force that he stopped. Six years of war. Fifty million dead. Britain bankrupted. Eastern Europe imprisoned. In this milieu, his knowledge was beyond price.

He continued walking more thoughtfully. He was treating this delusion as if it were reality, but what alternative was there? He was clearly going through some escapist wish-fulfilment fantasy, as there were few people as well-equipped as himself to provide useful advice about what to do over the next few years. He might as well enjoy the opportunity and see what happened.

Winston Churchill. The obvious name came to mind. After a while, Don dismissed the idea. In 1934 Churchill was in the political wilderness, a notorious Jeremiah, always prophesying war. He would be convinced readily enough by Don's story but it was unlikely that anyone would listen to him. He needed to speak to someone with authority, but not a politician who might consider only the party political implications. After a while, he made up his mind and walked with more purpose, staring with fascination at his surroundings. The relative absence of motor vehicles made the walk more of a pleasure than he would have expected, but he had to smile wryly as he encountered his first trams. He recalled reading recently that London was considering the reintroduction of a tram system and wondered if the old tracks were still there, buried under the tarmac. He crossed the Thames by Blackfriars Bridge, noting with a pang of nostalgia the steam train chuffing its way across the railway bridge to his right. He had forgotten, though, just how smoky the air would be, and how grimy the buildings in their layers of soot.

The porter at Imperial College was suspicious. 'The Rector is a busy man. He isn't accustomed to seeing people without appointments.' His look clearly suggested that anyone as strangely dressed and dishevelled as Don, still perspiring from his long walk, would be unlikely to be granted such an honour.
'Do you have an envelope I could use?' Don asked politely. The porter grudgingly passed one over. Don opened his wallet and slipped something inside the envelope before sealing it. 'Could you take this to the Rector, please? I am certain he will want to see me.' He tried his most confident smile. With more grumbles and suspicious looks, the porter bade him wait and disappeared inside the building.

Henry Tizard was irritated but clearly intrigued. 'What's all this nonsense about?' He asked coldly, holding up the 2002 pound coin.
Don did not immediately reply, but instead passed over his digital watch. Tizard looked at it with incredulity, his pale face even more tense than usual, fierce eyes glinting through metal-rimmed spectacles. Don opened his holdall and took out the notebook computer.
'Let me show you what this can do.' He said calmly.

Don reflected with some amusement that for all Tizard's reputation for being penetrating, tough and prickly, he looked decidedly nonplussed now.
'Very well, then,' Tizard said abruptly, 'for the sake of argument, let's accept your story that you're a visitor from the future. What do you want? Why have you come to see me?'

'The second question is easier to answer than the first, Sir Henry,' Don began, then realised his mistake as Tizard frowned. 'I'm sorry, of course you haven't been knighted yet.'

There was a glint of amusement in Tizard's eyes. 'Indeed I haven't,' he growled.

Don ploughed on. 'You are chairman of the Aeronautical Research Committee and shortly to become chairman of the Committee for the Scientific Survey of Air Defence, which will among other things sponsor the invention of radar.' Seeing Tizard's expression, Don hurried on. 'You are one of the most respected scientists in the country and your word carries weight with politicians as well as your peers. Besides,' he added, 'I knew where to find you. As to what I want, that's hard to say. Perhaps, above all, to give a warning.'

'What kind of warning?'

Don spoke slowly. 'The War to end all wars isn't over yet. This is no more than a pause in the struggle. The worst is yet to come.' He leaned back in his chair and then paused as an increasing distraction claimed his attention.

'Before I begin,' he said apologetically, 'do you think I could have something to eat and drink?'

The meeting had taken weeks of argument, demonstration and persuasion to organise, and was being held in conditions of absolute secrecy. Don had not been introduced to anyone present, but Dunning had warned him about that.

'They haven't been able to ignore the evidence you brought with you, which is why they are coming,' he explained, 'but they are acutely sensitive of the prospect of public ridicule if news of the meeting leaks out, so they won't officially be here.'

Tizard had introduced Charles Dunning to Don a few days after what Don had come to think of as his 'reversion'. A neat, well-dressed man of about his own age, Dunning was self-effacing but had an air of quiet authority. He had described himself as a civil servant, but his reticence combined with his remarkable ability to make things happen suggested to Don that his particular branch of the civil service probably had no official existence. He had rapidly organised some rooms close to Whitehall in which Don had been spending most of his time, and had turned up without warning to take him to this meeting.

Dunning had assured him that although no politicians were present ('This is being kept away from them until their advisers know what to make of it') the meeting included highly influential civil servants and military advisers ('They won't be in uniform, but you'll probably be able to pick them out').

So far Don had related, for the umpteenth time, the story of his strange reversion and his summary of the events of the next decade. He had then spent a considerable time fielding detailed questions, many of which he found surprisingly difficult to answer. He somewhat ruefully realised the extent to which general background knowledge tends to be frustratingly unspecific.

The air was thick with smoke, cigarettes vying for pre-eminence with pipes and cigars. Don felt ill, but was too nervous to ask for a window to be opened. The chairman of the meeting was a lean, grey-haired man wearing the authority of one whose judgement was unquestioned. He had chain-smoked cigarettes throughout the meeting.

'Very well, we have heard Dr Erlang's account. Let us assume for the purpose of this meeting that it is accurate. Certainly there are enough straws in the wind to make his story credible.' He began ticking them off on his fingers. 'Last June Hitler and Mussolini met in Venice. At the end of that month, Hitler purged Rohm's faction from the Nazi Party.' (Don tried to recall when the phrase 'Night of the Long Knives' had been coined). 'In August, the Austrian Chancellor, Dolfuss, was assassinated by a Nazi and in the same month Hindenberg died and Hitler immediately combined his position as Chancellor with that of the Presidency. He is clearly well on the way to becoming the unchallenged dictator of Germany. In the light of Dr Erlang's revelations, what response should we make?'

There was a rather uncomfortable pause. Clearly, no-one wanted to appear foolish or gullible. Finally, an elderly man who had not yet spoken removed his cigar and cleared his throat.

'The key problem is clearly the German Nazi Party in general and Hitler in particular. Japan is a separate issue of lower priority. The question must be: how can we stop Hitler?'

An obviously cultured younger man, whom Don had tagged as a Foreign Office official, elegantly waved his cigarette holder and begged to differ.

'From what we have heard, the Nazi Party is an inevitable expression of German frustration at the outcome of the Great War, and Hitler no more than a demagogic catalyst. If he fell, he would be replaced by someone else with similar ambitions.'

'But perhaps by someone more reasonable, less megalomaniac.' This from a rather earnest, pipe-smoking individual whose application of hair cream did not entirely stifle the exuberance of his light brown curls.

'But Hitler's paranoiac megalomania will be the cause of his downfall. A more rational leader may still wish to expand Germany's boundaries but would make fewer mistakes in so doing. Even with Hitler's misjudgements, we have heard how close Germany will come to winning the next war.'

'But if only half of what we have heard is correct, Hitler is appallingly evil.'

'All the better. It gives us a much less ambiguous target. A more reasonable man might be much harder to turn public opinion against, particularly in America.' The last speaker was clearly military, although Don was unable to guess the Service.

'Could the League of Nations be used in some way?'

'No fear', retorted Diplomat with feeling, 'If we try to encourage them to take a more active role, they would just expect us to contribute most of the military forces. We could end up being dragged into a war anyway, in circumstances not of our choosing.'

'Is there no way we can persuade the Germans away from their folly? Show them our evidence? Get them to see reason?' Creamed Curls was sounding desperate. Military Man was unmoved.

'War appears inevitable. Dr Erlang is the biggest secret weapon we will have. His existence must not be revealed.'

There was a thoughtful pause. Chairman broke the silence. 'I agree that the consequences of revealing Dr Erlang's existence are too incalculable to be risked, in terms of public opinion as well as German reaction. Events would be set off on an entirely new course which could result in a much more disastrous outcome for this country. And the interests of this country must be paramount in our minds.'

Don shuffled, feeling he ought to protest, but was stilled by the murmurs of agreement around the table. Chairman was warming to his theme.

'Let us consider the situation. We are warned of a terrible war which we, none the less, will win. It is therefore to our advantage to take no radical steps which might affect the outcome, but to make whatever adjustments appear necessary to our policies in order to reduce our losses and end the war in a more favourable position.' There was much nodding around the table.

'Some gentle nudges on the tiller,' murmured Diplomat, 'take in a reef here or there. Changes which, begging your pardon' – this to Don

– 'would do no harm even if your promised apocalypse turns out to be a damp squib.'

'We are agreed then,' stated Chairman with justified confidence. 'It might be helpful for us to have a preliminary tour around our foreign and defence policies in order to identify areas which could do with attention.'

'Mustn't forget the empire,' observed a man whose ruddy face was emphasised by his white hair, 'incredible about those Japanese. I wouldn't have thought they would have the nerve, let alone the ability, to pose any risk to ourselves or the Americans.'

'I agree entirely,' smoothed Diplomat, 'but from what we have heard, the errors which cost so dear - beg pardon, will cost; or should it be would have cost? These tenses are becoming confusing. No matter – the forecast problems in the Far East should be easy enough to correct with better preparation.'

'That depends,' responded Ruddy Face, 'the Navy can't be expected to deal with Japan at the same time as Germany and Italy. It would be highly dangerous to risk war with Japan unless we could be assured that America will fight with us.'

'From what we have heard,' commented Chairman, 'that should not be too much of a problem.'

There was a thoughtful pause.

'Are we agreed on that?' Enquired Chairman. Emphatic nods. 'Very well then, let us turn to the German question. What are our options.'

Creamed Curls was still optimistic. 'We could speed up re-armament and take a tougher line with Hitler; aim to stop him at some point before the attack on Poland. Perhaps the re-occupation of the Rhineland? The crisis over Czechoslovakia?'

'That would only postpone the conflict' (this from Elderly Cigar) 'and it's not feasible anyway unless we have full backing from France.'

'Can't we attempt to convince France of the need to re-arm and take a strong line as well?'

Elderly Cigar looked incredulous. 'My dear chap, have you been over there? Read their newspapers? Listened to their politicians? They are perpetually torn apart by conflict between left and right-wing groups and have no political stability at all. And while most countries are pulling out of the Depression, French production is still declining. What's more, they were so traumatised by the slaughter of the Great War that they would do almost anything to avoid conflict. They intend to hide behind their Maginot Line and haven't the will to confront anything. I am actually astonished that they are apparently going to stick to their treaty obligations and back us over Poland.'

Chairman frowned. 'Very well then, what other options do we have?'

Military Man had no doubts. 'Re-arm more quickly and effectively, persuade the French to do the same – as far as possible – and concentrate on defeating Germany as soon as possible after 1939, when they're still busy with invading Poland and simultaneously covering the Russians to ensure that they don't advance too far.'

'Risky, given German strength and French weakness,' murmured Diplomat. 'Let's face it, it's clear that in order to guarantee German defeat, we would have to bring the Russians in against them. This will only happen if Germany attacks Russia, and Germany won't do that unless France is defeated first.'

Everybody looked at Diplomat. He waved his cigarette holder. 'One of our most vulnerable points will be after the defeat of France. According to our friend here, nobody knows what would have happened if Hitler had invaded us in 1940, with our Army defeated and its equipment lost.'

'They would never have got past the Navy.' Ruddy Face's allegiance was now clearly identifiable.

Chairman was interested. 'What do you suggest?'

Diplomat smiled, rather enjoying the limelight, thought Don. 'I propose that we stay away from European entanglements and let Hitler do what he likes on the Continent. He will have no reason to attack Britain and will not be able to if we prepare our defences against invasion. There is still a good chance that Russia will defeat him single-handed, only much weakened. We can then step in to put things right.'

Creamed Curls was indignant. 'We can't do that, it would be legally and morally impossible given our treaty obligations.'

'What's more,' added Elderly Cigar, 'Hitler's desire for conquest appears to be insatiable and there will still be the risk that if he can secure his position in Europe, Germany will turn on Britain. Furthermore, as he grows in power so will his influence here. Nazism already has many supporters.'

There was silence as thoughts turned to the frequent, well-attended meetings of the British Union of Fascists.

'And not all of his supporters are down at the level of Mosley's Blackshirts,' murmured Diplomat.

'Quite so,' said Chairman, a little sourly Don thought. 'We need a way of minimising our losses without breaking our treaty obligations.'

'Try this one for size,' offered Diplomat. 'We refrain from giving that expensive guarantee to Poland – seems a daft idea anyway as we could never do anything effective to defend them and the Treaty of Locarno doesn't commit us to guaranteeing their boundaries. That means that we don't have to declare war until the Germans charge through the Low Countries on their way to France. It will then be too late for us to get any substantial part of our Army over before the French are defeated. Then we could sit, honour satisfied but with defences intact.'

Another pause, this time more encouraging.

'I like the sound of that,' from Elderly Cigar.

'So do I,' said Ruddy Face 'and I suggest a refinement.' Enquiring looks. 'We prepare instead to pinch Norway from under the Nazis' noses. If Hitler follows the script, we will be fully engaged in battling his invasion of Norway just at the point that he moves on France, so we will have a cast-iron reason for not coming to France's aid. Holding Norway will incidentally save us a great deal of trouble later on.'

Creamed Curls winced and objected. 'How do we know that the Germans will still invade Norway just before attacking France, if we're not already at war with them over Poland?'

'We don't,' said Diplomat, 'but we can take steps to ensure that they do. Suppose they were made aware that we would certainly declare war if they attacked France, and would then seek to ensure that Norway remained friendly to us? That would give Hitler enough incentive to catch us on the hop by invading Norway first. Ironically, our interests and those of the Nazis would be identical at that point: to prevent us from becoming involved with the fighting in France.'

Chairman waited for further contributions, but no-one seemed inclined to take the argument further. 'Very well, gentlemen. We seem to have arrived at a consensus over the broad thrust of our policy. I suggest we cancel any other commitments in order to continue these discussions next week.'

That evening, Don bought a copy of the *Daily Mail* on his way back to his rooms. 'GENERAL STRIKE IN SPAIN' announced the headline. And the sub-heading, 'Sound of firing heard in Madrid.' This would be the abortive precursor of the Spanish Civil War, he thought, with an attempt to form a Catalan republic leading to a battle in Barcelona. The real fighting would start in the following year.

Another headline caught his eye; 'NATION DEMANDS MORE AIR DEFENCES'. It seemed that the Conservative Party conference had passed a resolution expressing 'grave anxiety in regard to the inadequacy of the provisions made for Imperial defence.' Neville Chamberlain, the Chancellor of the Exchequer, had tried to fend off criticism by describing the government's plans to increase home defence aeroplane squadrons from forty-two to seventy-five over a five-year period. The Party was obviously not so easily satisfied. Sir Arthur Steel-Maitland, a former Cabinet Minister, claimed that air attacks would be so sudden and destructive that within forty-eight hours of war having been declared, one or other side would be annihilated.

That, thought Don, showed a remarkable lack of comprehension of basic statistics about aircraft, bombloads and the amount of destruction which bombs could cause. He read on. Lord Lloyd pointed out that Britain's armed forces were so weak that the country was 'no longer in a position to guarantee the safety of our sea routes and food supplies.' That struck much closer to home, he thought. If war was inevitable, as the country's most influential observers seemed to believe, much needed to be done.

Don walked to the window and looked down into the street. As on the previous few nights, an anonymous car was parked opposite the entrance to his building. A brief flare within it marked the lighting of yet another cigarette. Someone was keeping an eye on him and didn't care if he knew it.

Dunning dropped in a few days later, as usual without warning. Don had been using the unexpected free time to walk around 1930s London, re-learning the city he had previously known so well. He did not enjoy cooking and was finding the limited variety of eating places a distinct drawback; no Chinese, no Indian, no pizzas, even a burger would have been a welcome relief. The pubs were no help either; meals weren't available, and the restricted choice of beers (mostly mild or India Pale Ale) didn't much appeal. He noted that despite his frequent absences, Dunning clearly expected him to be in, and wondered about the extent of the surveillance he was under.

'Just thought I'd drop in to see how you're managing.' Dunning said pleasantly.

'Well enough Charles, but I'm becoming increasingly concerned about the policy decisions being made.' Don had been worrying for days, and knew that the situation would slip out of his grasp if he kept silent. 'The powers-that-be seem set on allowing this war to happen and in using my information merely to fight it more efficiently.'

Dunning raised an eyebrow but did not comment. Don leaned forward urgently.

'They have no conception of the horrors this war will bring. Millions slaughtered in Nazi concentration camps simply because of their racial origin. Tens of millions of Russians killed. There has to be a way to stop it.'

Dunning looked at him thoughtfully. 'I agree with your sentiments, Don, but what can be done? You have said yourself that international tensions are such that, one way or another, Germany is bound to try to avenge the crippling penalties of Versailles. Do you suppose that other countries will voluntarily give back the territories Germany has lost? Perhaps in your time governments are more rational, less nationalistic, but there is a tide rising in Germany which will not be held back by the threat of war. This boil has to come to a head before it can be lanced.'

Don said nothing, feeling overwhelmed by a sense of hopeless inevitability.

'Japan is an even worse case,' continued Dunning. 'They may not have a defeat to avenge but they are looking to expand their empire and are chronically short of the raw materials they need, which happen to be conveniently available in nearby territories occupied by the USA or European countries. Conflict is becoming increasingly inevitable.'

'It just seems so absurd, pressing on down the road to war knowing full well what the cost will be.'

'Perhaps the world has to go through this experience,' Dunning said gently, 'before nations are ready to put conflict behind them as a way of solving problems.'

Don thought of Korea, Vietnam, Bosnia and the Middle East, and put his head in his hands.

'In any case, by helping this country to win the war more quickly you will be reducing the period of suffering to a minimum.'

Don sighed. 'Very well, it doesn't seem as if I have any other option.'

It was clear that much discussion had been going on in the week since the previous meeting. Chairman seemed quite jaunty. 'Let me begin by summing up. We agreed last time that we would make no changes to our existing foreign policy but we would take care to ensure that our political masters enter into no further commitments, with particular reference to Poland. What we need to do now is to concentrate on any fundamental changes we should be making to our Imperial defence policy in order to come out of the forthcoming conflict as well as possible. Dr Erlang, do you have any observations to make?'

Don, who had firmly placed himself by a window which he had managed to open slightly, wondered briefly what conclusions they had reached already. They seemed remarkably confident of their ability to cope without detailed advice once they had grasped the basic issues. Still, he had already prepared what he was going to say.

'I will start with defensive measures before going on to the question of offensive action. First of all, top priority has to go to the measures needed to repel an invasion of the British Isles.' He had their full attention. 'This will involve a sophisticated aircraft detection and fighter control system backed by plenty of fighters, and fast bombers capable of attacking any invasion fleet. Strong fighter defence will also be necessary to provide cover for the naval units which will be engaged in attacking enemy vessels. Finally, mechanised divisions containing tanks, artillery, anti-aircraft vehicles and armoured troop transports need to be held in south-east England to respond rapidly to any landings. Above all, timely and accurate information will be needed to guide the defence effort so a robust communications network needs to be set up and thoroughly tested. I don't just mean telephones and radios, but a co-ordinated, multi-service system for gathering information from a range of sources, analysing it and ensuring it is passed on to the relevant military commands as quickly as possible.'

Much thoughtful nodding around the table.

'The next priority will be to prevent the North Atlantic supply lines from being cut by submarine warfare. It nearly happened in the last war and is still the biggest threat.'

Ruddy Face stirred uneasily and appeared to be about to say something. Don continued quickly. 'I know the Navy feels confident that sonar – I mean Asdic – is the ultimate answer to submarines, but I can assure you that it isn't that straightforward.'

Ruddy Face looked appalled, but at a gesture from Chairman held his tongue.

'Air cover is the key to defeating submarines,' continued Don, warming to his theme and slipping into lecturing mode. 'Maritime patrol squadrons should have priority in being issued with long-range aircraft. Incidentally, it would be advisable to hang onto those bases in the Republic of Ireland, and not allow the politicians to give them up before the war.'

'Noted,' observed Chairman drily.

'Land-based air cover won't be enough. Cheap aircraft carriers will also be needed to accompany convoys.'

Creamed Curls was becoming increasingly agitated. 'But bombers will surely be the main means of fighting war. They should have priority over any other type of aircraft.'

'They will be important,' conceded Don, 'but once again it's not that simple. Bombing has the potential to cause great destruction, but as a war-winning weapon it will not be as effective as many people fear.'

Don saw real alarm on Creamed Curls' face and remembered the bitter inter-service rivalry which had followed the end of the Great War, with the two older services trying to return to their pre-war pre-eminence and the newly-formed RAF fighting to preserve its independence. The RAF under Trenchard had taken to proclaiming the theories of Douhet and others who argued that bombing would be so destructive that it would supersede other methods of fighting. It had therefore become an article of faith in the RAF that the bomber would always get through, and could win wars by itself. He had a distinct feeling that Trenchard and his followers would be acutely unhappy about the message he was bringing.

'Turning to other issues,' Don continued, 'there are some basic questions of changes in military organisation and equipment which will be needed to enhance war-fighting capability; above all, the closer integration of the three armed forces in developing combined arms tactics, with a particular emphasis on amphibious warfare. Put briefly, you will need to develop the capability of transporting armoured divisions overseas and putting them ashore on an unprepared coast, closely supported by aircraft sufficient to overwhelm local defences and attack enemy troop concentrations and strongpoints.' Don recalled the chaos which had affected the Norwegian and Dieppe landings and added: 'It will also be prudent to acquire during peacetime detailed maps, photographs and other information about areas in which you may need to fight, with particular emphasis on coastlines.'

Varying degrees of interest, scepticism and dismay were evident from around the table.

'What about the Empire?' Asked Ruddy Face, returning to his theme of the previous week.

'Actual defence will mainly be provided by aircraft, ships and troops which can be put in place shortly before war is due to start. However, it will be important to prepare the ground to support the defences. This means, for example, building substantial bombproof storage for fuel and ammunition, storing plenty of food, providing sufficient airfields complete with shelter for the aircraft, providing submarine pens where appropriate, and so on. As much military equipment as possible should be pre-positioned ready for troops to use when called up.'

'Some of that has been done,' observed Chairman, 'but the cost is considerable.'

'But probably not as much,' interposed Diplomat, 'as losing the colonies.'

'There is another alternative,' Don said hesitantly. Chairman looked wary.

'I have already indicated to you that, from the late 1940s onwards, Britain starts giving independence to its colonies. It could be argued that there isn't much point in fighting for them now, if we're going to give them up soon afterwards.'

Ruddy Face appeared close to apoplexy. Even Diplomat seemed ruffled. 'Quite out of the question, dear chap. There is tremendous popular, and therefore political, support for the Empire. Just last week the government's modest inclination toward giving India more home rule was roundly condemned by the Conservative Conference.'

'Besides,' added Chairman, 'we could hardly simply cut the colonies free and abandon them to German, Italian or Japanese invaders. We would be honour-bound to offer them support against a common enemy.'

Don gave up. Shortly afterwards, the meeting broke up and Dunning accompanied Don back to his rooms.

'I feel boxed in, Charles. Every attempt I make to reduce the scope of the next war seems to be blocked.'

'But for very good reasons, I'm sure you realise. It raises interesting questions about the extent to which knowledge of forthcoming events enables us to alter them. In detail, yes, but the broad sweep of historical events seems to have a momentum of its own.'

Dunning changed the subject. 'With the basic policies decided, it's time to get down to details. It's unlikely that you'll be meeting that particular group again. Instead, we aim to get our specialists to extract all the information you can provide; painlessly, of course! To help with that, a change of scene has been arranged. You're off to the countryside.'

The house was large and sited somewhere in the Berkshire countryside. Don wasn't sure exactly where, as the car journey had been at night. The absence of the large, reflective road-signs – that he was used to taking for granted – disorientated him, and he was able to recognise few landmarks on the way. The grounds were spacious, surrounded by a high fence topped with barbed wire. No other buildings were visible from the grounds. The only break in the fence was at the main driveway, guarded by a small gatehouse, occupied continuously by men who were evidently soldiers despite their civilian clothes. It did not take Don long to realise that he was effectively a prisoner.

A few days after arriving, he returned from a pre-lunch stroll around the grounds to be met at the entrance by Dunning. With him was Mary Baker, an attractive, dark-haired woman whom Dunning had introduced as 'your secretary, assistant and general factotum'. Don had not been aware that he needed a secretary and suspected that she was yet another pair of eyes to watch him. It was noticeable that at least one of them was always around. He sometimes wondered if he was becoming paranoid.

'Some people to meet you, Don,' Dunning announced. 'I've put them in the lounge and I'll introduce you in a moment, but I thought I'd better explain who they are first. They represent the intelligence branches of the three Services and will be solely responsible for interviewing you about developments in their areas. For obvious reasons, we want to keep contact with you to as small a group as possible. They will all have rooms here, and will be alternating between staying here to talk to you and going off to use your information where it matters.'

They had reached the door of the oak-panelled lounge and Dunning shepherded Don inside. He was immediately the focus of intense scrutiny from three pairs of eyes.

'May I introduce Peter Morgan, RAF; David Helmsford, RN; and Geoffrey Taylor, from the Army. Needless to say, neither their ranks nor their uniforms will be evident here.'

Formalities over, Don settled down over tea to study the new arrivals. They all appeared to be in their late thirties or early forties, unremarkable at first sight except for the air of sharp intelligence common to all three. They had clearly been fully briefed on his background and were consumed with curiosity.

Morgan, slim and fair-haired with an air of boyish enthusiasm, was first to speak. 'We've been trying to work out which service you're least popular with,' he said with a grin. 'The Navy, for insulting their beloved battleships by insisting on the importance of aircraft carriers; the Army, for dismissing their equally beloved horses in favour of clanking machinery; or my lot, for shooting down the bombers and, to add insult to injury, advocating the transfer of the Fleet Air Arm to the Navy.'

Don smiled. 'Well, gentlemen, who's going to be the first to give me a going-over?'

They all grinned in response. 'David tried to argue that the Senior Service should take precedence, but Peter and I sat on him until he agreed to draw straws,' drawled Taylor, 'as a result of which you have the pleasure of starting with me.'

'Seriously, you needn't worry about offending me,' Taylor said after a long lunch filled with speculation, debate and above all, questioning of Don. 'I'm an engineer and have little time for the prejudices of the well-bred cavalry. Anyone with any sense can see that machine guns and artillery have done away with horses in the front line; they just make big targets and can't dive for the nearest shell-hole when they come under fire. Unfortunately many of the senior staff grew up worshipping horses and have tried to pretend that the Great War was an aberration.'

'It's not just the tanks,' interposed Don, 'everything else needs to be able to accompany them at the same speed and with armour protection; artillery, anti-aircraft guns, infantry, supplies and even engineers.'

Taylor laughed. 'I know. Fuller has been arguing that for years and we have been holding annual exercises with mechanised formations. Hobart introduced a real novelty in this year's exercise by making extensive use of radio communications between tanks. The main problem we have is in deciding the right proportions of the kinds of tanks we will be making; slow heavily-armoured ones to accompany the infantry and fast lightly-armoured cavalry vehicles.'

'Neither. If the tanks are too specialised you'll never be able to depend on having the right types available when you need them. In one respect, the tank enthusiasts are right to draw parallels with naval practice; like battleships, tanks need a good balance of characteristics – fire-power, armour, speed - so they can cope with whatever comes up.'

Taylor grunted and filled his pipe. His brown hair and neat moustache were unremarkable, but his powerful build and air of calm competence were impressive. 'I'm putting together some detailed information about our current plans for you to comment on. However, to turn for the moment to infantry equipment, I'm afraid your pleas for adopting a small-calibre automatic rifle have not been well received by the Master General of the Ordnance. He is adamant that we have too much invested in the three-oh-three calibre to be able to afford to change, and that designing a new automatic rifle and a new cartridge would take too long anyway.'

'I was afraid of that, but I have some alternative ideas...'.

The next morning was the Navy's turn. 'The first problem is our relationship with Germany,' said Helmsford. He was tall and dark with a habitually sardonic expression, and inclined to choose his words with care. 'We've been considering a naval treaty with them to try to limit their plans for expansion.'

'I advise you to forget it. It will only bring criticism on Britain for recognising formally Germany's breach of the Versailles Treaty, and we know that Hitler will build anything he wants to anyway.'

'What about wider international agreements? As you must know, we are deep in preparation for the second London Naval Conference due to be held next year, and one of the main issues is the size and gun calibre of new battleship construction. And I have to add that your scepticism about the value of battleships won't get a favourable hearing – the Admiralty will never agree to stop building them while everyone else is carrying on. However, the cost of these ships is so high that we are pressing for the smallest ships we can – ideally around twenty-five thousand tons and with twelve-inch guns – but the Americans are pushing for much larger ships. '

'I'm afraid they'll win. On the other hand, that can be turned to our advantage. If we manage to win agreement to thirty-five thousand tons and fifteen-inch guns – which should be quite feasible – we could save a huge amount of time and money by reusing fifteen-inch turrets from existing, obsolete ships, and incidentally save ourselves the trouble of maintaining and manning them. We can use the resources saved to concentrate on aircraft carriers.' Don warmed to his theme; 'The Navy did actually accept the reuse of the old fifteen-inch turrets from the *Courageous* and *Glorious* to arm their last battleship – the *Vanguard* – so all I'm suggesting is to incorporate those into the new design, and scrap the five old 'R' Class battleships so their turrets can be reused as well; really, they contributed – will contribute – next to nothing to the war. And frankly, the old fifteen-inch will be much more reliable than the new fourteen-inch you're planning.'

Helmsford considered. 'That might just be acceptable. But as for your other comments about the importance of anti-aircraft over surface fire, you had better be warned that I'm a gunnery officer by training!'

Don grinned. 'Sorry, but the evidence is clear. Aircraft are a much bigger threat than surface ships to warships, so it's essential that all ships have good AA armament – and that includes directors as well as guns. In any case, even against surface targets, the hit probability of a destroyer's guns is so low that they would do better with eight four-inch dual-purpose guns rather than four, low-angle four-point-sevens – the rate of fire is so much higher.'

Helmsford grimaced doubtfully. 'People will need a lot of convincing. And you say that the capital ships should have nothing bigger than four-point-sevens as secondary armament?'

'Yes, definitely. Give them modern, heavier shells by all means, but a well-designed twin turret in that calibre will be much faster-firing and more effective than those dual-purpose five-point-two-fives, as well as being lighter.'

Helmsford sighed. 'All right, I'll do my best, but I never thought you would present me with such a headache!'

Morgan was his usual ebullient self. 'You're quite right about the direction of aircraft design, of course. I've been to see the aeroplanes just about to set off from Mildenhall on the England-Australia race. Those sleek de Havilland Comet monoplanes are beautiful!'

'And they'll win!' Don grinned. 'But aircraft are only a part of the story. The key to success is to choose the right engines and concentrate on developing them by specifying them for future front-line aircraft. Another important issue is armament. Next comes the priority given to different aircraft types, and I'm afraid the RAF won't like them.' Morgan raised an enquiring eye. 'Fighters come first, which means that for once the politicians' preference is correct, albeit for the wrong reasons – they only like them because they're cheap and quick to build so they can meet their promises to build up the number of RAF squadrons more easily. But maritime patrol planes come next, and then some modern carrier-borne fighters and bombers. They all have a higher priority than the RAF's beloved bombers.' They were soon deep in conversation.

**Spring 1935**

Days became weeks which rolled into months. Winter came and went. The bare trees allowed a wider view of the countryside, but still no other buildings could be seen. Don was occasionally taken out by his minders, as he thought of them, to visit a nearby pub or cinema, but was never let out alone. He sometimes joked about the degree of custodial care, but Dunning was too serious about it to be amused.

'You must realise that your safety is of vital importance – you're probably the most valuable person in the country.' Furthermore, Don added silently, no-one else must know of my existence.

Newspapers were his other contact with the world outside. He found the old-fashioned sentiments and phrasing, the innocent adverts rather touching, but was amused to note unexpected portents of things to come. He had not been aware that Scotland Yard had been experimenting with an autogyro for observing 'traffic-congested areas' and possibly tracking 'car bandits'. A report of a German aeroplane powered by a 2,500 horsepower 'steam turbine' and capable of travelling at 230–260 mph for sixty or seventy hours appeared more optimistic, although Don was again surprised to read a report that an American steam-powered craft had flown three times already. He wondered if newspaper reporters in the 1930s were more or less gullible than those in the 2000s, or more willing to make things up. It also occurred to him that Dunning need not worry about his spilling the beans to any reporters. They would probably write up his story, but with zero impact on the public.

In the spring and early summer of 1935, Don began to notice a sharpening of interest and concern on the part of his team of interviewers. The reasons were evident enough in the newspapers. He had already been proved right in his prediction about the Saarland, which in January voted to return to Germany by 90.36%. On March 15th Hitler announced military conscription and an increase in the size of the German Army to thirty-six divisions; 'The Times' military correspondent stated that, with nearly 400 machine-guns, the German army was well-equipped defensively 'but it is hardly to be expected that an army... long restricted in developing heavy artillery and tanks, should have anything like an equivalent power of taking the offensive.' Don groaned. The complacency was almost comical.

Clearly, however, someone in the government was becoming worried. On the twenty-eighth of the month, Anthony Eden travelled to Moscow to discuss the European situation with M. Litvinoff (Soviet Commissar for foreign affairs) and spoke to Stalin. He established that there was 'no conflict of interest' between the governments. More accurate than they realise, Don thought; at least in the short term.

On April 7th, elections were held in Danzig – a predominantly German enclave within Poland and next to East Prussia – which had been detached from Germany and given Free City status after the Great War. The Nazis increased their vote by eight percent but despite intense propaganda, including visits by Hess and Goebbels, they failed to gain the two-thirds majority necessary to change the constitution in favour of Germany.

The Foreign Office stepped up its activities; between 11th and 14th April Britain, Italy and France met at Stresa for a conference on the European situation, which led to an expression of 'complete agreement'.

'All this diplomatic posturing will get them nowhere,' grumbled Don, reading the morning papers in bed.

'What do you expect?' asked Mary. 'They are politicians and diplomats. Even if they know that their efforts are likely to prove fruitless – and I doubt they've been told – they'll still try. It's what they're there for.'

Don was never quite sure on whose initiative his relationship with Mary had begun. In darker moments he suspected that she had been chosen for her good looks and her willingness to lie back and think of England. At other times he was merely thankful that she was there. Usually serious, quiet and attentive, with a core of sadness which was never far from the surface, her occasional smiles sparked a glow of warmth in him and their partnership gave a structure and dimension to his life that had been missing for a long time. In fact, as time went by it was his past life which took on the aspect of a dream, something less real than his fantastic present. He now felt at home in the 1930s, and he tried not to think too much about how he had arrived there. Whenever his thoughts drifted in that direction, he felt he was teetering on the edge of an abyss.

Mary's voice wrenched him back to the present. 'I wonder if Churchill's been told about you,' she mused, studying another paper. 'He's warning that if German air strength continues growing at its present rate it will overtake Britain's within three or four years.'

'True enough,' said Don, 'but I suspect that he's not been included in the "inner circle" yet; he had a reputation for sounding off about the Nazi threat for years before the war. Our lords and masters are anxious to avoid prejudicing the natural development of events – except in a few specific areas – so that my predictions remain valid for as long as possible. I expect they'll wait until he becomes Prime Minister before letting him in on the secret.'

'Now there's a paradox for you; Churchill is supposed to come to power because of the military defeats suffered by Chamberlain's government. If your advice is followed, the defeats shouldn't happen, so how will Churchill become PM?'

'Somehow,' said Don grimly, 'I have a feeling that it will be arranged.'

'And there's something I've been meaning to ask: what about the wider paradox? Suppose any one of your grandparents were to be killed as a result of the changes you're causing? Or that your parents never meet? What will happen to you?'

'Good question. I've given it some thought myself. Of course, I could just disappear in a puff of smoke, but that wouldn't be the end of the problem; if I'd never existed, I couldn't have returned here in the first place, so none of the last few months could have happened, so I couldn't have changed events, so I would have lived to return here – and so on. The thinking becomes rather circular.'

'So where does that leave you?'

'There are just two possibilities: either all of my forebears survive and my parents meet up as before regardless of all the changes, or the parallel worlds theory is correct.'

'The what?'

'Parallel worlds. The idea is that there is an infinite number of worlds existing in parallel in some undetectable dimension, each different in some small way from the next. They are connected by an equally infinite number of branching points; occasions when something different happened and changed history. So my return to the past would have kicked me onto an entirely different branch; what happens here can't affect the world I came from, that just continues as before on a parallel track.'

Mary snuggled up to him. 'Well, just make sure that you stay on this track from now on!'

**Summer 1935**

Time seemed to pass with ever-increasing speed. Intensive consultations with his military interviewers were interspersed by anxious scanning of the news as the European tragedy began to unfold. The celebrations in early May to mark the Silver Jubilee of the King and Queen included reviews of Britain's military and naval forces. Shortly afterwards Lord Londonderry, Secretary of State for War, announced a trebling of the strength of the Royal Air Force based at home to 1,500 machines by March 31 1937; the existing thirty-four airfields were to be increased to sixty-five and in addition, seventy-one new squadrons were to be formed.

Charles Dunning was naturally reticent but could occasionally be prompted into revealing progress. 'The Defence Requirements Committee has been considering how to act on your advice,' he said, 'although we did of course have to disguise it as the strongly-held views of the best military minds. They have agreed that the Army should be restructured to concentrate on armoured warfare including capacity for amphibious landings and the development of close co-operation with the RAF. An experimental paratroop brigade is to be formed and secret trials of the rectangular wing-parachute you sketched are due soon. The Fleet Air Arm is to be handed over to the Navy within the next few months; Coastal Command will remain with the RAF but under Naval operational control – that took a hell of a lot of haggling and a number of premature retirements to achieve. The discussions over the Naval Treaty are working out as you suggested and the Royal Marines are being strengthened, with their amphibious role being more clearly defined. Radar is coming along fine; Tizard sends his best wishes, by the way.'

'What about the basic education and training side? We will need far more electrical engineers and factory capacity in order to keep up with the demands for radio and radar systems.'

Dunning grinned sardonically. 'Much more difficult – did you ever see the educational establishment move quickly? We've made a start, though, in offering generous bursaries to able students in these areas, and will be identifying electronics shadow factories as well as those for weapons production.'

The military contacts were more forthcoming. Geoffrey Taylor, despite his cautious and deliberate manner, had obviously warmed to his task. The Army's biggest deficiency – the development of competitive, reliable tanks – was being tackled with vigour. Tank design was assigned to a planning body including Vickers, the only private firm with substantial tank-building experience, car firms to provide mass-production expertise, military officers and the Ministry. An integrated family of armoured fighting vehicles was being developed with reliability, ease of use and maintenance and the ability to be upgraded as top priorities. New artillery, mortars, anti-tank weapons and small arms were being designed.

News on the aircraft front was also encouraging. Morgan reported the selection of the Rolls-Royce PV12 Merlin and the sleeve-valve

Bristol Hercules (still some months away from running) as the RAF's future front-line piston engines. Napier had been assigned to develop Whittle's centrifugal fan gas turbine, and advanced project teams at Rolls-Royce and Bristol were working with the Royal Aircraft Establishment to develop Griffith's axial flow turbines for jet and turboprop engines respectively.

Fighter guns were a priority; as well as developing the 0.303 inch, a slightly larger version of the Browning (the 'Vickers-Browning') was being designed to take the Vickers 0.5 inch cartridge, somewhat smaller than the American equivalent. Hispano-Suiza in France were being pursued for a licence for their new 20 mm HS-404 cannon which was still in the process of being designed, and the development of a belt-feed mechanism for it was being given a high priority to ensure that both could enter service by the end of the 1930s.

Meanwhile, development of the Spitfire and Hurricane had been given top priority with arrangements already underway for their mass production. Don was acutely conscious of the fact that as soon as war was imminent, the War Ministry would be inclined to freeze current designs in the interests of achieving mass production. Accordingly, he discussed with Morgan the types of aircraft which would have a long service life to ensure that they would be in production by 1938. Among other proposals, de Havilland was to be strongly encouraged to design a wooden, twin-engined high-speed unarmed bomber as soon as possible.

Helmsford was equally encouraging about the Navy's plans. The fifteen-inch gun battleship design was proceeding well, as were the new aircraft carriers with their angled decks to enable planes to land without crashing into the ones waiting to take off ('steam catapults were considered, but would have taken too long to develop'). Don had advised against the armoured decks used by most RN war-built carriers because of the loss of hangar space and aircraft capacity. Just as important were the aircraft for them; Bristol had been given the contract to develop Hercules-powered fighters and multi-role torpedo/dive bomber/reconnaissance planes, with as much commonality as possible.

Otherwise, concentration in the naval field was on enhanced anti-aircraft and anti-submarine capabilities, with advanced fire-control systems, the commissioning of Bofors to speed up their development of 57 mm as well as 40 mm automatic guns and the development of ahead-throwing anti-submarine mortars (Don's mention of the 'Squid' promptly led to the name being adopted) with their associated pencil-beam Asdic sets. Don had been surprised to discover that ahead-throwing weapons had already been built and tested, but development was just about to be abandoned when his arrival led to a re-think.

By the autumn of 1935 the international situation was clearly worsening. On September 5th Italy walked out of the League of Nations Council meeting called to discuss the Italo-Abyssinian crisis. This was followed in October by an Italian attack on Abyssinia, countered by the urgent reinforcement of British forces in the Middle East. In November, German army recruits were required to swear allegiance to Hitler as well as to the nation. Don read the news with a mixture of anxiety, despondency and an uncertain hope that perhaps, this time, he could reduce the scale of the suffering to come. Mary was a patient, unfailing support.

'You have done everything you can,' she said for what was probably the hundredth time, 'you know all the arguments for keeping your existence secret. There is too much hatred and frustration bottled up for anyone to prevent what is going to happen. All you can do is to try to ensure that it is ended quickly, with an outcome that keeps Russia out of as much of Europe as possible.'

'I know, but I feel so helpless. It's not just the big picture, it's the personal aspect as well.' Mary took him in her arms, feeling the tension slowly leaving him as she stroked his neck.

'It's your parents you're thinking of again, isn't it? It must be so hard for you.'

Don grunted wearily. 'Fortunately they're still young children. I can't help wondering about them, although I know Charles is right when he tells me to leave them alone.'

'Well, what would you gain from seeing them? They're just like any other children, and won't even meet for years yet.'

He sighed reluctantly. 'I suppose you're right, but I still feel I should be introducing them to each other, or something!'

Mary grinned. 'From what I know of young children, that would just put them off each other for life!'

**Spring to Autumn 1936**

In the following year the pace of events quickened, although not all of them were concerned with the impending conflict. In January King George V died, and Don winced at reading the praise heaped upon his heir, the man who would not become King Edward VIII.

Spring saw rapid developments. In March, the political Left won the Spanish elections; yet another harbinger of war. In the same month, Hitler repudiated the Treaty of Locarno and sent German troops into the Rhineland, previously demilitarised following the last war. As a result of their ineffectual response, the French government was voted out of office in May in favour of Leon Blum's left-wing Popular Front. Churchill warned that failure to match Hitler's growing military strength could end in disaster for Britain. A government White Paper on defence, published in March, identified weaknesses and proposed increased spending. Newspapers were filled with concern about the adequacy of the country's defences and the threat of war.

Far from being worried, Dunning seemed quietly pleased. 'Every time the Nazis make an aggressive move that you've predicted, your stock goes up and your recommendations are given even more attention. People are feeling increasingly confident about being able to cope with the future.' No doubt, thought Don rather cynically, the attention isn't doing Dunning's status any harm either. However, his evident good humour paid off in a special treat; an unexpected trip for Mary and himself.

Dunning refused to state the destination or purpose, but the big Humber cruised steadily south until it reached Southampton late in the afternoon. Dunning led them to the water's edge near packed crowds and they looked out over the Solent. By now, Don knew what to expect. The weather was cool and cloudy, but the sun broke through as a huge passenger liner steamed slowly down the Solent.

'The Queen Mary!' Mary said, 'how wonderful!'

'Off on her maiden voyage,' added Dunning, 'first Cherbourg, then on to New York. Sure to win the Blue Riband.'

Don watched the magnificent ship with a strange mixture of emotions. Awe, at the majestic vessel. Excitement, at the noisy pride of the crowds. Perhaps above all, nostalgia, for an era he had never known. He thought about Jumbo Jets crammed with bleary-eyed, irritable passengers, and sighed.

The summer of 1936 saw no relief from the steady build-up of tension, as piece after piece dropped into place. In May, Italy conquered Abyssinia. The next month, Leon Blum's Popular Front government gave way to concerted strike action by signing the Matignon Agreement, giving French workers high pay for shorter hours and further damaging an already lamentable industrial performance. In

July, a right-wing revolt erupted in Spain; the Spanish Civil War had begun. In August, the Berlin Olympics were held.

The bad news wasn't restricted to Europe. Throughout the summer and autumn, Arabs rioted against the growing numbers of Jews in Palestine; British troops were involved. Don felt particularly low when he read this news.

'We haven't even begun this war yet, but more are already being lined up.'

He had to explain this to Mary; wars after 1945 in which Britain would not be involved had understandably been of little interest to the interviewers. Mary seemed particularly thoughtful.

'My mother was Jewish,' she said. Don looked at her speechlessly, thinking of all she had heard about the Holocaust. She raised her arms and shrugged helplessly. 'Why does the world have to be like this?' Don had no answer.

October 1936 saw a huge Nazi rally in Nuremberg and clashes between Mosley's Blackshirts and anti-fascist demonstrators in the East End of London. At the beginning of December, Mary found Don looking at the newspaper, sadness on his face.

'What's the matter?' she asked quickly. Don gestured at the paper. Mary looked at the item featured large on the page. The Crystal Palace had burned down.

'I never saw it,' said Don regretfully. 'It was the first thing which made me realise what had happened to me. And I never went to see it.'

## 1937–1938

The winter was marked by major events at each end of the social scale; unemployed workers marched from Jarrow to London, and King Edward VIII abdicated in order to marry Wallace Simpson. For Don, a much more significant event took place. On 1st January 1937 the Washington and London Naval Treaties expired and the keel-plates of the battleships *King George V* and *Prince of Wales* were laid at Walker-on-Tyne and Birkenhead respectively. So much was in Don's history; but these were to a different design, guided by his advice. It was the first concrete evidence he had received of the impact he was making.

The months skimmed by, a continual round of meetings with ever more urgent questions being asked as the nation's defence expenditure rose rapidly in the face of the German threat. Don found it more and more difficult to offer helpful advice. He felt drained dry of everything he had ever learned about the personalities, policies, strategies, tactics, equipment and events of the period.

Every now and then, his absorption was punctuated by a news item; the bombing of Guernica, the destruction of the Hindenburg at Lakehurst, the coronation of King George VI, the fall of Blum's government, followed by further rapid changes of government in France. The Japanese onslaught on China opened yet another chapter in the growing volume of the world's suffering, while European leaders scurried to and fro, meeting Hitler, trying to avoid the inevitable.

In early 1938 Dunning announced, with unusual good humour, that they were going on a tour, chaperoned by Geoffrey Taylor and himself.

'Something of a working visit,' he qualified apologetically, 'but I'm sure you'll find it interesting.'

Their first stop turned out to be an almost deserted rifle range 'somewhere in Surrey.' A small group of Army officers was huddled around some objects on a bench. Don was introduced as 'a senior civil servant in the Ministry' and the group parted to show him the weapons gleaming against the wooden bench. A Bren light machine gun was instantly recognisable. The warrant officer picked up a smaller weapon lying next to it. It was a short, brutal looking rifle, all metal pressings with a minimum of wood, a curved magazine jutting down behind the pistol grip.

'This is the new BSA rifle, called the Besal for short, which it is,' he laughed, ignoring the groans from the others. 'Action based on the Bren, but turned upside down and located within the stock, behind the handgrip. Calibre three-oh-three inch, self-loading with semi-automatic fire only. Empty cases are ejected straight upwards, but are deflected to one side by this rubber-padded underside of the cheekpiece, which can be instantly flipped over for left-handers. Weight ten pounds with a full fifteen-round magazine, which is interchangeable with the thirty-round Bren magazine. Like a go?'

Don declined, mildly alarmed. He had studied armaments, but firing them was something he had no experience of. The WO seemed disappointed, but not surprised. Doubtless his opinion of civil servants had just been confirmed. Taylor did not hesitate. He picked up the Besal, cycled the action with brisk efficiency then fired a rapid series of shots at the distant target. Don retrieved a distant memory; the Besal had actually been a simplified machine gun based on the Bren, which had not been adopted. Oh well, fairly close, he thought.

'This other beauty is the new Solen sub-machine gun,' continued the WO. Don, who had been slow to clap his hands over his ears when the Besal fired, barely heard him but hastily covered his ears again as Taylor picked up a weapon even uglier and more brutal looking. 'Based on the Solothurn SI-100 but simplified by Enfield for mass production. Chambered for the nine-by-twenty-five millimetre Mauser Export cartridge, longer and more powerful than the Luger round used in most such weapons. Gives it an effective range of around two hundred yards, which is enough for most purposes. Available with a wooden stock, like this one, or a folding metal one.' Taylor enjoyed this one even more, firing off the 32-round side-mounted magazine in short, controlled bursts.

Next came a conventional-looking self-loading pistol. 'Based on the American Colt M Nineteen-eleven, modified to fire the nine-by-twenty-five millimetre cartridge and with a two-row magazine holding fifteen rounds.' Dunning stepped forward this time, raised the gun, pulled back and released the slide, then fired off the entire magazine in a seemingly interminable string of concussions.

Dunning was smiling as they left. 'We've told the Army that these are meant for paratroops and marines, who'll need lots of firepower. Of course, we're preparing to mass-produce them instead of the Lee-Enfield Number Four bolt-action rifles.' Taylor snorted amiably, but made no comment.

The next stop was in Dorset, at another army camp busy with construction work. Some tanks were visible as they travelled through the site.

'This must be Bovington Camp,' guessed Don. Taylor merely smiled and led him into a large hangar-like building. An armed guard checked Taylor's and Dunning's passes carefully. Inside, some large shapes were covered with tarpaulins. A few men were sitting on boxes nearby, playing cards by the light filtering down from the skylights. They jumped up when they saw Taylor and moved to the shapes. Taylor was clearly enjoying himself, Dunning following quietly behind.

'We'll start with this one.' The tarpaulin was pulled away, revealing a low squat tank, the sloping armour giving a streamlined look. 'This is the Crusader. Eighteen tons, with two inches of armour on the turret and the frontal plate, one inch elsewhere. Engine at the front, beside the driver – a three hundred horsepower six-cylinder in-line unit; half a Rolls-Royce Merlin, actually. This leaves the rear half of the vehicle clear for the fighting compartment, in this case with a three-man turret mounting a two-pounder gun firing ammunition compatible with the Bofors forty millimetre AA gun – it makes resupply easier.' Don caught Taylor's wink as he remembered suggesting just that, in place of the very similar two-pounder ammunition historically used. 'Thoroughly tested in a wide variety of conditions and about to enter mass production in three different factories.' He moved on and more tarpaulins fell.

'All of the rest are based on the same chassis. The Comet anti-aircraft tank, with two twenty-millimetre Oerlikons in a power-driven turret. The Cromwell assault tank, with thicker armour – up to three inches – and a twenty-five pounder field gun in the turret. The Centaur self-propelled gun with the new sixty-two pounder field gun in an armoured compartment. It's a four-point-seven-inch gun firing the same shells, at a lower velocity, as the new navy dual purpose gun – which has incidentally also been adopted as the Army's heavy AA gun – and replaces the old five-inch sixty-pounder. Next comes the Cavalier tank destroyer with the new seventeen pounder – essentially the new three-inch high-velocity AA gun – behind an armoured shield. Last but not least, this Covenanter armoured personnel carrier, with a high, extended body carrying ten infantrymen.'

Don remembered the arguments about the anti-aircraft guns; his insistence on replacing the planned massive 3.7 inch with a smaller and much more mobile gun, which could do double duty as a tank/anti-tank gun, had evidently paid off.

They moved away from the men to more shapes at the other side of the hanger. Taylor spoke more quietly. 'Versions with more armour and more powerful guns are already fully developed, but we're keeping them back until we need them. We're also well advanced with testing the chassis of the next generation forty-tonner, with a turret large enough for the seventeen pounder gun or even bigger if required.'

They approached the other vehicles. The small Daimler Dingo armoured reconnaissance vehicle was instantly recognisable, but the big, low-slung six-wheeled armoured cars were not.

'These are made by Humber,' announced Taylor. 'Turret interchangeable with that in the tanks, so they can use similar armament. We're also developing a range of cross-country lorries using the same mechanicals.'

Don was in good humour after his tour around the Army bases. The following week, Helmsford arrived to brief him about progress with naval developments. Construction of the new battleships and aircraft carriers was proceeding apace, and the first of the fast, light carriers built on hulls originally intended for cruisers had been laid down. The new frigates, very light cruisers with four twin 4.7 inch dual-purpose turrets, were also taking shape. Then Helmsford changed the subject.

'There's something I've been meaning to ask you about. You mentioned two new German battlecruisers – what were they called?'

'Scharnhorst and Gneisenau,' Don replied promptly. 'Fast well-armoured ships, over thirty thousand tons, nine eleven-inch guns. They should have been commissioned by now, but I've not read a peep about them in the press. Have our agents reported anything?'

Helmsford looking at him curiously. 'No, they haven't,' he said. Dunning suddenly leaned forward, some sixth sense warning him. Don felt a sudden chill. Helmsford continued. 'We've been watching the German dockyards carefully, even 'accidentally' overflying them with photo-reconnaissance aircraft. The Germans are not building any more big ships. Nothing but small destroyers and submarines.'

Don stared aghast. 'But we've done nothing…nothing that could cause them to change their naval strategy as drastically as this.'

Dunning's breath hissed between his teeth. 'If you were helping Germany instead of us, would you advise them to build big ships?'

Don looked at him helplessly. 'No,' he said. 'They were a waste of resources.'

Helmsford passed him a photograph. 'What do you make of that? It was taken in the Baltic.'

It was an oblique view of a sleek hull, low in the water, topped by a slender fin. There were no guns or other distinguishing features, except for a periscope-like object with an unusually massive head. Don stared, appalled.

'It's an Elektroboot – a high-speed submarine,' he whispered.

'When are they supposed to emerge?' Dunning asked sharply.

Don swallowed. 'Nineteen forty-five.'

The three men looked at each other, none wanting to put into words the icy certainty forming in their minds. Eventually Dunning spoke.

'That's torn it,' he said quietly. He looked at the white-faced Erlang. 'They've got someone like you, haven't they? Someone just like you.'

# CHAPTER 2 - PRELUDE

**Spring 1938**

Don felt a powerful sense of déjà vu. The smoky room was the same and, with the exception of Elderly Cigar, the men were the same, despite the passage of time. It was the first meeting of this group Don had attended for over three years; he still did not know the names of the men, although Dunning had told him that the group was called the Oversight Committee. Unlike the air of perplexed scepticism which had greeted his previous visits, the mood was one of anxious tension. Chairman drew deeply on a cigarette.

'We've all heard the evidence, and have agreed that it's a strong indication that the Nazis are also receiving advice from the future. We now need to review the impact on our strategy.'

No-one spoke. Even Diplomat looked grim and worried. Don realised that they were upset not just by the threat of a suddenly uncertain war, but by the concepts that they were trying to grapple with. Their known, predictable world was becoming dangerously unstable. They had lost control of their situation and no longer knew what to do.

Don cleared his throat. 'I have been giving some thought to this. We essentially have a three-level problem. First, what would Hitler have done given the sort of knowledge I have. Second, what would he do if he also knew that Britain had similar foreknowledge of events. Third, how would his actions be affected if he also knew that we knew that he had such knowledge?'

Diplomat recovered a little of his sense of humour. 'If he knows that we know that he knows that we know…' he murmured. Chairman glared briefly at him then turned to Don with something of the air of a drowning man thrown a lifeline.

'Let's take the simplest case first. How would you have advised Hitler?'

Don settled into his lecture. 'There were certain key strategic errors which lost Germany the war. Declaring war on the USA was one of the biggest and certainly the most unnecessary in terms of Hitler's objectives.'

Military Man frowned. 'What about the attack on the Soviet Union? You've always said that Germany would have lost that war even if the Americans and ourselves hadn't invaded France.'

'It wasn't the attack that was the mistake, but the aftermath. Many of the states of the Soviet Union were sick to death of the Russians in general and Stalin in particular. The invading German army was welcomed with open arms in many places. If Hitler had offered states such as the Ukraine and the Baltic countries independence under an overall Reich oversight, regardless of whether he intended to stick to it, he very likely would have had firm allies against Russia. Instead, he treated them as underpeople and unleashed the SS on them. As a result, he managed to weld the Soviet Union together into a formidable and single-minded enemy. That lost Germany the war, not just on the eastern front but altogether.'

There was a thoughtful pause. 'That seems to be poetic justice,' observed Diplomat, 'but I'm not sure where it takes us.'

'What about the potential for alliances?' The curls were still creamed if somewhat greyer. 'Can't we tie the Soviets to us now in order to pre-empt Germany's non-aggression pact with them?'

Military Man was dismissive. 'Given Stalin's purges of the officer corps, the Soviet armed forces are more of a liability than an asset, and will be for some time to come.'

'They're unlikely to want to get involved unless they are convinced that they're being directly threatened in any case,' added Diplomat, 'on the other hand, they could be useful in restraining Japan.'

'What chance is there of bringing in the Americans?'

'None. Roosevelt is sympathetic, but America in general is more isolationist than ever before.'

There was a pause broken by Chairman, who turned to Don. 'Go on', he said grimly, 'what else?'

Don shrugged. 'Letting Britain off the hook in nineteen-forty was a major mistake, of course. More thorough prewar preparation would probably have led to the defeat of Britain.' Ruddy Face shifted uncomfortably. Don went on hastily. 'The emphasis on high-performance submarines rather than heavy surface ships is clear. We can also expect to see heavy bombers entering Luftwaffe service; that was one of the few technical areas the Germans never got right. Finally, I expect much attention is being given to tank landing ships and the like. And when it comes to tactics, they will have two priorities; the neutralisation of the Royal Navy with mines, submarines and air attacks to prevent interference with an invasion, and the capture of the British Expeditionary Force. They will not permit a Dunkirk this time around.'

Chairman looked at him sourly. 'Is that it?'

'Basically, yes. The Germans didn't make many mistakes in fighting the war. Fortunately for my time, the ones they did make were big ones. There is one thing that I'm finding it hard to understand, though.' They looked expectantly. 'The Nazis were utterly reviled and rejected in my time, nowhere more so than in Germany. They were so sensitive about militarism, I simply can't understand how any educated German from my time could help Hitler to win the war.'

The others looked uncomprehending. 'If he's a German, he'll support the Germans, surely. In fact,' Chairman gestured at the photographs of the electroboat, 'he obviously is.'

Creamed Curls leaned forward anxiously. 'What can we do to stop them this time?'

'Some of the actions we're already taking. If we keep our army out of France and prepare our defences we can still make a German invasion difficult if not impossible. The advanced anti-submarine equipment and methods we are working on should be able to cope with the electroboats, albeit with much more difficulty. Unfortunately there's nothing we can do about the other matters. In fact, if the Germans advise the Japanese about the outcome of their attack on America, they might refrain and thereby keep the Americans out of the war altogether.'

Diplomat leaned back thoughtfully. 'I'm not certain the situation is quite as bad as that. For a start, the Japanese are both suspicious and arrogant, and probably won't believe the Germans unless they provide them with incontrovertible evidence, which they may be reluctant to do for the same reasons that we're keeping quiet about you.' He carefully fitted another cigarette into his holder. 'I have also been studying all the information you've provided about Hitler. He is clearly not entirely rational and might not be prepared to listen to sensible advice. His racism is so intense, so integral to his entire philosophy, that he might not be able to refrain from his treatment of Jews and the eastern peoples.'

Chairman sighed. 'And that's the easy situation? Now, what's likely to change if Hitler knows that we know?'

'That could depend to some extent on when he knows. So far, we haven't done anything publicly except amend the battleship armament calibre from fourteen to fifteen inches, which is subtle enough to be missed. The longer we can keep him in the dark the better. That means concealing some of the new developments for as long as possible. Once my opposite number sees the angled decks on the aircraft carriers, the proverbial will hit the fan.'

The others looked momentarily mystified, then Ruddy Face grunted. 'That won't be long, then. The first two Ark Royal class vessels are due for completion this year.'

'Have you noticed any alterations to German actions which might indicate that they know about you?' Chairman enquired.

Don considered. 'There's a lot happening but it all sounds familiar.' He started ticking points off on his fingers. 'Hitler is now exercising personal command over the armed forces, has set up a Cabinet Council to advise on foreign policy, forced the Minister of War and the Army Commander-in-Chief to resign together with many other senior officers unsympathetic to Nazism. He is putting heavy pressure on the Austrians prior to declaring the union of Austria with Germany. Business as usual.'

'So what is he likely to do when he does find out?' Creamed Curls was sounding increasingly anxious.

'Almost impossible to say. He first has to assess what we're likely to do. We considered our strategic options the last time we met, and Hitler will be faced with the same possibilities. As far as he's concerned, those could range from our declaring war over Czechoslovakia to staying out of the war altogether. When the truth dawns on him, he ought to be a very worried man.'

Hitler wasn't worried yet but Konrad Herrman certainly was, albeit for quite different reasons; he was not a naval expert and the significance of the amendment to the details of the Second London Naval Treaty had passed him by. He was reviewing his personal strategy for at least the thousandth time since waking up seventy years in his past, and was increasingly aware of the tightrope he was walking. He lay back on his bed and sighed, feeling sick and weary to the core, and thought through the arguments again.

The demolition of the Berlin Wall had shattered the prison in which he had spent all of his adult life, and had enabled him to resume his academic career. He had been brought up by his grandparents, his mother dying in the aftermath of the Red Army's final onslaught on Berlin, his father in the Soviet prison camp he had been taken to within weeks of Herrman's birth. His youthful interest in history had been encouraged by his teachers and had secured him first a place as an undergraduate, then as a postgraduate researcher, and finally as a professor. That was when the trouble started. His curiosity had unveiled inconsistencies in the official version of the Great Patriotic War; his stubbornness had led him to investigate areas frowned on by the Party. The result: rapid deflection into a routine clerical post away from sensitive material. His young wife had been unable to stand the shame and had left him to bring up Stefan alone.

Stefan. He was able to think of his son now without anguish, just a deep, sad, sense of loss. The boy had been brilliant; sharp, keen, full of life and laughter. And fatally impatient. Herrman thought of the Wall again and felt the familiar tension in his stomach, the hate slowly burning. Stefan had been one of its last victims, unable to wait to be freed by the changes already in the air. Herrman tensed his muscles for a few seconds then released them with a deep sigh. He was right. His past must not be repeated. Stalin must not win.

He rolled on his side, trying to shut out the memories of the terrible photographs, the appalling names. Auschwitz. Belsen. Buchenwald. Treblinka. Could he do it? Could he stop all of this from happening again? Was it possible to find a middle way between the excesses of Hitler and Stalin – to preserve Germany but use the influence given him by his unique position to steer the country down a more civilised road? He didn't know, but he felt his determination firming afresh; he was going to do everything he could to try. First and foremost, for Germany to stand any chance against the Soviet Union, Britain had to be knocked out of the war as soon as possible.

'It's happened then.' Mary walked into the library, holding a message slip from the communications unit based at the house. 'Hitler moved into Austria on March the fifteenth, exactly on schedule.'

Don nodded resignedly. As he had predicted, all of the efforts of von Schuschnigg, the Austrian Chancellor, to preserve his country's independence had failed. A last-minute attempt to hold a plebiscite to determine the wishes of the people had been blocked by German pressure, which had then forced the resignation of von Schuschnigg in favour of the Nazi, von Seyss-Inquart. Anschluss – the incorporation of Austria into the Reich – had followed.

She sat in an easy chair and looked at Don. 'Next will come Czechoslovakia. Are we sure that the politicians will keep us out of this one? From what you said before, there's quite a risk of war.'

'I think we're safe. Chamberlain is no war-monger, and I know that the Foreign Office has been pressing him not to get Britain involved. The only reason that Chamberlain is trying to mediate is that he's afraid that if Germany does invade Czechoslovakia, France might feel bound to go to her defence, and Britain could be dragged in later. If all goes well – for us, that is, not the Czechs – Hitler's informant will have no reason to suspect my existence from any changes in our policy.'

'Is there any risk that the Czechs will fight this time? They've been making a lot of defence preparations.'

'They did last time, but it won't do them any good. Germany is too strong for the Czechs to stand up to alone. Even if they do fight, and Germany defeats them militarily, I can't see that making much difference to subsequent events. Poland will be next on Hitler's list, to enable him to get at the Soviet Union.'

'Does that have to be so? The German propaganda only seems concerned about the position of Danzig and the treatment of Germans within Poland. I would have thought that a diplomatic solution would be possible.'

Don sighed. 'In a sensible world it would, my love. But the Germans have been demanding the reunification of Danzig with Germany, plus access through Poland to Danzig, since before Hitler came to power. Hitler would prefer to gain this without fighting, of course, but this would effectively cut off Poland's access to the sea, which is too vital to their economy for them to agree to. In any case, Hitler would only use any Polish concessions as a springboard for a later attack. German hatred of the Slav peoples has a long history; the Germans have regarded Eastern Europe as territory for expansion since the Teutonic Knights first invaded centuries ago.'

Mary walked over and slipped her arm around him. 'Sometimes it seems so unreal. Here we are, in the peace of an English springtime, talking about the certainty of a horrible future. It seems almost…biblical, like the Apocalypse.'

Don thought of the nuclear weapons programme and gripped her hand. He had not wanted to give encouragement to the atomic research which had been in progress anyway, but the thought of Hitler's adviser providing him with such a weapon chilled the blood.

'Let's hope you're wrong,' he whispered.

Herrman was feeling nervous, as he always did before meeting Hitler. He was uncomfortably aware of the dissonance between his knowledge of the crimes committed on Hitler's orders, and the way in which this extraordinary man seemed to look on Herrman as a personal totem, a sign from above of Hitler's destiny. This evening the Fuhrer was with Göring, both of them in high good humour.

'Have you seen this?' Hitler waved a press report. 'Franco's showing the way, and proving you right about the bombers!'

Herrman looked at the paper, which reported the results of three days of bombing raids on Barcelona. Nearly a thousand were believed killed with thousands more injured. No wonder Göring was looking smug, he thought. Successes for air power meant a higher status for the Luftwaffe, and more influence for Göring.

'The prototype of the new Heinkel four-engined bomber is almost ready to fly, with the big Dornier following a few months later,' Göring stated. 'Thanks to your advice, Professor, there is little doubt that they will be successful. By the end of nineteen-forty we will have a force of heavy bombers capable of bringing Britain to the conference table on her knees.'

Herrman could not help pointing out the obvious. 'It won't be enough by itself.'

'Yes I know,' said Göring, tetchily. 'The new submarines are doing well on trials, I hear, but they will only be of use against Britain. The bombers will also have the power to reach out and crush Russia after Britain has surrendered.'

'But they will not be enough for that task, either.' Herrman ploughed on doggedly, unsure whether to be more worried about Göring's increasing irritation or the glint in Hitler's eyes. 'It is imperative to win the Soviet satellite states over to our side.'

Hitler stood abruptly, forcing Herrman to do the same. 'With your knowledge, we will deal with everyone who stands in our way. We have been given another chance to deal with the Slavs. We cannot lose this time. Why else would you have been sent to us?' He turned abruptly and left the room.

Göring eyed Herrman sardonically. 'Be careful, Professor,' he said softly. 'To survive here you need friends. With your support, my position will become unchallengeable. With my support, you can have anything you want. Just think about it.' He smiled benevolently and followed Hitler from the room.

Shaken, Herrman sat down abruptly. After such sessions, he could never decide whether his feelings of nausea were due to the release of tension or simple revulsion. Despite his fear of the casual, cruel power of Hitler and his cronies, he knew he could not give up. He was driven to try to achieve the best for Germany and the rest of Europe, whatever the cost to himself.

Don was feeling equally nauseous, but in his case it was due entirely to the rhythmical motion of the Hunt class corvette as it cruised down the Channel at twenty knots. It was a bright, fresh, April day and the sea seemed calm, but a steady swell was rolling in from the Atlantic. Helmsford, unfamiliar in naval uniform, stood easily beside him on the bridge and considered his distress.

'I think I should prescribe some medicinal brandy,' he said judiciously.

'Will that make me feel better?'

'Perhaps not, but it will at least take your mind off it.'

The commanding officer laughed. 'I hope this isn't putting you off the Atherstone. She's a beautiful little ship.'

'I'm sure Dr Erlang appreciates her,' said Helmsford drily.

Don had as usual been introduced as a senior official in the Ministry and no-one except Helmsford was aware of the fundamental role he had played in specifying the design of the new class of escorts. Although generally similar in size and purpose to the historical 'Hunts', the design differed in many details. She included all of the wartime lessons that Don could recall, with an emphasis on anti-submarine and anti-aircraft armament, a hull designed for heavy-weather performance rather than the smooth-water speed of the traditional destroyer, and an accommodation layout intended to ensure reasonable comfort on Atlantic winter patrols. So the radar, two twin-4 inch, dual-purpose guns and multiple 40 mm and 20 mm automatics dealt with surface and aerial targets, while the forward-firing 'Squid', coupled with the pencil-beam sonar, saw to the anti-submarine role. Using one half of a destroyer's twin-screw powerplant, she was fast enough to deal with the new high-speed U-boats and a much more useful escort vessel than a destroyer, while costing far less to build. As a result, the corvettes were being built at three times the rate of destroyers, to the anguish of many in the Navy.

Helmsford led Don to the CO's cabin immediately behind the bridge and poured him the prescribed brandy from a bottle which he triumphantly produced from his briefcase. He seemed far more cheerful now he was at sea.

'Foresee all eventualities, that's my motto. Seriously, how do you like her?'

'Looks OK, but I'm not exactly an expert. The captain seems pleased, though.'

Helmsford grinned. 'Commanding officers always are. The important thing is how she performs against the electroboats. The rush job to produce high-speed submarines for target practice is on schedule, so he'll soon have something to get stuck into.'

'I didn't say anything about advanced submarines earlier on,' Don admitted. 'I couldn't see any point. We didn't need them, and if we built them the Germans would soon copy us.' He settled back into the only chair in the cramped cabin; Helmsford made himself comfortable on the bunk.

'We still don't really know what the new U-boats will be capable of,' Helmsford pointed out.

'We can assume that the combination of larger electric motors, larger battery capacity and streamlining will double their underwater speed to around seventeen knots. The boat in the picture seems to have a schnorkel as well, so it can run its diesels for cruising or recharging while staying underwater.'

Helmsford nodded. 'The combination of the big electric motors from the Thames class in a streamlined version of the small 'S' class hull should give comparable performance for our target, albeit without the range.' He leaned back on the bunk, sipping his brandy thoughtfully. 'It does seem strange, you know. All my training and experience, all the assumptions in the Service, lead to enemy battlefleets being treated as the major threat and our own capital ships as the best counter to them. Yet here we are, quietly preparing for an entirely different kind of war to the one my fellow officers expect. They would be horrified if they knew.'

Don grunted. 'As long as the equipment and training are provided, they'll cope. Lack of competence was not something that the Navy was accused of in my time.' He looked around the cramped cabin and smiled. 'Thanks for arranging this. I'll never be much of a sailor, but anything to get out of that house for a while.'

Helmsford looked at him sympathetically. 'I can imagine how you feel. If you like, I think I can arrange some more trips. The first of the new frigates is working up, with the battleships and aircraft carriers following shortly after, not to mention the assorted amphibious mongrels.' He grinned again. 'There can't be many people who can claim to have been responsible for the design of a whole new navy!' He fiddled with the glass for a moment then asked abruptly, 'what chance does Poland have?'

Don was surprised. 'Basically, none. They are surrounded by potential enemies with Britain and France too far away to be able to intervene. And although Poland has a large army, it is nothing like as well trained and equipped as the Germans'.'

Helmsford sighed. 'It just seems such an appalling mess,' he muttered.

**Autumn 1938**

Herrman stood in the warm August sunshine, peering over the desolate countryside; heathland scattered with groups of trees. A deep, rumbling roar like distant, continuous thunder slowly built in volume. Vague movement became visible through the screen of trees. The roar gained a hard, clanking edge and the ground began to shake. Herrman knew what to expect, but even so he found himself filled with an unreasoning, atavistic fear. He flinched as a line of tanks burst through the undergrowth like a pack of hunting dinosaurs, roaring towards his position at over thirty kilometres per hour.

Stadler laughed. 'Don't worry, they're on our side. But God help the troops who have to stand their ground against this lot.'

Over a hundred tanks were now visible, storming across the heath, fire blasting from their cannon as they passed in front of their viewing platform. Behind them came the boxy shapes of the armoured personnel carriers. As they came abreast of the platform, they stopped as one, hatches bursting open and troops tumbling to the ground, the air suddenly filled with the crackling roar of a thousand automatic weapons. A wave of self-propelled guns crashed into view, some heavy artillery, some with automatic anti-aircraft guns. They slewed to a halt and added to the appalling din. At the front of the platform, Hitler clapped his hands with delight while the generals beside him looked on smugly.

Stadler spoke in his ear. 'The boys are pleased with their new toys. Guderian is in seventh heaven.' Stadler's casual disrespect never failed to amaze Herrman. The SD man had been assigned to him only recently, the latest in a line of 'aides' whose job seemed to be to accompany him at all times.

They were attending the beginning of ten weeks of manoeuvres involving three-quarters of a million men. Hitler had been keen to see the first of the new armoured formations which Herrman had persuaded him to create. As ever, he insisted on taking Herrman with him. The firing suddenly stopped and the soldiers jumped to their feet and stood to attention. Hitler and the generals strode down from the platform to inspect the nearest men.

'All hand picked,' observed Stadler. 'Aryan supermen with perfect teeth.' As ever, his dark, brilliantined hair was perfectly slicked back, his black leather coat immaculate, his patrician features set in a complex expression that Herrman could only describe to himself as a varying mixture of boredom, arrogance, disdain and watchfulness. At the moment, bored disdain predominated.

'Göring won't allow this little show to pass without response. We'll be at an airfield within a week.'

In fact it took ten days before they stood on a bleak, windswept airfield, admiring the new Heinkel He 177 as it prepared for flight. Standing with a group of senior Luftwaffe officers was Vuillemin, the Chief of the French Air Staff, who was being impressed by the strength of the German military preparations in a calculated – and successful – attempt at intimidation. Herrman looked at him with interest, knowing that his worried report of his visit would influence France against going to war over Czechoslovakia. The Daimler-Benz engines roared into life, four propellers slowly accelerating in turn – Herrman's anxious pleas had led to the rapid abandonment of the plan for coupled engines, as well as the need to strengthen the plane for dive-bombing. The huge plane bristled with turrets mounting the new Rheinmetall-Borsig MG 131 machine guns. It was clearly in a different league from its predecessor, the He 111.

'I've just realised,' remarked Stadler over the thundering engines, 'why the Kriegsmarine has so little influence.' Herrman waited for the punchline. 'Their toys don't make enough noise!'

They watched the big Heinkel lumber along the runway before lifting off and climbing away with surprising speed. As it disappeared into the distance, an assortment of other aircraft roared low overhead. Herrman automatically identified formations of Messerschmitt Bf 109s, Junkers Ju 88s, Focke-Wulf Fw 187s, Dornier Do 217s and the sole prototype of the new Focke-Wulf Fw 190. They circled the airfield then all landed in neat sequence, pulling off the runway to allow the He 177 to land, which it did with immaculate timing just as the Fw 190 took its place in the line-up. As the Heinkel rolled to a halt, the crews of all of the planes jumped out and stood to attention beside them.

'Trust Göring to put on a show,' Stadler commented as the portly General strode jovially beside Hitler to view the aircraft. 'Somehow I can't see Raeder getting the Führer to look at submarines.'

## Spring 1939

Judging by the volume of tobacco smoke, the Oversight Committee had been in session for some time when Don was invited to join them. They were no longer surprised when he immediately opened a window, despite the slight chill in the spring air. Chairman gestured genially at him, and Don judged that the atmosphere was more relaxed than before.

'It might be helpful for us to review our discussion. I understand that so far there has been no deviation from your predictions?'

Don leaned back in his chair, his expression thoughtful as he reviewed the last few months. The latter part of September 1938 had seen frantic diplomatic activity, sparked by a Nuremburg Congress speech by Hitler in which he demanded that 'the oppression of three and a half million Germans in Czechoslovakia shall cease and be replaced by the right of self-determination'. Three days later Chamberlain, alarmed that Germany was on the point of starting a European war, had flown to Munich to see Hitler at Berchtesgaden; the first of a rapid round of shuttle diplomacy involving the French and Italian leaders as well, and culminating in the Munich Conference in which the other European powers acquiesced to the transfer of German-populated parts of Czechoslovakia to Germany. This outcome had been greeted with widespread relief in Britain, despite Winston Churchill denouncing it as a servile act of appeasement. On 1st October, German troops had marched into Czechoslovakia and met no resistance.

Several months of uneasy peace had followed in Europe, punctuated in November by the savage German reprisals against German Jews following the shooting in Paris of von Rath, a German diplomat, by a Polish Jew. Mass emigration of Jews from Germany had resulted, encouraged by the Nazis (who confiscated their property) but limited by the willingness of other nations to absorb large numbers of refugees when they were themselves still suffering from unemployment. The Jews' favoured destination of Palestine was no help to the British who had been given a mandate by the League of Nations to manage the country; violent clashes with the resident Palestinians were intensifying.

Then on March 10th, less than two months ago, the Czech crisis had erupted again. Dr Tiso, the Slovak premier, was arrested on orders of Dr Hacha, the Czechoslovak president, for attempting to establish an independent Slovakia. Tiso visited Hitler a few days later; as a result, Hacha was invited to meet Hitler and forced to sign documents turning the Czech lands of Bohemia and Moravia into German protectorates. Prague was occupied by German troops on March 15th. Czechoslovakia had finally been dismembered.

Last of all, the long and bitter Spanish Civil War had finally ground to a halt on 31st March with the capitulation of the Republican government to Franco's forces, much to the jubilation of the supporting Italian and German governments.

Don was jolted from his thoughts as Chairman impatiently cleared his throat. 'Yes, I haven't noticed any changes in the pattern of events so far.'

'Good. Now Czechoslovakia's out of the way, Hitler's beginning to shape up to Poland.'

Don nodded. 'I read of his Reichstag speech the other day, denouncing the non-aggression pact with Poland and calling for the annexation of Danzig. On top of his demand for the return of German-speaking regions of Poland, he's on course for an invasion in September.'

'Is there nothing we can do to warn the Poles?' Don was amused to note that Creamed Curls had somehow retained his hopeful optimism.

'They know about the danger, all right,' said Military Man, 'I was over there the other week with the military attaché. The trouble is that they are banking on their alliance with France to deter Germany, or if the worst comes to the worst, they think they can hold out against the Germans until the French can come to their aid. Unfortunately, they don't appreciate the speed of the blitzkrieg they are about to face so they don't realise that they won't have time to mobilise their forces properly.'

'Can't we at least get them to mobilise in advance?'

'The problem with that is that it would raise the level of tension considerably as it's the final stage before a declaration of war, so France is pressing Poland not to do it. In any case, it would only delay the inevitable. The Poles simply don't have the modern equipment, tactics or trained manpower to hold out for long, despite their undoubted courage and determination. Whatever we were to do at this stage, it's too late to save them from their fate.'

'At least we've managed to dissuade Chamberlain from guaranteeing their independence this time, which was quite a struggle. There's a lot of political pressure to be seen to be taking action to stop Hitler's escapades.' This from Diplomat. 'He wanted to give guarantees to Rumania and Greece as well, after the Italians invaded Albania. He's becoming very irritated with us, but of course we can't yet tell him about Dr Erlang – it would be difficult to do so, bearing in mind that he needs to step aside once war commences.'

'What about the Soviet attitude?'

Diplomat shrugged. 'We have been trying to involve them in some sort of agreement for collective security, but they remain as impenetrable and paranoid as ever. They won't believe anything we tell them as they're convinced, not without cause, that we'd like to see them and Germany fight each other to a standstill. One side benefit of refusing to guarantee Poland is that we've thereby avoided annoying the Russians, but persuading them to commit themselves to an agreement is another matter. The Poles, of course, are in any case refusing to co-operate over any plans which would involve Russians moving into their territory to help defend them.' He sighed. 'Then there's the Finland problem. We know that Russia plans to invade later this year, and that there will be strong pressure to go to Finland's aid, but we must resist that at all costs – it would be disastrous to be drawn into a war against the USSR.'

Chairman intervened. 'France is still shaky, despite the failure of the general strike last autumn. They are uneasy about their treaty with Poland, and would be very reluctant to get involved without us. They're much more worried about Italy's territorial claims against them. And Spain has no interest in anything other than recovering quietly from their civil war. As for Italy – did you say it was next month they're due to sign a treaty with Germany?'

Don nodded. 'Mussolini will be determined to link Italy with Germany. The Albanian coup, following on from his Ethiopian success, will have boosted his confidence. He seems to be spoiling for a fight with France.'

'Let's turn to Ireland. Our first real change in policy was the decision to refuse to hand back the Irish bases. That took a lot of work with the politicians, who wanted to keep the Irish happy. And now we have IRA bombs going off in London.'

Don was unconcerned. 'As I recall, that happened anyway. Nothing will appease some sections of the Irish while partition remains in force. And the bases will be very valuable in a year's time.'

Chairman sighed. 'Very well, then. What about outside Europe?'

'No real change in China,' commented Military Man, 'the Japanese are continuing with their invasion despite constant harassment by Chiang Kai-Shek's forces and the Chinese Communists. It's just guerilla warfare, though, they can't stand up to the Japanese in open battle.'

'And the American attitude?'

Diplomat looked thoughtful. 'Roosevelt's speech to Congress in January was a hopeful sign, but it doesn't seem to have had much effect on the generally isolationist view. And the Nazi sympathisers have a high profile there.'

Don recalled that Roosevelt had warned of the dangers from aggressor states and suggested that the possibility of America's remaining isolated from the troubles of the rest of the world had become much reduced. On the other hand, right-wingers such as Charles Lindbergh, the pilot who had become a national hero after his solo transatlantic flight, had a lot of influence.

Chairman looked at Don dourly. 'There is, of course, one other possibility which we have so far not considered. What if other countries have been blessed with visitors from the future? Russia? Japan? America?'

The Committee looked at Don in consternation. 'That has occurred to me,' he said slowly, 'but so far I have seen no evidence to support the idea. On the other hand, we might well not find out until the fighting starts.'

Chairman surveyed the Committee intently before bringing the meeting to a close. Don was aware of a heightened tension – shared in it, in fact – and realised that they were all beginning to brace themselves for what lay ahead. The time for theorising was coming to an end. The necessary preparations were well in hand. Europe's inexorable slide to war had become a free fall.

## Summer 1939

'I still don't think this is a good idea.' Don was feeling grumpy, probably because he had been standing in the rain in a crowded Hyde Park for the past two hours. Dunning was more philosophical.

'It's the price we have to pay,' he said. 'Chamberlain was most annoyed that we dissuaded him from giving his guarantee to Poland, and he insisted that the King's review of the National Defence Forces went ahead in order to try to frighten Hitler. Extended the scope, in fact.'

Don grunted irritably. An apparently endless stream of first aid, fire service, ARP and other civil defence volunteers had marched through the Park past the King's saluting stand. What bothered him most, however, was the grand finale. He didn't have long to wait. A growing roar, partly mechanical, partly from the cheering crowd, preceded the arrival of most of the 1st Mechanised Division. The two observers watched with mixed emotions as the first reconnaissance units came into view, pennants proudly flying from the aerials of the little Daimler

Dingos. Hard on their heels came the big Humber armoured cars, two-pounder guns poking menacingly forwards. Last, filling the air with their thunder, came rank after rank of Crusader tanks.

'Thank God we managed to hold back the other tracked vehicles. It's bad enough giving the Germans a free view of this lot.'

'Don't thank God,' corrected Dunning, 'thank the Oversight Committee.'

His last words were drowned out by the roar of aero-engines as formations of warplanes flew low overhead, beneath the cloudbase. A fleet of Hurricanes, Spitfires, Blenheims, Hampdens and Wellingtons filled the sky. Don anxiously studied the Hampdens. The other aircraft would look familiar enough to anyone of his time, but thanks to his advice the Handley Page bomber was significantly different, with its circular-section fuselage, big Hercules engines and power-operated dorsal and ventral gun-turrets.

'Sorry about the Hampdens,' shouted Dunning. 'It was hard enough keeping the RAF from including Reapers, Mosquitoes and Herefords, but we managed to persuade them that it wouldn't be in the interests of national security. And of course, the Fleet Air Arm wanted their Beaufighters and Beauforts to join the fun as well. Had to promise them a separate naval review to pacify them.'

Don grimaced. The Gloster Reaper was an historical design which had been brought forward at his recommendation. A single-seat long-range fighter, its twin Merlin engines gave it a phenomenal performance and the quartet of Hispano cannon under the nose provided firepower to match. The Mosquito was very much as he remembered it, whereas the Hereford was a variant of the Hampden with a solid nose packed with machine guns, powerful anti-tank guns installed in the bomb bay and additional armour protection for the ground-attack role. He wasn't sure if Bristol had been influenced to name their new carrier planes after historical models, but in any case the Beaufighter and Beaufort were very different. The former was a single-engined, single-seat fighter-bomber based on Bristol's historical Type 153 design study for a Hercules-engined fighter. The Beaufort, a single-engined, multi-role two-seater, was as similar as possible, using the same engine installation and many common parts to ease maintenance in service.

Dunning suddenly rummaged in an inside pocket. 'By the way, I think we've identified your friend.' He produced an envelope which Don opened under cover of Dunning's umbrella. In it was a photograph of a man in civilian clothes standing in a group of men, mostly in German military uniform, except for someone standing close to him who was wearing a leather coat.

'Part of Hitler's entourage. We have several photographs of him, but so far have been unable to find out who he is. All we know is his name: Professor Herrman. He holds no official position and we've been unable to trace his background.'

Don stared at the photograph with sudden intensity, as if to try to read the man's mind. The picture showed a tall, slim, bespectacled figure in his late sixties with light, probably grey, wavy hair. He seemed preoccupied, somehow depressed.

'It would fit Hitler's character to want to keep a chap like this around him. Probably makes him feel more confident.'

What are you doing? Don thought. What is motivating you? Do you remember the Cold War, the Common Market, German reunification? What is in your mind?

Herrman was feeling bored. He studied the photographs again and looked up at Stadler.

'I can't tell you much,' he said hesitantly, 'but I believe these ships carried few aircraft because of the weight of their armoured decks. They were never as effective as the Japanese or American carriers.'

He pushed back the photographs of the *Ark Royal* and *Illustrious*. They had all been taken at flight-deck level so that the angled deck was not obvious. Herrman was not to know of the efforts the Oversight Committee had put in to ensure that no more revealing pictures emerged. Neither did he realise that the biplanes carefully parked on the decks bore no resemblance to the fast monoplanes with which the navy pilots were practising away from prying eyes.

Stadler sighed. 'Very well then, do these jog your memory? They are the new battleships *King George V* and *Prince of Wales*.'

Herrman shrugged. 'The names are familiar, but I really can't tell you much about their strengths and weaknesses. I seem to remember that they had a lot of trouble with their main armament. It was a new design, and kept breaking down in action.'

Stadler looked at him in astonishment. 'But these use old guns and turrets from Great War ships. That's why they could build them so quickly.'

Herrman frowned, confused. Stadler pushed forward some pictures of the Hyde Park Review. 'What about their mechanised division?'

Herrman studied the photographs and his confusion increased. 'Six-wheeled armoured cars? And these tanks have sloped armour! I'm certain that something is wrong here.'

Stadler looked at him intently, then drew some more photographs from his briefcase. 'These were taken with great difficulty at an army training ground by a sympathiser of Irish origin. What do you make of them?'

Herrman's breath hissed out at the sight of the box-shaped parachutes. He scrabbled quickly through the photographs, stopping at a slightly blurred close-up of the back of a paratrooper. The Besal rifle slung over his shoulder was clearly visible, the brutal appearance of the bullpup quite unlike any rifle which should be in existence. Herrman stared at it in growing horror.

'Oh my God,' he said slowly.

Himmler was coldly furious. 'So all of the time you have been telling us that you can give us the key to world domination, the British have had someone doing the same for them?'

The two men did not reply. Herrman noticed that the SD man's normal air of ironic insouciance was not in evidence. Himmler paced in agitation.

'Does this change our plans? What threat can the British mount against us?'

Stadler diplomatically let Herrman reply. 'It's difficult to say. We have discussed it, of course, but it is difficult to see how the British could stop us on land. If they warned the Poles, I can't see that making much difference. Our armed forces are far too strong for them. In any case, the British have refrained from giving any guarantee to Poland and the French are keeping very quiet about their old treaty. The signs are good that they will not even declare war this time.'

Himmler glared at him. 'What about us defeating the British?'

'That will be much more difficult. They will certainly be better prepared for an invasion. I still think, though, that our new submarines will be more than a match for them. We can still starve them to the negotiating table.'

Himmler stared coldly at them. 'I don't think you realise how serious this is. It isn't just a question of military advantage. The Führer is convinced that your arrival is a sign of his destiny.' He made a rapid decision. 'Tell no-one of this. I will put some trusted men onto examining the military implications and planning appropriate measures.

In the meantime, no-one – and I mean absolutely no-one – is to be informed.'

**Autumn 1939**

'The French are panicking, as expected.' Dunning had become quite philosophical about the onward march of events during his years of association with Don. 'Germany's non-aggression pact with the Soviet Union is causing some real flutters.'

Don grunted. 'Well it might. Nine days to go. Let's hope to God that someone's sitting on Chamberlain to make sure that he doesn't make any last-minute commitments to Poland.'

'Well in hand,' murmured Dunning absently. 'Do you think there's any chance that France will honour their treaty and declare war on Germany, even without us?'

Don shrugged. 'We're in uncharted waters, so anything's possible. I very much doubt it, though. They know they're in no shape militarily to take on the Germans, so they'll find any excuse to wriggle out of it. Their Foreign Minister is still strongly in favour of reaching some sort of deal with Germany even though their Premier is made of sterner stuff. Makes you wonder how Bonnet and Daladier can live together in the same government. Still, I gather Diplomat is trying to get them to agree a common sanctions policy.' He looked at his watch and sighed. 'The *Schleswig-Holstein* should be on her way to Danzig by now.'

Dunning nodded. 'She was missing from her Swinemunde moorings this morning, according to a reconnaissance report. We're expecting to receive a sighting report from Danzig at any moment.'

Don nodded tensely. The *Schleswig-Holstein* was an old battleship that Germany had been permitted to keep after the First World War. Her visit to Danzig was prearranged and ceremonial, but she was a 'Trojan horse', with over two hundred marines on board to supplement the hundreds of German troops who had been surreptitiously infiltrated into the supposedly demilitarised 'Free City' over recent months. In addition, regular German Army forces were poised to cross the border from East Prussia into the Free Zone around Danzig. When the old battleship opened fire on the Polish military transport depot on the Westerplatte, by the docks, it would be a giant starting gun to mark the beginning of the Second World War.

Käpitan zur See Gustav Kleikamp checked his watch. The time was 4.47 a.m. on Friday 1st September. From the bridge of the *Schleswig-*

*Holstein*, the long red brick wall marking the boundary of the Polish base on the Westerplatte was just three hundred metres away. He turned to the gunnery officer and gave the order.

The ship shook as the four 28 cm guns opened fire, shattering the silence with a massive blast, their 240 kg shells screaming towards the base at over 800 metres per second, the shock wave from the muzzle blast alone flattening buildings en route. The Westerplatte erupted with flame, smoke and earth as the shells hit home. In the sudden silence following the first salvo, the battleship's 5.9 cm secondary guns made themselves heard against the background of the tearing sound of the 2 cm AA guns, all firing at the beseiged base.

The Marine-Sturmkompanie had disembarked from the battleship a couple of hours before and was now a few hundred metres from the Polish base, waiting for the firing to stop so they could advance. The Leutnant in charge turned from observing the destruction on the Westerplatte to watch the *Schleswig-Holstein*, waiting for the next salvo from the big guns. He gasped in disbelief as two huge columns of water suddenly rose from the side of the ship, followed a second later by the blast of high explosives. At first, the old battleship seemed unperturbed, but as the Leutnant watched, the ship gradually tilted towards him and, in what seemed an impossibly short space of time, capsized with majestic dignity.

The Leutnant turned to face his stunned men, and realised that they would lose all heart if he didn't act immediately. 'Advance,' he shouted, and rising to his feet led his men towards the railway gate. There was a blast as explosives placed by an advanced team flattened the wall by the gate and the marines rushed through, only to tumble to the ground, shot or shaken by the hail of automatic fire from the Polish defences. The battle for the Westerplatte would be a long one.

As dawn broke on September 1st the Oberleutnant looked down on a misty landscape as his Junkers 88 led the Staffel towards Krakow. As the bombers neared the city, the small dots which were Polish defensive fighters rose to meet them from Balice. The obsolete PZL P11 fighters struggled for altitude but the Schnellbombers, the fastest in service in the world, simply increased speed and flashed past them, turning to line up on the airfield. The Oberleutnant's orders had been clear; the Polish airforce had to be wiped out. As he aimed the bomber at the airfield buildings and the few aircraft left on the ground, he heard over the radio the crisp interchanges of the Fw 187 pilots as they dived from high altitude on the Polish fighters. His air gunners wouldn't need to expend any ammunition on this sortie.

The Major of the Pomorska Cavalry Brigade of Army Pomorze in northern Poland watched through binoculars as the leading German armoured cars came into view. He noted they had only four wheels, and identified them as SdKfz 221s, lightly armoured and armed only with a machine gun. Unimpressive they may be, but he had more sense than to try to charge them with his cavalry. He gave a command and one of his men ran, crouching, towards his position, carrying the long Maroszek rifle which had only just been taken off the secret list. The soldier lay down beside him and worked the bolt to load one of the long 7.92 mm cartridges into the breech of the rifle. The calibre was the same as the standard infantry weapons but the cartridge was much bigger, propelling the armour-piercing bullet at 1,200 metres per second, enough to punch through the SdKfz's armour at several hundred metres.

There was a moment's silence before the vicious crack of the anti-tank rifle. Momentarily deafened, the Major saw the armoured car lurch off the road, black-clad figures jumping from it into a hail of light machine gun fire. The cavalryman reloaded and fired with methodical care until all three 221s lay abandoned, their surviving crews gone to ground. In the sudden silence, the louder rumble of tracks could be heard and the first of a line of squat, massive shapes emerged through the smoke of battle. Rapid fire from the Maroszek had no effect and the leading tanks started spraying the Polish positions with machine gun fire. The Major gave another command and his troops withdrew to where their horses were tethered. There would be other opportunities for combat on more even terms.

The Oberleutnant in command of the Panzer III tank felt confident as he led his troop towards Piotrkow. His 1st Panzer Division had punched through a gap between the two main Polish forces, Army Lodz and Army Krakow, and was almost half way to Warsaw. The Poles were fighting furiously but most of their weapons were incapable of harming the massive new battle tanks.

The sound of firing ahead grew in intensity and the commander dropped down into the turret as bullets began ricocheting off the armour. As he did so he spotted the compact shapes of tanks ahead and to one side. He shouted a command to his gunner and felt the turret traverse; the long 5 cm gun muzzle seeking its target. An earsplitting clang signalled a hit by one of the Polish tanks, but a shouted enquiry determined that his crew were unharmed; the shot had failed to penetrate. His own gun barked in reply and he could see through his periscope the Polish tank lurch to a halt, smoke pouring from the hatches. Through the dust another shape emerged. 'Right, aim right!' he shouted and the gunner responded.

Half a kilometre away, the crews of the Marder SPGs in a Panzerjäger unit observed the battle with interest, picking out with some difficulty the small Polish tanks from the big Panzers as they manoeuvred in the smoke and dust. Suddenly, the Oberleutnant spotted a column of the Polish 7TPs approaching the battle and gave a quick order. The long barrels of the 7,5 cm guns in the Marders tracked their distant targets. At a range of one kilometre, the Panzerjägers opened fire. Less than one minute later, there were no Polish tanks remaining.

Dunning was grim faced. 'It was Helmsford,' he said. 'He warned the Poles in enough time for them to be able to smuggle a couple of torpedoes and their firing mechanisms, probably dismantled, into the Westerplatte.'

'Helmsford?' Don was aghast, 'surely it could be a leak from the German side?'

Dunning shook his head. 'It turns out that Helmsford's wife has Polish relatives. He admitted passing on the warning about the *Schleswig-Holstein.*'

'What's happened to him?' Don had come to like and admire the dour sailor.

'Don't ask, but you won't be seeing him again.' Dunning looked tired. 'Just to be on the safe side, we've run a detailed security check on all those with inside knowledge. I think he's the only weakness.'

'I didn't think there were that many. I thought I was the number one top secret.'

'You are, but the knowledge you brought is too valuable to too many people to keep it entirely under cover. That little computer of yours, for instance. The boffins were absolutely ecstatic once they found out how to use it. The Royal Aircraft Establishment has been using it to speed airframe and engine design work – it's like magic after relying on log tables and slide rules. Now the intelligence people have sorted out code-breaking programmes which will speed up cryptanalysis no end. Even your little pocket calculator is being pressed into use. The boffins have been suffering acute frustration in trying to copy them, but there are too many unknown technologies involved.'

Don shrugged. 'I'm sorry I can't help there, but electronics was a closed book to me. Apart from the general importance of preparing for mass production of radio and radar equipment, the only thing of importance I could remember was the resonant cavity magnetron; I know it was essential to make compact, short-wavelength radars but I've no idea how it was designed.'

'They're working on it,' Dunning said absently. 'Have you heard the latest news from Poland? Despite the sinking of the *Schleswig-Holstein*, the fighting is going more or less as you predicted. The Poles used the warning they received to mobilise fully but the Germans are of course much better equipped than they were in your time so they're carving through them just the same.'

Don shuddered, trying not to think of the suffering being inflicted on the Poles, and changed the subject. 'Do we have any details about the German equipment?'

Dunning opened his briefcase and took out some photographs. 'I brought these along to show you. They've been collated from various sources, both Polish and German.'

Don examined them carefully. It was easy enough to tell the source of the pictures; the German ones showing triumphant soldiers, often in appropriate poses, the Polish ones snatched photos taken in battle or close-ups of wrecked equipment.

'Apart from their use of the Czech TNHP38 tank, they appear to have standardised on one main tank,' he noted. Dunning nodded.

'They call it the Panzerkampfwagen Three. In comparison with the description you gave us, it seems to be bigger and the shape is clearly different, with the glacis plate and turret front being sloped, but they've kept the engine at the rear and the front machine-gunner next to the driver.'

'The guns are obviously bigger as well. That looks like a long-barrelled five centimetre piece.' He sighed. 'That makes a mess of my plans. You'd better bring the Mark Two version of the Crusader into production as soon as possible; the Mark One will be outgunned.'

'Already in hand. The turrets of the Mark Ones will be fitted to the Humber armoured cars and the hulls used for the Comet AA tanks – very frugal! Take a look at these.'

The next series of photographs showed self-propelled field artillery and high velocity anti-tank guns, air defence tanks with quadruple automatic cannon, and armoured personnel carriers.

'They don't seem to have too many of these, and have concentrated them into hard-hitting armoured divisions. The Poles have nothing that can stand up to them. The Germans also have other mobile divisions relying on wheeled vehicles which have much greater range and speed and are causing chaos in Polish rear areas.'

Don looked at the photos, feeling depressed. Even the armoured cars looked formidable in the brutally functional way that only German designers seemed able to achieve. Dunning picked out another one.

'I'm sure you'll recognise this.'

It showed a dead German soldier, sprawled on his back. Lying across his body was a compact, efficient-looking rifle, obviously automatic, with a long, curved magazine in front of the pistol grip. Don winced.

'The Sturm Gewehr Fourty-four,' he sighed, 'four or five years early. That will cause us problems as well. What about aircraft?'

'So far, not so very different. The Messerschmitt One-oh-nine is the main fighter and the Junkers Eighty-seven Stuka has been doing most of the tactical support, with the Junkers Eighty-eight very much in evidence too; it seems to have reached service more quickly than in your time. The main variation seems to be the adoption of the Focke-Wulf One-eight-seven instead of the Messerschmitt One-one-oh. Any ideas about that?'

'Not really. The Messerschmitt wasn't a particularly outstanding aircraft, as I recall, but it proved very versatile so it stayed in production for a long time. The Focke-Wulf must be something special. I seem to recall that the prototypes were fitted with rather low-powered engines, but I assume they've rectified that by now. It looks smaller than the One-one-oh and is probably quite a bit faster. Any sign of heavy bombers?'

'Not in action, but there are reports of four-engined aircraft being seen near Luftwaffe bases. They seem to be working up towards operational readiness.'

Göring was not pleased. The Polish operation had come before he was ready to launch the new Heinkel bombers into battle, and although the Luftwaffe had acquitted itself well, he felt that an opportunity to demonstrate its invincible power had been missed. On top of that, this freak from the future seemed to be hiding something. If only he could get him to himself for a while at Karinhalle; but Hitler would never permit that. He kept Herrman always within reach, so Göring had had to come to Berlin.

'You still haven't explained to anyone how the British failed to declare war in support of the Poles,' he remarked lazily, 'this sanctions agreement with France is hardly the same thing, is it?'

Herrman blinked nervously. He could have speculated at some length as to the reasons, but the warning from Himmler was still fresh in his mind. Göring may be powerful, but Himmler was to be feared.

'It may signify nothing. Chamberlain was out on a limb in any case when he gave that guarantee to Poland. It might have taken something very small to deter him.'

'Ah, yes, your butterfly theory.' Göring was amused by the notion that an apparently insignificant change could ultimately lead to major consequences. But then, Herrman was not a clear expositor of chaos theory.

Herrman decided to cover his bets. 'Of course, one possible explanation is that the British have also received information from the future. That could affect their strategy.'

Göring was startled. 'Is this possible? Do you have any evidence for it?'

'Any change in predicted British policy might signify either that something we have said or done has had an effect on their thinking, or that they have a source of information of their own. There's no knowing which is more likely in this case, but I think we should keep our options open.'

He sat, hoping that his perspiration was not evident, that he had given himself a get-out if the facts became known. Göring was not fooled. The man was clearly lying, but why? The truth slowly came to him.

'You know, don't you?' He said softly. 'They have one of you. He is guiding their thinking just as you are guiding ours.'

Herrman said nothing, but his expression revealed all.

'Now why should you keep quiet about this? Ah yes, of course, friend Himmler. Doubtless he has had a word in your ear.'

Herrman still said nothing and Göring considered his tactics. 'On balance, I think Himmler is right to tell you to keep quiet.' He smiled and Herrman shivered. 'We shall keep this to ourselves. But I expect a clear briefing from you on what the British can be expected to do next.'

Don looked over the coast from his viewpoint on the South Downs, shivering slightly in the fresh autumn breeze. Mary, Dunning and Taylor stood beside him. An ordinary tourist could be expected to enjoy the sight of the Downs sweeping down to the sea, but this group was looking with other eyes.

'The combs you can see leading down towards the coastal railway line are essentially dry valleys.' Taylor was in lecturing mode. 'As you can see, we are constructing several railway spurs up them. These apparently go nowhere, but in fact are intended to be firing points for railway guns. In fact, when we were investigating possible sites, we were surprised to discover an existing section of track with a large shed at the end, which contained a nine-point-two inch gun from the Great War. Still in perfect working order, and maintained by an old guy whom everyone had forgotten about.'

Don smiled. He recalled hearing this story in his previous existence. Taylor went on.

'We have a crash programme to produce more railway guns for coast defence purposes. The Navy have passed over all of the seven-point-five inch guns from the four Cavendish class cruisers which they're converting to light aircraft carriers. We've put them into high-elevation mountings which give them considerable range.' He turned to point to some tiny buildings almost obscured by vegetation. 'Some of the small blockhouses for machine guns and anti-tank weapons are visible, forming a line along the coast designed to provide interlocking arcs of fire. We're doing our best to conceal them in various ways. If you look carefully, you can also pick out some horse-shoe shaped mounds not far from the road, over there. They are intended as gun emplacements for field artillery.'

Mary was listening with interest, this tour a rare outing for her. 'Wouldn't it be better to have the defensive lines further back? Then you would have more time to put the guns in the right position, once you knew the direction of attack.'

Taylor did not look surprised. All of the regulars at the House had become used to her perceptive questions.

'We do have another line, much further inland, and some armoured divisions will be held back from the coast. History tells us, however, that the best chance of thwarting a landing from the sea is to hit it as soon as possible, before the invaders have a chance to become organised and established. We hope we can rely on aerial reconnaissance and other means to give us enough warning to get the guns in place. And of course, the Air Force is practising tactical co-operation with the Army and Navy in order to ensure that the enemy are given no peace from the moment they set sail.'

They all looked at the peaceful scene for a while. Don realised that they were all probably thinking the same; trying to imagine this stretch of British countryside covered with black-crossed tanks, a scene of ferocious fighting, Luftwaffe planes dicing with the RAF overhead. They returned to their car in silence.

'So now we have Poland, and the British and French cower behind their defences, bleating about sanctions!' Herrman couldn't decide whether Hitler was angry or triumphant, and decided he was both. Hitler fixed him with his stare. 'They didn't guarantee Poland's safety and left me a clear field to attack. Why were you wrong?'

Herrman stammered the same sort of rationale he had used with Göring, but added, 'there are now strong indications that they are obtaining guidance from the future in some way.' He held his breath and waited. Hitler was silent for a moment and Herrman suddenly realised that Stadler had been right to warn him; this had come as no surprise to Hitler, so one of his sources must have informed him already. Then Hitler smiled grimly.

'So the Gods are restaging the contest? They want us to fight again! What reason could they have, except that they were dissatisfied with the outcome last time? Very well, we will give them a battle that will gladden their hearts.' He considered for a moment, pacing around the room. 'The question is: do we start with Norway or with France? The British will be expecting us to attack Norway, and may be better prepared to come to its aid, especially as they won't have most of their army locked up in France. To attack France first might surprise them.'

Herrman felt emboldened to intervene. 'Why not ignore France and Norway, and go straight for Russia instead? Then there wouldn't be the risk of facing a war on two fronts.'

Hitler considered this for a moment. 'There would still be the risk of being stabbed in the back by the French if we committed our forces in Russia. Besides, I have a score to settle with France. I am very much looking forward to signing their surrender in the same railway carriage they forced us to use after the last war! And with your help, defeating the French will be even quicker and easier than it was in your time. That will show the Generals that I know what I'm doing!'

'Well then, the British must know about me, or at least that you have someone like me. So they will be aware that we will be trying to outguess them. It is even possible that they have decided to stay out of the war altogether. There was a view held by certain postwar British historians that it was a mistake to get involved. The cost to Britain was appalling, and the Cold War outcome not much better than a Europe dominated by Germany; which will eventually happen anyway, in economic terms at least.'

Hitler considered this as he paced. 'Given their international obligations, I don't see how they can avoid coming to France's assistance. They would lose too much face. But if they intend to defend France, why didn't they declare war over Poland, which would have given them plenty of time to bring their army across the Channel? It's possible they may be planning to strike a deal after France's defeat; I would be generous and it would only cost them a few colonies, plus Edward back on the throne and a sympathetic government. A small price to pay in comparison with what they would lose in the war. They have no ties to Norway, though, and it need not be a *causus belli*. If I could take Norway first, it would be a clear warning to Britain and would still be useful later on in threatening the supply route to Russia.'

Hitler became more animated as he developed his thesis. 'Raeder has been arguing the case for securing bases in Norway anyway, if only to keep Britain out – we can't let them bottle up our ships in the Baltic while denying us the winter route for supplies of Swedish iron ore. We can't trust Norwegian neutrality; the British would try to stop the iron ore supplies anyway.' He stopped pacing as he came to his conclusion. 'If the British don't want war they may ignore our move on Norway. If they do, then being tied up in Norway will keep them out of France, making our task there easier.' He turned suddenly and faced Herrman. 'What do you think?'

Herrman stood silently for a moment, suddenly struck with the thought that this could be one of the pivotal moments in European history. He had no doubt that Hitler still regarded him with a kind of superstitious awe, and would listen to his views.

'Britain has been spending large sums on armaments and is clearly preparing to fight if need be. There is no indication that they are building any heavy bombers, though, of the sort they used to attack us. And they have kept their army in their own country. They may be glad of the excuse to avoid becoming entangled in France. We must remember that most of the prewar British government wanted to reach some sort of deal with us rather than go to war. They have been quick to build new battleships and aircraft carriers, but they will be more useful against Japan than us. It is possible that they would like to avoid war.'

Hitler stood in thought for a moment. 'Very well, then. We will put them to the test. Norway it is – but we will leave the attack until just before we invade France, to give the British no time to deal with both problems!'

## CHAPTER 3 - ENGAGEMENT

**May 1940**

The Wellington maritime reconnaissance aircraft cruised at 10,000 feet over a murky North Sea. The pilot peered through the gloom of early morning, beginning to feel stiff and tired after several hours of patrolling, a daily routine which had lasted for weeks. Behind him, the crew in the converted bomb bay were warming themselves with hot tea, feeling the cold despite their thick clothing. Suddenly, one of the crew leaned forward to look intently at the cathode ray tube in front of him.

'I think I have a contact, sir!'

The officer in charge of the radar crew came forward to look, while the other members of the team adjusted their instruments, trying to extract the maximum information from the signals caught by the long aerials above the fuselage. After a moment, the officer switched on the intercom to the pilot.

'I think we've found what we're looking for. It looks like a group of ships, bearing one-two-two degrees, range thirty-five miles. Not far off the Norwegian coast.'

'Roger. We'd better take a look.'

The heavy plane banked in a wide curve, then began a long slow descent to the contact.

Don stood at the window, looking out over Whitehall and feeling depressed despite the bright May morning. He gulped the last of his coffee and turned to Charles Dunning.

'How much longer are they likely to be?'

'Have patience, they've had a lot on their hands with the politicians. It was bad enough persuading them not to get involved with Russia over Finland; when the Finns surrendered, they made all sorts of carping remarks about why their non-interventionist advisers suddenly wanted them to give guarantees to Norway; and now April has passed without the predicted invasion, they are questioning our judgment.'

'They are going to go in if Norway is attacked, though?'

Charles poured a fresh cup of coffee. 'They finally agreed to. We made them understand the strategic importance of Norway to our own security, and the importance of the winter iron-ore route from Narvik to Germany. They accept that we would be in much weaker position against Germany if Norway fell to them. The problem is that the Committee has anxieties about the whole issue.'

Don frowned. 'Surely all the preparations are in hand?'

'More than. In fact, everyone is becoming rather tired of sitting around waiting for something to happen. There certainly won't be the fiasco that happened in your time. We have one big disadvantage, though; we're not currently at war with Germany, so we can't pre-empt their action. We have to wait until they attack and, what's worse, wait until the Norwegians ask for our help. Chamberlain and Halifax won't have it any other way. The only concession we've managed to extract is that we won't be giving the Germans a long period to consider our ultimatum; we'll go in immediately we're asked to.'

'The Germans will still have had time to get themselves established.'

'Quite. And they'll know we're coming. It won't be easy to dislodge them.'

The Lieutenant-Commander squinted through the periscope, his view intermittently obscured by the choppy sea.

'Bring her up a bit,' he called. As the periscope head rose higher, he felt a surge of excitement. The smudge of smoke that had caught his attention was clearer, and underneath, squat, powerful-looking shapes were beginning to emerge.

'Warships, heading our way. Down periscope. Steer eighty degrees.'

The tension rose as the minutes ticked by. The commanding officer waited patiently until the calculated moment.

'Up periscope.' He scanned the scene for a few seconds. 'Down periscope.' He turned to the navigating officer. 'Set a course to get us out of the Skagerrak as soon as possible.' To the radio operator; 'encode the following message for transmission as soon as we're out of the way: two pocket battleships and smaller craft heading north at position fifty-eight degrees five minutes north, eleven degrees and fifteen minutes east.'

He looked down pensively at the chart. The ships were on course for Oslo.

'Now I wonder what they're up to this time?'

Chairman looked up as Don and Charles entered the room.

'Good morning, gentlemen. I'm sorry to have kept you waiting. We've been rather busy this morning.' They murmured their acknowledgements and sat down. Chairman looked around the table.

'I would like to review the current situation and the arrangements in hand, to see if our adviser has any comments. I'd better start. We've had a difficult time with the Chiefs of Staff, who are still inclined to take a blinkered view of their Services, but they did at last agree a coherent command structure with joint planning between all three Services and clear lines of control and communication once we go in. At least everyone should know what is expected of them, and of the others involved.' He turned to Diplomat, who spoke slowly, studying the end of his cigarette with elaborate casualness.

'We have received reports from the British ministers in both Copenhagen and Berlin, who have picked up warnings of an impending assault on Norway. Troop concentrations have also been reported in German ports, as well as a build-up of substantial forces on their western borders; they appear to be fully mobilised to launch attacks either to the West or the North, or both, as they choose. We've relayed strong warnings to Norway and an assurance of immediate aid if requested. The problem is that the Nygaardsvold government is both strongly neutralist and passivist, and they don't want to believe us. We've used what military contacts we have with the Norwegians to spread the warning as far as possible, in the hope that some at least of their commanders won't be caught unawares. We've even used court contacts to get a message through to King Haakon, to warn him that the Germans are planning to capture him. The problem is that apart from their coast defence forts, they don't have a lot to fight with.'

Chairman nodded, and looked at Ruddy Face, who cleared his throat.

'The assault force and covering naval units sailed yesterday and will soon be in position off the Norwegian coast. The aircraft carriers *Ark Royal*, *Invincible* and *Courageous* will be operating in a group with the battleships *Hood*, *King George V* and *Prince of Wales*, staying a hundred miles offshore at the latitude of Trondheim. Further south, *Repulse* and *Renown*, together with the carrier *Furious*, will be stationed about fifty miles off Bergen to intercept enemy naval units. The heavy cruisers *Berwick* and *Cornwall*, together with the light carriers *Vindictive* and *Hawkins*, will be covering fifty miles off Narvik. The main assault forces will move into position twenty-five miles from Narvik and Trondheim respectively by the early hours of tomorrow morning. They will be supported by the old battleships *Warspite* at Narvik and *Malaya* and *Queen Elizabeth* at Trondheim. Following the main assaults we are planning to secure Bodø and Tromsø to ensure that we have complete control over the northern part of the country. After that we can turn our attention to Bergen and Stavanger.'

'Where are you planning to land?' Don had clear memories of the problems that had occurred in his time due to over-cautious landings far from the objectives, giving the troops an almost impossible task in slogging through snowbound countryside, often in blizzard conditions, with totally inadequate equipment.

'At Narvik the Germans will only be able to land lightly-equipped troops so we're going straight into the fjord under air cover and naval bombardment and landing the Marines at Øyjord and Haakvik, flanking the Narvik peninsula and about three or four miles away from Narvik itself. Incidentally, the terrible winter we've just had has helped enormously with training. Many of the Marines are now competent on skis and the rest have snowshoes.'

Don nodded. 'And Trondheim?'

'Same principle of landings a few miles either side of the city, although we expect much stronger opposition. It will be particularly dangerous entering Trondheimsfjord if the Germans have managed to seize the defending forts, so we're sending in Special Forces by submarine to secure those first. Once we're into the fjord, one of the key targets will be the airfield at Vaernes. We might secure the ports at Namsos and Åndalsnes later, but that's not vital.'

Don remembered the ill-fated landings at these ports, far from Trondheim itself.

Military Man took over. 'The First Armoured Division will be landed at Trondheim. We are also planning some paratroop drops to secure critical points. Once the city and the airfield are in our hands, the Division has orders to proceed south towards Dombås then down the Gudbransdal towards Oslo. Along the way, they should link up with the Norwegian government and the bulk of whatever Norwegian forces survive the retreat from Oslo. Once we have secured that link, together with Stavanger and Bergen, we will have effective control of all except the south-eastern lowlands around Oslo. That's when we expect the major battle. By then, the Second and Third Armoured Divisions will have taken over from the First, supported by three motorised infantry divisions. The First Armoured will be withdrawn to England to re-equip, leaving their equipment behind as an attrition reserve.'

'What about communications and specialist equipment?'

'There are plenty of radios and a well-practised communications network, with interlinking possible between the Services. As at Narvik, all infantry will have snowshoes and we are including some ski-troops, although if the Germans delay their attack for much longer they will hardly be necessary. Thanks to your warnings, we also have a good supply of detailed maps and photographs of the operational areas.'

Military Man handed over to Creamed Curls.

'Coastal Command is keeping a close watch for German shipping movements, with torpedo-carrying Hampdens standing by in the Orkneys. As well as the maritime reconnaissance aircraft, we have some new versions of the Wellington with radar adapted to detect aircraft, and these are patrolling the southern North Sea. Photo-reconnaissance Reapers are carrying out at least one sortie per day, weather permitting, of all likely target areas in Norway and of the German ports and anchorages. We also have five squadrons of Reaper long-range fighters and a similar number of Mosquito bombers based in Scotland, ready to attack the Danish and Norwegian airfields seized by the Germans. Finally, we have several squadrons of Hurricanes with long-range tanks ready to travel to Norwegian airfields as soon as they are available.'

Don sat back, thinking the arrangements through, racking his memory for anything he might have overlooked. 'Air power is Germany's biggest asset; it's what made all the difference before. Attacking the German airfields to disrupt their activities has a high priority. Another thing; one problem common to both sides which the Germans may well have corrected was defective torpedo fuses. Losses to U-boats could be high.'

Ruddy Face nodded. 'All of our task forces have strong anti-submarine escorts including air cover, from the land as well as the carriers. We also have plenty of ships held back in reserve if we need to replace losses.'

As they left the Committee, Charles looked at Don, seeing his anxiety. 'Don't worry,' he said quietly, 'everything that you have warned us about has been dealt with. We are as well prepared as possible.'

Don sighed. 'I know. It's just that after all these years of preparation, the shooting is finally going to start. We don't know whether Hitler will go for Norway or France first. If he goes for France, we're in real trouble, as the politicians will come under severe pressure to divert our assault forces to help the French. Even if he goes for Norway, we have to sit on our hands and wait for the Norwegians to ask us to help, while the Germans can attack at their leisure.'

The Norwegian government was in disarray. The British warnings of German intentions had been clear, specific and urgent. So had the

German warnings of British attempts to drive a wedge between Norway and Germany, with the aim of acquiring Norway as an ally. Evidence had been collected showing that both sides appeared to be mobilising and dispatching naval units towards Norway. The Cabinet, headed by Prime Minister Nygaardsvold, were painfully aware of their country's unpreparedness to resist any attack. After long debate, Nygaardsvold turned wearily to to Defence Minister Ljungberg.

'We are agreed then. However unwelcome it may be, it appears likely that we are going to be involved against our will in a conflict between Britain and Germany. We cannot judge who is telling the truth, but assurances from Hitler have been proved in the past to be worth little. Furthermore, the British are urging us to mobilise, which they would hardly do if they were intending to attack us. In the circumstances, we have agreed that we should issue a general mobilisation order immediately. We can only pray that this will deter any aggression. If the Germans attack us, we will immediately ask the British for help. In the meantime, we had better prepare for the evacuation of the government and the Royal Family.'

There was a quiet tension on the bridge of the cruiser *HMS Sheffield* as it ploughed through the rough seas off the coast of northern Norway, just inside the Arctic Circle. The Coastal Command Wellington had relayed the course and speed of the force; they should intercept it soon. The lookouts stood with eyes glued to binoculars; it was early evening but at this time of year it never became really dark even at midnight.

The first alert was issued from the radar operators in the small cabin behind the bridge. In response to the Captain's order, the big cruiser turned and accelerated towards the coast. Shortly afterwards, the lookouts sang out their warning and the Captain picked up the big 7x50 glasses and focused them on the distant shapes.

'A cruiser, large single funnel, either *Leipzig* or *Nurnberg*, with five – no six, destroyers in company,' the First Lieutenant commented, 'heading for the Vest Fjord. Have to be on their way to Narvik.'

The Captain grunted. 'Make a signal to the Admiralty, Number One. There's nothing else we can do about it except watch.'

The German force was slowly lost from view as the ships merged with the rugged background of the Norwegian coast.

The Kapitanleutnant commanding U64 watched through his periscope as the British cruiser turned away from the coast and smiled grimly. Soon, he thought, very soon.

General Nikolas von Falkenhorst leaned back and stretched in his chair, feeling a curious mixture of tiredness, satisfaction and nervous anticipation. He had still not entirely recovered from the surprise of the personal summons from Hitler which had led to his being given overall command of Operation Weserübung, the invasion of Denmark and Norway. However, no officer of the Wehrmacht is disconcerted for long, so he had rapidly begun planning the assault in close co-operation with the Kriegsmarine and the Luftwaffe. His work had not been made easier by the close interest taken by the Führer in the details of the operation, and he had been forced to make certain changes to his initial plans, apparently at the behest of the elderly and rather academic-looking personal assistant who always seemed to be hanging around Hitler.

However, the die was now cast, the plans fixed, the orders given, the forces dispatched. Denmark was unlikely to put up any resistance, but the planning for Norway had been particularly thorough. Merchant ships loaded with concealed military stores were already in place in the target ports and other merchant vessels with Marine units in the holds were due to dock just before the main assault began. Paratroop units had been assigned to take every airfield in Norway to prepare the way for the fleet of over 500 Junkers 52 transports already loaded on their airfields. He had not been given many ground troops – these were on standby in the West – but there wasn't room to take many in the aircraft and ships available to him, and the number included some of the best; the Gebirgsjäger of the Second and Third Mountain Divisions under Feuerstein and Dietl.

Admiral Raeder had been particularly co-operative and virtually every major surface unit, as well as most of the submarines, was included in the operation. Literally above all, some 500 combat aircraft of Fliegerkorps X were providing cover; a mixture of fighters and bombers with an emphasis on anti-shipping capability.

The possible British response was a worry; reconnaissance had revealed a high degree of alertness in the Royal Navy, and Raeder had been concerned about the vulnerability of the northermost group assigned to take Narvik. However, the tanker with the fuel they would need for the return trip was due to arrive shortly. Von Falkenhorst checked his watch; 2.00 a.m. Three hours to get some sleep before the attacks commenced. Tomorrow would be a long day.

'Wake up, wake up, it's begun!' Don groaned and rolled over in bed as Mary shook him awake. 'Charles has just called.'

'Where?'

'Norway!'

'Thank God! What's the time?'

'Half past four. Come on, we're needed in the Ops Room.'

Don dragged himself out of bed and headed for the bathroom, thankful that he had insisted on a shower being fitted into their Whitehall apartment.

Half an hour later, they were gathered in the so-called 'Operations Room'; an underground office wallpapered with maps, situated close to a radio communications centre. Morgan and Taylor were already there in their respective RAF and Army uniforms, together with Harold Johnson, the stocky, dark-haired naval officer who had joined the group as the replacement for David Helmsford.

'The Oversight Committee is meeting on the floor above if we need to communicate with them,' commented Charles. He turned to the military intelligence officers. 'What's the current situation?'

'Few surprises so far,' stated Johnson briskly. Don had not got to know him well; Johnson seemed uncomfortable with him and Don suspected that he regarded him as some kind of freak.

'Oslo is close to falling to a combined assault. German paratroops have secured Fornebo and Kjeller airfields and transports are flying in reinforcements. Two pocket battleships – we think they are the *Lützow* and the *Admiral Scheer* – have docked in the harbour along with other vessels, and somewhere between one and two thousand troops have disembarked.'

'No resistance from the coastal defences?' Don was surprised, remembering the massive damage inflicted by the handful of defenders in the Oscarborg fortress, who in his time had managed to sink a heavy cruiser.

'None. It seems the forts were taken by marines in a surprise attack before the ships went through.'

'What about the rest?'

'As expected. Trondheim, Bergen, Stavanger, Kristiansand and Narvik are all reported to be under attack by a combination of naval forces and paratroops.'

'Any Norwegian resistance?'

'Yes, some,' Taylor chipped in. 'Our warnings persuaded them to order a general mobilisation yesterday morning, so they were beginning to get themselves organised before the attack. Even so, they have little but small arms and a few artillery pieces to fight with. No tanks and no modern aircraft. The only blessing is that the King and the government just got out of Oslo by the skin of their teeth, after some fighting with troops who came from the German embassy.'

Reports continued to flow in during the morning, describing the progress of the German assault and the movements of British forces in response. At one point, an unidentified head popped around the door. 'The wireless is on. Can you turn on your loudspeaker?'

Mary reached over and turned up the volume as the familiar tones of Chamberlain came through. Don felt a pang of sympathy for the utter weariness and disillusionment in his voice. What he said sounded strangely familiar, and Don remembered another occasion, on a September 3rd 1939 long before he was born.

Chamberlain described how at four o'clock in the morning, British time, elements of the German armed forces had invaded Denmark and Norway. The Danish government had decided to make no resistance, but the Norwegians were attempting to defend themselves against the unprovoked attack. However, German forces had landed in several major cities and others had been bombed. He concluded:

'I have previously warned Herr Hitler that any such action would be regarded as unacceptable by this country, and have offered assistance to the government of Norway. At 4.30 a.m., the Norwegian government formally requested the assistance of His Majesty's government in repelling this invasion. That assistance is being provided as I speak. Consequently, this country is now at war with Germany.'

Mary turned off the loudspeaker and Morgan leaned back with a sigh. 'That's it, then. The gloves are off at last.'

The Squadron Leader shifted his position in the cockpit of the Gloster Reaper, trying to ease the stiffness of the long flight. His squadron had taken off from Wick early in the morning, within a few minutes of receiving the command to begin hostilities. They had been on standby for weeks, with plans prepared and maps and photographs of the target area studied. After two hours of cruising at an economical 250 mph, southern Norway was spread beneath them.

A sharp warning from his wingman alerted him to the distant shapes of aircraft ahead and below. He gave a brief command to his squadron, jettisoned the remaining drop-tank and pushed down the nose of the Reaper. The note of twin Merlin engines rose in pitch as the ASI swung towards and past the 400 mph mark. The aircraft ahead were clearly recognisable as Ju 52 transports, part of the shuttle service he had been warned to look out for, delivering reinforcements and supplies to the invading German Army. No fighter escort was evident so the lumbering transports would stand no chance. He armed the four 20 mm Hispanos and curved into the attack.

The Lieutenant-Commander brought *HMS Seawolf* back up to periscope depth for a final check. Once again he saw the purposeful shape of a pocket battleship approaching, this time heading south away from Oslo. The destroyer escort did not seem to have detected him.

'Down periscope. Stand by all tubes.' As the seconds dragged into minutes, a new sound familiar from training exercises slowly strengthened: the regular 'ping' of an Asdic pulse. They're not supposed to have that, he thought. We can hear their pulse before they will be able to hear the echo, but for how long?

'Up periscope.' A further pause, the tension palpable. The Lieutenant-Commander tried to ignore the daunting head-on view of a destroyer racing towards his position, and concentrated on the big ship beyond. 'Fire one – two – three – four; Eighty feet; Down periscope; Steer one-eighty; Full ahead both.' The commands rapped out in rapid succession and the boat started violent evasive action as the destroyer raced overhead. A few terrible seconds of silence, then the boat was hurled down and sideways as the huge hammers of the shock-waves from exploding depth-charges slammed into the hull. He watched the gauges anxiously; this close to the Swedish coast, the Skagerrak was shallow and he must be close to the bottom. On the other hand, this would make Asdic much less effective.

'Stop both; Silent routine; Damage report.' The boat slowed, gradually sinking towards the bottom as the slight negative buoyancy took effect. Renewed pinging grew in volume and the crew held their breath. The destroyer was travelling slowly, listening for them. Suddenly two distant 'crumps' were audible through the boat and a cheer was quickly stifled. They had scored hits! The destroyer's screws speeded up again then faded into the distance as it turned to help the stricken pocket-battleship. The *Seawolf* bumped gently onto the bottom.

'Periscope depth; Slow ahead both.' The view through the periscope showed a cluster of destroyers making for their listing charge. 'Down periscope: Fifty feet; Steer two-seventy; Half ahead both.' The *Seawolf* slipped away, back to the safety of the North Sea.

Fornebo airfield was a scene of organised chaos as the Ju 52s landed, were frantically unloaded by teams of soldiers and took off again; a steady stream of lorries shuttling supplies into Oslo.

Messerschmitt Bf 109s from the nearby Kjeller airfield cruised high overhead, guarding against surprise attacks from the Reapers which had lived up to their name in the terrible toll they had already taken of the vulnerable transports. The Gefreiter sat at the controls of the Flak 38, 2 cm cannon pointed skywards, and watched over the scene idly, with a professional soldier's ability to relax when opportunity presented.

A sudden change in the note of the circling fighters caused him to look up in surprise, to see them racing away to the south; they must have spotted some of the marauding British fighters. As they disappeared over the horizon he relaxed back into his seat and looked again at the airfield, just in time for sudden, rapid movement to catch his eye. He sat frozen for a second then shouted 'Achtung! Achtung!' and swung the Flak cannon around towards the sleek twin-engined aircraft racing across the field at tree-top height, their bomb-doors open. The first three planes were already past before he was ready but he centred the fourth in the Flakvisier and sent a deadly stream of cannon-fire into its path. The plane staggered, debris flying from it, then fell onto the airfield, ripping through a collection of Ju 52s before exploding at the edge of the field.

A sudden silence fell and the Gefreiter looked around cautiously. Curiously, there appeared to be no other damage; had the other planes not dropped any bombs? He thought back and recalled seeing many small objects falling from them. An unloaded Ju 52 revved its engines and taxied to prepare for take-off, the pilot anxious to leave the field before more bombers arrived. A sudden blast under one engine blew off the undercarriage and the plane lurched to a halt, the wing crumpling as it hit the field. As the Gefreiter watched in astonishment, another blast caused earth to erupt over some stacked supplies at the edge of the field.

The hundreds of mines scattered by the Mosquitos, fitted with combined contact, tamper and time-delay fuzes, closed Fornebo and other key airfields for a vital twenty-four hours.

The Captain stared out into the night, cheeks burned by the strong wind blowing through the slit windows in the armoured conning tower as *HMS Renown* steamed due east at thirty knots. The Coastal Command radar report of movements south from Trondheimsfjord had been received nearly three hours earlier and the huge battlecruiser was straining to make the interception. Further out to sea, her sister-ship *Repulse* was escorting the aircraft-carrier *Furious* as she prepared to launch a dawn bomb and torpedo strike on the target.

'Radar contact, ships bearing fifty-five degrees, range forty thousand yards.'

The enemy ships – they could be no other, at this time and in this place – were evidently hugging the Norwegian coast as much as possible as they made their way to the safety of German waters under the cover of the night. The Captain was determined that they would not escape. He made some calculations.

'Inform me when the range drops to twenty-five thousand, or if they change course.' Assuming the enemy force was travelling south along the coast at around 25 knots, they were on a collision course and should close to fighting range in about twenty minutes. The Captain moved to sit in his chair, and waited.

Aboard the *Furious*, there was quiet activity as the Beauforts were 'bombed-up', half with 2,000 lb armour-piercing bombs, the other half with 18 inch torpedoes. A flight of Beaufighters stood on the flight deck, ready to repulse any air attacks as the short night ended. One by one, the Beauforts were lifted up onto the windswept deck and moved into position behind the catapults. They would launch at first light.

Forty miles away, dawn was breaking as the call finally came: 'Targets bearing fifty-five degrees, range twenty-five thousand yards.'

The Captain felt the tension surging as he ordered action stations and forced himself to relax. 'Can the gunnery radar separate the targets?'

'Yes sir. One smaller vessel in the lead, one larger return in the centre, then two other smaller targets on the flanks.'

A classic defensive pattern. The latest intelligence reports indicated that the large ship was almost certainly the pocket battleship *Graf Spee*. The Captain took a deep breath. 'Engage the largest target.'

A brilliant flash split the night as the four forward fifteen inch guns opened fire at high elevation; their colossal blast was felt rather than heard. A long minute followed as the shells, each weighing nearly a ton, took their ordained ballistic path through the night. Then a message from the gunnery radar: 'Shell splashes, two hundred yards over.' The heavy guns fired again, the start of a tactical battle between the gunnery officer, trying to guess where the target would be a minute later, and the enemy ship's captain, trying to guess where the next salvo would fall. But all the time, the range was shortening, and the odds improving in favour of the hunter. Soon, the battlecruiser would be able to swing to starboard and bring all six heavy guns to bear. With its lower speed, thinner armour and smaller guns, the pocket battleship was doomed.

Three torpedoes from a spread of four struck the starboard side of *HMS Furious* as the first flight of Beauforts was preparing for take-off. The old ship was not designed to withstand the blast of the powerful warheads and the crew of the *Repulse* watched in horror the scene revealed in the dim morning light as the *Furious* listed slowly away from them, aircraft sliding off the deck into the sea. Two of the escorting destroyers raced away to sea, vengefully hunting down the hidden U-boat, as the others drew alongside the stricken carrier to take off the crew. The captain of the *Repulse* watched the scene grimly and with a heavy heart ordered his ship to turn away. With an enemy submarine in the area, he could not risk stopping his valuable battlecruiser to help. He ordered a course to rendezvous with the *Renown*.

'Cease fire!' The silence that followed the order was eerie after the half-hour of deafening gunfire as the *Renown* engaged the pocket battleship and her escorting destroyers with both main and secondary armament. The *Graf Spee* was sinking, the destroyers disabled and burning, as the big ship turned away. There had been warnings of submarines in the area and the Captain wanted to put as much distance as possible between his ship and the scene of battle before the flames and smoke brought unwelcome visitors.

'Message from *Repulse*, sir.' The seaman handed him the message apprehensively and the Captain glanced at it quickly. The *Furious*, gone! He looked at the paper numbly for a moment then turned to order a course to the rendezvous.

'Radar report, sir. Aircraft approaching from the south-east.' That had to be the Luftwaffe.

'Warn the Gunnery Officer to prepare for air attack.'

The *Renown*, like her sister-ship *Repulse*, had been extensively modified before the war and was well-equipped to deal with enemy aircraft. Apart from improved armour protection both ships had been fitted with a new secondary battery of sixteen 4.7 inch dual-purpose guns in twin mountings, together with their associated triaxially-stabilised radar-assisted directors to provide accurate fire-control of targets moving in three dimensions. Any aircraft penetrating the first line of defence had to face a formidable battery of 40 mm Bofors guns. The Captain felt confident as his ship prepared for action.

In the 4.7 inch turrets the crew sweated to clear away the last of the semi-armour-piercing shells used to engage the destroyers, and waited to receive the time-fuzed high-explosive anti-aircraft shells. The 62 lb shells and the brass-cased propellant charges were delivered separately from the shell-rooms and magazines below the turret but were put together in a setting tray beside the breech.  At the last possible moment, a fuze-setter at the front of the loading tray automatically adjusted the time fuze to explode at the calculated position of the enemy aircraft, then the shell and case were tipped into the loading tray behind the breech, from which they were driven into the chamber by a spring-powered rammer. The breech-block slammed shut and the gun was ready to fire. A practised crew could fire fifteen shots per barrel per minute, until they dropped with exhaustion.

'The aircraft have separated into two groups, sir.  One group is staying at high altitude, the other is diving to low altitude.'

'Bombers and torpedo planes, I expect. Concentrate on the torpedo planes, they're the most dangerous to us.'

'Yes sir, they'll arrive first anyway.'

The Captain moved to the bridge wing and looked aft for the pursuing aircraft. He saw the small shapes silhouetted against the early morning horizon.

'Junkers Eighty-eights, I think,' someone commented. The Captain ordered the ship to make a small turn to port in order to allow all of the secondary armament on that side to bear. As the ship steadied on her new course, the 4.7s suddenly erupted into rapid fire and a few seconds later the air around the planes became speckled with HE bursts. With all eight guns firing at a combined rate of two rounds per second, the Captain calculated that over 7,000 lb of HE shells were exploding around the aircraft each minute. First one, then another of the shapes trailed smoke and fell into the sea. A third exploded instantly from a direct hit. As the survivors approached, the Bofors guns joined in the barrage, each gun firing at 140 rounds per minute, their tracers streaking menacingly over the sea. One plane hit the sea in its efforts to avoid them, two others collided.  The remainder dropped their torpedoes at extreme range and turned for safety. The crew cheered as the ship turned back onto its course, away from the torpedoes.

'Sir, the bombers!'

The bridge crew looked up at the shapes high above, already being engaged by the starboard battery.

'Dornier two-one-sevens, I think.'

The Captain focused his binoculars at the planes, brilliantly lit by the morning sunshine which had yet to reach sea level. As he watched, smaller shapes detached from the aircraft, falling rapidly away. They seemed to be trailing smoke. The ship heeled as the helmsman threw it into a steep turn to avoid the bombs, which still had a long way to fall. The Captain watched incredulously as the bombs turned in their flight to follow them, trailing their smoke. He suddenly realised what was happening.

'Hit those aircraft! They're guiding the bombs in!'

Even as he spoke, he realised that it was too late. The first bomb, suddenly looking hideously massive, hit amidships. It punched through the armoured deck and detonated a fraction of a second later in a boiler room, sending steel fragments slicing through decks, bulkheads and boilers, causing a massive explosion as the boilers burst. The second bomb landed directly alongside the ship and exploded underwater, staving in the torpedo protection. As the Captain watched in horror, a third bomb struck aft, penetrating through the ship and detonating immediately forward of the rudder, wrecking the steering and inner propeller shafts and opening the hull to the sea. The ship shuddered to a halt, crippled, and the Captain realised instantly that this close to enemy-held territory, she would never make it back to port. All he could do was save as many of his men as possible.

The reconnaissance Beaufort swept down the Ofotfjord towards Narvik in the dawn light, weaving through the flak bursts from the Kriegsmarine ships and drawing a hail of small-arms fire from the Gebirgsjäger positions around the town. The observer calmly gave a running commentary over the R/T:

'Four destroyers in the Ofotfjord off Ballangen, ten miles from Narvik, guarding the access from the sea. One cruiser in the Herjangsfjord about one mile north of Narvik; two destroyers in Rombaksfjord to the north-east. Infantry established around Narvik and across the Rombaksfjord toward Elvegaardsmoen.'

The commander of the incoming flight of Beauforts acknowledged and the planes diverted to the north to approach Herjangsfjord over the mountains. The reconnaissance plane had meanwhile climbed to a safe altitude and circled the area, guiding the attacking planes in. The first that the anti-aircraft gunners of the *Leipzig* knew of the attack was when the planes dived on them from the north, instead of the south-west direction that they had anxiously been scanning. The light cruiser was a sitting target, and the 2,000 lb semi-armour piercing bombs carried by the Beauforts made short work of it for the loss of only one Beaufort. As the *Leipzig* listed, burning, the reconnaissance aircraft made its way over to Ballangen to guide in the next flight onto the helpless destroyers. The destroyers in Rombaksfjord would be next, the ground troops last.

The *Warspite* cruised up the Ofotfjord just before midday, past the burning wreckage of the destroyers. She had been delayed by the need to clear mines from the entrance and by the intensive anti-submarine efforts made by the escorting destroyers and aircraft from the light carriers. Approaching Narvik at the end of the Ofotfjord, she turned to port into the Herjandsfjord, the Gebirgsjäger watching in horrified fascination as the four massive turrets swung with leisurely menace, the barrels of the 15 inch guns seemingly shortening to invisibility as they aimed straight at them. The improvised cover which was all they had had time to devise suddenly seemed horribly inadequate.

Spray flew over the bows of the tank landing craft as it ploughed past Narvik toward Øyjord on the other side of the Rombaksfjord. The colossal detonations of *Warspite*'s huge guns had been reverberating around the fjord for almost an hour, and the Sergeant-Major, bracing himself against the hatch of the Cromwell assault tank, felt briefly sorry for the German troops on the receiving end. A sailor positioned in the bows signalled to him. One minute left.

He felt the butterflies fluttering in his stomach and wished he had time for another visit to the heads, but it was too late now. He took comfort from the massive bulk of his assault tank, with its 25-pounder gun thrusting forward. The tank's engine was warm and revving as the craft grounded. The ramp crashed down and the driver threw the tank into gear, the vehicle lurching over the ramp and into the shallow water beyond. Water streamed from the front of the tank as the tracks scrabbled it to the shore. On both sides, the Sergeant-Major could see other craft landing, disgorging a mixture of Cromwells and Covenanter armoured personnel carriers, each with a section of Marines.

The Marines had left their Covenanter on the outskirts of Øyjord and moved carefully through the village, alert to any ambush. The Sergeant crouched beside a building, knowing that its wooden construction would give no protection but feeling comforted by the cover. His section clustered around him, bristling with Solens, Besals and Brens. With hand signals, he sent one group led by a corporal around one side of the building while he led the remainder around the other.

He spun round at a sudden blast from one side, in time to see an arcing tracer impact the front of the Covenanter. A violent explosion shook the APC, which sat burning, obviously wrecked. The chatter of automatic fire snapped at his attention and he hurled himself to the ground as the air around him crackled with supersonic bullets. It seemed, he thought crazily, as if Øyjord might be occupied after all. He gripped his Solen and looked round at his men, who were returning a hail of fire towards the concealed German positions. It was not, he thought, going to be an easy day.

The Wellington patrolled its regular beat over the North Sea, festooned with the aerials of the new air observation radar. The aircraft's modest performance was slowed still further by the extra drag, but this was of no account to the RAF. What mattered was the plot being kept on board, tracking air movements over Norway and directing the relentless Reapers onto promising targets. The Nazis must, the pilot thought, be heartily sick of the way the virtually uncatchable fighters pounced without warning anywhere above Norway.

'Aircraft heading west over the North Sea.'

The senior officer went to look at the CRT, then frowned.

'Have we identified them?'

'No, there's no IFF response.'

He watched the blip on the screen as it grew closer. It was not large, but was beginning to show that there was more than one plane. He walked over to the R/T.

'Hello, Argus calling aircraft heading west from Bergen at angels fifteen; please identify yourselves.'

Silence.

The officer felt his unease growing. 'Where are the nearest Reapers?'

The operator sat still, suddenly pale. 'Too far,' he said quietly.

'Pilot! Bandits approaching from the west. Break off the patrol and take evasive action.'

The lumbering aircraft lurched to one side and dropped toward the sea, winding up to a shuddering 250 mph.

'Those bandits are doing at least four hundred.' No-one could hear the operator's whisper; they didn't need to. The four Fw 187s streaked towards the fleeing plane, guided faultlessly by the radar receivers they carried, tuned to the frequency of the Wellington's set. The officer suddenly guessed what was happening.

'Turn off the radar!' He yelled.

He was far too late.

'So far so good.' Mary was studying the latest situation reports and plotting the positions of the British units on the large map of Norway which dominated one wall of the Operations Room. 'Narvik and Bardufoss airfield are secure and the Marines have linked up with the Norwegians in Hegra fort. Dietl and the Third Mountain Division have been forced over the border into Sweden.'

'Where doubtless they will not be interned for long,' commented Charles drily. 'Still, if they do hang around there, it will give us a good excuse to go into Sweden after them and put the iron ore mines into protective custody.'

'What about Trondheim?' Don was bleary-eyed and dishevelled, having been forced to catch up with lost sleep during the day.

'Trondheim is ours but we took heavy losses. The Marines managed to neutralise the coastal forts and paratroops seized the airfield. But those radio-controlled bombs caused havoc until the carriers mounted standing Beaufighter patrols to knock down the Dorniers at a distance. Then the Germans started providing fighter escorts and the air battle is still raging. The first Hurricanes are operating from Vaernes, though, which is shifting the balance in our favour. The First Armoured is pushing up the valley towards Dombås, but the Germans are putting up a tough rearguard action so progress is slow.'

Johnson was moodily studying a map of the North Sea on the adjacent wall. 'Naval losses have been heavy on both sides. Our submarines and torpedo planes scored a number of successes and the Germans only have one pocket battleship, a couple of cruisers and some small destroyers left, but we've lost *Furious*, *Vindictive* and *Sheffield* to submarines, plus *Renown*, *Malaya*, *Cornwall* and several smaller ships to those damned radio-controlled bombs.'

'It could have been worse. At least the main covering force has stayed intact.' Mary should have been a diplomat, reflected Don, or maybe a counsellor, if such a role had been thought of. Johnson brightened.

'Yes, after some terrific battles. The Beaufighters and the new carriers have really proved themselves; they're claiming twenty-three Dorniers for the loss of only three fighters, and the anti-aircraft escorts have claimed another nine. On top of that, they sank three U-boats.'

'We've probably got the measure of those bombs for the time being,' commented Charles. 'The control frequencies have been identified so we can jam them, at least until the Germans find out and change the frequencies.'

'There have been some other nasty surprises, though. We didn't know the Germans had such good Asdic; it has cost us at least three submarines. And their Panzerfausts are costing us dear in hitting our armoured vehicles.'

'How are the Norwegians doing?' Enquired Don. Taylor pulled a face.

'They never really had a chance to mobilise and they've been pushed up the Gudbransdal past Lillehammer, but General Ruge is pulling the remnants together and we've flown them crate-loads of PIATs to give them some chance against the Panzers. Many of them are skilled skiers, though, so they're doing a great job of reconnaissance and screening wherever we've been able to add them to our forces.' Morgan looked up from the reports on operational readiness.

'The Luftwaffe was badly handicapped by the job the Mosquitos did on the airfields, but they're getting back into full swing now, with Messerschmitts operating from the Oslo fields. They're now too well defended to risk repeating the operations. However, we started on Bergen and Stavanger yesterday.' Johnson looked worried again.

'These are trickier, they're so much closer to the German airfields. We're going in, though, with *Warspite* and *Queen Elizabeth*, and the covering fleet is moving south to give them support. We've doubled the escort screen, but even so we're expecting a monumental air and sea battle before the Marines even land. What's worse, the Germans have had time to take over the defensive forts. We're planning to attack them with Beauforts carrying the new one-ton armour-piercing bombs, but there's no guarantee they will knock them out.'

Don grimaced, remembering a long-ago visit to Bergen, the charm of the medieval wooden dockside buildings of the Bryggen. They were hardly likely to survive the coming battle. He tore his mind away from the memory and turned to Mary. 'Anything happening elsewhere?'

'Bodø and Tromsø are in Norwegian hands, and oddly enough the Germans have heavily bombed Namsos and Åndalsnes despite the lack of any military activity there.' Don winced, thinking of the little towns, their wooden buildings so vulnerable to attack, smashed because of their significance in another time, another war. He realised that Mary was watching him anxiously, and forced a smile. 'Who was it who said that no plan of battle ever survives first contact with the enemy? At least, we're doing a whole lot better than we were in my time.'

Nothing seemed to be moving in the valley below. The little village of Kvam nestled on the northern slopes of the Gudbransdal, above the River Laagen. The railway line from Dombås to Lillehammer also hugged the north bank, with a station just where the river divided around a large island about half a mile long. Beyond that, the river curved southward out of sight. The Lieutenant lowered his field glasses and spoke to the radioman behind him.

'Tell them it's all clear.' He looked through the glasses again and murmured to himself. 'Neither the Norwegians nor, thank God, the Germans have reached here yet from Lillehammer, and if the remnants we drove out of Dombås came this way they haven't stopped. We should have time to set up a strong defensive position.' He turned to his platoon. 'Sergeant, stay here with the radioman and two others. The rest will return with me.'

The Norwegians were exhausted after days of heavy fighting and nights of retreating, always being pushed back by the heavily-armed enemy; every move under observation from the ubiquitous Fieseler Storch scout planes, always the possibility of a fighter or bomber attack. Still, they were intact as a fighting force under the grimly determined leadership of General Ruge, and their King and government were with them. The portable anti-tank weapons flown in by the British had surprised the Germans and made them more cautious, buying the Norwegians precious time in their retreat.

The small force moved up the valley towards Kvam just before dawn, hoping to reach shelter before the accursed scout planes started hovering over them. The Kaptein in command of the forward reconnaissance unit moved warily up the road toward the village, then halted as he saw movement by the road ahead. He reached for his glasses and saw the flag being waved; it was a Union Jack.

Late in the afternoon, the leading elements of the German force followed the same route. They too were tired, but buoyed by success and the steady flow of supplies reaching them. The British may have dislodged the small forces that took the coastal towns, but a full Division of the Wehrmacht was a different matter altogether.

Sudden bursts of automatic fire echoed across the valley as the flanking ski troops high up the valley sides reached the first Allied outposts. The troops on the road hastily ran for cover to either side, just as the first mortar rounds fell around them. They stayed low as the first of the Panzers drove past them, straight up the road to Kvam, followed by a line of armoured vehicles.

The blast of an explosion under the first tank reverberated around the valley as the mine detonated. The tank slewed sideways then stopped, one track torn off. The second tank tried to manoeuvre around it but there was a sharp 'bang-bang' of a high-velocity anti-tank gun and the impact of its shot against armour and the second tank stopped abruptly; a hole punched in the side. The Panzers were beginning to close up behind the blockage when, with a rising snarl of aero engines, four Hurricanes flew low up the valley behind the column; the tearing sound of multiple machine guns, each firing twenty rounds per second, sending exposed infantry flying in bloody disorder. Flame flashed from the wings of the planes as rockets sped forward and down, tearing the column apart with a series of ripping explosions. The hammering of Flak cannon spread through the column and a Hurricane lurched off course, crashing into the valley side.

The Division was just beginning to collect itself after the assault when the first of the barrage of sixty-two pounder artillery shells from the Centaur SPGs began to fall. Kvam would not be a pleasant memory for the Wehrmacht.

'Not again,' groaned Don, 'what is it this time? Is the battle for Kvam over?' Charles stopped shaking him and stood back, his expression grim as Don straightened up from being slumped over the table in the Ops Room.

'Kvam has been held all right; the Germans have retreated beyond Tretten and are being driven back to Lillehammer. But I didn't wake you to tell you that.' Don sat upright, sleep vanishing rapidly from his thoughts, and waited. 'Hitler obviously decided that he'd heard enough bad news from Norway. He attacked in the West half an hour ago.'

Hermann was feeling equally sleepless as he sat at the back of the Command Centre, listening to the flood of messages and orders as Fall Gelb, the assault in the West, neared the end of its third day. Stadler strolled over and sat beside him, lighting a fresh cigarette.

'Don't look so worried. Everything is going to plan.'

'Almost too much so. Didn't the British warn the French? And why aren't they coming to their aid? They must have known what was going to happen.'

'Now there are two interesting questions. We have captured some papers which show that the British did indeed warn the French of our thrust through the Ardennes, but the French ignored it. They didn't think it was possible; their high command was too complacent and far too slow to react when the blow fell. As to why the British aren't charging in to help the French, well, it could be pique. After all, the French refused to support them over Norway because the British wouldn't support the French over Poland. Or on the other hand, it could be realism. They must know that they can't stop us now, particularly not with some of their best Divisions tied down in Norway.' Herrman shifted uneasily. 'The Führer is still angry about that. He had high hopes for Weserübung.'

'Don't worry about that now, he has other things on his mind. He has given the General Staff four weeks to conquer France, which at the present rate of progress will be more than enough. After that, he will turn his attention to Britain. I wouldn't be surprised if Britain falls before Norway does.'

The mood in the Ops Room was sombre as the sweeping arrows indicating the German advance were marked on the map of France. Don tried to suppress his imagination, to forget the turmoil and tragedy represented by those bold lines, the death and despair flooding the country as the waves of terrified refugees fled before the armies. He struggled to regain his academic objectivity, to remember that this was all part of the plan. He cleared his throat, trying to sound calm.

'The Germans seem to have stuck to the Sichelschnitt plan, with their main thrust along the Ardennes axis followed by a northward curve to the Channel ports.'

'Presumably with a different motive this time; they're not trying to trap us, just to keep us out.' Don noticed that even Charles was beginning to appear slightly unkempt. The tension of the past few days was distracting all of them from normal habits.

'Any news from "Those Above Us"?'

Charles smiled wearily at the reference to the Oversight Committee. 'They're still fighting their biggest battle so far to prevent the politicians from sending help to France. Even though they know it can't affect the course of the war, Chamberlain and Halifax are desperate to show that we're trying. So far we've managed to persuade them that, now we've got the Germans on the run in Norway, it would be fatal to take the pressure off, so they've agreed that our help should be limited to air support. The RAF has been staging attacks on Luftwaffe airfields and trying to pick off German air raids. They've also tried to have a go at the advancing Wehrmacht but it's incredibly difficult. The battlefield is moving so fast that it's impossible to obtain reliable information about enemy movements. France's military command structure seems to have collapsed.'

'Even faster than it did in my time. The Germans are better prepared and equipped, of course, and the French didn't even have the benefit of being on a war footing when the blitzkrieg started.'

Charles shrugged. 'We warned them as strongly as we could, but they seemed to be so appalled at the prospect of another war that they didn't want to believe us. Still, look on the bright side. It will all be over for them a lot more quickly this time.'

'Yes,' said Mary quietly, 'and then it will be our turn.'

That evening, Don, Charles and Mary walked back through the darkening streets to their apartment building. Newspaper salesmen were locatable by their brief, unintelligible cries, the just-readable placards telling of successes in Norway, disasters in France. The last light of evening shone on the aquatic shapes of the barrage balloons high above in the multicoloured sky. A few cars grumbled and whined past, their hooded headlamps no more than dim gleams. Don looked puzzled for a moment, then laughed. Mary looked surprised and relieved, and hugged his arm. 'Share it with us!'

Don smiled. 'This scene looked so familiar and yet unfamiliar at the same time. It took me a few seconds to work out why. I've seen countless old films of wartime London; but always in black and white!'

Charles laughed, then seized the moment. 'I've been meaning to tell you something.' Enquiring noises. 'My lords and masters have decided that you need a change of scenery. They're replacing me with a new watchdog.' This time the noises were dismayed. 'Don't worry,' he added hastily, 'I know who they've got in mind and he's a splendid chap. Very keen to meet you. His name's Philby. Kim Philby…Don, whatever's the matter?'

They sat tensely in Charles's flat, trying to absorb the implications of Don's revelations about the Soviet agent working within the British security services. 'It's hard to judge how much he knows,' said Charles slowly. 'Your existence is still officially top secret, with cover stories always used to explain our inside knowledge. He has only been told that he is to act as liaison with an important intelligence source. There can be no doubt, though, that anyone in his position would have pieced things together long ago.'

Don took another large swig of whisky. 'We can assume that whatever he knows, the Russians know. God knows what effect this will have on our plans, but we can be sure of one thing. The Oversight Committee will not be pleased.'

They were not. There was an atmosphere of barely-suppressed outrage in the familiar room when Don finished his tale. He wasn't sure from their instant responses whether they were more upset about the impact on their plans, or that one of their own kind had proved treacherous. Don cleared his throat and continued.

'He's not the only one, of course. I've been racking my brains overnight to remember all of the others. Guy Burgess, Donald Maclean and Anthony Blunt I'm certain of. I know there were one or two more, but it's such a long time ago for me that I can't be sure who they were. I think one of them might have been called Liddell, and there was a chap called Hollis who was always under suspicion; though I don't think anything was ever proved.'

Chairman was icy. 'They will be moved into less sensitive areas and closely watched, of course. More to the point, what effect will their spying have on Russian policy? I agree we have to assume that they know at least the broad outlines of the story.'

Charles cut in. 'I've been thinking about that. If they believe what they have been told, they will have been taking precautions by moving strategic industries eastwards and building up their forces in readiness. This may not be a bad thing; otherwise the Wehrmacht, with their advanced knowledge and equipment, would be in a position to roll over them and knock them out of the war. There could actually be advantages in leaving one of the traitors in a suitable post so we could choose what information to leak to the Russians.'

The tension in the room relaxed a little as the Committee considered the suggestion. Chairman looked around the table, gathering assent. 'Very well, then, work out the details and let me know.' He turned to Don. 'However, we wanted to talk to you anyway about another matter. Norway will soon be ours. We think that the Germans are only resisting in order to keep us distracted. France is evidently heading for a rapid defeat but that isn't our Government's fault. Chamberlain's prestige took a hard knock when he had to declare war, but there's been no reason to criticise what he's done since, so there is no great call for his resignation. He seems to have rallied his spirits and is determined to stay on. Churchill is now in the Cabinet as First Sea Lord, of course, but as things stand there doesn't seem any prospect of his becoming Prime Minister.' Chairman stopped and looked at Don thoughtfully.

'That could be serious,' Don said slowly. 'Chamberlain always wanted to deal rather than fight, and Halifax as Foreign Secretary was even more keen on appeasement. There was some feeling in my time that if Churchill hadn't taken over in 1940, the Government might have decided that with France gone, there was no point in continuing the war.' He leaned back in his chair, considering. 'The question is, will Hitler give him the option? What does he want to do? Will he be satisfied with ending the war with us in order to concentrate on Russia, or will he want to defeat us first? Either way, I believe that we must have Churchill in charge, otherwise everything becomes totally unpredictable.'

Chairman looked at him grimly. 'In that case, there is only one option. Chamberlain and Churchill must be told the truth. And you will have to tell them.'

Mary handed Don the large whisky even before he sat down. 'How did it go?' She asked quietly. Don took a large gulp, leaned back with a sigh.

'About as badly as expected. Chamberlain went white and seemed to be in shock. Even Churchill was speechless for a while, although I soon saw the beginnings of a gleam in his eye. I could tell he was bursting with questions, but biting his tongue out of respect for Chamberlain's feelings.'

'What was the outcome?'

'Hard to tell. At first Chamberlain wanted to bluff it out, claim it was a ridiculous tale. The computer subdued him – Churchill was fascinated by it – but I think what upset him most was the clear determination of the Oversight Committee. I still don't know who they are, but he obviously does and he took them very seriously. In the end, he said he would need time to think about it. I have a feeling that it's going to be all right, though.'

'Why's that?'

'On the way out, Churchill turned and winked at me.'

Mary laughed. 'With him in the saddle, I think our lives might be in for a change!'

## June 1940

A fortnight later, Don and Charles were unexpectedly summoned to the Oversight Committee in order to review the strategic position in the pause following the fall of France and the victory in Norway. Don was rather surprised by the summons, even though he was by now familiar with the Committee's occasional need for reassurance, but his surprise redoubled when he entered the committee room to see a familiar figure wreathed in cigar smoke.

'Don't mind me,' the new Prime Minister said jovially, 'I'm just here to find out what's behind the news.'

Don collected his thoughts and duly delivered his assessment. 'On the face of it, the only strategic difference between the present situation and the one in my time is that Britain instead of Germany is installed in Norway. That alone is of great importance. However, the degree of preparedness for further action is considerably at variance. The Wehrmacht is much better equipped than in my time, with more and better armoured vehicles, anti-tank weapons and other small arms. The Luftwaffe is even more advanced, relatively speaking, with the first of the new four-engined bombers – the Heinkel One-seven-seven – in service and the Dornier Three-one-seven at an advanced stage of testing. Most seriously, the first of the Kriegsmarine's new electroboats are commencing operations. Fortunately, our preparations show even greater advances, probably because there was far more room for improvement.' He paused as Churchill grunted agreement. 'Aircraft production has concentrated on advanced types, with the Spitfire, Reaper, Mosquito, Hampden and Wellington in full production, plus the Beaufighter and Beaufort for the Fleet Air Arm. The Warwick is due to replace the Wellington on the lines in the next few months, and the Brigand, the de-navalised Beaufighter, has already replaced the Hurricane in production and will shortly be entering service as the RAF's tactical fighter-bomber. High-altitude bombers and jet combat aircraft are at an advanced stage of development. The Navy was hit hard in the battle for Norway, but it is still much stronger than in my time. There are far more aircraft carriers, for convoy escort as well as the main fleet, and all of the major warships are much better able to deal with air attack. Escort vessels are also far better equipped to deal with submarines. Most important of all, the Army is in infinitely better shape, with far superior weapons, most particularly the armoured fighting vehicles'.

Churchill interrupted. 'Will the Nazis invade, do you think?'

Don sensed the tension in the room and chose his words with care. 'I have no doubt Hitler planned to, before he knew of my existence. He will have been told that bolder action to close the net on the British Expeditionary Force to prevent its escape at Dunkirk, together with better preparation for an immediate invasion, would have stood a good chance of giving him a quick victory.'

'The situation is very different now, though. We have a far stronger army, with tactics successfully tested in Norway. There are three armoured divisions guarding the coast and another two in reserve behind the second defence line, supported by ten fully-equipped motorised infantry divisions and comprehensive mobile coast-defence and anti-aircraft artillery. We also have far larger numbers of Spitfires, and a new and very useful type of long-range fighter in the Gloster Reaper. It would be a huge risk for the Germans to attack us now.'

Churchill seemed dubious; 'Hitler enjoys taking risks.'

'Yes, but not over water.' Don laughed suddenly. 'He hates water!'

The Duty Group Controller looked impassively down onto the plotting table as the tension mounted in the Group Operations Room. Information about enemy aircraft movements was being fed through the Filter Room at Fighter Command HQ at Bentley Priory then transferred by WAAF plotters to the huge map of South-East England, the Channel and the Continental coast. The current plot showed streams of aircraft heading for England, apparently for a variety of targets. As usual, the current raid had been preceded by a cat-and-mouse contest between the Luftwaffe and the defence system, with Chain Home radar stations hit by low-level Ju 88 attacks and the back-up AEW Wellingtons the focus of sharp battles between attacking Fw 187s and defending Spitfires. The Controller considered the plot for a few minutes longer, then picked up a telephone and gave crisp instructions.

The Sector Controller of 11 Group grimaced as he studied an identical plot, then directed three Reaper and three Spitfire squadrons to scramble. The theory was that the Reapers would use their high attack speed and devastating cannon armament to concentrate on the bombers, leaving the slower but more agile Spitfires to take on the escorting fighters, but in practice the battles tended to develop into a free-for-all. The air battle had now been going on every day for three weeks and the strain was beginning to tell. His Deputy stood beside him and murmured thoughtfully.

'It looks as if it's the airfields again.'

The Controller nodded tersely. The Luftwaffe had been relentless in attacking the RAF defences at every opportunity; sneak raids to shoot-up fighter airfields supplemented by heavy attacks like this one, partly intended to damage airfield infrastructure, partly to draw defending fighters into the battle.

Don stood quietly to the rear of the balcony overlooking the plotting table, watching in fascination as the small tokens representing defending squadrons were placed on the map. Morgan murmured into his ear; 'Dowding is having to rotate squadrons with other groups every week to give them a chance to rest and build back to full strength. The fighters are taking a hammering but so far the supply of new aircraft and pilots is keeping pace. The Empire Air Training Scheme is delivering the goods. Just as important, the Luftwaffe is taking even heavier losses. They won't be able to keep this up for long.'

Don moved away abruptly; 'Let's go and see.'

Morgan studied his tense face thoughtfully and wondered what was passing through his mind, then nodded. 'I'll set it up for this afternoon.'

The airfield looked a mess. Black smoke rose from a few of the buildings and from a wrecked Spitfire which seemed to have crashed on landing. Weary AA crews, each man with a mug of tea and a cigarette, sat on their sandbagged revetments, surrounded by spent cartridge cases. The only sign of movement was a couple of camouflaged bulldozers, shovelling earth back into bomb craters. A steamroller waited under cover of some trees. Apart from the burning Spitfire, there were no other planes in sight.

'Over here!' Morgan was heading for the trees. As Don followed him, he became aware that a large mound under the trees was in fact a sandbagged blast pen, covered with camouflage netting. Inside nestled the sleek shape of a Spitfire.

'We've had to do this at all of the front-line airfields to protect against sneak raids. The vital services have all been moved underground, as well. Fortunately, the airfields are big enough that they can't easily be closed by bombing; the Spits can usually find a stretch of grass to land on.'

The pilot, a Flight-Sergeant, was standing by his aircraft, talking to the ground crew who were busying themselves with repair and maintenance. As he turned to meet them Don was struck by how young he was and how very tired, with red-rimmed eyes in a drawn face. Morgan chatted to him briefly, introducing Don in his usual civil-servant alias. The pilot did not seem very interested in him and Don could understand why. What an unnatural existence, he thought. Days spent sitting at readiness, waiting for the dread telephone ring that summoned them to scramble. A fast take-off and climb, eyes straining for a first sight of the enemy. Then a 'Tally-ho!' over the R/T, dots filling the sky like a swarm of flies, the fast streaks of Reapers diving on the bombers, followed by the vengeful German fighters, the sudden turmoil of combat, frantically trying to stay on the tail of his leader, perhaps a brief instant in which a black-crossed plane was in the right place for a burst of fire, the silence as the air seemed suddenly clear of planes, the battle having moved on. Then back to earth to sit and wait for the next call.

Don dragged his mind back to the present, aware that the pilot was looking at him oddly. 'How is the Spitfire performing against the German planes?' he asked quickly.

'Pretty well. A bit better than the one-oh-nine, a close match for the new one-ninety. The new engine improvements have helped a lot.'

'Higher octane petrol,' commented Morgan. 'It's enabled a higher boost pressure to be used; these Merlins are producing around twelve-fifty horsepower.'

'What about the guns?' Morgan looked at the three irregularly-spaced holes in the leading edge of the nearest wing, being carefully taped over by a fitter.

'Oh, these new fifties are great. They have a lot more punch than the old three-oh-threes. Nothing like the cannon in the Reapers, of course, but you can't have everything.' He invited them over to meet the other pilots, gathering wearily in one of the few remaining buildings which were still intact, although Don noticed that it had recently been repaired. He sat back and listened to their casual chatter, exchanging notes on the last battle, commenting on kills made, friends shot down as if they were talking about the weather.

As he absorbed the scene and listened to the familiar slang, Don felt a powerful surge of an emotion he could only describe as nostalgia. This is one of the defining moments of recent history, he thought. These dauntless young men, throwing themselves into lethal combat again and again against an equally skilled and courageous enemy; on their success depends the future of the air battle, the war, the shape of the world. He turned away, embarrassed by a sudden lump in his throat.

Don sat silently next to Morgan on the way back to London.

'Penny for them?'

Don stirred, momentarily lost for words. 'It's a strange feeling,' he said slowly. 'In a way I've lived through this before, at second hand. My past life seems like a dream now, but it meshes so closely with the present reality that… I still find it confusing.'

Morgan glanced at him sympathetically, then slowed the car as a building with a hanging sign came into view. 'I know an answer to that,' he said cheerfully, 'it's just about opening time!'

Herrman sat on the terrace by the FHQ Wolfsschlucht in Belgium, sipping morosely from a stein. As usual, he wasn't far from the Nazi bosses and as ever, the fact made him feel ill at ease. Where was the fearless young man who refused to toe the line for his communist bosses, he thought. Was the present situation so very different? It wasn't a new thought and the answer was the same, like a cold stone in his belly. The East German communists had been repressive and obnoxious, but the thread of decadent, depraved evil running through the Nazi hierarchy put them in a different league altogether. He thought of Faust and shuddered inwardly. He had made a pact with the Devil, indeed.

Stadler strolled onto the terrace and dropped into the next chair. 'That's that, then. Our lord and master has finally decided that England is too strong to invade.'

'What next?'

'We'll starve them out. Ports will be bombed, mines laid, and the new Elektroboote unleashed on their convoys. By your own account, we are much better equipped to do this than we were in your time.'

'True, but the British are also better equipped to prevent us.'

Stadler waved the objection aside. 'Britain is no threat without America. It has been decided that Russia is the more pressing problem. The Führer has always envisaged them as the enemy rather than Britain, anyway. And now their seizure of parts of Rumania puts them much too close to the Ploiesti oilfields. It is clear that they will carry on expanding westwards if we don't stop them. So we will.'

'Target dead ahead; range four hundred.' The calm voice of the radar operator crackled in the headphones. The pilot peered into the night for any sign of the intruder. Below, Southampton burned. The Ju 88 pathfinders had managed to overcome the jamming of their navigation beams and had placed their pyrotechnic target markers precisely on the docks. Now one of the Junkers was cruising around the devastation, guiding in the fast, high-flying He 177s whose bombloads were setting the city ablaze.

The pilot cursed under his breath as the range shortened with painful slowness. The new Mosquito night-fighters were already making a name for themselves, but his squadron had yet to convert from the pioneering Blenheims. Replacement of the turret by a pair of 0.5 inch Vickers-Brownings, aimed forwards and upwards, had added over 20 mph to the top speed, but the old plane was still only just fast enough.

A searchlight beam, probing under radar direction, briefly illuminated the Master Bomber plane ahead. The pilot put the Blenheim into a shallow dive, slipping underneath the tail of the Junkers. He looked up at the shape ahead and above, dimly discernable in the light of the blazing fires, as it drifting slowly into the sight markings on the canopy. A brief stab at the firing button sent a mixture of AP and incendiary projectiles into the belly of the target. He couldn't see whether they were striking home – tracers weren't used in order to give no warning to the target – but flame suddenly blossomed above him and the Junkers abruptly dived down and to starboard. The pilot followed him down, getting in a burst from the front 0.5s, then could only watch as the faster Ju 88 pulled away from him. He was still cursing his luck when the Junkers hit the ground in a flash of fire.

Charles held up the champagne bottle to confirm that it was empty, then grunted in disgust and heaved himself out of his chair to go in search of another. Mary unexpectedly giggled and leaned back in her armchair, kicking off her shoes.

'Why the unaccustomed hilarity?' Enquired Don, pronouncing his words with care.

'Why not?' She laughed. 'It's not often we have something to celebrate.'

Don looked at the somewhat battered copy of the decrypted message from Bletchley which revealed that Hitler had scrapped the planned invasion of England. 'I'm surprised they're still using Enigma, they must know we can crack it.'

'Not necessarily.' Charles reappeared triumphantly clutching a chilled bottle of Bollinger. 'It's still the best encryption machine around, and they've been changing the code wheels frequently. We wouldn't have had time to crack one code before the next was introduced if it weren't for your little machine – that they obviously don't know about.'

'It may not have been a bad thing if the Germans had invaded,' observed Don. 'We were ready to give them a good hammering this time.'

'I'd rather they stayed on the other side of the Channel.' Mary was sounding suspiciously dreamy. Don ploughed on.

'Hitler's obviously decided to close down our trade routes. Liverpool, Bristol, Southampton, all hammered. Several ships sunk by mines in the port approaches. Losses to submarines beginning to mount despite our precautions.'

'Oh, do stop being a Jeremiah for once. We've passed a turning point. Hitler can't beat us now.'

Charles laughed. 'Not even with Mussolini's help?'

Don joined in the laughter. 'Now there's someone who doesn't have foreknowledge, or he'd have stayed neutral. Seriously, though, talking about the Med., I'm glad the Committee was able to persuade Churchill not to attack the French fleet. We know they'll keep their word not to allow the Germans to get hold of their ships. It ought to make our conquest of North Africa that much easier.'

Charles smiled grimly. 'Just as well for Musso's peace of mind that he doesn't know what we have in store for him.'

'Enough!' Mary stood up determinedly. 'Bedtime, one and all. The Med. can wait till tomorrow.'

# CHAPTER 4 - MEDITERRANEAN

**Autumn 1940**

Peter Morgan peered through the side window of the Auster as the Army plane banked to circle the harbour. Valletta gleamed in the early autumn sunshine, stone buildings packed close to the water's edge, the massive walls of Fort St. Elmo dominating the entrance to the harbour. A flotilla of destroyers was visible, distributed around the harbour in case of air attack. A number of motor torpedo boats could also be spotted by the trained eye, hidden away in smaller creeks and inlets.

As the little spotter plane circled the area, the entrances of the submarine pens became visible. Morgan smiled to himself, remembering Don Erlang's insistence that these bombproof pens, started in the 1920s but abandoned as an economy measure, should be completed before 1940. He tapped the pilot on the shoulder to indicate he had seen enough.

The Auster returned to the west side of Malta to land, the three interlinked airstrips of Hal Far, Luqa and Ta Qali coming into view, and Morgan was able to check for himself the effectiveness of the camouflage netting protecting the substantial stone walls around the dispersal pens scattered about the edge of the strips. The menacing snouts of Spitfires became visible only just before the Auster touched down.

'Seen all that you wanted to?' The staff officer was evidently curious about the inspection tour by the RAF intelligence officer, but he kept his questions to the point. Morgan smiled.

'Thanks. You seem very well prepared.'

'You've only seen a part of it. Most of the work is underground. We have huge bombproof stores full of food, ammunition and aviation spirit. The ack-ack defences have been steadily strengthened as well.' He paused for a moment, then asked rather diffidently, 'do you have any news about more aircraft? The Spitfires are doing a terrific job of keeping the Eyeties away, but one squadron won't be enough if they get really serious about attacking.'

Morgan shrugged non-committally, well aware of the battle Don was fighting to persuade Fighter Command to release some of its squadrons, which now had little to do in England. 'The German enthusiasm for invading Britain seems to be cooling off, and their bombing is now mostly at night. I think there's a fair chance of some more day-fighter squadrons being released soon. In fact,' he added thoughtfully, 'things could become rather busy around here.'

'Just as predicted; they seem to be preparing for a long stay.' The Sergeant grunted, lying on his back to keep a better eye on the sky, as the Second Lieutenant continued to observe the distant activity through field glasses. The Italians were digging in at Sidi Barrani after a sixty-mile advance into Egypt. The much smaller British forces had retreated in good order, inflicting far more casualties than they sustained.

'Not much evidence of armour. Mostly those pathetic little tankettes.' The Sergeant snorted. The little three-ton vehicles had armour so thin it could be penetrated by armour-piercing rifle ammunition.

The Second Lieutenant slid back from the crest, and they stood up to walk back to the camouflaged vehicle parked in the wadi. Only as they came closer was the shape of the six wheeled vehicle revealed under the netting, based on the Humber scout car chassis but with turret and armour stripped off to produce a fast, lightweight vehicle, bristling with heavy machine guns, ideally suited to the needs of the Long Range Desert Group.

'OK chaps, we've seen enough here. Let's see how far south they've reached.' He consulted a map. 'Next stop Tummar.'

Tension aboard the frigate *HMS Dido* rose perceptibly as the dawn approached. The convoy had left the safety of Gibraltar far behind and was now only twenty-four hours steaming from Malta. With Sardinia to port and Sicily ahead, the close attention of the Regia Aeronautica was expected. The Executive Officer walked onto the open bridge and stood by the Captain.

'The Beaufighters dealt with the reconnaissance plane before it could see us, but that won't hold them up for long.' The Captain grunted acknowledgement and the two men stood for a while in silence, watching as the growing light steadily revealed the ships around them. The bulk of the carriers *Eagle* and *Courageous* dominated the centre of the group, with the menacing silhouettes of the battleships *Barham* and *Valiant* and the long lean shape of the battlecruiser *Repulse* in close support, surrounded by a defensive ring of frigates and destroyers. The twenty fast merchant ships, some bound for Malta, some for Alexandria, had their own circle of escorts a short distance away.

An Aldis lamp started blinking rapidly from the *Courageous*. A signaller brought them the message at the same time as their own radar room reported the news; a large force of aircraft had been detected heading towards them. The officers watched as Beaufighter after Beaufighter was launched from the carriers, climbing steeply into the rising sun on the threatening eastern horizon. The Captain sighed. 'Sound Action Stations. It's going to be a busy day.'

The crew of the *Dido* did not have long to wait. The Regia Aeronautica had been working on their tactics and the first wave of aircraft turned out to be a decoy to tempt the defending fighters away. The second wave of bombers and torpedo planes timed their attack to coincide with the absence of the main force of Beaufighters. Some more of the fast Fleet Air Arm fighters were launched in time to break up the attacks, their combination of speed, armour protection and heavy armament outclassing the best Italian planes, but the Regia Aeronautica attacked in such numbers that many of the bombers got through.

This was what the frigate had been designed for. The new class of ships bridged the gap between destroyers and cruisers; their combination of long range, high speed and powerful anti-aircraft and anti-submarine armament suiting them well to the fleet escort role. The barrels of the eight 4.7 inch dual-purpose guns lifted to train on the approaching high-level bombers while the Bofors guns concentrated on the low-flying torpedo planes.

The convoy erupted with a massed barrage of fire, the bombers almost disappearing in the rash of detonating shells which suddenly speckled the clear Mediterranean sky, laced by the trails of the Bofors tracers. The hastily recalled Beaufighters frantically dived through the flak, risking being hit in order to chase down the bombers before their fuel ran out. They well knew that if the carriers should be disabled, there would be no safe landing ground within range.

Bomber after bomber fell to the guns of the convoy and its fighters as the ships twisted and turned between the torpedo trails and the accurate high-level bombing. Silence fell suddenly, the crew of the *Dido* looking around tensely, deafened from their own gunfire. The only sign of the enemy was a few disappearing dots, left in peace by the fuel-starved Beaufighters now queuing up to land. The Captain looked hastily around the convoy. The carriers seemed all right. Smoke was billowing from two of the merchant ships, but only one of them seemed in real trouble. The convoy had been lucky. He checked his watch, and grimaced. It wasn't even ten o'clock. He knew from experience that there would only be a brief pause before the next assault. He had barely moved to his chair in order to rest his legs when the Aldis starting blinking again.

'Message from *Courageous*, Sir. Reconnaissance reports enemy battlefleet at one hundred miles, heading this way.' It was definitely going to be a long day.

The *Valiant* and *Barham* strained towards the Italian fleet at their maximum twenty-three knots. The Italian ships were faster; their four old battleships of the Cavour and Doria classes had been completely remodelled and rebuilt in the late 1930s and could manage up to twenty-seven knots. Three of them were believed to be in the attacking force, together with heavy cruisers and destroyers.

The *Repulse* paced the lumbering battleships, waiting to make her move. Capable of thirty knots, she could quickly reach the Italians but their 320 mm guns posed a danger to the battlecruiser's thinner armour. The *Repulse*'s role would be to wait until the battleships engaged, then use her speed to manoeuvre to attack them from the flank and cut off their retreat.

The Captain of the escorting *Dido* watched as two squadrons of Beauforts flew overhead, covered by Beaufighters cruising at higher altitude. The carriers had few of the bombers on this occasion because of the need for fighter defence, and the sixteen aircraft probably represented all that could be put into the air. A long wait followed and the Captain was reminded, not for the first time, of the aphorism that war consisted of short periods of panic punctuating long stretches of boredom.

A message was brought just as the Aldis lamps began to flicker. The Captain studied it with mixed feelings. The Beaufort attack had scored hits on the big ships and, although none appeared to be seriously damaged, the Italian fleet had turned away and was racing back to port. There would be no fleet engagement this time.

Stadler watched sardonically as Herrman downed another schnapps. 'You should be careful, my friend. You are beginning to live on that juice.'

Herrman shrugged. 'Why should you worry. In fact, why should anyone worry? I've done all I can. Now it's up to others.'

'You still have a… symbolic value in certain quarters. And who knows, some unexpected turn of events might jog yet another forgotten fact from your increasingly befuddled memory.'

'The war is not going well.'

'Oh, I don't know. Our attacks on trade are beginning to hurt the British badly. If this winter is as hard as the last one, they'll be cold and hungry by the end of it. Losing Norway was annoying, but we have France safely wrapped up. And thanks to you we have avoided many of the mistakes of your time. Our military industry is well organised, with production increasing steadily in preparation for the assault on Russia. We have more and better equipment, plus a clearer idea of our long-range strategy. This time there will be no disaster on the Eastern Front.'

'I'm uneasy about the Mediterranean. I'm not sure what the British might decide to do; there would be some logic in them abandoning it altogether to concentrate on North-West Europe and the Far East, but they don't seem to be doing that.'

Stadler sighed. 'The Führer is most irritated. Despite his best efforts, Franco will not co-operate in an attack on Gibraltar. After all we've done for him! The British have a stranglehold on his food supplies and have threatened to seize the Canaries. And now 'Il Duce' has not only refused our offers to reinforce his troops in Libya, he's attacked Greece against all our advice!'

Herrman snorted morosely. 'I did warn you.'

'I know. But we didn't want to reveal your existence to the Italians, and although it would have been useful to push the British out, the Mediterranean is only a sideshow. It's in the east that this war will be decided.'

'I hope you're right. Losing Norway throws one big unknown into our planning. The Mediterranean would be another. Events are beginning to drift away from my experience. The future is becoming less predictable.'

Stadler smiled. 'Let's hope so. We wouldn't want a repeat of your time, after all!'

The Observer in the Beaufort carefully checked his position on the chart then spoke to the pilot: 'Let's go down. I think we're there.'

The plane dipped down towards the Italian night, the shape of the land beginning to stand out against the sea. The dark lump of the Isolotto San Pietro loomed ahead, punctuating the threadlike walls of the Mar Grande, the outer harbour. Three miles beyond lay Taranto; guarding the entrance to the inner harbour. Remembering the reconnaissance photographs, the pilot banked to starboard towards the long mole cordoning off the Diga de Tarantola, where the battleships lay at anchor.

'Watch for the barrage balloons!'

The pilot lifted the nose of the plane, then settled into a steady run. Searchlights snapped on, alerted by the noise of the big Hercules radials. The pilot wove a little to throw off the defenders, then hit the bomb release button. For a few seconds nothing happened, then the harbour lit up under brilliant parachute flares, the huge capital ships suddenly standing out in sharp relief. The Observer checked them quickly.

'Six of them! The new *Littorio* and *Vittorio Veneto* are there as well as the older ships; we've got the lot!'

The Beaufort banked around the harbour, the crew holding their collective breath in anticipation. They did not have long to wait. From high above them, a streak of flame flashed down as the first of the rocket-propelled guided bombs plunged towards the harbour, its flaring motor marking its position for the bomb-aimer. A battleship shuddered as the huge bomb blasted through its armoured deck, detonating within the hull. Then another, and another, as the squadron of Beauforts methodically pulverised the pride of the Regia Navale. The night sky filled with the glowing tracers of AA fire as the relentless destruction ground on.

With the battleships burning and sinking in the outer harbour, the circling Observer directed the next attack onto the heavy cruisers; some in the outer harbour; some in the Mar Piccolo. The bombers were supplemented by low-level torpedo attacks to divert and confuse the furious AA defence. Finally came the oil storage depot and the pipeline jetty. By the time the Observer decided to leave, the flame and smoke over Taranto marked the funeral pyre of a navy.

The shockwaves from the destruction of the Italian battlefleet reverberated around Italian North Africa for weeks. Even in Tripoli, the capital of Libya some 800 miles from the front line at Sidi Barrani, a perceptible shudder of unease was felt.

The sentries guarding the harbour defences tensed as they heard the rumble of aero engines just before dawn, but no flares lit, no bombs dropped. They relaxed with sighs of relief, speculating on the likely destination of the mysterious aeroplanes.

The airfields of the Regia Aeronautica throughout Libya, Sicily and Southern Italy were soon left in no doubt. As dawn broke, the British aircraft struck. Hereford attack aircraft, surreptiously gathering for weeks in Malta and Alexandria, roared in at low level, rockets flashing from the wings, 40 mm and 0.5 inch automatic fire hammering from the nose. The neatly lined-up Italian warplanes were blasted into scrap before the startled airfield defenders were able to respond.

Freed from defensive duties, a wave of Beaufighters from the carriers of the Mediterranean fleet dived in to attack the AA defences of Tripoli; rocketing and machine-gunning them into impotence and clearing the way for the following Beauforts which dive bombed the main land defences with careful precision.

No sooner had the planes departed than a noise like a multitude of speeding trains roared over the bewildered defenders, erupting in devastating explosions as the eighteen 16 inch guns of the battleships *Rodney* and *Nelson* lobbed their one-ton shells onto the stunned Italians from seventeen miles offshore. Closer to home, a gunnery control officer with the Special Boat Service watched the destruction in awe from his camouflaged hideout, almost forgetting to send corrections to the battleships.

The Italian commanders frantically tried to contact their shore defence batteries but received only sardonic responses from the SBS troops sent in before dawn to capture them.

Troops guarding the outskirts of Tripoli listened to the uproar in shocked amazement, which turned into incredulity as the unmistakable rumble of tracked vehicles gradually drowned out the noise of the bombardment. The squat shapes of Crusader tanks, put ashore by tank landing craft from a convoy whose purpose had been one of the best kept secrets of the war, roared towards them out of the desert. They frantically ran to man their defences.

Those defences were not thorough, most of the 200,000 Italian troops in North Africa were based closer to Egypt. Furthermore, the Mk II Crusaders, with three inches of frontal armour and a high-velocity six-pounder gun, were virtually impervious to the standard Italian 47 mm anti-tank gun while able to penetrate the thinly-armoured Italian tanks at all battle ranges.

Accompanying the tanks were RAF officers in Covenanter command vehicles, providing forward air control for the circling Beaufighters. Whenever Italian defences seemed to be stiffening, a brief call from a FAC brought a pair of fighter-bombers hurtling down to rocket and bomb the hapless defenders.

The outcome was in no doubt. The British troops were few in number, but the quality of their equipment, training and experience coupled with the shock effect of complete surprise shattered the Italian defences. By nightfall, Tripoli was in British hands and the first ships of the Royal Navy were entering the intact harbour. Italian North Africa had been struck in the heart.

On the same morning eight hundred miles to the east, Lieutenant General Richard O'Connor, Commander of the Western Desert Force, launched the 7th Armoured Division against the Italians at Sidi Barrani. The Division was fully equipped with Crusader IIs, together with Cromwell close-support tanks and Conqueror SPGs. Tracks through the defending minefields had been cleared by Centaur ARVs modified for the purpose and armoured units had also been landed behind the Italian lines to create more confusion.

The Desert Air Force joined in the carefully co-ordinated attacks, with the new Brigands, which along with the Herefords formed the core of the Force and had the same shattering effect on the Italians as the Stukas had had on the Poles and French. Unnerved by the news from Tripoli, the Italians did not hold out for long.

As the infantry divisions mopped up the bulk of the Italian troops in Egypt, the armoured forces ground relentlessly into Libya towards Bardia, supported by tank landing ships hopping around the coast to deliver small tank units where they could do most harm. Simultaneously, heavy reconnaissance elements equipped with Humber armoured cars sped across the desert of Cyrenaica to the Gulf of Sirte, cutting off the Italian line of retreat along the coast road. The Humbers had considerably better speed, range and reliability than tanks, but could still match the best of the Italian tanks in a straight fight. Overhead, the aircraft of the Desert Air Force hung in the air like a raised sword, chopping down at the smallest sign of resistance.

Over the course of the next week, amphibious landings at Benghazi and Tobruk met with little resistance. Some of the Italian units fought with bitter determination, but the spirit of their army had been broken by the crushing superiority of the British strategy, tactics and equipment. The obliteration of Italian North Africa took just ten days.

'Hardly surprising, really. Even in my time, O'Connor inflicted a spectacular defeat on the Italians and might well have mopped them up before Rommel could arrive on the scene if Churchill hadn't insisted on diverting forces to help Greece. This time, the Italians were facing nineteen-forty-five level forces infinitely more capable than the Desert Army and Air force had been in my time. Rather like the French facing the Wehrmacht, only more so.' Don found it hard to feel the same sense of elation as his friends in the Ops Room, knowing only too well what lay ahead.

'Cheer up, for once!' Taylor was still beaming with delight at the stunning success of the Army. 'It isn't often we have something like this to celebrate!'

'I'd feel happier if we had better news from the Western Approaches. Those electroboats are arriving in numbers now, and they're every bit as dangerous as we feared. On top of the mining and bombing of ports, things are beginning to get tight.'

'We're learning fast how to deal with them,' claimed Johnson. 'It's largely a matter of developing the right tactics through experience.'

'And we're hitting back!' Morgan was also determined to keep the mood of celebration. 'The new radio navigation aids and Pathfinder tactics are really bringing results. The Gelsenkirchen oil refinery was obliterated the night before last.'

Taylor leaned forward, smiling at Don. 'So what's likely to happen now? Do we throw the Italians out of Greece or Ethiopia next?'

Don considered for a moment. 'That's going to be up to Churchill, but I'm afraid he's so pro-Greek it's going to be difficult to deflect him, despite the fact that Chamberlain was persuaded not to give his guarantee to the Greeks last year.'

Mary looked at him penetratingly. 'I have a feeling you have something else in mind.'

'Right. We are now sharing a frontier with the French in Tunisia. They've stayed loyal to the Vichy government, as has most of the French Empire. We are also keeping the best ships in the French Navy bottled up at Oran, under pain of destruction if they try to move. But de Gaulle has already taken charge in some of the African colonies. If he can lead a Free French force from Libya into Tunisia to persuade the government there to join him, that could start a domino effect which would give us the French Empire and much of her fleet without a shot being fired.'

Mary thought about it. 'That's way ahead of schedule, isn't it? French Africa isn't supposed to be taken over until after the Americans land in 1942. How will Hitler react to that?'

'Invade the rest of France. He only kept the Vichy government in being to keep the French Empire loyal to it and therefore out of the war. I think I'd better see Churchill.'

Very much later, Don staggered into their apartment and collapsed into an armchair, hand reaching blindly out as Mary put a glass of

Scotch into it. 'Where does the old man get his stamina from?' He groaned.

Mary perched on the arm of the chair and ruffled his hair. 'Did you win?'

Don smiled crookedly. 'An honourable draw. De Gaulle can have an armoured regiment with support troops and three squadrons of Free French Spitfires provided that most of the rest goes to Greece.'

'Is that safe? To take so much out of Africa?'

'Ought to be. Malta should be OK now, there's no reason for the Axis to attack it any more as they no longer have trade routes with Africa to protect. The Italians still have an army in Ethiopia and the Horn of Africa, but it's cut off and can do no harm to us there, we can mop it up at our leisure.'

'What do you think the chances are?'

Don took a long sip of whisky. 'Very hard to judge. The Germans made mincemeat of us in Greece last time, even took Crete which was unforgivable. Our forces are immensely more effective now, but the Wehrmacht is just as good, if not better. We only beat them in Norway because we committed far more forces, particularly armoured divisions. It was just a small sideshow to the Germans, who were concentrating on France. And this time the Germans will have overland communications and supply routes, while we'll be dependent on the sea.'

'You sound really worried.'

He sighed. 'Combat analysis after the war showed that a hundred German troops were as good as a hundred and twenty of any other nation's. That's still likely to be the case. It's not going to be easy.'

**Winter 1940–41**

General Ubaldo Soddu, the overall commander of the Italian forces in Albania, was not happy. Tasked by Mussolini with the subjugation of Greece, he had duly marched his divisions over the border in October, only to see them repulsed and pushed well back into Albania by the astonishingly aggressive Greek Army. Italian superiority in numbers, tanks, transport and aircraft were counting for nothing in the mountainous terrain. They could hold the lowlands all right, but to make progress they had to clear the Greeks from the mountains, and that was proving far more difficult than anyone had imagined. Worse still, the British were sending increasing numbers of aircraft to harrass his troops, as well as nasty little portable anti-tank guns. Still, the reinforcements on the way by sea should help.

His aide was looking nervous again, always a bad sign. 'What is it?' He snapped.

'The reinforcements, sir. It seems the British sent a naval force into the Adriatic – heavy cruisers and light aircraft carriers. They found the convoy.'

Soddu closed his eyes wearily. Would nothing in this accursed campaign ever go right? 'Go on. How many were sunk?'

There was an ominous hesitation. 'All of them, sir.'

At the end of the month, General Soddu was relieved of his command.

'I don't care about Il Duce's precious pride anymore! He kept us out of Libya until it was too late to come to his aid, because he thought he might win a famous victory. Now he's trying to keep us away from Greece. Doesn't the idiot realise that he can posture and pretend all he likes, his precious army has all the fighting ability of a flock of sheep?'

Rather unfair, Herrman thought. Some Italian units had shown bravery and determination. The terrain suited the Greeks, though, who were ferocious in defence. The Führer paced up and down; Herrman had never seen him so angry with his ally, for whom he had always had a soft spot.

'It would not be advisable to try to reinforce the Italians through Albania,' Herrman offered. 'There is only a sea route and the Royal Navy is too strong. Now Bulgaria has joined the Tripartite Pact, we can invade Greece through Thrace and Macedonia. Alternatively, we could invade Yugoslavia on the way. As I recall, that was a quick and painless campaign in my time; it was easy to turn the Serbs and Croats against each other. It left a serious partisan problem, though. The country is ideal for it.'

Hitler grunted. 'I didn't want to fight in the Balkans at all, but to neutralise them with diplomacy. I can do without any distractions from the preparations for Russia. Now the Italians have left me no choice. I can't have the British on my southern borders.'

He paced around the room, thinking. Herrman wondered if he would ever get used to the surroundings, which seemed to fit a standard pattern wherever he went; the heavy panelling hung with Nazi flags, the awful furniture and kitsch statuary, occasional paintings of triumphant Aryan warriors, contrasting with those of blonde maidens demurely revealing their charms.

The Führer stopped pacing. 'I'll give Yugoslavia one more chance to join the Pact. If they refuse, I'll take them!'

'They will agree, but there'll be a popular revolt against the government for doing so,' Herrman predicted confidently.

'So be it! I'm not wasting any more time than I have to on the Balkans.'

'The British will send troops to Greece if we invade.'

'Good! Let them see how they will fare against the Wehrmacht for a change!'

'We must defend the north-east! It has a strong line of fortifications, well armed. Besides, we cannot possibly abandon Thrace, Macedonia and Salonika. The people would never forgive us!' General Metaxas, the Greek leader, was clearly appalled at the suggestion. Geoffrey Taylor, leading the covert British delegation, was trying to balance firmness with reasonableness.

'I know the Yugoslavs have given assurances as to their neutrality, but we have it on the highest authority that they won't be able to stick to that. The Germans will brush them aside. Then they will be able to attack from the north, and cut off your troops in the north-east.'

'So you say!'

Taylor was feeling acutely uncomfortable. He knew that the defences of the Metaxas Line were dear to the heart of their architect. He also knew that Metaxas would be dead within weeks.

'We are organising the shipping to bring our divisions over to you. I have to tell you, though, that we will only deploy further west, on the Aliakmon Line and the border with Yugoslavia. We won't put any troops into the north-east.'

Metaxas nodded curtly. 'We can look after that ourselves.'

The Lochagos lay just below the crest, watching elements of the XL Mountain Corps of the Wehrmacht pressing relentlessly forward through the Monastir Gap linking Yugoslavia with Greece. The British SAS unit lay beside him, the forward air controller giving clipped instructions over the wireless.

They did not have long to wait. With a rising howl of Hercules engines (how appropriate, thought the FAC irrelevantly) a pair of Brigands swooped down on the troops, rockets rippling from underwing. The Greek Army captain shouted encouragement as the German troops dived for cover, then waited eagerly as the fighter-bombers lazily turned to begin a strafing run.

Suddenly, two similar-looking aircraft flashed down out of the cloud layer, heading unerringly for the unsuspecting Brigands. A brief hammering of cannon fire, and the British planes tumbled broken to the ground. No parachutes opened.

'Focke Wulf 190s! How did they...? The Germans must be using mobile radar! I'd better warn HQ.'

The leader of the SAS team stirred uneasily. 'Don't stay on the wireless for long. We know they have detection equipment.'

The FAC nodded and sent his message. Then he rose slightly to put the equipment away. There was an odd snapping sound and the FAC jerked violently then slumped to the ground.

'Get down! Sniper!' The experienced troops needed no telling. They slid backwards down the slope to make their escape. The SAS lieutenant looked back up at the still body of the FAC, and cursed. 'We've lost the wireless!'

'Not much use to us now,' his sergeant commented. 'We can do no more here.'

The lieutenant nodded and the small troop followed the grim-faced Lochargos away from the Gap.

The long barrels of the sixty-two-pounders gave the game away. Poking skywards at identical angles from the shapeless lumps of camouflage netting, they revealed the presence of a troop of Conqueror self-propelled guns, emplaced behind Vroia on the Aliakmon Line. Every few minutes new instructions came through from the Auster spotter plane, bravely risking flak and fighters to ensure the gunners hit the attacking German forces some eight miles away. The barrels shifted minutely, the guns fired a ragged salvo – deafening, metallic thumps – followed by a clanking of metal as the empty cartridge cases were ejected, clearing the breeches for the next shells waiting in the loading trays.

Despite the winter cold, the hatches and rear doors of the Conquerors were open to reduce the fumes in the fighting compartments. The crews froze as a sudden, violent hammering filled the air.

'Air attack!' The crews scrabbled frantically to slam the rear doors shut as a gunner in each vehicle struggled up into the hatch, grasping the handles of the Vickers-Browning 0.5 and swinging it skywards. Their accompanying Comet AA tank whose firing had alerted them was still engaging the diving aircraft with short bursts of the Oerlikons. Tracers laced the sky as the Conquerors joined in, as if trying the snare the enemy in a web of smoke. Rockets shot forward from the Fw 190s, an eruption of rapid explosions obliterating the vehicles in earth and dust.

Heads popped back out of hatches as the engine noise died away.

'Prepare to move out! Now they've found us their counter-battery units will be zeroing in!' The gunners needed no further encouragement, and the armoured beasts roared and growled as they lurched heavily out of their firing points, turned tightly on their tracks and lumbered ponderously away in search of the new firing position which had previously been identified for just such an eventuality.

Seven miles to the east, the Eighth Armoured Division was not having an easy time. The Aliakmon Line was not as well fortified as the Metaxas Line and the precious armoured units were being held behind the Line to race from place to place to cut off any threatened German breakthrough.

The driver of the Crusader II cursed through gritted teeth as he wrenched the steering levers back and forth, aiming the speeding tank for the narrow gap between two buildings of the burning, deserted village. Once through, he spun the tank with a violence which threatened to tear the tracks off, then nudged it slowly forward.

As expected, the first of the Panzer IIIs emerged through the dust and smoke of battle some three hundred yards away. A short command and the Crusader's six-pounder gun fired with an intense blast, rocking the tank on its suspension. The leading Panzer jerked to a halt, but two more appeared, one on either side, their guns firing heavy shells which collapsed the buildings around the Crusader.

'Get us out of here!' Yelled the Sergeant, who had collected much dust and rubble through keeping his head out of the hatch. As the tank ground slowly backwards, it tilted up to clear the rubble, then began to lurch down the other side. A solid armour-piercing shot slammed into the gun mantlet, knocking the turret completely off the tank. Almost simultaneously, a second shot smashed the frontal armour. The Crusader began to burn.

A thousand yards away, the gunner of the Cavalier waited tensely, straining to see through the dust. Grey shapes suddenly emerged into the open, muzzles raised as they headed towards the self-propelled anti-tank gun.

'Fire when you're ready!'

The gunner needed no urging, and the Cavalier lurched as the massive high-velocity cannon sent seventeen pounds of solid, hardened steel screaming towards the Panzers at nearly three thousand feet per second. The turret of one tank was smashed apart by the second shot; by then, the other tanks had spotted the Cavalier and opened fire.

Shellfire crashed around the SPG and the vehicle rang as a solid shot deflected off the thick, well-sloped frontal armour. The crew fired steadily, destroying a second tank. More of the Panzers emerged from the smoke.

'Watch out – they're flanking us!'

The side armour of the Cavalier was much thinner than the frontal plate and the SPGs could not risk being attacked from the flanks.

'Fire smoke and pull back – we've got to get out of here!'

The smoke mortars lobbed their screening shells out in front of the SPG as it reversed rapidly out of the battle line to seek a safer firing position.

'We can keep our end up in a straight fight; the problem is that the Germans keep on coming.' The staff officer was staring at the map in frustration. The steady onward thrust of the Axis columns was starkly displayed.

Taylor grunted in sympathy. 'The qualitative balance is close. The new version of the Panzer III has a seventy-five millimetre gun as well as thicker armour; it's more than a match for the Crusader II. Fortunately we brought enough Cavaliers over to stop the rot, but an SPG is never as good as a tank in a mobile battle. We've some new ammunition which will give our six-pounder tank gun enough punch to penetrate the German armour at long range but it's not over here yet. You're right about the numbers, though. Whenever we try to hold our positions we're in danger of being bypassed and swamped. We can't bring up reinforcements as fast as they can. I don't see that we have any option but to pull out.'

'To Crete, you mean?'

Taylor nodded. 'The Navy is standing by at some of the southern ports. I think the decision to evacuate will be taken soon.'

The contingency had been carefully planned for; Don Erlang's warnings about the danger of airborne invasion had been heeded. Four squadrons of Reapers had been assigned to Crete to cover the withdrawal from the mainland ports nearly two hundred miles away; six squadrons of Spitfires were also in place ready to defend the island from the expected attack. Air Vice-Marshal Park, fresh from his successful defence of South-Eastern England in the Battle of Britain, had instituted a scaled-down version of the air defence system, with radar coverage of the northern coast feeding information to a fighter control centre.

The Navy was also prepared. A force of frigates and destroyers, all with heavy anti-aircraft armament, escorted the vessels evacuating troops from Greece then patrolled the north coast of Crete. On the ground, the airfields, the weak link in Don Erlang's time, were heavily defended with batteries of 3 inch and 40 mm AA guns, with the perimeter of the fields guarded by Comet AA tanks, backed up by well-emplaced troops armed with heavy machine guns. If the Fallschirmjäger attempted to land this time, they would be greeted with an annihilating reception.

'Seems as if everything is in order.' Don was feeling particularly relaxed, enjoying a quiet Sunday morning in the apartment. He waved the latest report from Geoffrey Taylor, who had now moved to Crete.

'Do you think they'll try to invade this time?' Mary gave up trying to catch up with the latest opinion in the Sunday papers; the occasional groans and snorts of derision from behind the newsheets had been indicating a certain lack of patience with the jingoistic editors.

'Suicidal if they do; Hitler is bound to be aware of the appalling casualties his paratroops took last time and he will know that we're much better prepared now.'

'The papers seem to have got over their shock-horror at Britain's first defeat. Now they're going on about how the despicable Nazis were unsporting enough to send far more troops than our brave boys could deal with. Good news from Algiers, though.'

'Brilliant. Now the Free French are in charge of all of France's African empire, the rest of their possessions will fall into line soon.'

'What effect will the German takeover of the rest of France have?'

'Hard to say. They've really given themselves more of a problem. Now there isn't a legitimate French government to collaborate with them, they have to run everything themselves. And they weren't quick enough to seize the French ships in Toulon before they could be scuttled. While we have picked up the much stronger fleet in Oran as allies again.'

'How cooperative is de Gaulle likely to be now he has a large power base of his own?'

Don laughed. 'Time will tell. He's still almost completely dependent on us for arms, and desperate to see the liberation of France. I think he'll work with us until that's achieved.'

The insistent ringing of the telephone woke them early the next morning. It was Harold Johnson, on duty in the Ops Room. At first, Don was too groggy to grasp clearly what Johnson was saying.

'They've invaded, you say? Must be mad, with all our preparations. What d'you say? Not Crete? What…Malta?' As the enormity sank in, Don was temporarily speechless. Mary deftly acquired the phone and asked some crisp questions, then hung up. She talked swiftly as they dressed.

'They've thrown everything at it. The radar stations were taken out by special forces – presumably landed by U-boat – before dawn, then the paratroops went in at first light. They've succeeded in seizing at least one of the airfields and there are reports of transport planes delivering reinforcements, but reports are very confused. There are continuous air raids.'

Don was still bewildered. 'But why Malta? It doesn't make sense.'

Mary shrugged. 'Pre-emptive strike. Make it harder for us to invade Sicily.'

They found that Charles Dunning and Peter Morgan had already arrived at the Ops Room and were in the middle of an intense debate with Johnson. Charles turned to them. 'It's not looking good. After we kicked the Italians out of North Africa the Middle East Command judged that the threat to Malta had dropped to negligible levels and switched most of the forces to Greece and Crete.'

Morgan nodded grimly. 'There were only three squadrons of Spitfires left. Some of them managed to get airborne but without the early warning from the radar they were sitting ducks as they tried to take off. Most of them have already had it. The Luftwaffe has complete air superiority.'

'What about the AA defences?'

'Doing a good job as usual, but around the airfields they're distracted by having to fight off the paratroops.'

'What do we have in the way of ground forces?'

'Not much. And there's hardly any armour. There are some Comets at the airstrips and they chewed up quite a few of the gliders, but most of them seem to have been taken out by Panzerfausts.'

Mary looked at Johnson. 'What about the Navy?'

'Nothing but light forces, MTBs and the like. The destroyers are all around Crete. There are some subs there and the last report said they had sailed to intercept any Italian convoys, but there's such intense air cover that they stand little chance in daylight.'

The crew of the 57 mm Bofors gun were close to exhaustion. From their location under the massive stone walls of Fort St Elmo, by the entrance to Valletta's Grand Harbour, they had borne the brunt of air attacks designed to ensure that the naval forces could do nothing to interfere with the invasion convoys. In this, the Luftwaffe had been successful, but at a price: three Stukas had fallen to this Bofors gun alone in a day of almost continuous fighting. Now that the long-prayed-for dusk was falling, the crew began to relax. They were too tired to think of clearing away the piles of spent cartridge cases littering their gun pit.

Suddenly, the alarm bell rang again, followed by a unanimous chorus of groans from the various locations the members of the crew had chosen to lie down and rest.

'I don't believe it! They're not going to bomb us in the dark as well?'

The sergeant in charge of the gun listened to the field telephone for a few moments, then held his hand up.

'Listen, this is different. There's a report of naval activity, coming this way.'

Reluctantly, his crew gathered around the gun, heaving fresh three-round clips of ammunition close to the breech. Night fell with Mediterranean swiftness. The incessant noise of sirens, aircraft, bombs and anti-aircraft guns fell away, leaving only the more distant hammering of small arms from the embattled ground troops.

The Sergeant sat crouched over the telephone, listening. 'Range four thousand yards and closing,' he said quietly. Tension began to grow, adrenaline pumping away weariness yet again. The barrel of the Bofors slowly tracked across the entrance to the harbour, duplicating the actions in half-a-dozen other gun pits around the entrance.

Only because they were listening for it did the crew hear the coughing bark of a mortar, then several more. They held their breaths and waited. The parachute flares blazed out over the approaches to the harbour, throwing everything into sharp, black and white relief. For a moment, nothing was visible, then the stealthy movement of sleek, low-lying craft approaching the harbour caught the eye of the crew. Searchlights snapped on, wavered, held the craft, which began firing back at them; tracers streaking across the harbour.

'Open fire!' The order was hardly necessary. The Bofors began its harsh thumping, a rhythmical two rounds per second, each shot a curving arc of tracer across the bay, joined by others from neighbouring guns. Like candle flames to a moth, thought the Sergeant crazily, as the shells hit home on the frail Italian MAS craft, shattering them before they could make their escape. The slaughter was brief but complete, the last of the craft burning as the last flare guttered out. The crew were beginning to relax again when they were disturbed by a new sound; the booming of heavy naval gunfire.

By the evening, no-one had left the Ops Room and the atmosphere was dulled by prolonged tension. The map of Malta, hastily retrieved from storage, showed the relentless, creeping progress of the German forces, spreading out from the airfields to join the German and Italian troops landed by sea later in the day, once air superiority had been assured.

'It's a wall-by-wall, street-by-street, battle of attrition, now.' Charles' mood was sombre. 'At least this has kept down the air attacks on our troops. The forces are so intertwined no-one can tell where the front line is.'

'Any news of our reinforcements?'

'We've got some Reapers flown into Tripoli. They're beginning to mix it with the Luftwaffe, but our nearest naval forces are too far away to do much about cutting off the German supply ships. We have few forces of any sort west of Alexandria.'

The telephone rang, and Mary picked it up. After identifying herself she listened in silence for a while, but the others saw her body language and began to gather round.

'Thank you. Yes, please keep us informed.' She looked round the circle of faces, grinning broadly. 'It's the Free French! They sailed from Oran as soon as they heard the news. The *Dunkerque* and *Strasbourg* have already hit a major Italian supply convoy, and now their whole fleet is pounding the German forces on Malta. They borrowed some tank landing craft from Tripoli and their armoured regiment is about to land!'

The room erupted in amazement and delight. The *Dunkerque* and *Strasbourg* were the pride of the Marine Nationale, fast and powerful modern battlecruisers. Don was jubilant. 'I knew it! I knew I was right to fight Churchill over his plan to sink the French ships!'

By late evening the outcome was becoming clear. The Reapers had managed to provide air cover for the French operation until nightfall had removed the threat from the Dorniers and their guided bombs. The Germans were still resisting bitterly but were being driven back by the defending forces and the Free French, who were fighting with a ferocity born of hate and frustration.

Dawn brought the final messages to the bleary-eyed gang in the Ops Room. The last German troops had been cornered and surrendered. They had suffered sixty percent casualties; among the Fallschirmjäger, seventy-five percent. The German airborne had been broken as an effective fighting force.

Hitler looked coldly around the table at his senior commanders, reserving a particular glare for Admiral Raeder, who had been the strongest proponent of the Mediterranean strategy.

'So much for the grand ideas about conquering the Mediterranean and encircling Russia from the south! Without Malta, there is no chance of proceeding. We have even lost the chance of causing the British trouble from Syria, now it has declared for the Free French.'

Raeder stirred uncomfortably, but decided not to point out that that had been the almost inevitable consequence of the termination of the Vichy government and the total occupation of France by German troops. Hitler went on to his favourite theme.

'Now that the southern situation has subsided, we can concentrate on our two main objectives; the subjugation of Britain and the conquest of the USSR!'

Göring saw his opportunity. 'We continue to mine the approaches to British ports, and our raids on dock facilities are continuing virtually every night. They are receiving very little in the way of food or other supplies. As for Russia, we can switch our bomber forces to the east in twenty-four hours, as soon as you give the word.'

Raeder was not to be outdone. 'The new Type Ten Elektroboote, and the smaller Type Eleven coastal version, are now in full production and will replace every other type in service over the next few months. Already they are having a dramatic effect on the British convoys; they can slip in to attack at will. When we have a full force in operation, the convoys will be massacred.'

Herrman listened to the boasts with a weary cynicism. Raeder he respected, but he knew that the British would have anticipated the Elektroboote and would have counters to prevent their complete dominance. As for Göring, he had delicately tried to warn Hitler of his casual incompetence and inflated confidence, but to no avail. He was too valuable to Hitler as a trustworthy and popular colleague. Herrman was feeling uncomfortable; this rare meeting of the OKW – Hitler usually preferred to see his senior commanders separately – was being held in the Führersonderzug 'Amerika', the special command train currently parked in a mountain station in Austria. The bitter winter cold outside caused the windows to steam up, adding to the claustrophobic effect.

'Very well. We will leave sufficient forces to invest Britain, but will otherwise concentrate on the Soviet Union. Once we have defeated the Slavs, Britain will have to surrender. And I would rather they surrendered than were invaded and beaten, since then their empire would collapse and fall into the hands of Japan and America. I want a full-scale attack on the Soviet Union to take place as soon as the weather permits.' He turned to Brauchitsch. 'How soon will you be ready?'

The Army C-in-C tensed, and Herrman felt a glimmer of sympathy. Chosen by Hitler for his acquiescence to the Fürher's demands, Brauchitsch had a nervous disposition and suffered torments as a result.

'By the spring. Military production is now at a maximum and we will have twenty-five armoured divisions fully equipped with the Panzer Four entering service. There will also be a full complement of self-propelled guns and other armoured vehicles. A further seventy-five infantry divisions will also have full equipment, including Panzerfaust anti-tank weapons and automatic rifles, and we have stores of clothing and other goods for both summer and winter fighting. Lorries for keeping supply lines open are being stockpiled now.'

Göring stepped in. 'Needless to say, we can launch a thousand heavy bombers, both Heinkel One-seven-sevens and Dornier Three-one-sevens, with another thousand Junkers Eighty-eights. To cover them we have two thousand fighters, mainly Focke-Wulf One-nineties and One-eight-sevens.'

'Quite so,' interposed Himmler smoothly, 'but land conquered has to be held, without fear of insurrection. Plans for that are well in hand.'

Herrman felt a surge of uneasiness. He found the Gestapo leader every bit as chilling as his reputation and hated to challenge him, even with Hitler's protection, but felt compelled to speak.

'For the defeat of Russia to be certain, the subject states must be peeled away from their side and onto ours. It is important that we do nothing to dissuade them.'

The others looked at him with carefully concealed expressions and Herrman suddenly felt that he had been dropped into a snakepit full of spitting cobras and crushing pythons. He knew that they regarded him with a mixture of jealousy at his influence and contempt for his weakness, and that he only survived because of Hitler's protection. Stadler had once commented, in an unguarded moment, that, left to himself, Himmler would have quickly extracted every item of useful information from Herrman before eliminating him as a disruptive influence. With a feeling that he had nothing to lose, he battled on.

'We may not be finished with the Mediterranean yet, either. Britain will be keen to get Italy out of the war, and may yet invade Sicily.'

'Without American help? Surely not.' Göring was scornful.

Herrman shrugged. 'Who can tell? They are well-equipped and determined, and we all know about the morale of the Italian forces after their uninterrupted string of defeats.'

Hitler turned to Brauchitsch. 'Keep an eye on the situation, but I don't want to be deflected from Russia if at all possible. In the meantime, bring me your plans for the invasion. I want to go over them in detail.'

'One other thing.' Himmler was smoothness itself. 'Has Professor Herrman anything to say about the Leipzig experimental work towards producing an atomic bomb?'

For a moment, Herrman froze. He had known that this was bound to happen sooner or later, and had prepared his reply. He collected his thoughts and spoke carefully. 'I know about this work, of course, and it does eventually lead to weapons of high explosive power. The technical difficulties are enormous though, and in my time were not solved for many years; certainly too late for this war.'

Himmler persisted. 'Can the Professor not help us to shorten the period?'

'Unfortunately not. The technical details were the most closely guarded of military secrets. Even to try to reveal them earned an immediate death penalty. And I was only a historian, not a scientist.'

Hitler nodded understandingly and the meeting broke up. Herrman walked slowly back to his quarters, trying to put out of his mind Himmler's thoughtful, predatory stare. He knew that the Gestapo chief had not believed him.

Churchill gazed benevolently around the Oversight Committee. Don reflected that with his love of planning military strategy, he probably enjoyed these visits more than anything else; certainly more than the frustrating sessions with his Chiefs of Staff, who had the irritating habit of deflating his most brilliant inspirations by pointing out the risks and problems.

'Well then, we seem to have reached a temporary stalemate. I propose we end it immediately by launching a new offensive in the Mediterranean, to take Italy out of the war and bring Turkey in on our side. Before discussing the details with the more conventional bodies, I would like to have the views of this group.' He turned to Don Erlang. 'What do you think?'

Don had, as usual, been giving some thought to the matter in advance, and he was no longer overawed by the pugnacious Prime Minister. 'I think it would be helpful to start with a SWOT analysis,' he began, then paused at the blank looks around the table. 'Strengths, weaknesses, opportunities, threats,' he explained. 'Our strengths are well-equipped and experienced armed forces, capable of standing up to the best that the Wehrmacht can offer, given equal numbers. The country is now safe from the threat of invasion, and our forces in Norway and the Middle East are also secure. We hold the initiative in deciding where to fight the Axis forces next. Our opportunities to do so lie in two main directions: the continuation of the economic war against Germany by blockading maritime supplies and bombing strategic industrial targets, and by direct attack, probably in the Middle East, as you suggest.'

'What about threats and weaknesses?' Chairman sounded a little sour and Don guessed that he did not enjoy being displaced by Churchill.

'The main weakness is that we are not yet strong enough to contemplate invasions of Northern Europe from England or Norway, so we can't grapple directly with Germany. Furthermore, we're unlikely to become so without American help, and we can't guarantee that that will arrive. The most obvious threat is, of course, to our maritime trade. The bombing raids on the ports are causing major supply difficulties and, although we've managed to restrict the shipping losses so far, the new electroboats are appearing in numbers now, and are becoming a serious problem. In fact, if we can't defeat them then we won't be able to invade Northern Europe even with American help, because it would be too dangerous to transport across the Atlantic all of the American troops, equipment and supplies we will need.'

Churchill grunted. 'I'll leave that question until last.' He turned to Creamed Curls. 'Haven't we got the measure of the Nazi bombers yet?'

'They don't come in daylight anymore; they've found it too expensive. Their night attacks come in a few distinct patterns. First, there are the small-scale raids on our radar systems. These have become more problematical lately because they seem to have invented some sort of long-range air-launched missile. We suspect it homes in on radar transmitters. Certainly we've lost a few early-warning Wellingtons in the last month. Then there are the large-scale raids on docks, railway marshalling yards and military production plants by the big Heinkels and Dorniers, led in by pathfinders. These have occasionally caused significant civilian casualties, but that appears to be accidental. Finally there are the individual mining runs, what we call 'gardening', over our port approaches.'

Churchill glowered at him. 'You haven't answered my question!'

Creamed curls continued hastily. 'All of the old Blenheim night-fighters have been replaced with Mosquitos, and they're scoring heavily. What's more, they have the range to go over to the Continent and attack the German planes around their own airfields. Unfortunately, the German night-fighters are returning the compliment around our fields, as well as accompanying their bomber streams. Basically, it's a war of attrition. The Luftwaffe is suffering much higher losses than the RAF, but our transport system is taking a pounding.'

'What about our own bombing?'

'The Luftwaffe night-fighters have great difficulty in catching the Mosquito, and with the help of the new navigational aids we're having no problems in continuing a steady programme of precision attacks on industrial and military plants. The trouble is, the bomb load is rather small. The new Avro Manchester is flight testing at the moment and is expected to be in service by the end of the year.' He smiled as Don raised an eyebrow. 'Not the same plane as the one in your time. This one is streamlined and carries no defensive armament. It has four highly-supercharged Merlins and carries a crew of four in a pressurised compartment. It can reach forty thousand feet and nearly four hundred miles an hour.'

For once, Churchill looked impressed. 'Given a fleet of these bombers, and taking into account our continued blockade of Europe, what chance do we have of defeating Germany by economic means?'

Diplomat stirred in his chair. 'There's no doubt that we can do a lot of damage and cause shortages of certain strategic raw materials as well as food, and this might help to stimulate unrest in occupied countries. There is a limit to how draconian our blockade can be; we wouldn't want to antagonise Portugal or Spain, and deliveries there can make their way to Germany. And, of course, we can do nothing about supplies from the Soviet Union. The consensus is that with the newly conquered territories the Germans will be able to adapt and find substitutes. We just have to keep identifying these and bombing their production plants wherever possible.'

'Very well, then, what about other ways of taking the war to the enemy? We have all these fighter planes and soldiers standing around in England; they might be better employed attacking the coast of Europe.'

Don intervened hastily. 'The difficulty with launching significant attacks on the coast is that the Germans will be stimulated into improving their defences and thereby making it harder for us to invade later on. And sending fighters over to seek combat won't achieve much except losing valuable aircraft and pilots. It would be much better to send any spare armoured units or fighter squadrons overseas where they really are needed; we have no modern tanks or aircraft in the Far East at all.'

Creamed Curls looked agitated. 'We must keep an adequate reserve of Spitfire squadrons in England to dissuade daylight attacks, or even renewed plans for an invasion.'

'Granted. But we have far more than is necessary for that. Besides, we would have ample warning of renewed invasion plans. The vast quantity of barges and other craft would be obvious as soon as they began to be assembled. It seems pretty clear from all the intelligence reports that Hitler is now focusing on Russia.'

Churchill looked speculatively around the Committee. 'Let's consider the Far East for a moment. Do you think our defensive plans are adequate?'

Military Man nodded. 'I think so. We have built new airstrips on both Singapore island and in Malaya, the latter well away from the coast so they can't easily be seized by amphibious assault. They are all fully equipped with dispersal pens and other facilities. Likely invasion points, as well as the landward side of Singapore Island, are receiving field fortifications ready for emplacing artillery as required. Needless to say, the big guns are being modified and equipped with far more HE shells so they can help with landward defence.'

'What about the equipment?'

'We have started to ship heavy artillery over already and are planning for three armoured divisions by the end of the year, as well as seven infantry divisions. I should add that we are rapidly building up towards our target of ten armoured and forty infantry divisions overall, with improved equipment and the new main battle tank at an advanced stage of development. We are expecting India, Australia and New Zealand to provide a lot of the troops in the Far East.'

'How well equipped do you think they are to help us?'

'The Prime Minister will recall the Dominion Production Plans which we instigated,' interposed Diplomat. 'Australia is producing Hercules engines and Brigand, Hampden and Hereford aircraft to use them. They are also preparing to produce a range of small arms and the Crusader series of armoured vehicles. We don't think that bigger tanks will be necessary in the Far East.'

'Incidentally,' added Creamed Curls,' Canada is already producing Merlin engines and Spitfires, Reapers and Mosquitos.'

'How many aircraft will be based at Singapore?'

'We estimate a need for around thirty squadrons in Singapore and Malaya; about one third devoted to each of fighter defence, fighter-bombers and medium bombers.'

'I'll see that they're there by the Autumn. We don't want to repeat the catastrophe of Dr Erlang's time.' He turned to Ruddy-face. 'What do you think the Navy should be providing?'

'We can manage to send quite a lot. We lost some good ships in the North Sea last year but all of the new battleships and fleet aircraft carriers are now in service, and with the Italian and French navies removed as a threat and Germany possessing only a handful of ships bigger than destroyers, we face no real opposition in Europe. We should be able to send a large modern fleet whenever it's required, leaving the older ships in Europe to support amphibious landings and so forth. In addition, production of the new cruisers, light aircraft carriers, frigates, destroyers and corvettes is keeping up with demands, although of course it will be a different matter if Japan attacks us.'

'What about India?'

'There is some concern about the activities of Nehru and the Congress Party,' admitted Diplomat. 'I appreciate that independence is on the way, but we can't afford to lose them while we know that we will have Japan to deal with. Without India, we could never hold Malaya, Burma and Singapore against the Japanese and our communications with Australia and New Zealand would be jeopardised. India is also producing large numbers of troops.'

'Are you proposing to warn the Americans?' Don enquired.

Churchill regarded him thoughtfully. 'We have given them our considered opinion that Japan will attack both our forces and theirs by the end of the year. We have not yet told them about you. We have to be careful or they will just think we are trying to drag them into our war. I don't have to tell you that while Roosevelt is sympathetic, there is a strong isolationist sentiment in Congress. It is clear that they will not declare war on anyone unless they are attacked first. If they knew about you, they might become so alarmed that they would take diplomatic action to avoid the war with Japan. That would not be in our interests at all; it would be a disaster if Japan just attacked us.

So far, our efforts are concerned with persuading them to build military equipment for us. We could manage without it, but our orders are helping the Americans to build up their military production ready for when they will need it. Now,' he said with evident anticipation, 'let's turn to the Mediterranean. What's your view of the options?'

'We could invade Sicily and then go on to Italy, but it would take all of our offensive strength and the outcome would be uncertain as the Germans would inevitably become sucked in. You will recall that we couldn't hold Greece even after becoming established there. In my time, even with substantial American forces it was a long, hard battle. It would be better to choose a theatre where the Germans can't send land forces to, at least until the Wehrmacht is fully locked in to the Russian invasion.'

Churchill grunted irritably. 'That would exclude the Balkans as well. That only leaves us the Middle East. Syria is now ours, along with the rest of the French and Italian Empires, which gives us borders with Persia and Turkey, both of which also have borders with the USSR. If we're going to be helping the Russians, we need as many routes to them as possible.'

'Turkey would be difficult,' said Diplomat hastily. 'Now the Germans control Greece and Bulgaria on their western border, they will not be willing to join us in case of attack. Persia would be much safer. It would also provide a direct land link between India and the Middle East'

Churchill nodded, and turned to Ruddy-face. 'Now, what about the convoys?'

The old naval officer sighed and Don suddenly saw how worried he was. 'The new electroboats are proving a real handful,' he said slowly. 'The older boats have such limited underwater speed and range that they have to approach convoys on the surface, which makes them vulnerable. The new U-boats are so fast underwater and have such a long range, that they can catch a convoy without ever being spotted except when they come up to periscope depth. That's their only point of weakness.'

'Do we have the measure of them?'

'No.'

The Prime Minister nodded grimly. 'I feared as much. Then all the rest of this theorising could be pointless. If we can't defeat the U-boat scourge, we won't defeat Germany.'

# CHAPTER 5 - ATLANTIC

**Spring 1941**

Herrman had been thankful to return to Berlin from the claustrophobic atmosphere of the Führersonderzug in its Austrian mountain hideaway. The weather was still cold but there was the tang of spring in the air for the first time, and Berlin was surprisingly normal after ten months of war. No bombers had yet disturbed its sense of security and Herrman wondered briefly why the British were so carefully avoiding civilian targets; they had not been so scrupulous in his time. The war seemed to be proceeding in measured steps, more like a formal fencing match instead of the usual chaotic street brawl.

Even the the Kriegsherr, Hitler himself, and the OKW were playing a careful tactical game, always trying to outguess the British, even turning to Herrman from time to time to ask, what would he do, if he were Churchill's mysterious adviser? Herrman could never be sure. He had often tried to think himself into his opponent's shoes, sometimes with success, but the Britisher's experience, concerns and priorities would be so very different from his own.

This morning's meeting was mainly turning into another round of the perennial struggle between Göring and Raeder, ostensibly about the most sensible organisational arrangements for maritime aviation but actually, in the Reichsmarschall's case at least, about personal status and prestige. Hitler observed noncommitally while Brauchitsch was thankful to stay quietly in the background.

'Right from the start the Kriegsmarine opposed the formation of the Luftwaffe,' argued Göring scornfully, 'all you are doing is trying to win the same old battle. To divide control of the Luftwaffe will inevitably weaken it and cause a loss in operational flexibility. I have already appointed a Fliegerführer Atlantik to oversee our maritime squadrons; what more can you ask?'

Raeder was coolly logical, as always in the face of Göring's bluster. 'There are not enough long-range planes made available to do the job of locating convoys for the U-boats. They are hunting blind and often spend an entire patrol with never a sight of a ship.'

'What, even your precious Elektroboote?'

'Even them,' the Grossadmiral responded firmly, 'they are wolves among sheep when they find a convoy, but first they have to find it.'

'My bombers are much better employed hitting British trade where it can't escape: in the ports, dockyards and warehouses. It doesn't matter how many ships reach England if they are sunk at their moorings and their goods destroyed before they can be distributed.'

'One squadron of bombers more or less will make little difference to the degree of destruction you can inflict. It would make all the difference to our chances of locating ships at sea.'

'Everything that flies is mine! That is an unalienable principle!' As always, Göring fell back on bluster. Herrman suddenly became uncomfortably aware that Hitler was eyeing him sardonically. He knew what that meant. He cleared his throat, bringing a glare from Göring and an icy stare from Raeder.

'The important task is to sink ships as quickly as possible, however that can be achieved,' he temporised. 'If ships are sunk at a faster rate than replacements can be built for long enough, we will win. And if the total volume of goods reaching England can be kept below a certain level, England will starve. Even if that level is not quite achieved, getting close to it will mean that Britain will have no spare shipping capacity for armaments; it will all be needed for food.'

'And what are those critical figures?' enquired Göring.

'I don't know,' muttered Herrman. 'My specialities were in land and air warfare, I don't remember the details of the naval war.'

'Britain was importing 60 million tons of goods per year before the war, including half of her food needs,' remarked Raeder. 'We are certainly keeping the figure well below that now. And we estimate that America and Britain have a combined merchant shipbuilding capacity of about 700,000 tons per month; so we have to sink more than that.'

The Reichsmarshall suddenly changed tack. 'Very well,' he said expansively, 'I will assign another squadron of Dorniers to the Fliegerfürher Atlantik. I look forward to seeing the British brought to their knees very soon.'

Raeder glowered and Herrman realised that Göring had won again; while appearing to be magnanimous, he had kept his Luftwaffe firmly under his control. A squadron granted could be withdrawn again just as quickly.

The Fürher decided to take a hand. 'I am concerned about resources for our attack on Russia. We now know,' with a nod to Herrman, 'that while initial victories will be easy, finishing off the Russian bear will take longer than we otherwise might expect. On no account must our troops run short of vehicles and equipment; the factories must be going full blast from now until we have finally won.'

Raeder realised that he was being attacked from a different quarter. 'We must increase the production of Type Ten Elektroboote,' he almost pleaded. 'We achieved our target of three hundred U-boats at the start of the war but these were nearly all Type Sevens or coastal boats. They suffered so badly at the hands of the strong British escorts that we had to withdraw them to the North Sea. The Type Tens have the upper hand but the assembly yards are being pounded virtually every night and their training grounds in the Baltic are mined just as frequently. If we are to win this battle we must have more Elektroboote reaching the Atlantic; that means more production efforts and more guns and night-fighters defending the yards. At the moment we are only building fifteen each month; this must be doubled.'

Göring decided to rub salt in the wound. 'Fortunately, our bombers have also been engaged in mining the approaches to the British ports. Our latest mines are triggered by a combination of magnetic and acoustic fuses which are almost impossible to fool, and we are working on something even better; one which reacts to the rise in water pressure as a ship goes overhead!' He beamed triumphantly. 'I am reliably informed that more ships are being sunk by my mines than are falling to your submarines!'

'And what,' interposed Hitler, 'about the risks if the anti-shipping campaign is too successful? It is our one strategy which really infuriates the Americans. I hear that they are now helping to escort the convoys. If we start sinking American warships we could find ourselves at war with them, and that must not happen; we must deal with Russia first!'

'To avoid that, we need a quick victory, before Roosevelt can steer public opinion against us. Should we not also defeat the British before taking on the Russians?' Raeder, Herrman reflected, obviously felt that he had nothing more to lose.

Hitler waved dismissively. 'Ideally yes, but the forces required to fight them are substantially different. The only conflict is over the disposition of bomber aircraft and they are now flowing from the production lines.' He turned to Herrman. 'Remind me, did the U-boats of your time still rely on batteries?'

Herrman felt the tension growing and answered carefully. 'Yes, my Fürher. Refined of course, but with no wars, development slowed right down. The Walter turbine was a dead end – the oxidant was too unstable.' Hitler nodded and Herrman breathed an inward sigh of relief. Strictly speaking he hadn't even been lying; the German navy of his time had not aspired to nuclear submarines. Somehow, he didn't think the Nazis would appreciate the distinction. For the thousandth time, he wrestled with the spectre of nuclear war; was he right to withold information from the Nazis if the British, and through them the Russians, were working to make nuclear bombs? Might this war be even more catastrophic to Europe than the devastation he remembered? If only he knew what the British were doing!

The U240 ploughed through the North Sea in the pre-dawn gloom, the watch crew mentally preparing themselves for the order to submerge as the light grew. The Oberleutnant braced himself against the side of the low conning tower as yet another blast of spray hit them. Beneath his feet the big diesels rumbled steadily, sucking fresh air down the hatch and through the boat. He was well aware that darkness was no guarantee of safety, with the British patrol aircraft all fitted with radar, but he had some confidence that the Metox radar warning receiver would give him time to crash dive before being spotted.

He waited for as long as possible before diving. While his boat was an old-fashioned Type VIIC, it was fitted with a schnorkel so that the diesels could keep running underwater, preserving battery power until it was needed. Even so, once submerged the boat's speed would be cut and, worse still, his visibility limited to the constricted view through a periscope. An added irritation in such a rough sea was that the schnorkel head would keep dipping beneath the waves, causing the air supply to be shut off. The diesels would then promptly suck air from the crew compartment, sharply dropping the air pressure until the schnorkel surfaced, whereupon the air pressure would shoot up again. This did not, he reflected wryly, lead to a happy crew.

Less than two miles away, nemesis raced towards him. The Coastal Command Hampden bored in at low level, the radar operator tracking the clear blip of the submarine in his screen and shouting commands to the pilot. The new centimetric radar gave a precise bearing and worked on a wavelength too short to be detected by Metox. At a final shout, the Leigh light switched on, the brilliant beam outlining the U-boat dead ahead.

The Oberleutnant screamed commands at his crew as his mind spun with calculations; thirty seconds to dive, too late on this pass; fight the plane now, dive the instant it was past. How the hell had it found them? Why had the Metox given no warning? The 2 cm and 3,7 cm cannon opened up, sending a stream of tracer toward the racing plane. At the same instant, flame rippled from under the wings and small dark shapes sped towards the submarine. The rockets peppered the area like a shotgun blast, splashing into the sea and flashing overhead. One of the gunners suddenly shouted in triumph and the Oberleutnant could hardly believe his luck as he saw the plane turn away, flame streaming from an engine. He turned to yell congratulations to the gunners but was interrupted by an urgent shout from below. He scrambled down the ladder then stopped as he realised the problem. One rocket had neatly pierced the base of the conning tower, wrecking the lower hatch. The boat could not submerge.

The destroyer raced towards the coordinates radioed by the stricken Hampden. An S Class of First War vintage, she had been deemed too small for Atlantic duty and assigned to the East Coast. But not, reflected her commander happily, before being equipped for her task. Torpedo tubes had been landed and replaced with Squid anti-submarine mortars; the old 4 inch guns likewise gave way to automatic 57 mm Bofors, far more effective against aircraft and E-boats, and even against submarines when firing the armour-piercing anti-tank rounds. A battery of Oerlikons and last but not least a suite of Asdic and radar made her a devastating coastal combatant.

'Target dead ahead; range ten thousand.' He acknowledged the radar report and waited. The crew was already at action stations, excitement rising at this climax to an uneventful patrol. Dawn broke, sihouetting the unmistakable shape of a U-boat hurrying south-east back to base.

'Range six thousand.'

'Open fire!' Almost simultaneously he saw a flash from the submarine's deck as the main armament fired. In theory the U-boat's 8,8 cm gun was much more powerful than the Bofors; in practice, accurate shooting was difficult from a submarine and the stream of Bofors shells swept the German crew off the deck before the destroyer could be hit.

'He's not submerging!'

The lieutenant-commander grinned wolfishly. The U-boat must have a problem. Too bad, it couldn't outrun his ship! As the range closed rapidly his instinct was to ram, but that would mean weeks in a dockyard being repaired... 'Set Squid fuses to minimum depth!' He barely heard the acknowledgement, concentrating hard on the fleeing submarine. Squid was normally fired automatically by the associated Asdic set; as the sub was surfaced he would have to do it by eye.

'Fire!' A massive, multiple thud shook the ship and three huge black canisters soared over his head towards the U-boat nearly 300 yards away. They appeared to bracket the sub and there was a brief silence before the sea suddenly heaved and burst, obliterating the target. As the spray settled, the lieutenant-commander could see the U-boat heeled over, the bows slowly rising.

'Slow ahead both. Prepare to pick up survivors.'

There were not very many.

'Before we start this meeting,' announced Churchill, 'I have been advised that we need to clarify the status of this Oversight Committee, particularly now we have changed the membership.' He paused and looked around at the group; only Don Erlang and Charles Dunning remained, the others being replaced by Don's long-standing military intelligence liaison officers 'to keep it tight' as Churchill had said. Mary Baker was also present, ostensibly to take the minutes but in fact as the result of a brief campaign which the others had realised from the start they stood no chance of winning.

'Up to now it has been entirely unofficial and outside the normal structure. In view of the sensitive, if not sensational, nature of its business,' this said with a sardonic glance at Don, 'I still want to keep it secret and separate from other policy and operational committees such as the Joint Intelligence Sub-Committee or the Chief of Staffs Committee. I see your role as more of a personal advisory panel and accordingly this Committee will form a third top-level military committee alongside the Defence Committees for Operations and Supply, although for obvious reasons you won't appear on any published committee structure. Minutes of the meetings will go only to me. Any questions?'

There were none.

'Very well, I want to turn our attention to the Battle of the Atlantic. We all know that this is the battle that we cannot afford to lose, and I have set up a separate Battle of the Atlantic Committee to coordinate and review operations. The key factor is maintaining our imports at an acceptable level. Tremendous efforts have been made to reduce our needs, with metals being reused and virtually every available open space dug up for crops. However, we still need to import around twelve million tons of food per annum and a similar quantity of oil. Overall, we need not far short of thirty million tons to survive and have so far managed to achieve this. Assuming that America enters the war and we stage a joint invasion of Europe, their troops, equipment and supplies will generate additional shipping needs. I am not lacking in facts about the progress of the battle, but I want you to produce ideas about what we can do to ensure our victory. Who's going to start?' Churchill leaned back, puffing as usual at a large cigar.

Charles took up the challenge. 'Winning the battle is a complex problem. We need to do four things; reduce the number of sinkings, build more merchant ships to ensure that we keep ahead of the sinking rates, make better use of the shipping capacity we have by ensuring that the right cargoes are heading in the right directions, and reduce delays at sea and in port to make more use of the ships.'

'I know all that,' Churchill interrupted, 'the last three points are all being adequately dealt with by others. It's the first problem which concerns me; how can we sink more of these U-boats in order to keep our losses down?'

'Sinking U-boats is actually the least important matter.' Don said; Churchill made a disbelieving noise. 'No, it's true. We just have to stop U-boats sinking ships. There are several ways we can do this;' he began to count on his fingers, 'in the first instance, we need to reduce the number being built. The new Type Tens are prefabricated inland, with the sections brought to the dockyards for assembly. That means hitting the transport links as well as the dockyards.'

'We're doing that already,' Peter Morgan said quietly. 'It isn't easy. The Germans have concentrated their air defences around the dockyards and other key targets, and hitting them is increasingly expensive. Even the Mosquitos are suffering heavy losses.'

'I know, but it's vital to keep at it. The second stage is to prevent the boats reaching operational readiness by mining their training areas in the Baltic. The third is to prevent them from reaching the Atlantic by laying minefields and flying frequent air patrols in the Channel and the North Sea. The fourth is to hit them in their French harbours and, again, mine the approach routes to them. The fifth is to use intelligence data to route convoys around known U-boat concentrations, the sixth is to keep them submerged by maintaining long-range air patrols, which will reduce their speed and vision, and the seventh is to distract them with carrier-based planes and naval escorts if they do reach a convoy. If we manage to sink some U-boats in the process, all well and good, but that's a bonus. The important aim is to stop the U-boats from attacking so we can get those ships across with minimum losses.'

'How do our losses compare with shipbuilding rates?' Geoffrey Taylor enquired.

'So far, we're winning,' Harold Johnson chipped in. 'We're losing half a million tons per month, rising steadily as more of those electroboats come into service. Thanks to the mass-production techniques of the American shipyards we're building at around twice that rate, with the potential to build over one and a half million tons each month. The danger is that our losses are rising at a faster rate than our construction. If nothing happens to stop the trend, in a few months time the curves will cross and we will start to lose the war.'

Churchill nodded. 'Roosevelt has managed to deliver the Lend-Lease agreement and we have focused all our requests on new merchant shipping. Until now we've been paying for the ships by giving them naval bases in our colonies, but at least that means we don't have to divert our efforts into defending them.'

'After the convoy system, air cover is the main ingredient in dealing with submarines at sea,' said Don. 'I've been looking at the records of the Great War. After May nineteen-seventeen when the convoy system was adopted, only two hundred and fifty ships were sunk out of eighty-four thousand sailing in convoys; and only five were sunk by U-boats when air cover was present as well. This will still hold true even with more advanced technology.'

'So what are the priorities in increasing air cover?'

'Dr Erlang's prewar proposal for the Merchant Aircraft Carriers was invaluable,' replied Johnson. 'We had the materials available to convert a dozen large bulk carriers, mainly tankers, at the start of the war, and now have three dozen in service. Not a convoy sails without at least one of them, and their aircraft have proved highly effective at keeping enemy bombers and the older U-boats at bay, but are having problems with the new electroboats. To deal with them we need as many Sunderland and Warwick long-range maritime patrol aircraft as we can get, fitted with the latest weapons and detection equipment.'

Morgan shifted uneasily. 'But we desperately need as many heavy bombers as possible to carry out the raids on dockyards and other military targets in Germany and France. The Mosquito is a superb aircraft but it can't carry the heaviest bombs. We're developing some five-ton monsters which could easily be carried by those Warwicks, but Coastal Command has priority for them.'

'Bomber Command believes that Coastal Command activities are a waste of time,' remarked Churchill. 'All that swanning around and hardly ever seeing anything. I'm inclined to agree with them; at least with bombing raids the public can see that we are hitting back.'

Don sat up in some alarm. 'What can't be known is the number of U-boat missions which are disrupted by the subs having to dive whenever they see or hear an aircraft. That can be just as valuable as a sinking. Anyway, the Warwick isn't suitable; it's designed for flying low and slow. Wait for the Manchester; that's due to start reaching the squadrons in the summer and it can carry the five-ton bomb with ease.'

'What resources does Coastal Command have at present?' asked Charles.

'Ten squadrons of Sunderlands, slowly increasing,' answered Morgan, 'a similar number of Warwicks, including those based at Keflavik in Iceland, and another dozen squadrons of Wellingtons, although these are gradually being replaced by Warwicks. To cover the North Sea, the Channel and the Western Approaches there are twenty-two squadrons of Hampdens, some based in Norway, some in Ireland. They can be used for torpedo attacks as well as anti-sub work.'

'How many U-boats are slipping through the North Sea net?' Don enquired.

'Our best estimate is that two-thirds get through,' replied Johnson. 'There's a vicious little war going on in the North Sea, with E-boats and aircraft joining in. We've lost half of our fishing catch because of attacks on the fishing fleet, and had to stop much of the east coast shipping traffic.'

Charles nodded, his expression wry. 'Don't I know it! That's causing major problems for the railways; they're not structured to move goods in those directions, so this is causing all sorts of bottlenecks.'

'I'm still worried about the availability of anti-submarine warships,' said Churchill. 'I have to say I wanted to take up the American offer of fifty old destroyers, but you insisted that they wouldn't have been worth it.'

'They really weren't suitable,' agreed Johnson. 'We would have had to replace all their equipment and even then they wouldn't have been anywhere near as good as our corvettes. For the same reason we rejected the offer from smaller shipyards to mass-produce the whalecatcher design. It was simply too slow and too small to carry the weapons needed to cope with the electroboats. On the other hand, they're now producing a lengthened version with much more accommodation to act as convoy rescue vessels.'

'Poor quality warships are of little use,' added Don, 'in fact they're worse than useless because they take up precious resources to build and man. It's the same argument we applied to aircraft and tanks. Just building big numbers is no good if they only cost us lives and reduce the men's faith in success.'

Churchill raised his hands. 'All right, all right, I've heard you before. But I still think that any ship is better than none.'

'We have about a hundred and twenty escorts in service, mostly Hunt-class corvettes,' commented Johnson, 'and are building more at a rate of one a week. In addition we have a similar number of destroyers and although the build rate is much lower, many more are being released for escort duties now that the invasion threat has receded. We already have enough escorts to cover the convoys and we're beginning to form hunting groups centred on the new escort carriers.'

Churchill's face lit up. 'Good!' I have to confess that I have little sympathy with this defensive strategy of tying escorts down to the convoys. They should be out hunting submarines! We should also be using our fleet carriers to put an end to this menace.'

Don interrupted hastily. 'It's much too dangerous to risk fleet carriers in chasing submarines. The new escort carriers are designed for the task. They're small and very cheap because they're based on merchant ship hulls. And linking escorts to convoys is the best way of hunting U-boats; convoys attract them like wasps to a jam-pot. Even the hunting groups will accompany convoys, but they will have the flexibility to spend time in following up contacts.'

Churchill changed tack. 'What's this I've been hearing about a sudden increase in sinkings of escorts?'

Don pulled a face. 'It sounds as if the GNAT has arrived.' Quizzical looks. 'German Naval Acoustic Torpedo. They called it the Zaunkönig. Designed for firing by U-boats when submerged and being hunted. It homes in on the propeller noise of the escorts.'

'What are we doing about it?'

'We've already done it. Escorts are being equipped with Foxer; it's a towed decoy which makes more noise than the propellers.'

Johnson nodded. 'The trouble is it hinders sub-hunting so it's not popular with the captains. These sinkings are beginning to drive the message home, though. Tell me, Prime Minister; when can we expect to obtain bases in the Azores?'

Churchill grunted. 'We're working on it. The truthful answer is that Portugal will decide to abide by our ancient treaty when she sees that Germany can't win. That's not likely before the Americans come in.'

'I worry about that,' admitted Don. 'Hitler's declaration of war against the USA was so quixotic and counterproductive that I simply can't see him making the same mistake again. And if he doesn't, the Americans may ignore Europe altogether and concentrate on beating the Japanese.'

Churchill's expression was grim. 'I know. But you can be assured that I will be using every ounce of my influence with the President to avoid such an outcome.'

'Any indication of the range, yet?' The Hauptman was beginning to sound impatient as they reached the most dangerous part of the mission. A sprinkle of bomb flashes and the red glow of fires were visible to port through the thin cloud as the Junkers Ju 188 sped in a shallow dive towards the Mersey estuary. Liverpool and Birkenhead docks were receiving their usual pasting but, also as usual, the defenders were hitting back. A vivid mid-air flash followed by a cascade of sparks marked a bomber's fall. It wasn't the searchlights and flak that worried the Hauptman, however. Outside the flak zone, danger lurked.

'No indication yet,' responded the navigator. The Y-Gerät was an experimental, frequency-hopping version of the radio guidance and ranging system which was supposed to be immune from British interference. The problem was that it was far from fully proven in action and the Hauptman and his crew regarded it with justifiable suspicion.

The fast new bomber plunged through the cloud and emerged into gloom. With no lights and no moon, their chances of locating the correct spot without Y-Gerät were minimal. The tension grew as the Junkers slowly approached sea level, crew straining for the first sighting of land or sea.

'Still on course,' reported the navigator. 'No range indication yet.'

'Naxos warning!' shouted the pilot, the plane lurching as he pushed down the nose and opened the throttles. The gunner in the dorsal turret tensed, peering through the reflector gunsight. Below and behind him, the other rear gunner crouched behind another MG 131. The new radar warning receiver was able to pick up the latest British centimetric radar and its alarm sounding in the pilot's headphones meant only one thing; a night-fighter was on their tail.

The Hauptman levelled off at an indicated 100 metres altitude, not daring to go lower. He didn't want to take evasive action, either, if he could help it; they were too close to the target to stray from the Y-Gerät beam.

'Naxos strengthening!' The BMW radials howled as the Junkers sped at 500 kilometres per hour through the night. The fighter on their tail had to be a dreaded Mosquito; nothing else was so fast. Red streaks suddenly flashed past the plane from behind; the gunners instantly responded, the 13mm heavy machine guns drilling fifteen rounds per second at the muzzle flashes of the Mosquito's cannon. The Hauptman cursed and yelled 'cease fire!', hauling the bomber round in a violent curve to try to throw the night-fighter off his track. No point in trying to fight four 20 mm cannon with a pair of machine guns. With luck, the tracers of the return fire might have distracted the crew long enough to break contact. He held the nose of the Junkers up, compensating for a potentially fatal loss of altitude in the turn.

'Tell me when we're back in the beam!' He turned through a full 360 degrees, hoping this would return him to his track, only behind the night-fighter. At a yell from the navigator he levelled off, breathing hard.

'On target!' The Hauptman dropped the plane lower and at last spotted the faintest gleam of whitecaps below.

'Bombs gone!' The Junkers lurched upwards as the deadly pressure mines slipped into the sea; if all went to plan, into the narrow shipping lane leading into the Mersey. The Hauptman immediately hauled the bomber into another tight turn, this time of 180 degrees. Climbing slowly, he headed for home.

Don Erlang stood on the roof of the Liver Building, looking across the smoking devastation of Liverpool docks. At first, it did not seem credible that any practical use could be made of the port, but on closer inspection he was able to make out frantic activity around the merchant ships in Princes Dock below him.

'It may look a mess, and at times we've only had a dozen berths in service out of a hundred and forty four, but you'd be amazed at the speed with which damage is repaired and the berths made workable again. The Port Emergency Committee is doing a terrific job.' There was a distinct note of pride in the voice of the officer from the Liverpool command centre based in the building.

'Where are the warships based?'

'The main naval base is much further north at Gladstone Dock in Bootle. I expect you've heard of the Flotilla Club there; it's like the Windmill – it never closes! Smaller warships – minesweepers and the like – are mainly across the river in Wallasey and Morpeth Docks, but some use Albert Dock just to the south of us.'

Don took a final breath of air, even at this height polluted with the unmistakable tang of wet, sulphurous soot from the many fires doused during the night, then turned to go below.

'I'd better get to Western Approaches Command. They're expecting me.'

'I'll show you the way.'

Once out of the building they walked up Water Street, away from the Pier Head. All around them workmen laboured to clear the streets of rubble fallen from the great holes torn into the massive office buildings; incongruously, Don noticed a desk and chair, still perfectly placed, poised on the edge of a sheer drop. They stepped over lines of six-inch steel piping crossing the road, 'the water mains have been badly hit,' commented his guide, 'doesn't help the fire-fighters', then negotiated a crater in the road, some twenty feet across; 'looks like a two-fifty kilo job'.

'What effect is the bombing having on transport to the docks?'

'It's pretty bad. Most of the roads have been closed after the worst raids, and we've had a lot of unexploded bombs to deal with, which effectively puts more areas out of action. We're keeping on top of it though; the Luftwaffe won't close us down.'

'What about morale?'

His guide became more cautious. 'We're having some problems with rumour-mongering. We suspect the IRA are behind a lot of the alarms, with stories about trainloads of corpses being shipped out for mass burial, the introduction of martial law, food riots and so forth. We're doing our best to counter their propaganda.'

They turned left down Rumford Street. 'Here we are; Derby House.'

Don thanked him and walked through the stone-faced archway. He was met by a Wren who led him down to the lower ground floor, past massive blast walls constructed the year before when the Command had transferred from Plymouth. He was shown into an office with a huge window overlooking a wide, double-height room below. The walls of the large room were completely covered with painted charts of varying scales covering the North Atlantic and the seas around the British Isles. Wrens climbed up and down moving ladders in front of the charts, marking the changing positions of every ship, convoy and known enemy vessel.

The scene was at the same time familiar and strange; he remembered in his past life visiting this very room in the early 1990s, shortly after its restoration. Then, smaller paper charts had been stuck onto the walls and there seemed to be differences in the furniture layout which he couldn't quite pin down.

'Impressive, isn't it?' Don smiled and turned, recognising Harold Johnson's voice.

'Very. The nerve centre of Western Approaches Command. What wouldn't Hitler give to drop a bomb into the middle of this lot!'

Johnson shrugged. 'Temporary hitch. We have an identical set-up ten miles away in Knowsley if this is destroyed.'

'I'm sure that thought is a great comfort to the staff here,' Don said drily. 'How many are there now?'

'Around a thousand, mostly Wrens, but we also have the HQ of Fifteen Group Coastal Command based alongside the naval staff to ensure the best possible co-ordination. They include squadrons based in places from the Outer Hebrides to Ireland so they cover all of the Western Approaches. And that's not the only example of cooperation; there's a joint navy/air force anti-submarine school at Londonderry.'

Johnson turned to the door. 'I've arranged a meeting in another room so you can be brought right up to date by the intelligence staff. We can't stay here; it's the C-in-C's office!'

They climbed back up to a conference room on the ground floor. Don was introduced to Squadron Leader Blackett and Captain Swinton, senior officers from the Coastal Command and Navy intelligence staffs. At first he was slightly surprised by their age; he had become used to the idea that war was primarily a young man's business. Afterwards, he learned that they had been recruited for their experience in commanding ships and squadrons involved in the battle.

'The key to the battle is information, of course,' commented Blackett. 'We get a pretty good service from Bletchley but every now and then the gen dries up for a while.'

Don had a momentary vision of the codebreakers slaving over his computer, trying to keep up with the ever-changing German Enigma codes.

'The information isn't precise or topical enough for us to locate particular U-boats but we are often told about wolfpack concentrations in time to divert convoys around them.'

'Less often now, of course,' commented Swinton. 'The new electroboats stay underwater and hunt alone. Unlike the old tactics, they keep radio communications to an absolute minimum – just a high-speed burst transmission whenever they locate a convoy – so they're very difficult to track by huff-duff as well. Fortunately, they haven't yet realised that they can be detected when listening for directions; their receivers give out local oscillator radiation.'

Don nodded. High-frequency direction finders were a valuable aid to escort warships in pinpointing U-boat locations as they communicated with their base. 'How are tactics developing?'

Blackett grimaced. 'As soon as we perfect one technique, the Germans alter theirs so we have to begin again. One thing is certain: only the electroboats stand any chance of survival now. They use schnorkels to operate submerged virtually all of the time, switching to battery power only when they're preparing to attack. Even with the new three-centimetre radar which is just being introduced, a schnorkel is very difficult to pick up, especially if there's any sort of sea running. Aircrew are almost as likely to spot it by eye, especially if it dips underwater; that often sends a plume of smoke into the air.'

'Fortunately a schnorkeling sub is noisy,' commented Swinton, 'so we've developed the technique of sending a destroyer or two well away from the convoy to stop and listen. We're trying to develop better hydrophones. Unfortunately most emphasis prewar was on Asdic, but that has a much more limited detection range.'

Blackett nodded. 'We're experimenting with sonobuoys – floating microphones which can radio back the sound of submarine engines to attacking aircraft – and a magnetic anomaly detector which works in the same way as a magnetic mine fuse, indicating when there is a large mass of metal under the surface. There are big technical problems, though.'

'What about the relative success of methods of attack?'

The intelligence officers looked at each other. 'Confirmed U-boat sinkings are approximately evenly divided between ships and aircraft,' responded Swinton. 'The combination of Squid with depth-finding Asdic is still very effective, but the electroboats are so fast underwater that the corvette captains have to be very sharp to hit them.'

'Aircraft are at less of a disadvantage than you might expect. Because the submarines stay submerged their field of view is limited to what periscopes can provide and they often don't realise there's an aircraft overhead until the depth charges detonate around them. As for more deeply submerged boats,' Blackett paused and smiled rather mysteriously, 'the new mine is very promising.'

'Mine?' Don was puzzled.

'Code name. Actually we're giving the Germans some of their own back; it's an acoustic homing torpedo.'

'Are there enough escorts available?'

Swinton laughed ruefully. 'There are never enough, and never will be. We can provide at least half a dozen corvettes for the close escort of each convoy, and we're collecting the destroyers now being made available into hunting groups, each supported by an escort carrier. Their extra speed is useful in regaining station after chasing down contacts.'

'What about the range problem?' Johnson enquired. 'With all that dashing about they can hardly be expected to cross the Atlantic.'

'Not as bad as you might think. The corvettes have a very long range and can fight their way across the Atlantic. We have an emergency refuelling and repair base at Hvalfiord in Iceland but haven't had to make much use of it, although I expect the destroyers will be there more often. Another little secret is that we're developing refuelling techniques so the destroyers can top up from tankers in the convoy.'

'Are you doing this with aircraft as well?' Don enquired.

Blackett nodded. 'The Coastal Command Development Unit is practising in-flight refuelling techniques with Wellingtons. If we can perfect it, all Warwicks and Sunderlands will be fitted. It will make a considerable difference to their endurance.'

'None of this helps with one of our major difficulties, though,' Swinton said grimly. Enquiring looks. 'Mines. The Germans keep laying them in the Crosby Channel and even in the Mersey itself. Aircraft come over most nights and we caught some submarines slipping in to lay some as well. The subs are even more dangerous because they lay them more accurately.'

Don nodded. 'What types are they using?'

'We don't always know. All too often we only find them when they explode. We know they use magnetic triggers on some and we've developed effective sweepers. The problem is that they're now fitting them with counters. We can sweep them three times over and they don't react, but the fourth time they blow. We're losing far too many ships just when they think they've reached safety. If you can suggest a way of dealing with them, we'll all be very grateful.'

Don thought of the immense difficulty even 21st Century technology had in dealing with mines, and grimaced. Ultra-high definition sonar and remotely controlled mini-submarines were too much to ask for at this stage.

'I'm afraid you'll just have to step up the anti-submarine patrols around the estuary – perhaps a line of moored hydrophones might help – and keep the night-fighters on their toes. Otherwise, keep sweeping!'

Don and Johnson were walking back to their hotel through the blacked-out city when the air raid sirens began the unearthly wailing that sent shivers of dread up Don's spine. The few people left on the street headed for the nearest shelters, but to Don's surprise Johnson led him in a different direction. 'Something you'll want to see!' He called.

After a few hundred yards they were challenged by a sentry. Johnson spoke quickly to him and the sentry nodded. 'Right-oh, sir. You'll be needing these.' He reached down and held up two Army helmets. Don put his on, his perplexed glance at Johnson lost in the gloom.

'What do we need these for?'

Johnson bent down; 'These!' He held up a light, oddly shaped piece of metal. Don examined it but could make no sense of it.

'You ought to recognise it; you were responsible after all!'

This time Johnson didn't have to see Don's face. He chuckled and said, 'don't you remember some years ago describing the results of some German operational research to do with anti-aircraft fire against bombers?'

'I think so. You mean that time fuzes were a waste of time, so to speak?'

'That's right. Flak fuzes were set to explode the shells at the estimated height of the aircraft, but they had to explode so close to a big bomber to bring it down they virtually had to hit it. The trouble was, the fuzes weren't that precise, so almost half the shells burst before they reached the aircraft. The Germans found that they actually improved their strike rate by fitting simple contact fuzes.'

Don tapped the piece of metal. 'That doesn't explain this!'

Johnson continued, obviously enjoying the rare experience of telling Don something he didn't already know. 'We put that together with two other things you told us about; first, that if a flak shell scores a direct hit it can afford to be much smaller – about five pounds or so; and second, that very high velocity can be achieved by using discarding sabots.'

'But that was for anti-tank guns!'

'Principle still applies. We've designed a high-explosive discarding sabot shell to be fired from the big new four inch anti-aircraft gun; that's the four point seven inch sleeved down. Instead of the usual thirty-five pound time-fuzed shell, it fires a nine pound high-explosive discarding-sabot shell at a far higher muzzle velocity, which improves both the altitude performance and the accuracy, as the time of flight is much shorter. The only problem is that the light alloy sabot which holds the shell in the barrel falls back down again onto the gunners' heads. So we made it to break up into small pieces when it leaves the barrel. It's still advisable to wear helmets, though!'

Don thought for a moment. 'I'm impressed! That application never occurred to me. But don't you lose the morale effect of flak bursts near the aircraft?'

There was a grim smile in Johnson's voice. 'We thought of that as well. The reason the shell is a bit heavier than it needs to be is that it contains a big tracer, designed to ignite some way below the aircraft. There's nothing more off-putting to a pilot and a bomb-aimer than to see the shells curving up towards them – particularly in those German bombers where the crew all huddle together in the glazed nose! Of course, once the radar proximity fuze is perfected that will change matters, but for now this is doing pretty well.'

Ahead, there was a gleam of light reflecting from purposeful-looking machinery. They walked up to what was gradually revealed to be an anti-aircraft gun installation. After a few words with the crew, Johnson picked up something long and heavy and pushed it against Don's chest. He grasped the big case of a 4-inch round. At the business end, he made out the short, sharp point of the shell protruding from the cylindrical sabot.

'Any time now!' Johnson said. 'Stay and watch the fun!'

This was not Don's idea of fun but he could hardly make his own way back. One of the crew, who was wearing headphones, stiffened suddenly then called out, 'radar has them; they're coming right over us.'

'Load!' The command was immediate. Don heard the double metallic clang of the shell-case being flipped into the loading tray followed by the power rammer driving the case up into the breech. A loud electrical humming came from the mounting, which slewed suddenly, the gun elevating.

'Remote power control,' said Johnson, 'the nearby gun-laying radar provides height, speed, range, bearing and heading gen which are fed into a calculating machine which works out where the guns should be pointing. This then controls the gun aiming by signals sent over a land line. Each radar controls a battery of four guns, plus a searchlight.'

On cue, the searchlight snapped on just as the air raid sirens finally wound down. Don could faintly hear the distinctive, uneven drone of the German bombers at high altitude. The searchlight probed through the misty air, but Don could see nothing.

'The lights are more for morale purposes than anything else. On a night like this, they're not likely to spot a high-flyer, and the big Heinkels come in at well over thirty thousand feet.'

A brilliant flare suddenly illuminated the sky in the direction of the docks. Almost immediately, other flares became visible much further north.

'At least one of their marker planes got through,' commented Johnson. 'The others are probably our decoys. The Germans keep changing their flares and it's a constant battle to keep copying them.

To confuse matters further we've even built a 'decoy city' a few miles to the south; lots of fuel pipes to produce spectacular fires.'

Don was reflecting on the irony of the reversed roles, with the Germans and the British both applying experience originally culled from the Allied bombing of Germany in 1944/5, when the gun fired with an ear-splitting crash. Even before he had recovered, the empty shell-case was automatically kicked out, the next round slammed into the breech and the gun fired again. Less than three seconds later, the third shot followed. Don looked up into the sky; far above, he saw a red flare curving gently away as it faded into the night. Much later, a brief flash indicated where the shell had self-destructed as the tracer burned through.

The noise seemed to go on for hours, the crew frantically running to and from the ammunition store, throwing shells into the mechanism as the gun relentlessly blasted skywards. Five times, Don saw a brighter glare high above them, followed by a tumbling fire as a stricken bomber fell to earth.

Sudden silence. As his ears recovered, Don heard the dull thuds of explosions from the docks, saw the glow of fires in the sky. Around him, the gun crew were draped in postures of exhaustion.

'Twenty minutes,' said Johnson judiciously. 'Just keeping us on our toes. They'll be back at least one more time tonight.'

Don walked back to the hotel in silence.

'Message coming through; the convoy's under attack!' The radio operator's voice crackled through the headphones. The pilot acknowledged, leaned forward to flip off the autopilot and began to ease the Sunderland around onto the course being fed to him by the navigator.

The huge plane looked little different from the pictures Don would have remembered from his youth, but at his urging production had been held back to make some important changes. Four big Hercules radials provided far more power than the Pegasus of the original design. To take advantage of the power, the wingspan and fuel capacity had been increased and the hull lengthened. Armament had also been boosted considerably, as had equipment and pilot aids such as the autopilot. The result was a formidable long-range patrol aircraft, now coming off Short's production lines in significant numbers.

The plane had already been flying for many hours since leaving its base and was close to its rendezvous with the convoy homeward bound from Gibraltar. The ships had to sail far out into the Atlantic to keep away from the dangerous Bay of Biscay, before turning north to head for home.

The first sign of the convoy was an ominous smudge of smoke on the horizon. The pilot wiped the sweat from his brow – the hot sun turned the Sunderland's big cockpit into a greenhouse – and alerted the crew. Those resting, off-duty, in the narrow bunks now took their position by guns or portholes. The tension rose steadily as the plane thundered toward the beleaguered ships.

The convoy was a fast one and heavily protected by fleet destroyers and an escort carrier. As the Sunderland approached, the crew spotted one burning ship and a scatter of wreckage rapidly being left behind by the speeding convoy. A rescue ship was nosing around the wreckage. The destroyers were concentrated on the eastern flank but there was no sign of action – or of the escort carrier.

The Sunderland was equipped with short-range TBS radio and the pilot identified himself to the convoy escort captain.

'We've lost the carrier and three merchant ships. They sent Junkers eighty-eights over first to decoy our Beaufighters. We got two of the Junkers, but in the meantime Dorniers came in at high altitude and released some form of guided missiles from long range before turning away. The missiles homed straight onto the largest ships in the convoy. We could do nothing to stop them. Radio jamming didn't work'

The frustrated anger was clear in the captain's voice. The pilot could do little but acknowledge and assume a protective patrol around the convoy.

Several hours later, nothing further had happened and the Sunderland began its return to Berehaven. The naval base was a strange place, the pilot reflected. Located in south-west Ireland and greatly resented by the Irish government, it was effectively cut off from the surrounding countryside. It was known that the IRA kept the base under surveillance and suspected that they reported ship movements to Germany. The British government had prudently ensured that the base was defended by Canadian troops in order to minimise friction, but there was still a tension not present at mainland British bases.

'Radar contact dead ahead; range twenty miles!' The pilot was jolted out of his reverie and called his crew to battle stations as he started the Sunderland on a steady descent towards the sea. The ASV radar achieved its longest range at an altitude of a few thousand feet, but at that height lost contact due to sea clutter while still several miles away. The shortest effective radar range was achieved at sea level, with the target silhouetted against the horizon.

'Switch on camouflage lights.' The pilot still found it difficult to believe, but the Sunderland had been fitted with a number of lights along the wings and the fuselage. The boffins had apparently worked out that because aircraft always appear dark when seen at a distance against the daytime sky, they could be made harder to see by illuminating them.

The Capitano di Corvetta in command of the Marconi class submarine of the Regia Navale was pressing ahead with all speed to make contact with the reported convoy. A part of the Betasom force based at Bordeaux, he was tired of the ill-concealed derision with which the slow, comfortable Italian submarines were regarded by the tough 'sea-wolves' of Dönitz's U-boat fleet. Something caught his eye low on the horizon. At first he couldn't make out what it was, but the view through binoculars shocked him.

'Dive! Emergency!' He gripped the forward edge of the conning tower, cursing the lethargic diving speed of his submarine as the hull slowly slipped into the Atlantic. He turned to enter the hatch but was caught in a hail of fire as the four 20 mm cannon fixed in the nose of the Sunderland sprayed the boat.

The pilot grinned fiercely as the submarine grew to fill the windscreen, large conning tower still above the surface. The four 250 lb depth charges, on minimum depth setting, straddled the hapless boat and the rear gunner gave a yell of delight as the combined explosion lifted the submarine onto the surface. The pilot banked the plane around to see if another attack was necessary, then froze in disbelief as cannon shells tore into the fuselage behind him.

'Junkers! Four of them!' One of the gunners yelled as the dark shapes of the big long-range fighters swept past the Sunderland. The pilot dragged the plane round and down to sea level, heading for home at full throttle. He silently cursed the lack of attention of his gunners, realising that they had been distracted by their first attack on a submarine.

'They've split up,' the rear gunner's voice was under control now. 'Two coming in on the port quarter, two to starboard. I'll take the port.' The other gunners acknowledged and shifted their turrets to cover the starboard quarter. The Sunderland was heavily armed, with four 0.5 inch Vickers-Brownings in the rear turret and two in each of the two upper turrets, one behind the wing and the other just behind the cockpit. Even so, they could not match the cannon-armed Junkers in range and hitting power.

The pilot began a game of cat and mouse, turning into or away from the repeated German attacks to confuse them, keeping always just above the sea so the attackers could neither get underneath him nor dive from above for fear of hitting the water. The contest seemed to go on for hours, the desperate pilot dully aware of the Sunderland shuddering under the frequent cannon strikes, the rapid hammering of the defending guns and the continuous background howl of the abused engines. Cries of pain from injured crew, yells of triumph from gunners, scarcely distracted him from his concentration on judging which way to turn, when to turn… and then there was silence.

The co-pilot came forward and slumped heavily into the seat next to him. The pilot scarcely dared ask.

'We've beaten them. Shot one down and damaged another. The others have gone – probably getting low on fuel. But we've lost Jackson. Merrit and Walker are badly hit, and the rear upper turret is knocked out.'

They scanned the instrument panel apprehensively as the pilot eased the engines back to a steady cruising hum. One fuel tank had been hit but there should just be enough to get them back to base. They looked at each other with that mixture of emotions so common after battle; shock at the encounter, relief at having survived, guilt about their friend who had not – and near-total exhaustion. The Sunderland droned north into the evening, a bubble of life and death traversing the vast uncaring ocean.

**Summer 1941**

The large meeting room in the Liver Building was crowded. Naval staff sat on one side of the long table. They were flanked and faced by a motley collection of men in a wide variety of clothing. Nearly two hundred of them packed the room, sitting behind the table and standing against the wall. They were merchant navy captains and they were not happy.

Their grumblings fell away as the C-in-C Western Approaches rose to his feet. After some initial words, he came straight to the point.

'I know you don't like having to wait for such a large convoy to be assembled, and that sailing with so many ships causes problems,' the Admiral said quietly. 'I want you to understand why we're doing this. You all know that your chances of survival are much better in a convoy than on your own. What you may not realise is that the bigger the convoy, the better we can protect you. A convoy of two hundred ships can be given four times the number of escorts than one of fifty ships, yet has only double the perimeter to patrol. Furthermore, we are able to provide two MAC ships to provide continuous air cover throughout the voyage.'

This time the murmering was of appreciation. The captains knew all about the benefits of air cover.

'To add to that, we are assigning a hunting group to the convoy; with five destroyers and an escort carrier.'

The murmur became a buzz of excitement.

'Finally,' the Admiral continued smoothly, 'We have a whole squadron of long-range maritime patrol aircraft with the sole task of protecting your route all the way across the Atlantic.'

With the dour captains showing as much enthusiasm as they were ever likely to, the Admiral chose his moment to hand over to the Convoy Commodore and depart. The Commodore was a tough-looking weatherbeaten man in late middle age. His approach was rather different.

'There are other benefits to large convoys that the Admiral was too polite to mention,' he began. 'For a start, a U-boat can only sink so many ships in one attack regardless of the size of convoy, so there's safety in numbers.'

The mood sobered instantly.

'We have also managed to include five rescue boats to haul you out of the water, so with luck and hard work we can better the average fifty percent survival rate following a torpedoing. What I am about to tell you now will minimise the chance of that happening to you, as long as you follow my instructions to the letter.'

He had their full attention as he took them through the rules and procedures governing the convoy. After he had finished, the Captain in charge of the escort took over, stressing the vital need for maintaining position. His concluding remarks were grim.

'Remember these words all the way across: "Straggle and Die!"'

The bellow of the Pegasus radial engine filled the cockpit as the Swordfish struggled off the deck of the MAC ship and climbed with painful slowness to 2,000 feet. The observer settled back, feeling thankful yet again that this plane was one of the latest models with a well-heated, enclosed cockpit. It was theoretically early summer, but convoy OB150 was far to the north of the Great Circle route in the hope of avoiding U-boats, and a typical Atlantic storm was lashing the ships. Only the slow take-off speed and short deck run of the Swordfish allowed it to fly in these conditions; the fast monoplanes on the escort carrier stayed in their hanger. At least they had a hanger, the observer thought. Their MAC ship was one of the early ones consisting simply of a flight deck with arrester gear, bolted on top of a large grain carrier which still was able to carry its full commercial load, although it was now in ballast like most of the ships in this outbound convoy. The planes lived on deck, normally tied firmly down in conditions like these.

The Swordfish carried eight armour-piercing rockets underwing and four 250 lb depth charges under the fuselage. It was further burdened with ASV radar and a Leigh light, as were all anti-submarine aircraft these days, but in the almost perpetual daylight at these latitudes visual sightings were still the most common way of spotting the faint track of a schnorkeling U-boat. The observer picked up the binoculars and began a systematic search as the pilot commenced his 'Viper' patrol; cruising around the convoy at visibility distance.

The Captain in charge of the close escort watched the old 'stringbag' perambulating around the convoy, travelling perceptibly slower into the wind than with it, and smiled in appreciation. Those boys seemed able to fly in virtually any weather and their appearance was a great boost to the morale of the convoy. He settled back into his high chair on the bridge and surveyed the scene. Huge Atlantic rollers swept by in the shrieking wind, lifting and dropping the corvette, spume blown from the crests spraying the windscreen. The convoy's ships were visible as the corvette crested each wave, struggling to maintain station.

The enclosed bridge on the new Hunt class corvette was still highly controversial in naval circles but the improvement in the comfort and effectiveness of the bridge crew was immense. The Captain had spent too many North Atlantic patrols on windswept open destroyer bridges to want to return to them, and now that initial detection was usually achieved by HF/DF, radar or Asdic, the need for maximum field of view had declined.

The Captain reflected that many other things had changed in nearly twenty months of war. At first the sheer numbers of U-boats had achieved significant successes, mainly against ships sailing alone. As the importance of sailing in convoy had been realised, losses had dropped sharply; the MAC-based Swordfishes keeping surfaced submarines at bay while the new 'pencil' Asdic beams and Squid mortars proved devastatingly effective against submerged U-boats once the escort commanders had learned how to get the best from them. Surface attacks at night, often by groups of submarines, had been held off by radar-equipped escorts like his own, later supplemented by Leigh-light Swordfish. The Battle of the Atlantic was being won very comfortably, until recently... he bit somewhat harder on his pipestem as he thought about the new threat – the high speed electroboats.

A towering column of spray from the convoy caught his attention in the same instant that the lookout shouted a warning. It was unmistakable: the signature of a torpedo strike.

'Sound action stations.' The clamour of the alarm bells rang through the ship, urging the crew to their positions. The Captain sent a brief message to the other escorts then settled back to wait. There was little else to do; there was no indication of where the torpedo had come from and the escort would have to wait until some sign of the lurking menace was detected. He had time to think that the crew were better protected as well; the gunhouse for the forward twin 4 inch mounting was now fully enclosed against the weather with ready-use rounds clipped to the inside, and the Squid teams were relatively well-sheltered behind the bridge. He settled back again and started brooding about that submarine. How on earth had it been able to aim with any accuracy in this weather?

The Korvettenkäpitan heard the dull boom of the explosion and smiled as the crew of U470 cheered. Four G7a torpedoes fitted with FAT pattern-running controls had been fired blind into the convoy from a range of more than 5,000 metres. The torpedoes were set to travel straight for a certain distance before beginning a zig-zag pattern which took them repeatedly through the convoy until a hit was achieved or they ran out of fuel. It was the ideal weapon for when weather conditions were too poor, or the escort too strong to close in for an aimed shot.

The torpedo tubes were rapidly reloaded by the powered system introduced on the Type X, and the Elektroboot crept in closer, staying below the turbulent waters of periscope depth and relying on the Balkon hydrophone system instead.

'High speed screws, coming this way.' The Korvettenkäpitan frowned; they could not possibly have been detected, it must just be bad luck that they were in the path of a destroyer sweep. The lound pinking of Asdic interrupted his thoughts; they were close to being detected. Irritated, he manoeuvred the Type X around to aim at the oncoming warship.

'Fire a T5.' The Zaunkönig acoustic homing torpedo sped from the tube, curving around to home in on the noise of the cavitating propellors above them. The detonation a minute later brought further cheers from the crew, and the commander confidently steered his boat through the escort screen and into the convoy, switching on the Nibelung active detection and ranging set, which enabled accurate torpedo firing without needing to use a periscope.

The Captain looked around at the devastation in his convoy with anger and disbelief. OB150 had already lost four ships and an escorting destroyer, and not a single sighting of a submarine had been reported. Furthermore, the escorts now had to trail Foxer decoys which rendered their own hydrophones useless. He wanted to send his ship racing around after the hidden submarine, do anything rather than simply sit and wait, but there was no point in any action beyond the intensified Asdic sweeps around the perimeter of the convoy. Another Swordfish had managed to take off and both planes were now skimming over the water, straining to spot a periscope or a torpedo track that would give them some clue as to where to hunt.

U470 went deep and slipped away from the convoy, all torpedoes expended, with six merchant ships and a destroyer to show for it. At least thirty thousand tons, the Korvettenkäpitan reflected: a third of the way towards his Knight's Cross in one attack! He set course for Lorient.

The convoy regrouped and continued westwards; the crews wary and mentally bruised. They had a long way to go to reach America.

Herrman emerged blinking into the early morning light, and looked round for signs of the night's devastation. The deep bunker had protected him from the bombs but he had still been able to feel the ground shake with their detonations. Somewhat to his surprise, Dönitz's Kerneval headquarters at the mouth of the Scorffe was untouched, but a heavy pall of smoke hung further inland.

'Lorient copped it last night, as well as the new pens,' Stadler commented. Herrman thought about the little fishing village of Keroman nearby, the site of a massive project to build bomb-proof submarine pens.

'Was much damage done?'

'Quite a lot. They were using heavy bombers to drop some really massive bombs. Paid for it, though. The bombers were Vickers Warwicks – too low and too slow to get away from our night-fighters so a lot of them didn't make it home. Unfortunately, we lost some of our planes also; it seems the RAF tried to protect their bombers by mixing Mosquito night-fighters in with them.' Stadler turned away. 'Come inside and get some breakfast. There's a meeting immediately afterwards.'

Herrman sat at the back of the conference room, observing the Befehlshaber der U-boote in action with his Operations Staff. The Admiral was brisk and to the point; his small staff, young, able and displaying the fanatical enthusiasm inspired by their leader.

'We have been asked to review the current position for the benefit of our guests from Berlin,' Dönitz inclined his head towards Herrman and Stadler. 'Käpitan Godt, could you summarise?'

Godt, the Admiral's Chief of Staff, radiated quiet competence. 'As you must know, the first phase of the fighting, after a good start, was increasingly hindered by the British deployment of air cover for their convoys. This made it difficult for our boats to pursue convoys on the surface as they were frequently forced to dive. Our planned night-time surface Rudeltaktik, which the British call 'wolf packs', also received severe setbacks because of the increasing use of radar by their escorts and aircraft. However, the tide of battle is beginning to flow in our direction.'

Dönitz nodded briskly. 'My compliments to xB-Dienst, they are doing a great job in breaking the convoy codes and warning us of likely targets.'

Herrman leaned forward. 'But how certain can we be that the British are not reading our codes?'

Godt was surprised. 'How can they be? The new M-4 cypher machine is unbreakable.'

'I wouldn't be too sure. We have received intelligence reports that the British have acquired copies of the code machines and are able to break the codes quite quickly each time they are changed.'

'That would be unfortunate but not as critical as it might have been,' commented Dönitz. 'The Rudeltaktik required frequent radio transmissions to coordinate mass attacks, but the new Type Tens hunt alone. They only need to send a brief sighting report via Marine-Kurier, which is a short burst transmission, and then to listen out for information about convoy locations. That is hardly enough to betray their location.'

'I hope you are right,' muttered Herrman. For once, his loyalties were undivided. The rapid defeat of Britain by the U-boats would reduce the risk of nuclear weapons being developed and used.

'It is fair to say,' Godt continued delicately, 'that we could do with more support from the Luftwaffe. KG Forty is based at Bordeaux under the Fliegerfürher Atlantik but the aircraft available are not always suitable and there are other problems.' Herrman raised an eyebrow. 'Their maps and codes are different from ours which makes coordination very difficult. We really need more of the long-range Dorniers and Heinkels to carry out reconnaissance. Admittedly the change in British convoy routes to the north gives less scope for aircraft but we know the RAF is developing in-flight refuelling. If the Luftwaffe would do the same, their planes could cover the whole ocean.'

Dönitz nodded. 'Any assistance you can offer in that direction would be much appreciated.'

'We really need to keep every convoy under continuous attack, to achieve a Geleitzugschlacht,' continued Godt, referring to the travelling convoy battle doctrine required. 'That means keeping as many U-boats as possible up where the convoys are. Among other things, it means avoiding the time and risk involved in bringing the boats back to base to rearm and refuel. We are aiming to achieve this by means of the Type Twelve supply U-boats, and are also gaining some assistance from Spain in arranging for boats to be refuelled in the Canaries. Unfortunately, Franco is coming under increasing pressure from the British to stop this.'

'To make rendezvous in mid-ocean implies radio contact,' observed Herrman. 'That is bound to be vulnerable to code-breaking, or just to radio direction-finding.'

'We are aware of that,' commented the Admiral, 'but warfare cannot be conducted without risk.'

'There have been reports of more local problems.' Stadler's interruption was the more surprising for its rarity.

Godt looked at him warily. 'There has been some activity apparently due to the French resistance movement in the west-coast ports, if that is what you mean, but that is little more than an irritation.'

'What aid are they able to give to the British?'

'Some minor sabotage. Possibly of more damage is information. It seems possible that they are providing some sort of markers to guide in minelayers.'

'Have there been many losses to mines?'

'Not many. We use Sperrbrecher to clear minefields each time a boat is expected in or out. The British mine technology is not as advanced as ours; we are able to sweep most of them.'

The rest of the meeting was concerned with operational details. Herrman eased back, worrying about the battle, recognising as clearly as Dönitz that this was one of the key battles of the war; the one Germany had to win to be safe from American involvement. Listening to the streams of facts, figures and operational orders, he wondered just what was going on out there.

The Commander of the *USS Anderson* peered anxiously through binoculars at the approaching convoy. OB150 had taken a pounding already with fourteen ships lost in three separate U-boat attacks. Only in one case had the escort even detected the electroboat – a brief sighting of a periscope – but the boat had disappeared before an attack could be launched. Still, he reflected, the storm had now swept on westwards and the calmer weather would aid air operations. He was uneasily conscious that his ship, a big new destroyer of the Sims class, had been designed with the emphasis on gun and torpedo action and was not well equipped to deal with submarines. However, she represented the best the USA could offer in supporting the Royal Navy in the western leg of convoy defence. So far, no USN vessel had actually engaged a U-boat. Sooner or later, the Commander was grimly aware, the time would come; and America's neutrality would be strained even further.

'Acknowledge the signal from the *Anderson*. Tell them we have now refuelled from a convoy tanker and will be staying on until we meet the next west-bound convoy.' The Captain of the hunting group settled back in his chair and sighed, conscious of little but extreme tiredness. The voyage had been one of the most frustrating he had ever made. The appalling weather had rendered the escort carrier useless and severely hindered sub-hunting. A year ago, it would also have prevented U-boats from attacking; but the electroboats could seemingly locate and attack convoys from deep, regardless of the weather. Now the seas were calmer, his Beauforts were scouting far and wide while the MAC ships' Swordfishes circled the convoy more closely.

'Signal from the *Kingston*, sir. HE detected at long range to the south. Could be an electroboat.'

The K-class destroyer had been ordered to wait well behind the noise of the convoy, listening on its sensitive new hydrophone array.

'Order *Jervis* to assist and try to triangulate that HE. Alert the Beauforts.'

A long period of waiting followed. The Captain estimated the times required; say half an hour for the fast destroyer to get away from the convoy and start listening. More time until the faint traces of hydrophone effect could be cross-correlated with those from the *Kingston*. More time still to locate the submarine and attack. He waited, patiently.

'Signal from *Jervis*, sir. HE detected and confirmed with *Kingston*. Location about thirty miles to the south-south east. They are on their way.'

Tension began to rise on the bridge, but only slowly. Such detections did not often result in sinkings; the cursed electroboats were far too elusive.

'Message from the Beauforts, sir. Schnorkel head spotted; it disappeared before they could get there. Sonobuoys being dropped on the estimated location.'

More waiting. The tension built slowly, washing away the accumulated tiredness of days and nights of frustration. The Captain thought about the problems of the crew in the cramped little aircraft, trying to make sense of the hydrophone readings from the pattern of sonobuoys. Unlike the big Warwicks, the Beauforts could carry very few of the sonobuoys; another Beaufort, armed with depth charges or a homing torpedo, would be circling nearby.

'Message from the Beauforts, sir. Position triangulated; torpedo dropped.'

The tension rose until the Captain could almost hear it. One minute passed; two. He thought of the ugly little acoustic homing torpedo, questing blindly through the dark water, spiralling after the unsuspecting U-boat.

'Message from the Beauforts, sir!' The signalman's voice was pitched high with excitement. 'Underwater explosion observed!'

The tension released suddenly. The tired bridge crew, officers and men, grinned at each other. The message could only mean success; the torpedo had found its target, completed its suicidal mission. The Captain felt a quiet satisfaction, but at the same time, a feeling of anticlimax. This was nothing like the war he had expected, of blazing guns and desperate attacks to depth-charge or ram the enemy. There was something cold and clinical about the destruction of the U-boat. Fighting was becoming less human; the machines were taking over. He pushed the thought from his mind and turned to broadcast the success to the crew. The lift would keep them going, keep them alert, ready for the next time. There would be plenty of next times.

## CHAPTER 6 - BARBAROSSA

**Summer 1941**

The first light of dawn glinted through the canopy, bringing with it a perceptible rise in tension in the cramped cockpit. The big Heinkel had been droning steadily eastwards for hours; the crew mostly silent, preoccupied with thoughts of the day ahead and its larger implications, or just dozing after their late night take-off. Around them, the sun revealed the scattered shapes of more of the big bombers, beginning to close into formation after the long flight.

The terminator slowly moved towards them, revealing the featureless Russian landscape passing below. From this height, few details of human activities could be seen, despite the clear air promised by the Truppenwetterdienst. Ahead, a smudge of smoke gradually formed; their target moved steadily towards them as if they were suspended in mid-air while a huge map was rolled beneath them.

'Watch out for fighters!' The Hauptmann did not really expect to see any. The Russians would have had no warning, and he doubted if they had any fighters capable of reaching the fast, high-flying bomber. In any case, the Soviet Air Force would soon have troubles of its own. He smiled at the thought of his comrades in the fast bombers and heavy fighters which would even now be launching the first of their carefully coordinated attacks on the Soviet airfields.

The task of his formation was very different. Along with every other Heinkel and Dornier Kampfgeschwader which could be spared from the war of attrition against England, his Gruppe was to penetrate deep into enemy territory, to destroy strategic targets such as factories and communications centres. In his case, it was a tank factory on the northern edge of the industrial city below. The Heinkel banked slightly as the Gruppe formed up and commenced its bombing run.

Far below, the factory workers on their way to take over from the night shift looked up in puzzlement at the thin, straight clouds of the contrails approaching the city. No engine noises could be heard. The silence was not to last for long.

Silence was the last thing on the mind of the Scharführer as his Panzer III crashed through the scrubby woodland. He snapped a command and the tank ground to a halt on the edge of the pastureland. Before him, fields sloped down to a small village, clustered round a bridge over the winding river. Beyond the village, on the other side of the river, small shapes were moving towards them. He scanned them through his field glasses and identified them immediately: T26 light tanks, still out of effective range. Around them were Soviet infantry, walking towards the village.

His radio crackled as the Sturmbannführer in command of the Waffen SS unit gave instructions. His troop roared forwards, going flat out to reach the bridge before the Soviet tanks, while behind him he heard the first crash of covering fire from the supporting Panzers, firing high-explosive shells to pin down the enemy infantry and leave the tanks exposed.

The Scharführer reached the bridge and crossed first, holding his breath in case it had been mined. Normally they would have sent in Pionieren to check, but the proximity of the Soviet forces compelled urgent measures. The bridge had to be secured before the Soviets blew it, otherwise there would be a delay while bridging equipment was brought up to span the swollen river, and the instructions had been clear: no delays!

Safely across, his troop deployed at the edge of the settlement, ignoring the bewildered and terrified Polish villagers who rushed between the houses, still not realising what was about to happen. The T26s were now only a kilometre away, in plain view as they rolled steadily towards the village, undeterred by the shellfire. The Scharführer allowed himself a brief moment of sympathy for the Soviet tank crews; they were hopelessly outclassed, their armour vulnerable to the Panzer's powerful 7,5 cm gun, while the T26's 45 mm was unable to penetrate the Pz III's thick frontal armour. They couldn't even run away, being considerably slower. However, there was a job to be done.

His tank shook as the gun fired with a deafening bang. He watched the tracer curve swiftly towards the target and grunted in annoyance as it kicked up dirt ahead of the lead T26. A second shot hit the tank full on and it lurched to a halt, smoke pouring from the blown-open hatches. No-one got out. Beside him his comrades were firing steadily and the remainder of the Soviet tanks were soon disposed of. The Scharführer had not even noticed them returning fire; if they had, it had done no damage.

The action over, the Panzers stopped engines to conserve fuel and stood guard while the rest of their Kompanie moved to join them, together with motorized infantry and anti-tank troops to secure the village. In the sudden silence, a sound like a fast-approaching express train could be heard. The Scharführer had time to shout a warning before the first artillery shell crashed into the village. The tanks 'buttoned up' rapidly, hatches slamming shut as they prepared for a grim wait. They were safe from all but a direct hit on their thin upper armour – an unlikely chance – but the tension was nerve-racking as the big Panzers shook and rang with the detonations of the artillery barrage aimed at destroying the bridge. In the brief pauses between explosions, the screaming of the helpless villagers could be heard.

At the edge of the wood, the Sturmbannführer was speaking urgently on the radio as he watched the destruction of the village. So far, the bridge had not been hit, but it was only a matter of time. The infantry and anti-tank troops in their more lightly armoured vehicles waited by the edge of the wood while the remaining tanks raced forwards to cross the bridge while they still could. He watched, scarcely able to breathe, as they rumbled across in quick succession. A sudden flash from the village and a shouted curse were enough to tell him that one of the Panzers had been hit.

A flicker in the sky caught his eye; a quick check through the glasses brought a sigh of relief as the Fieseler Storch spotter plane cruised over in the direction of the Soviet artillery unit. The Sturmbannführer settled back to watch.

Fifteen minutes later the bridge was, incredibly, still standing, but the village was totally wrecked. The Sturmbannführer wondered idly what had happened to the villagers. The twenty-one surviving Panzers of his Kompanie were through and deployed beyond the village, away from the artillery fire. He was becoming nervous; it was not good to have the tanks separated from the infantry and anti-tank troops. He looked up at the snarl of engines overhead and saw the deadly shapes of Fw 190s streaking towards the Soviet positions. Through the glasses he could see the yellow identification stripe of all Luftwaffe Eastern Front aircraft and the rockets under the wings. Minutes later, a pall of smoke rose in the distance and the shelling abruptly stopped. Half an hour later, the entire Waffen SS force was across and the bridge secured against counter-attack. By then, the leading tanks were already out of sight.

Herrman sat gazing out of the window, scarcely noticing the East Prussian landscape as it slid smoothly past the Führersonderzug. It was the early morning of Tuesday the third of June and Barbarossa had been underway for forty-eight hours. Hitler was on his way to the new eastern Führerhauptquartier near Rastenburg, from which he intended to oversee the conquest of the Soviet Union.

The train was buzzing with the news of the early breakthroughs by the Wehrmacht. The leading Panzergruppen were already nearly 200 kilometres from the start lines, slicing through the stunned and confused Soviet troops with scarcely a pause. Herrman felt remote from the celebrations, feeling an odd mixture of detachment and tension. At last it had started, the war against the hated enemy towards which he had been guiding Hitler for the past seven years. He should be delighted, but instead he felt anxious, even depressed. The dice had been thrown in the greatest gamble of the war.

He thought back over the past few months of diplomacy and deception. Until the attack started, every effort had been made to reassure Stalin about Hitler's intentions. The Moscow mutual assistance treaties of August and September 1939 had been followed by Soviet-German Pact of February 1940, exchanging Soviet raw materials and foodstuffs for German military equipment and industrial machinery – the latter being unaccountably slow in arriving. Relationships had remained good for the first half of 1940, Molotov even sending congratulations to Hitler on the success of the German invasion of Western Europe. However, tensions had begun to arise from the two countries' overlapping spheres of interest, particularly Finland and south-eastern Europe. In June 1940 Stalin had demanded territory from Romania, which aroused Hitler's concern about the vulnerability of the vital Ploesti oilfields.

No sooner was the conquest of France complete than Hitler had ordered OKH to begin detailed planning for the invasion of the Soviet Union. His target date had been May 15th 1941; in fact, the assault had been delayed a fortnight by the consequences of a late spring thaw after a severe winter, exacerbated by exceptionally wet weather, which had combined to cause swollen rivers and flooded plains. Even now some of OKH had argued for a further delay to ensure that conditions were suitable for the Panzers, but Hitler would wait no longer.

Herrman's main concern had been whether Stalin would act on any warnings from the British. In his time, the Soviet response to the invasion had proved ineffective for a variety of reasons. Although the Soviets had vast quantities of equipment, most of it was obsolete and the Soviet army had been misled by their experience of the Spanish Civil War to discount the use of integrated armoured divisions, so their handling of armour at operational level was hopelessly inferior. Stalin's purges of the late 1930s had also deprived them of most of their able officers and left the rest too frightened to take any initiatives which were not sanctioned by their political commissars. Last, but far from least, the disposition of the Soviet forces had been much too far forward to allow a flexible defensive response, since Stavka, the Soviet High Command, had assumed that operations would build up gradually with front-line forces acting to disrupt enemy attacks while protecting their own mobilisation in the rear areas.

As it was, he need not have worried. The Soviets were faring no better now that he recalled from his studies; in fact, if possible rather worse because the German equipment was so much better. The Wehrmacht's armoured divisions had punched through the unprepared Soviet front in several places, with some forces turning back to encircle the trapped Soviet troops in a classic Kesselschlact, or cauldron battle, giving them no choice but surrender or annihilation. Stavka had not previously prepared a plan for strategic defence so the Soviet forces' response had been disorganised and chaotic. The only question was, this time, could the Germans keep it up long enough to force the Soviet Union into defeat?

The mood in the War Room was sombre. Churchill had convened a meeting of the Oversight Committee deep in the Whitehall bunker where they could examine the huge maps of central and eastern Europe fixed to the walls. The stark, curving arrows showing the movement of armies spelled out the grim story of Soviet disaster.

'Stalin didn't take any notice, then.' Dunning commented.

'Evidently!' Churchill was in a sour mood. 'We told him everything we possibly could, except for the source of our information.' This with a glance at Don. 'I can't understand why he left his troops so vulnerable.'

'I can. Stalin is suspicious beyond the point of paranoia. I gather that there have been so many attempts by our diplomats to persuade the Soviet Union to join our side that he probably regards any anti-German information from us as just more propaganda. Even in my time, Stalin ignored warnings from his own intelligence sources in Japan and Switzerland. He just didn't seem to want to believe it would happen.'

'The attack has come earlier than in your time, has it not?' Enquired Taylor. Don nodded.

'Hitler originally intended to attack in May, but was deflected until late June by the Balkans campaign, which in my time went on for much longer. This time, he must have been anxious to start as soon as the weather permitted, knowing what was to come in the autumn.' Don could still remember the haunting images from the Eastern Front, first of vehicles stuck in deep, sticky mud after the autumn rain had destroyed the unpaved roads, then the immobility of frozen men and machinery in the bitter winter to follow. 'Hitler will want victory as quickly as possible.'

'What are his chances of succeeding?' Churchill's inevitable question caused a sudden stillness in the room. Don chose his words with care.

'Clearly, he is much better equipped than before, although initially that shouldn't make much difference. The string of German victories in the first few weeks were so swift and comprehensive that the Soviet forces could hardly be destroyed any more than they were then. The crunch will come later on. Can the initial momentum be sustained over those vast distances, with vehicles inevitably breaking down and wearing out in the harsh conditions? Can the German supply lines keep pace with the armoured divisions given that there are no decent roads and the railways are the wrong gauge? How will the Germans treat the non-Russian peoples? Can the Luftwaffe stop Stalin moving his strategic industries east of the Urals? Will Hitler decide to go straight for Moscow this time and, if he takes it, will Stalin surrender? Perhaps the most ominous sign is that, despite knowing everything we know about what happened in my time, Hitler nevertheless believes he can do it.'

Churchill grunted acknowledgement. 'All imponderables, as you say. We must concentrate on what we can do to help. I have already publicly offered our support and intend to declare an alliance with the Soviet Union. What can we send them that will be of most use?'

Don grimaced. 'Almost everything, I imagine. What they will need most urgently is equipment to counter the Panzer Divisions. We can fly PIATs over via Norway – the Russian anti-tank rifles will be virtually useless against the Panzer Threes. Then self-propelled anti-tank guns; all the Cavaliers we can spare. And fighter-bombers equipped with rockets – as many Brigands as possible.'

Churchill nodded. 'That's more or less what the Chiefs of Staff recommended.'

'The important thing is for Stalin to hold on. The Germans and the Russians fight different kinds of wars. The Wehrmacht has never fought a campaign lasting more than a few weeks; everything is geared towards the Blitzkreig concept, which involves an attack so sudden that it paralyses the enemy command centre. They can't regroup because every time they try, the Panzers are behind them again. Eventually opposition collapses because the HQ can give no useful orders and the troops' morale is crushed.'

'So we have seen for ourselves, with our victories in North Africa.'

'The point is that German industry and logistics are geared up for short, sharp campaigns. Unless my opposite number has persuaded them to make some drastic changes, their war economy is inefficient and will remain so until Speer is given the job of sorting it out, late in the war. Even the army is not well organised for a long campaign; their main repair workshops are back in Germany, which isn't much use when the front's a thousand miles away. The Russians, on the other hand, are best suited to a long war of attrition. They have space, resources and people to spare. Quite simply, Hitler either wins quickly or not at all.'

Churchill turned to the other members of the Committee. 'So ignoring the political side of what Stalin might decide to do, what are the chances of a quick German military victory?'

Geoffrey Taylor shuffled some papers. 'Our best estimates are that the Germans have committed twenty Panzer divisions with a total of four thousand tanks. As many as half of these are the latest version of the Panzer Three, with the remainder being earlier versions – still more than a match for almost all of the Soviet tanks – and some of the older Czech tanks. The Russians have far more – estimates range over twenty thousand – but they are nearly all obsolete except for a few of the new T Thirty-fours and KV Ones. What's worse, the Russians have no idea how to use them effectively. The Russians have a similar advantage in infantry divisions, but again their equipment is outdated and they are badly led. They're little more than cannon fodder.'

'It's much the same story where aircraft are concerned,' said Peter Morgan. 'Huge numbers, but qualitatively no match for the Germans and largely wiped out by the Luftwaffe on the first day anyway.'

Churchill was silent for a while. 'So,' said slowly, 'the only hope is that the distances involved will frustrate the Nazis before they have time to compel Stalin to surrender.'

'The other hope we have,' added Don, 'is that he has no reason to surrender. If he does, he's as good as dead.'

The Oberst stood on the roof of his Panzerbefehlswagen, field-glasses trained east over the vast, rolling plains of the Ukraine. Far behind him, the distant mutter of artillery fire signalled the destruction of yet another encircled Soviet unit, cut through then bypassed by his own Panzergruppe.

With a rare few moments for reflection in the frantic, headlong campaign, he had a strong sense of being part of some huge, dispersed machine. In a wide screen around him were the Panzer IIIs of the leading Kompanie. Somewhere out ahead of him were the armoured cars of the Panzeraufklärungsabteilung, their occasional terse reports crackling on the radio. Further ahead still, the Fieseler Storchs hunted, seeking out Soviet troops and defensive positions, while far above the fast photoreconnaissance aircraft tracked the movements of armies and the Fw 190 fighter-bombers cruised, waiting for the call which would bring them hammering down on any points of resistance, or much less frequently, pouncing on any of the few remaining Soviet aircraft which tried to hinder their passage. Behind him was the rest of the Panzergruppe; not just tanks, but Panzergrenadiers in their Personenkraftwagen, Panzerjäger units with their Marder and Jagdpanzer self-propelled anti-tank guns, together with artillery, engineers, signals units, medical units and the all-important supply organisation.

At that thought he grimaced. The machine had some problems, and worst of all was the supply situation. The further and faster the armies moved forward, the more difficult it was to ensure the supply of fuel, ammunition and other necessities. Despite commandeering every available lorry capable of managing the conditions, the Wehrmacht was in danger of running out of steam. Far behind him, he knew that engineers were racing to convert the Soviet railways to the German gauge in order to push forward railheads to shorten the travel distance of the lorries. In an emergency, the Luftwaffe could arrange vital deliveries. But it was still very tight. Now the plains were drying out, dust was beginning to form, penetrating the air filters to wear out the engines and sharply increasing the wear rate of tank tracks. There was indeed some grit in the machine.

His thoughts were interrupted by a sharp note of urgency in the radio report from the reconnaissance unit, then a sudden silence. He swept the horizon with his glasses and spotted a smoke column forming in the distance. Seconds later, the heavy thumps of gunfire reached him. He dropped down into the command vehicle and issued instructions over the radio net. The Panzer Kompanie burst into life and moved off, splitting into three groups; one headed for the smoke, the others diverged to either side.

The big, eight-wheeled Panzerspähwagen burned fiercely. Close by, two of the smaller four-wheeled vehicles were visibly wrecked. There was no sign of life. The Oberst shifted the glasses to the small copses about a kilometre away, calculating distances and angles. 'That one, I think,' he muttered to himself, and switched on the radio. The Panzers moved to surround the copse. The Oberst frowned; one of them was exposing his flank only 500 metres from the copse. He reached for the radio again but was forestalled by the sudden boom of a heavy-calibre gun. He looked up in time to see the Panzer shudder to a halt, smoke already seeping from it. There was still nothing visible in the copse.

On his command, the Panzers poured high-explosive shells into the copse, blasting the trees to splinters and setting them ablaze. After a few minutes, a massive shape lumbered forward out of the flames, a type the Oberst did not recognise. The lead Panzer promptly fired and the Oberst watched incredulously as the armour-piercing shot bounced off the tank's glacis plate. The Soviet tank returned fire and knocked out another Panzer with a flank shot; the others hastily traversed their vehicles to gain the protection of the thicker frontal armour and retreated up the slope. After a few minutes it was clear that they had a stand-off; neither side could penetrate the other's frontal armour and the Soviet tank was even able to shrug off hits on the side armour. The Oberst gave more instructions. The Panzers ceased fire to conserve their ammunition and waited.

Half an hour later, the Jagdpanzer rumbled up to join the Panzers. When he had first seen them, the Oberst had thought they were an unneccessary extravagance. With a huge 8,8 centimetre Flak cannon mounted in an armoured box on a Panzer III chassis, they had seemed far too powerful to deal with the relatively thinly-armoured Soviet tanks which the Germans had first encountered. He was beginning to realise that the OKH knew what they were doing. The Hauptmann in charge of the Panzerjäger unit strolled over to the command car and climbed up beside the Oberst. He studied the Soviet tank, still motionless in front of the copse.

'Ah yes, one of the new KV One heavy tanks. Only a medium-velocity seven point six centimetre gun, but very good armour all-round. Still, we have the right medicine for it.' He walked back to his vehicle, which edged forward up to the crestline. The KV1 turret turned towards them as the crew spotted the movement and the Oberst was irresistably reminded of a cornered, dangerous rhinocerous sniffing the air for enemies.

The sound of the 8,8 cm gun firing at close range was so loud it hit him like a physical blow. Just over a second later, the 9.4 kilogramme shot smashed into the KV. To the Oberst's astonishment, after a few seconds the Russian tank returned fire. The exchange continued for several more shots, one bouncing off the Jagdpanzer's well-sloped armour, before the Soviet tank fell silent. The Panzers approached cautiously and gave the all-clear. The Oberst ordered his driver to approach the KV and got out to examine the tank. It was much more massive than the Panzer III, although as the Hauptmann had said, its gun was shorter and less powerful. The Panzers' 7,5 cm projectiles had gouged the surface of the armour but failed to penetrate; of the four visible 8,8 cm strikes, only the last had succeeded in dealing a fatal blow. The Oberst whistled between his teeth, and returned to his vehicle in a thoughtful frame of mind.

The village burned, flames and smoke rising into the summer sky. Men were moving back to a line of vehicles, preparing to move off. From where the villager lay, concealed in some undergrowth, he could see still figures, like ragged bundles of clothing, lying on the ground. It was quiet, since the shooting had silenced the screams of the women and the cries of the children.

It was pure chance that he had been working in the copse when the Germans came, surrounding the village before anyone could escape. He continued to watch as with much revving of engines the small convoy drove away. Nothing moved in the village.

The man lay there for a long time, unable to move, his limbs frozen in shock and despair. He had played no part in the war; like many other Ukranians he and his neighbours had hated the brutal, all-embracing power of Stalin's Russia and had welcomed the Germans as liberators. The first wave of troops had swept past the village, ignoring the awestruck peasants. Stalin's appeal to the people to wage a merciless struggle against the invaders had been scoffed at.

Since then, ugly rumours had begun to circulate, causing a growing feeling of unease: rumours of senseless killing and torture on both sides, of the brutality suffered by many civilians, especially those of Jewish descent. Worst of all, a name whispered to him by a Ukranian Jew who passed through the village a few days ago, fleeing with his family: SS Einsatzgruppen.

Eventually, the man rose to his feet and walked slowly to the village to search for the bodies of his wife and son. After he had buried them, he knew what to do.

The conifers shaded Herrman from the summer sun as he walked around the narrow, winding roads within the 'Sperrkreis I' security fence. He felt relaxed by the warmth, his mind in neutral, slipping idly through random patterns; forgetting for a while where he was and why he was there.

'May I join you or is this a private expedition?' Stadler's sardonic voice jarred him back to reality.

'Please yourself,' he said resignedly.

His guard and companion fell into step and they walked for a while in silence.

'I've noticed you're inclined to spend more and more time on these solitary rambles. Is this a sudden urge to commune with nature or achieve athletic prowess perhaps?'

Herrman laughed shortly. 'Hardly that. It's just that there isn't much else to do, cooped up in here. I hardly have a function anymore.'

'Oh, I don't know. The Führer likes to have you at his nightly table talks in the tea house. I'm sure you remain a constant source of comfort and inspiration to him.'

They walked on in silence for a while, past the cinema and towards Göring's house. Herrman tried in vain to recover his earlier equanimity, the presence by his side a silent but continuous pressure. Eventually he stopped with a sigh. 'I have this terrible feeling of having set some huge juggernaut into motion, then watching it veer off course toward destruction.'

The SD man's eyebrows lifted. 'My, you are in a pessimistic mood. I can't think why; the news from the front could hardly be better. All three Army Groups are ahead of schedule and the Soviets have taken appalling casualties. They've lost thousands of tanks and aircraft and hundreds of thousands of men – in fact OKH reckons they're past the million mark. And there's no sign of any slowdown. Long before autumn is here, we'll be in Moscow and the Soviets will have run out of equipment and men.'

'Unfortunately they can replace both at an astonishing rate, and still have vast stretches of territory to fall back into.'

Stadler started walking again and Herrman reluctantly followed. They turned left at the crossroads to walk past the Keitel Bunker, the sun strong on their backs. 'Is this the same man who has spent years convincing our Führer of the evils of Stalin's system and the importance of crushing it? What has changed?'

'Nothing in principle. It's the practice that bothers me. These Einsatzgruppen.'

'Ah-ha. Your liberal sentimentality is surfacing again. You really must do something about that.'

Herrman shook his head. 'It isn't even that, although God knows I can't see the point of killing all those civilians just for the sake of it. No, it's the consequences that bother me. Our troops were welcomed with open arms in the Ukraine, the Baltic states, even in eastern Poland, God help us. With the right handling, we could have had all of those nations on our side, fighting alongside us. Instead, we're turning them into implacable enemies, with partisan activity already being reported. It just increases the depth of enemy territory we have to operate in. On top of that, the order for the liquidation of all captured Red Army political commissars just stiffens their resistance. I've explained all of this to Hitler, countless times. I can't understand why he won't listen.'

Stadler laughed grimly. 'Actually, that's your fault. With your information, he's been able to plan a decisive campaign with much better equipment and the power to sustain the effort for as long as it takes. He is quite certain of victory so sees no need to make concessions to the Untermenschen.'

'I would feel more confident of that if only I could stop him from interfering. The OKH and the Army Group commanders know what they're doing – they're the most capable set of professional soldiers on Earth.' They bore left along the main road, passing between the Kasino and the Wehrmacht-Adjutant's office.

'The Führer's bold and inspired guidance has led the Wehrmacht to historic success.' Herrman glanced at him but there was not the slightest trace of irony in his expression. Stadler was too good at his job to reveal anything.

'His bold and inspired political leadership has, yes. It's just that as soon as the armies start rolling, he turns into a nervous meddler.'

The SD man glanced around hastily. 'I'd be a little more judicious in my choice of words, if I were you. You might be favoured but you're not immune.'

'Then there's his siege mentality,' Herrman ploughed on regardless. 'All he cares about is establishing defensible eastern boundaries which include sufficient economic assets. He doesn't seem to realise that unless he completely destroys the Soviet regime, they'll just lick their wounds and rebuild their forces, safe behind the Urals, ready to continue the struggle. This obsession with capturing Leningrad and the Ukraine instead of aiming straight for Moscow.'

'Well, you won that one, at least.'

'Only just, and only because the entire General Staff was behind me.'

Stadler laughed. 'That isn't necessarily a recommendation, in the Führer's eyes.'

'They know what they're talking about,' Herrman continued stubbornly. It was as if the frustrations building up inside him had to be released. 'It's standard and well-tried doctrine to choose a Schwerpunkt for maximum effort and stick to it, instead of dispersing the Army across half Russia. If we try to grab everything at once, we run the risk of ending up with nothing.'

'But you've said yourself that the longer we give the Russians to recover from our onslaught and organise their defences, the harder the job will be. We have to seize as much as we can, while the initiative is ours.'

Herrman sighed. 'I know. Perhaps we have bitten off more than we can chew. I did want Hitler to wait until after the British were defeated before opening up a second front.'

Stadler laughed. 'Well, Guderian agreed with you there, and much good did it do him. Besides, you are forgetting that your own information correctly indicated that the Soviets were in the middle of a military restructuring and had just begun to re-equip. They would have been a much tougher target had we waited a year. And then, the Führer is impatient.'

'I know.' Neither of them needed to comment on Hitler's obsession with his health and mortality, his nervous determination to achieve as much as possible while he still could.

They stopped outside the liaison barracks where they both lived. 'Look on the bright side,' Stadler said expansively, 'we're winning the war, it's summer, and we are staying for free in a delightful resort.' Herrman laughed reluctantly. The Rastenburg FHQ was a scatter of camouflaged bunkers and other buildings hidden in a wood and surrounded by several layers of security.

'I didn't know it was possible to suffer from claustrophobia out of doors. Still, it's nice to know some things are still predictable.' Stadler raised an eyebrow. 'The Führer called this place 'Wolfsschanze' in my time, too.'

The mood of Hitler's daily Lagebesprechung was buoyant, as usual. Keitel and Jodl, respectively Supreme Commander of the Armed Forces and Head of Operations in the OKW, were not inclined to be critical. In any case, there was no apparent reason to be so. Herrman had been invited to attend, for once; possibly because none of the more forceful OKH or Army Group commanders, with whom he might agree, were present. After a rambling discourse from the Führer on the Wehrmacht's successful implementation of his ideas, the question turned to future priorities.

'We have agreed,' this with an ironic glance at Herrman, 'that the current priority remains the destruction of the Soviet forces which are now concentrated for the defence of Moscow. Now the conversion of the railway gauge has been completed as far as Smolensk, OKH has stated that the army will soon be sufficiently rested and reequipped to begin Operation Typhoon.'

The obsequious Keitel nodded happily, for once able to agree with both his Führer and OKH. 'It will be better to secure Moscow while we have them on the run and before the Siberian troops can be deployed. At this time of the year, we are assured of plenty of daylight and good flying weather for Luftwaffe support.'

'What is the current assessment of the balance of forces?'

Keitel turned to Jodl, who did not need to check his notes. 'Casualties have been higher than we might have expected, given the scale of the Soviet defeats, simply because the political commissars ensured that their troops kept on attacking even in the most hopeless situations. However, we are back up to twenty-five Panzer and a similar number of motorized divisions, together with fifty infantry divisions. Half of these are in Army Group Centre, which will be heading straight from Smolensk to Moscow and will therefore face the toughest resistance. While the bulk of the Soviet troops are being pinned in front of Moscow, the Panzer and motorised divisions of Army Group North will be aiming to circle behind the city to cut off any further reinforcements. The northern infantry divisions will remain in holding positions for the time being. Meanwhile, Army Group South will be continuing the destruction of the relatively strong Soviet forces in the Ukraine.'

'And the Soviets?'

'They are in such a mess that I doubt if they know themselves. At the beginning of Barbarossa they had around three hundred divisions, including fifty armoured. Their casualties and equipment losses have been almost incredible and what they have left is mostly disorganised. They have twenty to twenty-five divisions in Siberia, but are hesitating to move them because of the potential threat from Japan. We believe they have managed to raise another twenty divisions, mostly of infantry, to block the way to Moscow. Nevertheless, the current estimate is that Moscow will fall two weeks after Operation Typhoon begins.'

'And after that?'

'The plans are for a double encirclement of the remaining Soviet forces. Some of the Panzer and motorized divisions will head north to cut off Leningrad and, with the aid of the Finns, crush the defending troops there against the anvil of our infantry divisions already in place. The remainder will head south-east to meet a north-eastern thrust by Army Group South. By the end of September, we should have destroyed all organised opposition and be in control of Russian territory up to the Volga. That will give us time to consolidate our position before the worst of the weather sets in.'

Herrman felt moved to contribute. 'The Russians will not be stopped by winter. Unless we can persuade the Japanese to attack, they will have reinforcements from Siberia as well as many new divisions raised by the spring, equipped from the factories they have moved east of the Urals.'

Hitler was dismissive. 'The Japanese will not attack; they still remember the bloody nose they received from Zhukov in Manchuria when they adventured there a few years ago; besides, they are fully engaged in China and the rest of their attention is on the south. But it does not matter. By the spring, our forces will be still stronger and equipped with tanks and aircraft which will beat anything that the Russians have. They may not know it yet, but they are already finished.'

The Major commanding the Panzer IV Kompanie of the 900th Panzer Brigade stood in the turret and watched with quiet satisfaction the retreat of a force of Panzertransportwagen half-tracks in the valley below. They were fleeing in good order, keeping well ahead of the pursuing T 34s. The Major scanned the advancing mass and estimated there were at least a hundred of the fast Russian tanks, some with tankriding infantry clinging to handholds on them. He shuddered briefly at the sight; scarcely a satisfactory substitute for armoured personnel carriers.

He calculated that it would be at least ten minutes before action commenced, so he settled back to wait. His force was now just a few kilometres from Moscow, after fifteen days of hard fighting. The Russians had thrown everything at the advancing Germans; troops not yet trained, tanks straight off their Moscow production lines. They had help, too; suicidal soldiers equipped with British PIATs had hidden as the wave of Panzers swept past then emerged to knock out a tank with monotonous regularity. To prevent this, Panzergrenadiers had had to be sent to clear the ground first, but this had slowed the advance and led to heavy casualties among them from machine gun and artillery fire. It was all rather difficult and depressing.

The same could be said for the increasing numbers of Bristol Brigands, flown over from Norway, which for the first time had posed an aerial threat to the Wehrmacht formations. One had been shot down near his unit the other day, and the Major had been surprised to find that the pilot had been British. Apparently, the original plan to hand them over to the Soviet Air Force had been abandoned because of the shortage of time for training.

The Soviets had been learning, too. Their tanks no longer offered convenient targets by cruising along crest lines, and their initial total disorganisation had been replaced by more systematic tactics, concentrating on punching into the side of the advancing Panzer streams, cutting off the leading units from their support. He smiled mirthlessly. This time, they had tried the ploy once too often.

As the first T34s crossed his path, he glanced to either side at his comrades just below the crestline. The 900th was a special Panzer Brigade, made up exclusively of armoured warfare instructors gaining first-hand experience, and they had been given the new tank, already dubbed Panther, to try out. Now was the time. He issued a terse instruction over the radio net and all twenty-two of the formidable forty ton Panzers edged forward to expose their turrets. On the far side of the valley a kilometre away, he could just make out movement as their fellow Kompanie took up position.

'Start with the lead tanks,' he instructed the gunner. 'Bearing one hundred degrees, range six hundred metres.' Electric motors hummed as the huge turret swung and steadied, the long barrel of the 8,8 cm cannon questing forward.

'I see him.'

'Fire at will.' The vicious bang as the gun fired was echoed almost immediately as his comrades opened up. Tracer after tracer streamed towards the hapless T34s which slowed and milled in confusion, uncertain of the source of attack. Tank after tank stopped, smoke pouring from them, as the heavy, high-velocity shot slammed home. The T34s' well-sloped armour could not save them; the Major watched in astonishment as a tank turret was blasted clean off.

Some of the Russian tank crews spotted the half-hidden Panthers and returned fire. The Major was momentarily stunned by a huge clang which shook his tank, and a blurred image of a shape flashing past him. It took him a second to realise that his tank had suffered a direct hit, but the Panther's 10 cm of sloped armour had deflected the shot. A shade further over, he reflected, and the ricochet would have taken his head off.

An urgent call shifted his attention back down the valley. More shapes could be seen rumbling belatedly to the rescue of the slaughtered T34s. 'KV1s!' he said out loud, 'this is getting interesting!' The Panther eased forward into a new firing position. This would be a real test of the new tank's mettle. Having lost the element of surprise, they would have to slug it out with the formidably armoured Russian heavy tanks.

'Armour piercing. Bearing thirty degrees. Range about twelve hundred metres. Fire at will.' The cannon banged again and again, until the Major felt deafened even with his headphones on. His gunner stopped firing when smoke and flames obscured the view. The Germans waited for a while, but none of the KV1s emerged. As he looked down at his tank, he saw the scars of two more hits. He looked along the line of Panthers. All of them began to move forward, unharmed.

The Generalmajor of Army Group Centre's staff concluded his summary of the progress of Operation Typhoon. The visitors from OKH, he noted, appeared to be reserving their judgment.

'So while acknowledging that progress varies across the front according to local conditions, Army Group Centre appears to be about five days behind schedule,' the Generalleutnant leading the group commented. 'What are main factors causing that?'

'It is a combination of factors. On the material side, the appearance of the British PIATs and Brigands was an unwelcome surprise and has led to noticeable Panzer losses. What is worse, they have enforced a change in tactics which costs time. The introduction of these 'Katyusha' artillery rockets was also unexpected and is causing problems, particularly for the infantry. The launchers are very mobile and the arrival of scores of high-explosive warheads simultaneously has a bad effect on morale. As far as armour is concerned, the Panzer Three is as well protected as the T34 and the latest version with the long seven-point-five centimetre gun is much better armed, so it can kill T34s at one thousand metres while remaining safe down to five hundred. However, they are having a real problem dealing with the KV Ones. The gun/armour balance is such that each can start hurting the other at about five hundred metres. The Jagdpanzer and the new Panther tank easily have the measure of even the KV – the eight-point-eight centimetre gun with the new sub-calibre ammunition can penetrate at over one thousand metres while they are virtually immune to anything the Russians can throw at them – but they are only now being introduced in some numbers. Tactically, the Russians under Zhukov are learning fast. They are making much more use of minefields and covering them with anti-tank guns and artillery. They have also become good at deception, building false defence lines for us to attack while concealing the real defences which then take us by surprise. This is inevitably slowing down progress. It appears that the entire population of Moscow has been mobilised to build earthwork defences and the Russian soldiers fight with fanatical courage until they are surrounded, when they give up quickly.' He looked round at his audience for emphasis. 'In many ways, this is more like a seige than the open-country fighting we have become used to, so there are no quick solutions.'

The Generalleutnant nodded. 'Army Group North are facing less resistance in their drive to cut off the city; that seems to have taken Stavka by surprise. Let's hope that the predilection of the Russians to surrender when surrounded applies to the whole city. We are already receiving reports of civil disorder since their Government fled to Kuybyshev; the city authorities have declared martial law.'

The sunshine gleamed on the feathers of the ducks as they squabbled over food. Don and Mary watched for a moment, enjoying the simple pleasures of a warm summer's day, before strolling on around St James's Park.

'It seems hard to believe, that it can still be so peaceful here,' Mary murmured. Don grimaced and nodded. The newspaper reports were still fresh in their minds: the appalling losses suffered by the Russians, now amounting to millions dead or captured, the apparent destruction of Stavka's ability to put up any effective defence and, perhaps above all, the photographs of the ranks of massive Panther tanks, lined up in Red Square.

'Does it mean the end for Stalin, do you think?'

Don considered. 'It's hard to be certain about anything to do with Russia. What we do know is that he hasn't surrendered yet, nor do I believe he will. After years of repression, his government isn't exactly loved by his people and the only thing holding them together is their determination to fight to preserve the Rodina, the Motherland. If Stalin gives up, all that will collapse and he would probably be killed by his own side before the Germans could get at him. His only hope of survival is to hold on to power and maintain the tight communist discipline. He's not alone in that, of course, the commissars and the entire communist party structure know that they would go down with him, so he should be able to keep the apparatus of state control effective.'

'But can he still make any sort of defence?'

'His government has withdrawn to the Volga, but that line is the next obvious German target so I wouldn't be surprised if they have to move further east still. One benefit is that Stalin started transferring weapons factories far to the east several years ago. Given time, he will have the men and equipment to reconstruct a substantial army. And of course, the aid from the USA and ourselves should help.'

Mary laughed grimly. 'If we can still get it to them.'

Don nodded. 'The sea route to Murmansk could be vulnerable to air attack if the Luftwaffe base themselves in Finland. The Germans will probably try to cut rail communications with the port in any case, but thanks to the new railway connecting Murmansk with Archangel that will be difficult. The Americans can ship their supplies to Vladivostok for another few months but that will close as soon as the Japanese attack. The only other possibility is the southern route, via India, which doesn't have a high capacity. Basically we need to get as much to them as we can, while we can. It's just as well Churchill has been placing orders for military equipment with America; we can divert those orders straight to Murmansk. One other consolation is that the Germans won't be launching any attacks in winter, so the Russians will have a few months to recover.'

'There are still a couple of months before the rains are due.'

Don sighed grimly. 'Indeed there are. The Wehrmacht will need some time to recover and regroup, but it's not hard to guess what they'll do next.'

It made a pleasant change for Herrman to be in Berlin. Hitler was rarely there, spending most time at the Rastenburg FHQ or his retreat at Berchtesgaden, but he had returned for the celebrations of the fall of Moscow and to confer with the Party and Wehrmacht leaders over the next moves. Herrman took every opportunity to stroll around the streets, enjoying the holiday atmosphere in the great capital city, as yet apparently untouched by war. The shops were all open and stocking a wide range of goods, although with some exceptions, he noted. The British blockade of Atlantic and Mediterranean sea routes had cut off supplies of some goods, as had the war with the Soviet Union, but produce from Italy and Greece varied the home-grown foods. He could not escape his destiny for long, however; every day, there was the war.

'After seizing Moscow, the army is already back on course to take Leningrad and the Crimea, encircling and destroying the Russian forces there. Next we will press on to the Volga and kick the Russian Government out of their new capital. By then we will have seized nearly half of all Soviet production facilities. Then our army can enjoy a well-earned winter rest.'

Hitler was evidently in a particularly omnipotent mood and not without reason, Herrman reflected. The imposing meeting room in the Reich Chancellery was filled with senior officers of OKW, OKH, OKL and OKM.

'Not so for the navy and air force, however! England still holds out, and a maximum effort must be made to enforce our blockade. Every merchant ship that gets through must be regarded as a defeat in battle, for every one brings to the English what they need to defy us for a little longer. The only exception to this maximum effort shall be the bomber groups on the Eastern Front, which must keep pounding the remnants of the Russian forces and their industrial capacity. Meanwhile, the army must be preparing itself to crush the final Russian resistance in the spring. The new Panther tank has proved itself to be more than a match for the best Russian tanks, and this will be steadily replacing the earlier Panzers in our tank armies. The conversion of the railways will continue so that we can take our supplies up to the front line, and partisans will be dealt with ruthlessly. This does not mean that the military will get everything that you ask for. We must remember the ordinary German people. We cannot just print all the Marks we need, because that way lies inflation, and we have all seen the devastating effects of that under the Weimar Republic. Production of military equipment will be limited to what we calculate we need to finish this war, so that our people can continue to enjoy a good standard of living. We will never again subject the German people to shortages and rationing.'

Afterwards, Herrman circulated somewhat reluctantly among the assembled uniforms, clutching a glass of champagne that he supposed had been filched from some unfortunate chateau. There was a palpable buzz of excitement and confidence in the air, with officers chatting animatedly.

'You must feel rather outnumbered by all these uniforms.' Herrman turned to meet the eyes of a Generalmajor.

Herrman smiled slightly. 'I have become rather used to that in recent years.'

'Yes, I must confess I have been intrigued by your attachment to the Führer's staff. I know you're not an intelligence man, or a doctor, or anything like that. You're something of a mystery man.'

Herrman laughed rather uneasily. 'Nothing mysterious about me. I just bring an historical perspective to the great events we are living through.'

'Interesting. I thought our Führer was more interested in the future than the past.'

'Excuse me.' Stadler's voice was firm and cold. 'Professor Herrman's presence is required.'

'But of course,' the officer murmured. Herrman was conscious of the man's eyes on his back as he walked away.

'Who was that?'

'His name is Oster. He is one of Canaris's Abwehr men, running their Central Department. Don't talk to him; the Abwehr is politically unreliable so they haven't been told about you.'

'I see.' Herrman did indeed. He was well aware of the intense rivalry between the SD and the military's intelligence and counter-intelligence organisation, only held in check by a relatively good working relationship between Admiral Canaris and Obergruppenführer Heydrich, the head of the RSHA, the Reich Central Security Office, of which the SD was a part. He recalled that much of the opposition to Hitler had its roots in the Abwehr, who in the nature of their work were well aware of the atrocities being committed by the Nazis.

The gathering was suddenly interrupted by the wailing of sirens. Stadler looked astonished. 'An air raid warning? Here? How ridiculous!'

Herrman was aware that British bombing of Germany had been restricted to precisely defined military and industrial targets, carefully avoiding city centres. The gathering was clearly reluctant to break up and descend to the bunkers, so the party went on. Curious, Herrman walked to a tall window overlooking the city. Searchlights were leaping up into the night and the distant rumble of gunfire was audible. He watched, fascinated, his first view of a bombing raid. For a while, nothing much seemed to be happening; then a vivid, multi-coloured glow lit the window.

'My God, they're coming here!' Stadler was incredulous and there was an unprecedented touch of panic in his voice. 'Come away from the window and down to the shelter. NOW!' He hurried Herrman away in an iron grip. Just as they reached the door, the building shook to a massive blast. Herrman glanced back and saw glass flying across the room from the window he had been standing by.

'They must be mad!' Stadler seemed caught between astonishment and fury. 'Hitler will smash London for this!'

A sudden thought almost stopped Herrman in his tracks. 'Yes,' he said slowly, 'I expect that's exactly what Churchill wants!'

Don and Mary stood at the window of their darkened apartment, looking at the clear night sky revealed by the blackout.

'Peaceful so far,' she said.

Don was subdued. 'Not for much longer. Hitler is bound to retaliate soon.'

'Is it worth it? Sacrificing this beautiful city?'

'It had better be. Churchill would never admit it publicly, of course, but diverting the Germans into attacking our cities is the only thing that might take the pressure off our ports and shipping, as well as convincing the Russians that we're still fighting and won't abandon them.'

She sighed. 'History seems to be repeating itself in so many ways, despite all of your efforts. We were doing so well until a couple of months ago. Now there's a real threat that Hitler will finish off the Russians and turn his full force onto us.' She paused for a moment, then continued hesitantly. 'There's something I've been meaning to tell you. I'm afraid I've been rather careless. I'm pregnant.'

For a moment Don did not reply. Then he took her in his arms and held her close. His thoughts were in turmoil, but above all he felt a powerful, unaccustomed surge of tenderness and protectiveness. His voice was muffled by her hair. 'Then we'd better make sure this will be a world worth bringing our child in to.'

# CHAPTER 7 – CO-PROSPERITY

**Winter 1941-42**

The morning air was cool and fresh; the sun was just beginning to penetrate the light mist. The guard paused in his rounds, enjoying the first moments of a day which promised to be warm and sunny. The long stretch of featureless runway slowly crystallised out of the haze, with surrounding trees and buildings taking firm shape.

The planes he was guarding were clustered neatly, wingtip to wingtip, as ordered by the base commander. International tension had been steadily mounting and the brass were apparently afraid of sabotage. Certainly there had been unaccustomed activity around the base in recent weeks, with many new aircraft arriving and much effort put into training. He hated to think how much fuel was being burned up.

A sudden roar of engines jarred him out of his semi-reverie, and he turned to see the ungainly four-engined plane warming up ready for take-off. The guard watched as it slowly taxied down to the end of the runway then turned in his direction. The four undercarriage legs, one beneath each engine, were unmistakable.

The engine note hardened and the plane began to roll, gathering speed with relentless determination as it sped down the runway. As it flashed past the guard, the tail slowly rose then the whole aircraft gradually lifted itself into the air.

The guard watched with interest as the Vickers Warwick vanished in the haze, puzzling as everyone had been about the presence of the aircraft. The official word was that it was on loan, together with its crew, for some sort of evaluation exercise. All the same, it seemed very odd to see an RAF plane in Oahu!

Several hundred miles to the north-west, Vice-Admiral Chuichi Nagumo was feeling acutely nervous. His flagship, the giant 40,000 ton aircraft carrier *Akagi*, moved easily through the heavy seas. His fleet had adopted the daytime cruising formation an hour before and was now spread over an area of the Pacific with a front and depth of some sixteen nautical miles.

Closest to the *Akagi* were the five other aircraft carriers which, along with his own, were the home for the 465 aircraft of the First Air Fleet: the equally huge *Kaga*, the 30,000 ton sister ships *Shokaku* and *Zuikaku*, and the 20,000 ton *Soryu* and *Hiryu*. In the past, he had been comforted by the thought that even the smallest of these was similar in size to the British Royal Navy's new Ark Royal class carriers. As the time for action approached, his anxiety grew beyond the help of such thoughts.

He peered ahead to where Rear Admiral Omori in the light cruiser *Abukuma* commanded the nine escorts of the 1st Destroyer Squadron; five of them were spread in a screen a few miles in front of the carriers, the other four were ten miles further ahead. In between were the heavy cruisers *Tone* and *Chikuma*; trailing the carriers by some four miles were the reassuringly massive Kongo class battlecruisers *Hiei* and *Kirishima*. Scattered around the fleet were the tankers necessary for them all to make the 3,000 mile journey from their bases.

Nagumo cast his mind back to the arguments that had raged at the highest levels in Japan about the impasse the country faced. He had not been party to them himself, of course, but Admiral Yamamoto, the Commander in Chief of the Imperial Japanese Navy, had said enough to give a flavour of what had happened.

The Army had been mainly responsible for pressing for war. Their territorial ambitions had already led to the effective annexation of Manchuria and a long drawn out invasion of China. Last summer, they had also moved into French Indo-China. Japan saw herself as the natural leader of Asia and deeply resented the attempts by the Western powers to block the expansion of her power, most recently by refusing to sell her the raw materials her economy needed.

The Navy was not so belligerent, Nagumo reflected, but had been insulted by the West's refusal, at a series of naval disarmament conferences, to countenance Japanese equality in warship numbers.

The result of the West's intransigence was that Japan was now cut off from the supplies of oil and other raw materials readily available in the western colonies of the East Indies – temptingly within range of Japanese military power. Japan was slowly strangling for lack of these materials. At the same time, the Americans had announced a massive naval expansion programme of over two hundred warships, including seven battleships and eighteen aircraft carriers, to add to the hundred and thirty ships already being built and more than three hundred and fifty in service. By the time this was completed, the US Navy would be far too strong to attack.

The choice had been stark. Japan either had to give in to Western demands, renounce her expansion plans and withdraw from China, and thereby suffer an appalling loss of face throughout Asia, or attack now while the British were locked in a death struggle with Germany and before America's naval expansion could take place.

Nagumo remembered the Admiral's face as he had explained the situation. Yamamoto, who had spent time in the USA, had had no doubt that a war would have to be over quickly, because in the long run America's industrial might would far outperform Japan's. The gamble was that a knock-out blow against the American fleet and the rapid conquest of the remainder of the West's Asian colonies would give Japan enough time to secure her supplies of raw materials and to throw such a strong defensive ring around her new possessions that the Americans would be forced to accept the new status quo instead of continuing the battle.

It was this reasoning that had led Yamamoto to plan the bold step of an attack on the American naval base of Pearl Harbor in the Hawaiian Islands. The base was essential to American naval operations in Asia and most of the US fleet was based there.

'Climb Mount Niitaka'. The message from Japan, ordering the attack, had arrived on December 1st. Nagumo grimaced, remembering the mixture of emotions with which he had received it. He was not an expert in naval aviation, but nonetheless had been entrusted with the task of striking Japan's most daring blow. It was more responsibility than he could easily cope with.

The course of his fleet had been carefully plotted to minimise the risk of discovery. The usual shipping lanes kept to the south of the Hawaiian Islands so the fleet's route had curved well to the north, through turbulent seas which had made refuelling a nightmare. The fleet was sailing under strict radio silence, but a stream of messages came from Japan, relaying the latest information from spies on Oahu, the island which included Pearl Harbor.

'The tankers are moving into position for the final refuelling, sir.'

Nagumo nodded acknowledgement. It was the morning of December 6th. Soon it would be time to assemble the crews and tell them, at last, what it was they were there to do.

'It's absolutely monstrous! Do you know how long it takes to build a golf course?' The visitor was red-faced with indignation, moustache bristling. The Brigadier in the Royal Engineers tried to appear sympathetic. He was too tired to be good at it. He uttered what he hoped were a few soothing platitudes, well aware that the bulldozers had moved in before the august members of the Golf Club Committee could organise in its defence – because he had so arranged it.

The plans had been around for years, he knew, but so massive was the complacent inertia that procrastination had delayed their implementation – until General Wavell had arrived: he had been appointed overall Commander-in-Chief and armed with draconian powers and instructions signed by Churchill himself.

Brigadier Simson sighed and walked around to look at the large maps of Singapore and South-East Asia on the wall. Wavell had given him the authority and resources to put his long-planned defence measures into effect. The last of the additional airfields was well under way, the field fortifications facing Malaya across the mile-wide Johore Strait almost complete. With the accelerated shipments of troops, guns, tanks and aircraft now streaming into the island, as much as possible was being done. Even the 15 and 9.2 inch coastal artillery, most of which could be trained to fire inland, had received large quantities of anti-personnel shells together with some fuses labelled 'Variable Time', although the security surrounding them suggested something more than a conventional time fuse. Finally, some large cruisers and a couple of light aircraft carriers had arrived only the previous week.

'So far so good,' he murmured.

Geoffrey Taylor, who had sat quietly at the back of the room, observing the confrontation with wry amusement, grunted agreement. 'It's the preparedness of the new troops that worries me the most. They'll have to get used to jungle fighting in a hurry. Still, the Japs had no experience of that until earlier this year, either, so there's hope yet. And they're far better equipped with automatic weapons.'

Simson nodded. 'This might not be much like the African desert, but the Australians and New Zealanders are good soldiers and they'll adapt quickly enough. It's Siam that worries me more. Any news from there yet?'

Taylor shrugged. 'I gather it's hard going. They don't want to believe us, as usual.' He thought back over the past few months of planning and diplomacy. The first crisis had actually come nearly eighteen months ago, when the Japanese had started to put pressure on the French Vichy government over access to French Indo-China (an area later to become better known as Vietnam). While all of the other French colonies had come over to the Free French, Indo-China was more isolated and vulnerable to Japanese invasion. Churchill had taken the view, with some reluctance, that the Japanese occupation of Indo-China would have to be accepted even though it put Japanese forces much closer to Malaya. It would be fatal to trigger war with Japan without the certainty of American involvement.

This left only independent Siam between the Japanese and Malaya. Taylor strolled over to stand beside Simson, studying the map of South-East Asia. The bulge of French Indo-China loomed ominously over the Gulf of Siam. Siam itself stretched down the narrow Isthmus of Kra, separating the Gulf from the Indian Ocean, before reaching the border with Malaya, at which point the peninsula widened again before narrowing to the island of Singapore at its tip.

The defence of Malaya was complicated by its long, exposed coastline and by the fact that it wasn't one country. Apart from the Straits Settlements of Singapore, Penang and Malacca, which were British colonies, the rest consisted of the Federated Malay States, which were closely tied to Britain, a group of more loosely associated states in the north, and Johore, the most independent of them all. The fact that Johore was the state closest to Singapore had been a potential headache but fortunately the Sultan was a generous supporter of the British and had willingly cooperated in the defensive measures currently underway.

According to Don Erlang, Siam was due to receive the main bulk of the Japanese invasion force with landings at Singora and Patani, while a smaller force landed at Kota Bharu just inside Malaya. The problem was in stopping the landings in Siam, the closest of which would be sixty miles from the Malayan border, over bad roads. So far, the Siamese had been most reluctant to conclude a defence agreement and appeared to be putting their trust in the goodwill of Japan.

'Whatever happens,' Taylor said thoughtfully, 'we've got to hold them as far from Singapore as possible. They mustn't get hold of our airfields.'

Simson nodded. 'That would put their aircraft far too close to Singapore. After all, as our naval colleagues keep reminding us, the importance of Singapore lies in its value as a naval base. If it's too dangerous to keep ships here, there's not much point in staying.' He sighed and picked up his cap. 'Care for a drink?'

Taylor shook his head. 'No time. I'm flying up to Alor Star in less than an hour.'

Simson's eyebrows rose. 'Right up at the sharp end? Well, good luck then. I'm afraid I've still got a lot to do at this end. As well as the military defence, I've been asked to advise on civil defence. Officialdom claims that the ground is too waterlogged to dig air raid shelters. Has nobody heard of reinforced concrete buildings?' He snorted in weary disgust and left.

An hour later, Taylor was flying over the dense greenery of the Malayan peninsular. It was not as impenetrable as it looked, he knew. The roads were good and were often lined with rubber plantations spreading out for half a mile or more to each side. Movement through the plantations was easy and, despite some official views, tank operations quite feasible. The roads also suited the Japanese secret weapon for rapid troop movements, he thought wryly. Who would have imagined that bicycles would be so useful?

At least, Wavell's unexpected appointment had brought some energy into the defensive preparations and begun to heal the rift between the forces, which had led to a complete lack of cooperation over defence planning. The Air Force, after years of losing bitter arguments with the Army and Navy over the best way to defend Malaya, had even started to build their own airfields very close to the coast where the Army could not easily defend them. Fortunately, this had been caught in time and the new airfields were carefully sited and well defended. They also had enough aircraft, thanks to the prewar planning which was now resulting in Brigand fighter-bombers streaming from their Australian production line to support the Hampdens and Sunderlands already established at Singapore.

Taylor himself, with his mandate from Churchill, had enforced the integration of the intelligence services, and it was to keep up with the situation on the ground that he was now flying north, to the closest point to the expected Japanese landings in Siam. He closed his eyes and tried to relax. He didn't expect to get much sleep over the next few days.

'It seems a terrible risk, not to give the Americans more warning.' Harold Johnson was looking moodily into bottom of his teacup, as if trying to see the future in the leaves. He had dropped in to Don Erlang's flat, restless and needing to talk as the tension increased.

Don didn't mind seeing him. Following his marriage to Mary – an event which had caused him a disconcerting mixture of joy and confusion about the potential time paradox implications – Mary had gone very reluctantly to stay with relatives in the country for the remainder of her pregnancy.

He nodded sympathetically realising that Johnson, as a Navy man, was feeling the current crisis more deeply than the Peter Morgan and Geoffrey Taylor, and was resenting the fact that he had been ordered to stay in London while the others were where the action was, or at least was expected. 'I know. All those battleships lined up like sitting ducks. We've been through it all before, though. If the US Navy got wind of what was happening, they would sail their battlefleet out to meet the Japanese. A fleet of old dreadnoughts against the most powerful naval air force ever assembled! The Americans would lose all their battleships beyond hope of recovery, and suffer far worse casualties. Believe me, keeping them in Pearl Harbor is the least costly option. Most of them will be salvaged after the attack.'

'Can't we send them out of the way? Tell them that the Japanese are advancing from the south?'

Don grimaced. 'That's the tough one. If the fleet sails, the chances are that the Japanese will call the whole thing off, which will lead to massive uncertainty. At least we now know what they plan to do, and can prepare accordingly. Alternatively, they might switch their attack to the shore installations, which are much more important to the American war effort than the old battleships. At least Peter's Warwick ought to give them enough warning to get their fighters airborne and their anti-aircraft guns manned, which should minimise the damage.'

Johnson nodded gloomily. 'I suppose you're right. It doesn't seem decent, though, treating those grand old battlewagons as bait.'

You don't know the half of it, Don thought. He kept trying to suppress the memories of the *USS Arizona*, in which over a thousand Americans lost their lives, and the horrifying story of the *West Virginia*, from whose salvaged hull the bodies of many sailors who had been trapped in air pockets were recovered months later, some by a calendar with seventeen days marked off after December 7th. Not for the first time, he felt a wrenching sense of futility and despair. Sleep did not come easily, and he missed the quiet reassurance of Mary's presence.

'Any news of our Eastern Fleet yet?'

Don shook his head. 'Thankfully, not since they left Colombo. As far as anyone knows, they're heading on a goodwill tour to Australia before arriving at Singapore in January.'

Johnson perked up a bit. 'Four carriers and four battleships!' He gloated. 'That's going to give the Japs a nasty surprise.' He looked thoughtfully at Don. 'Why wasn't this done in your time?'

Don shrugged. 'A combination of reasons. Partly because the new ships weren't ready so early, but also because of the threat from the German capital ships which kept the best British battleships in home waters. Malaya has also benefitted from our improved equipment situation, which has enabled us to divert more resources to the Far East. There was a hell of a battle with those who wanted us to send as much stuff to Russia as we could, but fortunately the Americans have taken on much of that burden.' He leaned back in his chair. 'It's going to be interesting to see what happens.'

'Target bearing three hundred degrees, sixty miles range. It's big – looks like a whole fleet.'

The radar operator's voice was calm and controlled. The pilot acknowledged and swung the big Warwick around to an easterly heading, away from the advancing Japanese fleet.

'Do we alert Pearl Harbor?'

The RAF intelligence officer who had accompanied them on the long flight from England responded carefully. 'Not yet. Maintain radio silence. They mustn't know they've been spotted.'

Peter Morgan was not enjoying this assignment. Playing the innocent guest among the friendly Americans did not come easily. He had told himself that, of course, it wasn't as if he was certain about what would happen. Perhaps the Germans had warned the Japanese – perhaps the attack would never take place. The cluster of blips on the screen told him otherwise. The Japanese were exactly where they should be, and precisely on time. Now he knew that some of the people whose hospitality he had been enjoying would be dead within hours.

Morgan ran the calculations through his mind. The first, most devastating wave of the Japanese air attack was due to hit Pearl Harbor and Oahu's airbases at 8 a.m., on the morning of Sunday 7th December – just five hours away. Normally it took three and a half hours for a battleship to get underway from a cold start, but in an emergency they could get moving in under an hour. The Warwick was five hundred miles from Oahu, so it could not land for two and a half hours. At that hour it would literally be very difficult to wake people up to the danger. The alarm needed to be raised just after 7 a.m. to give the Americans time to mobilise their defences without the risk of any battleships sailing out to the acute vulnerability of the open sea. To ensure that happened he would need at least half an hour to persuade the Americans that they were in danger. That gave him an hour to lose.

'Keep them on the screen at this distance. Let's keep a close eye on them for a while.'

The pilot and co-pilot exchanged puzzled glances, then shrugged. It had been made very clear to them who was in charge of this mission.

'Do you think they will take any notice?'

Stadler shrugged and shifted his feet closer to the fire. He held up the glass of schnapps to the flames before swallowing it in a gulp. 'Who cares, my friend? We have little in common with the Japanese, for all that they are supposed to be our allies. Ugly little yellow people – Untermenschen if ever I saw them. Our Führer has also gone off them somewhat after they refused to join us in the attack on Russia. The chances are that we will end up fighting them, after we have beaten everyone else. So whether they go ahead with their attack on the British and Americans or not, it's all the same to us.'

Herrman was feeling increasingly nervous as the hours stretched on, and for once had drunk little. 'What really matters is, will the Führer declare war on the USA this time? Surely he won't make the same mistake again?'

Stadler waggled a less than sober finger at him. 'Let's hear no talk of mistakes – our Führer does not make mistakes. However, the situation is not as clear-cut as it might seem. The increasing boldness of the American fleet in defending Atlantic convoys against our U-boats is causing great irritation, for all that it is largely ineffective. And it is the Americans who are supplying most of the materials that keep the British going. What's worse, much of it is now being diverted to help Russia! The Führer regards the American problem as a boil that needs to be lanced.'

'Surely he'll wait until after they are fully committed in the Pacific? After all, what is Churchill likely to fear most? With the Russians virtually finished, he knows that he can't hope to survive without the Americans on his side.'

Stadler frowned suddenly. 'The Russians might not be all that finished, just yet.'

Herrman's surprise was clear. 'I thought we'd driven them back over the Urals?'

'So the glorious Wehrmacht has. Unfortunately, they don't know when they're beaten. Stalin won't allow any talk of surrender – we have reports that several members of the hierarchy incautious enough to raise the possibility of discussing terms have not been heard of since. And the party officials know exactly what would happen to them if Russia surrendered – it would be a race as to who strung them up first, the Gestapo or their own people. So they're keeping everyone bottled up, while rebuilding their armaments from the new eastern factories.'

Herrman frowned. 'Haven't we moved our air bases far enough forward to attack them?'

Stadler regarded him sardonically. 'Have you forgotten already? You were the one who warned us about the weather. An atrociously wet autumn followed by a bitterly cold winter. Everything is frozen solid. Any vehicles or aircraft out in the open have to keep their engines running all night or they'd never start them again, and they have to move around from time to time or they'd be frozen to the spot. This is not good fighting weather.' He poured himself another shot of the clear, fiery liquid. 'Then again, there are the partisans.' He sighed and rested his head against the back of the armchair. 'They show a most irritating persistence.'

'I did warn you of the consequences of letting your thugs loose on them.' Herman's tone was bitter.

'Unfortunately it isn't that simple. All it takes is for some of our men with...' he gestured vaguely '... less delicate sensibilities, shall we say, to become a little overenthusiastic with security measures. The next thing you know is that some of our men are killed in reprisal. So of course, our troops respond by obliterating a village or two to teach them the consequences of such ungrateful behaviour. Then word spreads and more partisan activity happens.' He waved his glass about. 'It is all very tiresome.'

Herrman wearily closed his eyes. It was all happening again, he thought. If the Wehrmacht couldn't finish off the Russians before they had time to regather their strength, the battle could go on for years. And if the Russians were to win the contest while the Americans concentrated only on the Pacific, the avenging Russian armies would roll all the way through to the Atlantic coast. What to do? Every path seemed fraught with danger. He felt the beginning of yet another migraine attack.

Patchy fog surrounded the ships; heavy clouds massed above. The patrolling fighters were only occasionally seen as they swooped down low over the convoy. As night approached, Vice-Admiral Ozawa, Commander-in-Chief of the Southern Squadron and given the task of protecting the invasion fleet, allowed himself to feel relief. He would shortly lose the fighters back to their base on Phuquok Island, but gain the protection of darkness as the ships approached the coasts of Siam and Malaya.

Since leaving port on the 4th of December with over twenty-six thousand troops of the 5th and 18th Infantry Divisions, tension had steadily increased. So far, they seemed to be undiscovered. One unidentified aircraft had strayed too close at around midday, but the fighters had despatched it rapidly.

He gave the order to the transports to split up into their separate detachments and head for the three landing points, then signalled the rest of the covering force: 'The main business from now is to proceed to Kota Bharu to cover the landing of the Katumi Detachment. Pray for the success of the disembarkation.'

Ozawa carefully reviewed the task ahead. Kota Bharu was assigned only a small Detachment of three transports, but was the nearest point to the big British airbase several miles inland. This had to be captured quickly to enable the Army Air Force to mount operations in support of the invasion, so the assault force was timed to go in first – even before the planned attack at Pearl Harbor – in order to provide maximum surprise. The assaults on Siam would go in a few hours later. They would then be able to use the airstrip at Singora, but that was far cruder than the British facilities.

He was not particularly concerned about the presence of the British heavy cruisers at Singapore. Two of the eight-inch gun County class were reported, together with two of the newer six-inch gun ships. His flagship *Chokai*, a heavy cruiser of the Takao class, could outgun any of them, and he had two layers of cover; nearby was Rear Admiral Kurita's 7th Cruiser Squadron with the four vessels of the Mogami class, and acting as distant cover were two more Takao class ships and the battlecruiser *Kongo* and battleship *Haruna* under Vice-Admiral Kondo. Furthermore, a minefield had been laid between the island of Tioman and the Anamba Islands, across the most direct route from Singapore to the landing beaches, and there was a patrol line of submarines just to be certain. The aircraft carriers would be unable to stop the landings, which would all be over by dawn.

He began to relax a little. The worst problem now facing them seemed to be the heavy seas, which would interfere with smooth disembarkation. But that wasn't his problem.

Geoffrey Taylor squelched through the mud towards the looming shapes barely visible in the pouring rain. The journey from Alor Star to this northernmost point of Malaya, the closest the British could get to the main landing point of Singora, had not been pleasant. For the armoured vehicles which now lined the road, to reach Singora before the Japanese established themselves would be a major task.

'Hop aboard sir! It may not be comfortable but at least it's dry.'

Taylor acknowledged the young Captain's offer and clambered up the side of the big Humber armoured car before dropping down through the turret hatch. The six-wheel-drive vehicles had been reckoned the most likely to get to Singora quickly. He noted that this was the latest Mark III version, with the bigger fourteen pounder gun capable of firing a large explosive shell or the new APDS shot. Introduced a few months ago in the Crusader II tank, the bigger gun was simply made by increasing the calibre of the previous six pounder, so the two guns were interchangeable. The Humber was more than capable of looking after itself against the mediocre Japanese tanks.

'Will the Humbers be OK in this weather?' He asked dubiously. 'I gather the roads are pretty awful on the other side.'

The Captain shrugged. 'I expect we'll soon find out. Any news yet?'

Taylor shook his head. Operation Matador, the advance into Siam to forestall a Japanese invasion, had been planned for months. The only problem was the diplomatic nicety of invading a neutral country which hadn't asked for help. Norway all over again, he thought. We really must stop being so squeamish. At least, one glove had been taken off with the shooting down of the reconnaissance plane; now they could shoot back. He was more than a little suspicious of the reason for the orders which had taken the Hampden so unnecessarily close to the Japanese fleet, which the radar-equipped Sunderlands had been tracking from a safe distance…

The radio headset crackled and the Captain put it on and listened for a few seconds. Then he turned to Taylor with a grim smile. 'We're on. Invasion ships have been reported inside Malayan territorial waters off Kota Bharu with more approaching the coast of Siam.'

Taylor mirrored his grin. 'I gather your loader has a bad case of the runs.'

The Captain eyed him speculatively. 'You didn't find me by chance, did you?'

Taylor's grin widened. 'I don't like leaving anything to chance. Let's go!'

The soldiers on duty at Kahuku Point, on the northern tip of Oahu, were bored. They had been out on a training exercise since 4 a.m., manning the Opana Mobile Radar Unit. Since the big British plane they had been warned about had passed by on its way back to Hickham Field half an hour ago, nothing had flickered on the screen.

One of the GIs leaned forward, puzzled.

'What do you make of that?'

A smaller dot had appeared on the screen from the north, as if following the track of the Warwick.

His companion grunted. 'Check with the others.'

In due course the other two units confirmed that they too had made the same contact.

'Better report it. Then we can start packing up.'

Their stint ended at 7 a.m. Two of the units shut down ready to leave. The third pair of soldiers left their set on a while longer, waiting for the breakfast truck.

The exclamation of astonishment came from one of the soldiers at 7.06 a.m., precisely.

Peter Morgan controlled his temper. The young Lieutenant in front of him was clearly worried, but reluctant to act.

'It is very early on Sunday morning, sir. My superiors are probably all asleep at home.'

'Look at it this way,' Morgan said reasonably. 'If I'm wrong, you can blame me for insisting that the alarm is given. If I'm right and you don't act, you'll go down in history as the one man who left Pearl Harbor open to disaster.'

The Lieutenant gulped unhappily. The Britisher's fierce intensity unnerved him. 'Well, I don't know…'

The phone rang.

Commander Mitsuo Fuchida stared down on Oahu from the cockpit of his bomber. The cloud formations above the island which had been visible from far away had now broken up and the morning sun shimmered across the sea. Visibility was perfect, the surf breaking on Kahuhu Point clearly visible. The reconnaissance aircraft which had preceded the air fleet had reported no aircraft carriers in harbour, which was a blow, but several battleships. Good enough; he was going in. He scanned the sky, looking for the dots of defending aircraft ready to pounce. Very soon, he would need to decide which plan of attack to execute.

The time was 7.40 a.m. The sky was clear. Fuchida pulled open the cockpit and fired the single 'Black Dragon' signal flare which indicated a surprise attack. His formation of Aichi D3A dive bombers, Mitsubishi A6M fighters and Nakajima B5N attack bombers, some carrying bombs, others torpedoes, began to move into their attack positions.

Fuchida frowned – the fighters had not responded. Irritated, he fired another flare. The fighters reacted – but so did the bombers, as two flares meant 'surprise lost' and a different attack formation. Fuchida grunted in annoyance – now both the dive and torpedo bombers would attack simultaneously instead of in the coordinated way planned.

Pearl Harbor crawled into view on his port quarter, the lines of battleships moored by Ford Island clearly visible. As he began to lead his formation around to line up on the great base, movement caught the corner of his eye. He looked down, puzzled.

The Allison engine screamed as if in unearthly rage, dragging the P-40 upwards and forwards into the sky, hurtling towards the clusters of dots gleaming in the morning sun. In his headphones the pilot could hear the constant stream of profanity from his wingman. Nerves were stretched close to snapping by the sudden alarm at Wheeler Field, the desperate rush to fuel the planes, arm the guns, take off, take off!

Behind him, some three dozen sleek fighters, all of the P-40s that could be scrambled, fought to catch up. Further behind still trailed however many P-36s had managed to get airborne.

Shouts and screams echoed over the intercom and he glanced in his mirror. The P-36s were under attack! He could see the swarm of dots which must be Japanese planes surrounding the struggling American fighters. No time for that now – his business was ahead of him.

Fuchida urged the Nakajima onwards, the airframe shuddering as it approached its maximum speed of 200 knots. Ahead and to one side, he could see the Aichis preparing to dive. Suddenly, his plane juddered and lurched as if in pain, and strange shapes flashed across his field of view – fighters with long, pointed noses, not the blunt radials of the familiar Mitsubishis. The Americans were amongst them!

The Japanese formation, shredded and dispersed by the P-40s' attack, pressed on to the target. The quiescent ships suddenly erupted with anti-aircraft fire; first the five inch guns, their fifty-five pound shells bursting among the planes, then the 1.1 inch cannon in their quadruple mountings, hammering rhythmically as the gun crews raced to and fro with clips of ammunition; finally the rapid blare of the fifty-calibre Browning machine guns. Planes fell, bombs fell, torpedoes struck, mayhem ruled. The noise, smoke, shock and terror were indescribable. It was just past 8 a.m. on a sunny Hawaiian morning.

'They should have provided us with periscopes – it's just as well it's dark, otherwise I wouldn't be able to see a thing!' The navigator grinned at the pilot's idiosyncratic logic as rain sluiced past the Beaufort's canopy.

'Not to worry!' He called out. 'We can blow ballast tanks soon!' He continued to watch the radar screen as the Isthmus of Kra crawled below him. Somewhere up ahead should be some ships.

Admiral Somerville stared grimly at a much larger radar screen, which showed the Beauforts at the limit of detection. Soon they would be out of range and on their own. He sighed. 'It's a foul night. I hope the weather's better on the eastern side.'

'Not much, sir. There should be some breaks in the cloud and rain, but on the other hand they shouldn't need them. At least, there is good news from Kota Bharu. One of their ships tripped over our minefield and Brigands from the air base hit the other two with rockets before they could start unloading. All three ships were sunk and not many troops made it. The survivors have all been captured.'

Somerville grunted. He was not best pleased to be sending his airmen out to do battle while he was forced to remain in relative safety in the Indian Ocean, fifty miles off the west coast of Siam. His mighty battleships were useless there, hundreds of sea miles from the Gulf of Siam on the other side of the Isthmus of Kra. He fretted in the knowledge that action had already started. Still, he was forced to acknowledge the sense of his orders. He could not possibly have sailed the Eastern Fleet round the Malayan peninsula and past Singapore without the Japanese knowing all about it. For a little while longer, his presence would be unsuspected.

At midnight local time, the three transports of the Ando Detachment separated from the fleet and headed for Patani. About two hours later, the fourteen ships of the main invasion fleet dropped anchor opposite Singora beach, guided in by the lighthouse still innocently functioning. The ships rolled in the heavy seas and the freshening north-east wind dashed the waves against the sides of the vessels.

The Japanese soldiers gloomily contemplated climbing, heavily laden, down rope ladders into violently pitching small boats. This was not going to be fun. The only benefit was that the clouds had thinned sufficiently to allow a dim moonlight to illuminate the scene. A signal light flashed from the command ship, the *Ryujo Maru*, and the lowering of the flotilla of motorboats began.

A bright, fast-moving streak of light suddenly flashed across the sky.

'Look, a meteor!' Several voices cried. 'An omen!'

The light streaked towards the *Ryujo Maru* and disappeared. A second later, the night burst open in a ball of fire, the concussive thunder of the explosion rolling around the bay. As the Japanese watched in horror, more lights flashed in from the west, more explosions shook the fleet.

'Get loading now! Hurry it up!' The officers screamed instructions and the men were not slow to obey, the little boats on the heaving sea suddenly seeming much more appealing than the massive transports. The task of transhipment from the surviving ships was completed in record time.

The Captain of HM Submarine *Talisman* observed the carnage with interest through his periscope. His own carefully-aimed salvo of ten torpedoes had claimed four victims but had scarcely been noticed amidst the spectacular missile attack. The Japanese destroyers were dashing about frantically but posed no immediate threat. He decided to wait for his crew to finish reloading the six internal tubes, then see what was left.

'A pity we didn't have more Ospreys.'

Admiral Somerville grunted acknowledgement to the intelligence officer. The anti-ship missiles, guided by homing in on the reflected radar emissions from the Beauforts which carried them, had been devastatingly effective, but only a few had been ready in time, flown out to Columbo for the fleet to collect.

'Still, we've dampened their enthusiasm more than somewhat. The reports of the SBS reconnaissance units indicate that at least three quarters of the Singora ships were hit, and probably less than half the troops got ashore, without much heavy equipment.'

'What about Patani?'

'The *Tribune* got all three ships at Patani. The SBS finished off the few who got ashore.

'So now it's down to Operation Matador to clean up. Let's hope they get a move on before the Japs send in reinforcements.'

'Get that blackout fixed! Don't you realise there's a war on!' Brigadier Simson was being driven to distraction by the casual attitude of the Singaporeans to their terrible vulnerability. The problem was, he was aware, that deep down most of them couldn't really believe that they would be affected by war. To them, the war was something that happened thousands of miles away, while they continued to enjoy all of the privileged lifestyle that the wealthy colony offered.

Robinson's, the huge modern department store and restaurant whose air-conditioned luxury made it the central focus of white Singapore, continued to trade as usual. The cream of local society still headed out to the Sea View Hotel for Sunday morning drinks and the ritual singing of 'There'll always be an England'. And it was far too hot and humid to think of blocking the ventilation with blackout blinds.

As he jumped back into the car, Simson was stopped in his tracks by a new sound. An unearthly low moaning rose steadily to a chilling wail, lifting the hairs on his spine. The first air raid had begun.

JAPS DECLARE WAR.

Don stopped and passed a penny over to the newspaper vendor, eyes caught by the banner headline of the *Daily Express*. 'We fight Britain and America from dawn' the headlines went on, quoting Imperial Headquarters in Tokyo. NAVY BATTLE IN PACIFIC the paper continued more speculatively.

'I hope not,' Don muttered to himself, 'otherwise something's gone wrong.' He rapidly skimmed the paper, but it added nothing to the information he had been receiving all night. Pearl Harbor and Singapore bombed, but casualties were relatively light and the paper was full of praise for the exploits of the squadron of Mosquito night-fighters which had, just in time, been wrenched from a protesting Fighter Command and dispatched to the Far East. The landing at Kota Bharu had been defeated, but there was no reliable information about the situation in Siam. Don was momentarily surprised by the dates and times involved – the Kota Bharu assault took place on the morning of 8th December but some hours before Pearl Harbor was attacked on the 7th – until he remembered they were in different time zones.

He shivered and turned his collar up in the cold morning air, then walked on towards his flat. Not too much damage last night, he noted. The night-fighter force was steadily gaining in experience and reaping an increasing toll of the raiders, while the emergency services were becoming skilled at dousing fires and clearing away the rubble caused by the ones which got through.

Charles Dunning was waiting for him in his study. He had, it appeared, enjoyed more sleep than Don. 'The last piece of the jigsaw in place,' He commented.

'Not quite. Hitler hasn't yet declared war on the USA. Once he has, we can get down to brass tacks with the Americans.'

Charles nodded, thoughtfully. Discussions, both public and private, had been going on with the USA for a long time, and had been raised to a new level when Churchill and Roosevelt had travelled by warship to a meeting at Placentia Bay, Newfoundland, the previous August.

Don gratefully accepted a steaming cup of his own tea and settled wearily into the other armchair. The relationship between the two leaders was rather curious, he reflected. Churchill desperately wanted to recruit Roosevelt's, and thereby America's, participation in the war. Roosevelt was well aware of this and countered Churchill's jovial bonhomie with a degree of reserve. Both, however, were agreed on the importance of resisting totalitarian regimes, with Nazi Germany as the highest priority. Both men were also well aware that many in the American establishment considered the USA's interests in the Pacific to be more important, and furthermore were reluctant to do anything to help Britain retain its prewar colonial influence.

'So your Automedon ploy worked after all.' Charles' voice broke into his thoughts.

Don nodded. 'Looks like it.'

Charles was referring to a carefully leaked report which cast doom and gloom on Britain's ability to defend its Far East possessions against a Japanese attack, with the aim of inciting the Japanese to do just that. The code name had come from an incident in Don's time in which just such a report, being carried to Singapore in the freighter *Automedon*, was seized by a German commerce raider and found its way to Japan. The difference was that in Don's time, the loss was regarded as an intelligence disaster; this time, Churchill wanted Japan to attack in order to bring America into the war.

'The great unknown is still whether or not the Germans have warned the Japanese.' Charles was thoughtful.

'Not very convincingly, obviously, or they wouldn't have attacked. On the other hand, they might have had the same problems that we had with Stalin, who was suspicious of the warnings and didn't want to believe them.'

'From what you've told us of the political and economic pressures caused by the Western refusal to trade with them, they were being strangled anyway and probably thought they had nothing to lose.'

Don grimaced. 'The military are firmly in control, and they're a real death-or-glory bunch.' He threw himself wearily down into an armchair, feeling suddenly tired despite the earliness of the hour. 'So now it's the Philippines, Malaya, Singapore and all the rest all over again.' The names rolled through his memory; Corregidor, Bataan, Guadalcanal, Kwajalein, Guam, Iwo Jima, Okinawa. Ferocious battles against the most fearless and tenacious of enemies.

Charles studied his cigarette with unusual care. 'There is a good chance that the Americans will be better prepared this time.'

Don cocked an eye at him. 'Let me guess – the "special relationship" is it?'

'You could say that our leader was in a state of nervous excitement at Placentia Bay. He would have loved to tell Roosevelt all about you, of course, but was scared stiff that too much honesty about the battles ahead might have tipped the Americans towards negotiating with the Japanese instead of fighting them. It was no accident that you were left behind. Just the same, I'm willing to bet that the US received the benefit of some unusually accurate "intelligence reports".'

Don frowned. 'I rather hope they have. Far too many lives were lost because the Allies underestimated the Japs.' He winced as he remembered the racist rhetoric in British newspapers, whose editors were evidently convinced that the Japanese were inferior specimens of humanity, with particularly poor eyesight due to a lack of vitamin C, and with an industry incapable of doing more than produce inferior copies of western equipment.

Charles sighed. 'I wonder how Geoffrey and Peter are doing? I gather Geoffrey flew up to north Malaya and hasn't been seen since. Everything's in a state of confusion up there.'

'It's Peter I feel sorry for. We gave him a hell of a job.'

Dunning shrugged. 'It had to be done, and he was the only one to do it.'

His pass eventually accepted by the jumpy guards, Peter Morgan walked through the naval base towards the South-East Loch. There was surprisingly little damage and the all-important tank farm he had passed, holding fuel supplies for the fleet, was intact. The dockyards were jammed with ships showing varying signs of damage and the teeming activity around the base reminded him of a giant anthill.

From the quayside next to the *USS Pennsylvania*, which had survived virtually intact, he looked across to Ford Island, where the other battleships had been moored. As the reports had indicated, the capital ships had taken the worst of the pounding. The nearest one, which he had been told was the *California*, was low in the water and listing. Smoke was rising from some of the more distant ships, moored in three pairs, but although they had all suffered some damage only two were dockyard cases. The other four could sail and fight.

Morgan surveyed the scene with mixed feelings. There had been several hundred American casualties – here, at the airfields and among the fighter pilots – but this was far fewer than he had feared. There had been just enough time for the American defences to mobilise and disrupt the first attack.

The second wave of Japanese planes, arriving an hour later, had been decimated by the raging USAAF fighter pilots before they could reach Pearl Harbor, where the survivors were met by a concentrated barrage of fire. Little damage had been done, and there had been no third wave. The remains of scores of Japanese aircraft littered the island or lay hidden under the harbour waters. They had struck a heavy blow, but had been severely mauled in return.

'You're one of the English fliers, right?'

The voice jarred him and he cringed inwardly, bracing himself to confront the naval officer. I'm sorry, he felt like saying, I did what I had to. He stared in confusion as the American's grim, smoke-blackened face broke into a tired smile.

'Thanks,' he said simply. 'If it weren't for you guys we'd have been slaughtered in our beds. You did a great job.'

Numbly, Morgan shook the proffered hand and watched as the man walked away. The final irony, he thought. Judas becomes a hero. He walked slowly back to his temporary quarters at Hickham Field in order to complete his report for London. No doubt Churchill would be pleased.

'Gunner, fire! Reload canister!' The Captain's voice was barely audible over the hailstorm of machine-gun fire drumming against the Humber's armour. With scarcely a pause, the gun jerked backwards in its mounting, blasting hundreds of steel balls into the surrounding jungle. Taylor waited as the spent case was automatically kicked from the breech, then dragged another cartridge from the rack and slammed it into the hot gun. He swayed as the turret swivelled rapidly, co-axial Browning hammering. Another shell. And another.

Taylor was half-deafened, cramped, exhausted. The battle for Singora seemed to have been going on forever, after that reckless dash through the night, tyres slithering on the switchback mudslick that passed for a road. The Humbers had taken the lead, among them some AA versions, the deep roar of their twin Oerlikons occasionally heard as they scythed through the trees.

Following on behind were the six-wheeled APCs, each carrying a section of infantry. Still, as Taylor gathered from the brief reports he heard in his secondary role of Wireless Telegraphy Officer, the British column had hundreds of troops to fight thousands. Reinforcements were on the way as fast as the roads permitted. Meanwhile, the column had to hold on, to prevent the Japanese from securing a bridgehead.

'Dawn's breaking.' The Captain's voice was hoarse. 'Now at least we can see the little bastards coming.' There was a brief lull. 'My God, there are thousands of them!' The Captain's voice had risen sharply. Anything else he might have said was suddenly drowned out by a rippling blast of explosions which rocked the Humber, followed by a whining snarl.

'Beauforts! You beauties! The Navy's here!'

But that was only the end of the first phase.

The Captain of *HMAS Canberra* anxiously scanned the northern sky. The eight-inch gun heavy cruiser, along with her sistership *Australia* and the six-inch gun *Newcastle* and *Glasgow*, the light aircraft carriers *Manchester* and *Frobisher*, and a screen of frigates and destroyers, was heading north into dangerous waters.

Their route from Singapore had taken them around the Anamba Islands to avoid a reported minefield and they were now making a steady twenty-five knots to the area to the east of the Singora invasion beach. It was a risky gamble – Japanese submarines were known to be in the area, a naval covering force was lurking somewhere and Singora was within reach of enemy air cover – but risks had to be taken in order to prevent the Japanese from reinforcing their hard-pressed invasion force.

Far ahead, a lone Beaufort scouted for targets or enemy warships. Closer to the small fleet, two more aircraft flew anti-submarine patrol. High overhead, a quartet of Beaufighters provided top cover. Numbers were critical; the two small carriers, converted from cruiser hulls, could only carry a couple of dozen aircraft each, only half of which were fighters.

The Captain lowered his binoculars, feeling a little self-conscious. He was fully aware that the airborne radar of the Beaufort, and then his ship's on-board systems, would pick up any danger long before the human eye. Furthermore, the low cloud, rain showers and misty conditions that were helping to conceal them from prying eyes also blocked his own vision. But habit was hard to break.

By the route they had taken, Singora was some 600 nautical miles – twenty-four hours steaming – from Singapore. They had left at nightfall on the 8th and it was now midday on the 9th. About six hours to go. The Captain fervently hoped that the RAAF planes at Alor Star and Kota Bharu were ready to support them. He knew that the Eastern

Fleet, separated from him by the Malayan Peninsula, had left the area and was steaming rapidly southwards towards Singapore. Reinforcements from that quarter would arrive far too late.

The commander of the Imperial Japanese Navy submarine I-57 counted the ships carefully as they passed by him at extreme range. At their speed they were maintaining, together with their frequent changes of course, he reluctantly estimated that a torpedo attack was unlikely to be favoured with success. However, that was not, in any case, the main reason for his presence. With equal care, he composed his message.

'Urgent signal from the Beaufort recce plane, sir. A cluster of ships spotted on radar two hundred miles north, heading two-forty degrees. It must be the second wave of transports!'

'Very well. Steer three-forty degrees and maintain speed. Let's hope they haven't spotted the plane. I want to catch this lot napping.'

Assuming that the invasion fleet was travelling at 12 knots, the ships' courses were converging at a combined true figure of over 30 knots. Less than seven hours to contact; it would be dark when action was joined.

The Aichi E13A seaplane skimmed the surface of the sea at 120 knots, keeping below the clouds and, did the crew but know it, below the searching radar beams. The plane had been out for six hours already and would soon need to turn back to find the parent cruiser, a part of the screening force under Rear-Admiral Kurita.

A shout from the pilot jolted his two crew-members into full alertness, and they spotted the tell-tale wake of a big ship as the floatplane swept past. The pilot banked the Aichi round to follow up the track, while the radio operator prepared to make contact.

The Beaufort's radar operator cursed as the image in the cathode ray tube flickered and died. They were meant to remain on station a hundred and fifty miles ahead of the British fleet for several more hours, and the shortage of planes was such that a replacement flight would not be ready for some time.

After a brief, agonised discussion among the crew, the reconnaissance plane dropped to a lower altitude and started a visual search pattern.

The mixed force of Mitsubishi G3M and G4M bombers from the Genzan, Kanoya and Mihoro Air Corps Attack Groups had taken off from Saigon and Tu Duam airfields in the cloud and rain of the early afternoon. The message relayed from the floatplane had led to an adjustment in the course but much anxiety as to whether or not they would be able to find the reported British fleet. As evening approached, the skies began to clear and excitement aboard the planes rose sharply. Surely it would not be long before they found their targets!

'Action Stations – Repel Aircraft.' The bugle call echoed over the tannoy systems throughout the fleet as the radar reports came in. The carriers immediately changed course and increased speed, ready to launch aircraft. The first four Beaufighters were already warming up, ready to support the combat air patrol cruising at 15,000 feet, while the sweating deck crews heaved more fighters into position or stood ready to pull them off the lifts as they emerged.

The first attack wave consisted of over thirty of the older G3Ms, lining up a high-level bombing run from 10,000 feet. They never saw the first Beaufighters until they stooped like hawks, cannon hammering. The Mitsubishis had tremendous range, gained in part by savings on armour plate. The Hispanos' high-explosive and incendiary 20 mm shells glaringly revealed the downside of that particular compromise as the leading bombers exploded and burned.

By now, nearly all of the defending fighters had been launched but most were still climbing at full throttle. The battle that followed was a running one, each flight of Beaufighters attacking in turn as they reached the rapidly disintegrating bomber formation.

Twenty minutes later, the fighters broke off their attack as the remaining handful of bombers reached the fleet. The 4.7 inch guns of the frigates opened fire at 15,000 yards. The Japanese high level bombing attack required aircraft to cluster in close formation, flying straight and level before dropping their bombs simultaneously on a signal of the leader. This also made them beautiful targets for the naval AA gunners. No ships were hit and very few aircraft survived. The Beaufighters were pursuing the remnant of the Japanese force when the fifty low-level torpedo bombers arrived.

The *Canberra*'s captain watched the Mitsubishis closing in with mounting anxiety. He was well aware that a prewar study had revealed that the success rate for airborne torpedo attacks was only ten percent at 1,250 yards but increased to fifty percent at 750 yards and an alarming eighty-five percent at 600 yards. The aircraft had to be stopped at maximum range.

The cruiser held steady as the Mitsubishis approached at 100 feet, scarcely troubled by the few fighters able to reach them in time. Five thousand yards, four thousand, three.

'Now we'll see if it really works,' the Captain muttered. The big Australian cruisers had just emerged from a controversial refit which had seen all of their old 4 inch secondary armament stripped out and replaced by the new water-cooled 57 mm Bofors guns in eight stabilised twin mountings.

The starboard battery opened fire as one, the combined rate of fire of sixteen rounds per second creating a massive roar of sound. The sky filled with smoke trails as the day-tracers ignited, streaking towards the Japanese planes. The Mitsubishis wobbled perceptibly as the tracers flashed past, then one after another exploded or crashed as the six-pound shells struck home.

'The *Frobisher*'s been hit!'

The Captain swung round and cursed as he saw the old carrier swinging, slowing, listing. A column of water rose from the side as a second torpedo struck home. He knew immediately that she would never recover.

'Tell two of the destroyers to pick up survivors.' He was scarcely aware of his First Officer translating his command into specific orders. Half of his air cover was sliding beneath the waves. And they were six hundred miles from Singapore.

He became aware of cheers and cat-calls around him and turned to survey the scene. The attack was over, the remaining aircraft escaping into the gathering dusk. Reports came to him. The *Newcastle* had also been torpedoed but the much newer cruiser would survive, albeit with reduced speed. The returning Beaufighters were crowding the *Manchester*'s flight deck as they came in to refuel. Launching any aircraft from that ship would take some organising.

'Radar contact, sir. Several ships, dead ahead, range fifteen miles.'

The Captain swung round in surprise. To have arrived so soon, the Japanese ships must have been travelling much faster than he had assumed. A dreadful possibility grew in his mind.

'What speed?'

A few minutes silence as his officers calculated the rate of change of distance and bearing.

'Twenty-four knots, sir.'

The Captain cursed under his breath. Those weren't transports – they were warships. And they were hunting him.

The atmosphere in the War Room was tense with excitement. Churchill was in his element, poring over maps and charts of the Asian theatre and consulting the latest intelligence reports about naval deployments and military progress.

'So the rest of the cruiser force made it back to Singapore and has joined the Far East Fleet there. We now have the most powerful naval force in the area. The question is, how to use it to the best effect?'

The Prime Minister's first sentence had covered a minor epic, Don thought. Realising that there were no invasion ships to attack but only a large and hostile heavy cruiser force bearing down on them, the mixed British and Commonwealth fleet had turned back to Singapore. It would have been a relatively simple exercise if it were not for the torpedo damage sustained by the *Newcastle*. It would have been easier to have abandoned the vessel, but the fleet commander decided to fight for it.

The night action which followed had been intense and relentless. The Japanese ships were more powerful and numerous and were well trained in night fighting, but the British had the huge advantage of gunnery radar which enabled them to detect and hit their targets at long range. RAF Hampden torpedo bombers had also flown many sorties in support of the *Manchester*'s radar-equipped Beauforts.

The end result had been a battered but intact fleet which had eventually crawled into Singapore Naval Base on the morning of December 11th. Behind them lay a mauled Japanese cruiser force, of which two or three were believed sunk by aerial torpedoes. Losses among the British aircraft had been heavy.

'We may have kept the Japs out of Malaya, but the situation elsewhere is difficult.'

Harold Johnson's judicious words were, as usual, a model of understatement, Don reflected.

'Taylor's reports from Singora indicate that the invading force has been pushed further back into Siam, to join up with the smaller forces landed further north at several points on the Isthmus of Kra. A notional front line has been established with the Japanese defence centred on Nakhon, but the jungle means that the line gets a bit fuzzy inland. There are widespread reports of small-unit engagements across the isthmus as each side probes the other's defences, and there has been unremitting air fighting. There are some concerns about the attrition rate among our aircraft, although more supplies of Brigands are due from Australia.'

Churchill nodded. 'The Army and the RAF are doing well, although they will be further stretched if the Japanese drive west from northern Siam into Burma, as predicted. But so far the Navy has achieved little apart from the initial air attacks on the Singora invasion fleet, and the Americans are in dire trouble. We must help, especially since we must keep Roosevelt on our side in the hope that sooner or later America will be at war with Germany as well.'

Quite, thought Don. The American side of the Japanese operation was going to plan, apart from the more limited damage inflicted at Pearl Harbor. Japanese landings had already been made on some of the smaller Philippine Islands and air attacks had destroyed many American aircraft. Peter Morgan and his AEW Warwick, en route from Oahu to Singapore, had been on hand as planned to sound the alarm, so the contest had been less one-sided, with the Japanese also suffering heavy losses.

'What do you think?'

Churchill's question jolted Don out of his thoughts. 'There is no doubt that our Eastern Fleet is the biggest piece on the board at the moment. The IJN will be anxious to come to grips with it before the USN can recover from the Pearl Harbor damage. It could be a mistake to go out and fight them until we are ready to coordinate with the Americans. After all, they know exactly where we are and you can bet they'll have minefields and submarines in position to block any likely routes from Singapore. I think the main need is for aircraft to defend the Philippines and to attack the various Japanese invasion forces heading for it, or around it to Borneo and the Dutch East Indies. If the Philippines fall, the East Indies will follow and Malaya will become vulnerable again.'

Churchill gestured in exasperation. 'Aircraft, aircraft, that's always the problem. The Soviets are screaming for as many aircraft as possible, so are the Americans, yet we really need all we can make for ourselves.'

'The key to using our fleet,' Don mused, 'is to find an opportunity to strike when the Japanese will be most vulnerable – when they are about to launch another invasion.'

'Can you recall the sequence of events?'

Don shook his head regretfully. 'I wrote down all I could remember in the mid-1930s, but South-East Asia wasn't a particular specialism of mine. In any case, the changes which have already taken place will be bound to affect Japanese planning. The best approach will be to make use of our radar-equipped reconnaissance planes to cover the area and give advance warning of the next attacks. We have a squadron of Sunderlands at Singapore as well as Peter's Warwick.'

'Then we'll send some of the Sunderlands to Manila, with a couple of squadrons of Spitfires to defend the area.'

Don stirred uneasily. He well remembered the bitter arguments with Fighter Command, who had been keen to hang on to their squadrons in England, justifying their retention by sending them on largely pointless and expensive 'rhubarb' raids over occupied Europe. Four squadrons for Singapore was all the Spitfires that could be released. 'That could be leaving Singapore very exposed to daylight attack.'

'I know, but some risks have to be taken. The loss of the Philippines and the East Indies is a more immediate danger than bombing raids on Singapore. I will inform the Joint Chiefs of my decision.'

'That's more like it. A long hot soak, clean underwear and a large scotch.' Geoffrey Taylor settled luxuriously into the liberally cushioned chair with every sign of having settled in for the duration – of the bottle, at least.

'I hear you've been having some exciting times.' Peter Morgan had been considerably cheered to see his old colleague again. At last, he had someone to whom he could talk freely, who would understand the tension and the constant, underlying guilt which had racked him since Pearl Harbor.

'I thought it better to get some first-hand information about what was going on. Very difficult to form a clear view from several hundred miles away.' And it had certainly been first-hand, he thought wryly. The fluid 'front line' combined with the Japanese tactic of small-unit penetration meant that there were no safe areas anywhere near Nakhon.

He shivered briefly at a sudden, intense memory; darkness, confusion, screams and shots sending a surge of adrenaline through his sleep-befuddled mind, the weight of the Solen in his hands, the bucking, hammering recoil, the contorted Japanese faces close enough to be illuminated by the flickering muzzle flashes. He abruptly shook his head and took a large swig of scotch. 'Meanwhile you, I suppose, have just being playing the tourist in your personal chauffeur-driven transport plane.'

Morgan grinned lazily. 'Something like that, yes.' The Warwick had been on duty whenever the weather permitted, ranging far across the South China Sea towards Borneo, constantly watching for the movement of Japanese ships; a duty which had only recently become less hazardous with the arrival from England of some Reaper aircraft for escort duties. 'Off to Burma soon, are you?' Morgan teased.

Taylor groaned. 'Give me a break. I've had enough of jungle for the time being. Anyway, they seem to be doing well enough without me.'

This time, the British had been expecting the Japanese to thrust westwards across the Siam-Burma border and had been able to call on well-equipped troops and air cover, aided by the American Colonel Chennault's 'Flying Tigers', to repel the initial attacks. As in the Isthmus of Kra, the jungle hid a conflict mainly consisting of a continuing series of intensely bitter engagements between relatively small numbers of troops.

'At least we don't have to worry about defending Hong Kong.'

Taylor nodded. The position of the colony would clearly be hopeless once Japan entered the war, so after a brief argument with a belligerent Churchill, Don Erlang had secured agreement to withdraw all regular forces the previous November. The local defence volunteers had followed instructions and surrendered after a brief token resistance in order to minimise casualties. 'The place seems a bit emptier than I remember?' Taylor's remark was a question.

Morgan nodded, serious. 'Singapore's defences have largely been stripped to support Burma on the one hand and the Philippines on the other. There are only a few Spitfires and Mossies available on the island – as well as the carrier planes, of course; the fleet refused to give them up.'

The war of attrition was continuing in the Philippines, with General MacArthur doggedly blocking the Japanese advances, greatly helped by the influx of British and Australian air power to supplement his own depleted defences.

'I hear fleet leave has been cancelled.'

Morgan nodded, his face suddenly sombre. 'There's every indication that the Japs are going to move south. And our cryptanalysts have identified their new flagship – the *Yamato*.'

Taylor winced. They had all been warned by Don about the massive Japanese battleships under construction, which dwarfed the treaty-limited ships being built by the other naval powers. At seventy thousand tons, *Yamato* displaced twice as much as the new British battleships. Her nine eighteen-inch guns fired shells weighing nearly one and a half tons – two-thirds heavier than the British fifteen inch – out to a range of twenty-six miles. Her armour protection was equally massive. No ship was unsinkable, but the *Yamato* was by far the most formidable battleship ever built. Her sister-ship – *Musashi* – was due to be commissioned later in the year. 'Rather them than me,' he muttered, thinking of the British crews.

Morgan raised his glass. 'Amen to that,' he intoned. They continued to drink in thoughtful silence.

Yamamoto had made his decision, not without some anguish. The American carrier force still lurked intact in the Pacific, a threat to Japanese operations against Midway and other Pacific islands. However, the need to secure the East Indies, with their oil and other vital resources, was paramount; and this was being blocked by the British Eastern Fleet. The Royal Navy must be forced to come out from the protection of Singapore and fight. The Pacific would have to wait.

From the cruising Beaufort, the South China Sea stretched like a vast steel sheet, gleaming in the evening sunshine. A pattern of markings marred the smoothness, white-streaked trails running in parallel. At the head of each was what looked like a small, pointed stick. From this altitude, the massive Eastern Fleet looked insignificant indeed.

The plane lost altitude, shaping its flight to head for the boxier stick which was its home, *HMS Manchester*. As they approached, the crew began to identify the ships. The four new fleet carriers, *Illustrious*, *Invincible*, *Inflexible* and the *Ark Royal*, were in a loose group in the centre of the fleet, with the smaller *Manchester* a couple of miles ahead.

Surrounding them were the massive shapes of the battleships: the flagship *King George V*, which had given its name to the class of 'KGVs', with her sisterships *Duke of York*, *Prince of Wales* and the new *Anson*, on her first commission. Ahead of the formation came the surviving cruisers: *Canberra*, *Australia* and *Glasgow*, joined by the Dutch *De Ruyter* and *Java*. *Newcastle* was absent, still being repaired in dock. In a screen around the fleet was a circle of Dido class frigates, and further out still were the lithe, restless destroyers. All in all, the pilot of the Beaufort reflected, it was the most impressive fleet the United Kingdom and Commonwealth had sent into battle since the Great War.

Admiral Somerville did not share the Beaufort pilot's complacent pride. The fleet had successfully negotiated the minefields, albeit with the loss of a minesweeper and a destroyer, and the circling Beauforts had suppressed any enemy submarine activity, but he was well aware that the worst was yet to come.

Long-distance radar contacts made by patrolling Sunderlands had been followed up by a photo-reconnaissance plane. The sweating pilot had flown his Reaper straight over the Japanese fleet, spearing through the swarming Mitsubishis at well over 400 mph with Merlins howling and boost gauges in the red. He had been too preoccupied to notice much about the ships, but the photographs he brought back sent a chill through the intelligence officers who examined them.

'They've sent the lot,' one said, his voice an awed whisper. There were transports in plenty, clear evidence of the Japanese determination to seize the East Indies with the minimum of delay, but it was the escorting warships which drew the attention.

'Six carriers. The two big ones must be the *Kaga* and *Akagi*. The other two the new Shokako class. And two smaller ones.'

'Look at those battleships,' another said. 'Four twin turrets in close pairs; they must be *Nagato* and *Mutsu*, with sixteen-inch guns. The two with six turrets have to be the Fuso or Ise classes, with fourteen-inch. There seem to be a couple of Kongo class battlecruisers with eight fourteen-inch – X and Y turrets are widely separated – and just look at that!'

Dwarfing the other battleships, the immense shape drew them all to peer in turn through the magnifying glass. The ship's huge beam tapered to surprisingly slender fo'c'sle before swelling out again to rounded bows. The massive triple turrets were unmistakable.

'It must be the new one, the *Yamato*.'

'Yes, but look at the size!'

Somewhat to his regret, Somerville had just had time to study the photographs before the fleet left Singapore. He was left, he reflected, between the devil and the deep blue sea. He had to try to stop the invasion but he also had to try to preserve his fleet. He would do very well to achieve either. There was a strong chance that he would fail at both.

The silence in the Ops Room was sombre. Don Erlang, Charles Dunning and Harold Johnson had spent several hours together in the claustrophobic space, collating the intelligence reports of the battle as they came in. They had been obtained at some risk, Peter Morgan flying his Warwick over the South China Sea to radio the messages back to Geoffrey Taylor, who in turn sent them on to London.

'That seems to be it, then. It's all over.'

Nobody felt inclined to add to Charles's conclusion. Johnson left the room for a while, and returned clutching a bottle of gin and some glasses. He poured large measures into each and passed them round.

'To Admiral Somerville and his men. May they rest in peace.'

His companions murmured assent and drank. Don pulled the paper towards him, studied the scrawled notes. The Allied fleet's advantages had been speed and radar. They had used the latter to keep out of reach of the Japanese fleet until dark, then had raced in to launch their aircraft, following up with a flat-out charge by the gun ships while the carriers retired. The radio-controlled bombs which had done such damage at Taranto had hammered the Japanese warships and had been followed up in a coordinated attack by torpedo planes.

The first waves had been concentrated on the carriers, to put them out of action before dawn. Two had been sunk, another two badly damaged. Attention had then switched to the battleships, especially the giant flagship. Damage had been done, with one Kongo sunk and the other, plus an Ise, sent limping homewards. By then, a third of the Beauforts were lost and the pilots of the remainder were collapsing with exhaustion.

Dawn had brought the response. First, a melee of aircraft over the Allied fleet as the defending fighters fought off the vengeful Japanese aircraft from their surviving carriers. As Don had expected, the Beaufighter had proved able to handle the Mitsubishi Zero. The British aircraft's greater weight and wing loading made it less manoeuvrable but faster in the dive, while the combination of armour and 20 mm cannon had proved decisive against the unprotected Japanese planes.

Then the gun ships were within range, the British battleships engaging their opposite numbers while the smaller warships tried to slip through to get at the transports.

No quarter had been asked or given, no pause in the action through a long hot morning, the faster British ships constantly manoeuvring, covered by destroyer-laid smokescreens through which their radar-directed guns could shoot. In response the Japanese cruisers and destroyers constantly tried to close the range to launch their massive 24-inch 'Long Lance' torpedoes, which totally outclassed the Allied weapons in speed, range and destructive power. The covering British destroyers were repeatedly hit and knocked out, leaving gaps in the smoke-screen through which the skilled Japanese gun crews immediately opened fire.

Don tried to imagine what it had been like for Admiral Somerville, standing on the bridge of his flagship, perhaps seeing the rippling flash of the distant *Yamato*'s gunfire, waiting an eternity before the gathering roar signalled the arrival of the massive shells. Could he even have seen them before they struck, he wondered? Somerville must have known that the KGV's armour was not designed to resist such an assault.

Reports from British survivors had described the duel, the KGV's old guns firing quickly and accurately at the Japanese flagship, shell splashes almost hiding the towering superstructure. It seemed that it had been the *Yamato*'s fifth salvo that had finally caught the KGV and slowed her. Three full broadsides had then straddled the British flagship. When the spray settled, she was already sinking.

Then the great guns had turned onto the other British capital ships, already locked in battle with the *Nagato*, *Mutsu* and the Ise class battleships. The *Ise* had been sunk and the *Mutsu* left dead in the water, but two more British battleships had been hammered to the sea floor by a hail of sixteen- and eighteen-inch shells before the Japanese Admiral broke off the action.

At last, it had finished. Strategically, the result of the Battle of the South China Sea had been a victory for the Allies. Persistent attacks by cruisers, frigates and Beauforts had inflicted such losses on the invasion fleet that it was forced to withdraw, covered by the remaining Japanese warships, among them the *Yamato*, battered but unbeaten. The British carriers, staying well back from the action, had been spared as the Japanese concentrated their power on defending their fleet against the onslaught of the gun ships. But the cost had been appalling. Initial estimates were that at least five thousand British, Commonwealth and Dutch sailors had died. Japanese casualties had probably been five times higher, mainly among the troopships.

Johnson slowly and deliberately swigged another large gin, then began reciting the names as if in prayer, his voice shaking with weariness and emotion. 'King George the Fifth. Duke of York. Anson. Glasgow. De Ruyter. Canberra. Six frigates and at least nine destroyers, God help me but I don't yet know their names.'

The others stood silently. Outside, a winter's dawn was breaking.

# CHAPTER 8 - SECOND FRONT

**Spring 1942**

A slow churning noise disturbed the evening air, followed by the shattering roar of a high-powered aero engine. A second engine joined in, then a third and a fourth. Still more added to the cacophony, until the air itself seemed to be shaking.

After a few minutes, the huge shape of the first Manchester bomber began to move slowly from its dispersal area to the end of the runway. Don Erlang watched with mixed emotions. Excited in his childhood by the stories of epic heroism in the fight over Germany, he had carefully assembled the Airfix kits in his bedroom before recruiting his father's aid to hang them from the ceiling. The Wellington, Stirling, Halifax and Lancaster had cast shadows on his imagination for years afterwards.

Later, he had found out that it wasn't quite as simple as that. The controversy which had gathered around Bomber Command's devastating raids on civilian populations had been the subject of his doctoral thesis. He could not help reflecting on the irony of the situation. In the hope of minimising the horrors of the war to come he had used his influence to counter the ambitions of Bomber Command, to give priority to the unfashionable Coastal Command and to developing army co-operation – even more hated by an RAF which saw its future in independent action, divorced from the other services. In the meantime, he had encouraged the development of precision night bombing techniques which would allow the small force of bombers to concentrate their efforts on military and strategic targets, sparing the cities the horrors of area bombing.

Then disaster had struck. Once Churchill had decided that it was essential to Britain's survival to deflect the Luftwaffe from attacking ports and dockyards and had launched the first attack on Berlin, the war of the cities had started. Since then, the desperate plight of the Soviet Union had kept up the pressure to be seen to strike hard at Germany, to encourage the Soviets to keep on fighting.

The wind created by the dozens of propellers chilled him, and he snuggled more deeply within his greatcoat. A more urgent roar came from the first of the Manchesters, and Don watched as it slowly gathered speed. There was enough light left to reveal a shape very different from those which had hung from his ceiling. The fuselage was sleek and slender, unmarred by gun turrets, the wings narrow and long, the four highly supercharged Merlin engines tightly cowled. This was an aircraft designed to travel far, fast and high, a kind of giant Mosquito relying on speed, altitude and the cover of night to keep above the flak and avoid the attentions of the Luftwaffe.

Don thought back to the briefing he had attended as an observer. The crews had been told that the target for tonight was an armaments factory in Berlin. The name of this most distant and heavily defended of targets always had a sobering effect, according to the Intelligence officer who had chatted to him afterwards. The night sky over Germany was the scene of a constantly fluctuating battle, as first one side then the other seized the advantage. The current odds were that of the forty-eight aircraft which had taken off from this airfield, one or two would not return.

Don waited until the last of the huge machines had vanished into the gathering gloom, leaving behind the smell of engine oil and high-octane fuel. Then he slowly walked back to his car, deep in thought.

The young mother groaned in exasperation as she tugged her unwilling daughter back from the shops. It wasn't as if they were poor, but with her husband away in the army she had to be careful about money. And despite nearly three years of war, there was still plenty in the shops – enough to tempt her daughter, at any rate.

She at last returned to the small flat she rented in the city suburbs. It wasn't much, but it was adequate and it had the benefit of a large basement with room for all the residents during the occasional air raid. She dumped her shopping on the kitchen table, passing her daughter a sweet to suck. She checked her watch. Time to catch the news. She switched on the wireless and waited patiently as the set warmed up.

The news was much the same as usual. Encouraging news about the fighting, exhortations from some minister about the need for more efforts to save, to produce, to economise. Nothing of interest. She sighed and started her housework, leaving her radio on for the illusion of company it gave. She wondered if the RAF would come to Berlin, tonight.

The navigator read the battle order again, just to be sure. Unlike the early part of the War, when each aircraft had found its own way to the target, their route was carefully specified. It did not follow a straight path, but zig-zagged in order to confuse the enemy about their intended target. In addition, they had been informed of diversionary raids being mounted by other units, all designed to draw the German night-fighter force away from them. There would also be some pressurised Serrate Mosquito night-fighters accompanying them on this trip, waiting to pounce on their opposite numbers.

He knew that the timing of the raid had been carefully calculated to ensure that the ten squadrons taking part passed over the target area in quick succession. The worry was always that the bombers would collide or bomb each other, but the Operational Research boffins had assured them that the risk was much lower than that of being attacked by a night-fighter, and the denser the stream of bombers, the harder the task for the German defences.

The navigator settled back in his seat, reflecting on the dramatic changes since he had first trained in an old Whitley. On a night like this he would have been chilled to the bone in the drafty fuselage despite an immense swaddling of clothing. Then came the Mosquito, which at least was kept warm by the engine radiators, buried in the wings on each side of the cockpit. And now the Manchester.

He looked around the small, pressurised and air-conditioned compartment, kept comfortable despite flying seven and a half miles high and with the outside temperature sixty below. The crew numbered only four: the pilot, flight engineer, radio/EW systems operator and himself, the navigator/bomb aimer. As they headed into the danger zone, the flight engineer would be spending much of his time on his stomach, peering through the small ventral observation dome, straining to spot any night-fighters trying their favourite trick of slipping underneath to use the upward-firing cannon they had been warned about.

He sighed. Berlin – that was a nasty one. There was a distinct chance that either they, or another crew in the squadron, would be shot down in flames over the target. The Germans had some new night-fighters that could fly as high as they could, and even faster. It was rumoured that they had recently shot down some Mosquitoes, a remarkable achievement given the difficulty in tracking the "wooden wonder" on radar.

Still, he consoled himself, it could be worse. As usual at such moments, he thought of his brother, serving in a sloop on Atlantic convoy work. Now there was a grim task, trapped for weeks on end in a pitching, heaving hull, forever cold and wet, and waiting for the next torpedo. He reflected again on how unreal his own war seemed. Living a normal life at the base, with the local pub to visit on off-duty evenings, flying off at dusk to unload several tons of bombs over Germany, then returning to sleep the rest of the night in his own bed.

He shook his head and turned back to his charts. One hour to the target.

Back in their flat, Don poured Mary and himself a large scotch before settling down with a sigh in his armchair. 'How's she been?' he asked. Mary had insisting on returning to London as soon as Hope had been born. She appeared as cool, calm and competent as ever, but Don was still trying to get used to the idea of being a father for the first time at the age of forty-eight.

'Fine. She went to sleep an hour ago.' She took a slow sip of the drink. 'How did it go?'

'More or less as expected. We went to Bomber Command HQ first and then on to an airfield to see the crew briefed. The takeoff was impressive...' his voice trailed away.

'Penny for them?'

He shook his head as if to clear it. 'I lived with all of this for years, when I was researching my thesis. It feels peculiar, to put it mildly, to watch it in real life, and know that it is radically different because of my own contribution. Different technically, at least. I doubt that the...' he groped for a word, gesturing vaguely, 'atmosphere, the mood, is different – I think that would have been pretty much the same in my time.'

'Does that ease your mind about what's happening?'

He sighed. 'I really don't know. At least the more rapid development of the navigation aids and bombing techniques means that the planes can virtually always find their targets, and I've been able to persuade Churchill to go for specific military targets rather than just flattening cities.' He snorted. 'Not that that was easy. The belligerent old so-and-so wanted to bomb them back into the Stone Age until I pointed out that history would say very unkind things about him if he didn't show more restraint.' He settled deeper into his chair and closed his eyes. 'Not that the Germans on the receiving end are necessarily aware of the difference. Many of those military targets are surrounded by housing, such as tonight's target factory in Berlin, and all the navigation aids in the world won't stop the bombs from falling on a wide area around.' He grimaced. 'Collateral damage, they used to call it in my time.'

'Göring isn't showing such restraint,' she pointed out, 'we are still getting raided every night.'

'True enough. Although if you look at the pattern of their attacks, they're very focused on ports, dockyards and the like. My oppo will be aware that the only chance they have of defeating us is to starve us into submission. And that's still not out of the question.'

There was a gloomy pause, each thinking of the implacable struggle spread across thousands of miles of ocean. Convoys with fast escort ships and merchant aircraft carriers, supported by long range patrol aircraft and the specialised hunter-killer groups, against the elusive new electroboats firing homing and pattern-running torpedoes, aided by the very long range radar-equipped four-engined Dorniers which fed sighting reports directly to them. Very occasionally, Dornier met Warwick or Sunderland and a strange battle took place, the gunners hammering away at each other as their ponderous craft manoeuvred for advantage, rather like sailing ships in Nelson's time, Don reflected. The Battle of the Atlantic see-sawed this way and that, each side gaining a momentary advantage as some technical subtlety was fielded, only to lose it as soon as a counter was designed. So far, they were surviving.

'It seems that your "oppo" has so far succeeded in persuading Hitler not to declare war on America, despite Dönitz's best efforts.'

Don sighed. 'True, and there's nothing that Roosevelt can do about that even though he recognises that Nazism is the greater long-term danger, the American people are too outraged by Pearl Harbor to want to hear about Germany. Their fleet got some revenge, but that hasn't satisfied them.' The USN's carrier force had located the battered Japanese fleet as it returned to base after the Battle of the South China Sea and the resulting slaughter had effectively eliminated the Imperial Japanese Navy as a major threat. 'Still, at least he's stepping up the anti-submarine patrols in the Atlantic, and calling for volunteers to help us with non-combat tasks.'

A knock on the door interrupted them. 'That'll be the babysitter. You'd better get changed. We're going out to dinner tonight. Peter and Geoffrey finally made it back from the Far East and want to catch up with the news that doesn't appear in the papers.'

Don brightened. 'Great! We'll have a lot to talk about.'

The Kapitan checked the information for the umpteenth time, then gave the command: 'periscope depth'. The Type X angled gradually upwards from the depths where it had been lurking, safe from detection, for the past eighteen hours. He grasped the periscope, spun a quick circle to check for trouble, then returned to focus on the vessel heading towards them. He grunted. 'Precisely as advertised. Load torpedoes.' For this special mission, the torpedoes had been kept out of the tubes for as long as possible so they could be carefully checked over before firing. The power loading system would make short work of the task.

He looked again at the ship; a large passenger vessel, travelling alone at well over twenty knots, relying on speed for defence. Normally, this would be safe enough, but the xB-Dienst had somehow acquired key information about this particular vessel: not just details of its route and timing but also that it was carrying some valuable cargo. Perhaps there were some important people on board? The Kapitan shrugged mentally. He had been sent out for this specific mission and knew what he had to do. He settled down to concentrate on the task.

The Heinkel 219 of Nachtjagdgeschwader 3 clawed its way up into the night sky, powerful Jumo engines straining under the high boost level, wide, paddle-bladed propellers flailing to find enough grip in the thinning air. The Oberstleutnant watched the dials carefully. The aircraft had been rushed through its development as a top priority project, and as always had its fair share of teething troubles. He glanced up through the thick glazing of the pressurised cockpit; nothing was visible but a sprinkling of stars. He checked the gauges again. Boost pressure steady, oil pressure steady, temperatures steady. Of the engines, anyway, he reflected wryly. Outside, it was well below zero and dropping fast.

The Horchdienst had issued a warning of a raid tonight, and initial reports indicated that a large force of bombers was heading towards central Germany. The pilot recalled his visit to an operations bunker, a massive building with a bombproof roof five metres thick. Rows of seats, raked as if in a lecture theatre, faced the huge translucent map on which Luftwaffenhelferinen used light projectors to indicate the air situation. The chief operations officer was stationed near the rear of the stalls, the broadcast officer on his right. In front sat the fighter liaison officers who kept in telephone contact with the airfields. Things will be buzzing in there now, he thought.

Behind him, the radar operator was looking around, enjoying the few minutes of relaxation before he would have to glue his face to the screen surround, trying to follow the elusive, flickering contacts through the haze of enemy jamming devices, gripping tightly to the set as the big Heinkel raced and slowed, climbed and dived, after their quarry. The new centimetric radar was capable of leading the night-fighter to within a few hundred metres of the target, but after that, visual contact was required for an attack. There were rumours that radar gunsights were being developed which would enable the fighters to open fire without even seeing their targets, but the Oberstleutnant would believe that when he saw it. There were even rumours of the new jet aircraft being prepared for night fighting, but for now day fighters had priority.

At least they were well equipped to deal with the British bombers, the pilot thought with grim satisfaction. Nestling in the belly of the plane was a pair of the massive new high-velocity Rheinmetall-Borsig MK 103 cannon, each capable of firing seven of the big three-centimetre rounds per second. These guns could outrange any conceivable defensive armament a bomber could carry and just a few hits would bring down the target. Behind the radar operator was a pair of the compact, fast-firing, low-velocity three centimetre MK 108s from the same maker, angled to fire upwards at fifty-five degrees in the 'Schräge Musik' installation, with an extra gunsight in the cockpit roof for aiming them. The 'Schräge Musik' was particularly effective, partly because the bombers offered a bigger target from below and were usually more visible as they were silhouetted against the stars, and partly because the night-fighters themselves were much less visible, lost against the dark ground.

The pilot looked again at the altimeter. Past ten thousand metres, and still climbing. They would need another two thousand to reach the usual altitude of their high-flying targets. He settled back to wait.

Geoffrey Taylor sighed appreciatively as he settled back to enjoy the precious brandy. 'Now that was a much better meal then I expected. What's all this talk of shortages and hardship, then?'

'Oh, that's real enough,' countered Mary. 'We are privileged to enjoy some luxuries, but you go out to see what ordinary people eat and you'll soon see what the problem is. How would you like a dinner of reconstituted dried egg powder, alternating with Spam and, for a special treat, some whale meat? Then of course, there are sausages – but it's best not enquire what's in them – and cheese; the ration is all of two ounces a week, the same as for tea. Most luxuries are just unobtainable. I heard of someone who was given a banana by an American the other week. She was so delighted she gave it to her child as a special treat. The trouble was, the child had never seen one before and tried to eat the lot, skin and all!'

Once the laughter had subsided, Peter Morgan put his glass down carefully. 'Well then, Don, what happens next?'

Don looked around the table at his friends, all together again for the first time in months. Peter Morgan and Geoffrey Taylor, both still tanned from their stints in the Far East, were in other ways as contrasting as ever. The RAF man was still slim and boyish but with grey appearing in his fair hair and lines of strain on his face. Geoffrey's powerful figure had thickened but his brown moustache still bristled as he puffed at his pipe ('I know, I know,' he had responded to Don's dire warnings, 'but when you consider all the other ways I'm likely to die in the near future, smoking is a minor threat'). Harold Johnson had thawed in the couple of years since joining the group but was still quiet and reflective, his underlying intensity only apparent at times of stress. Charles and Mary appeared least changed, he thought, Charles as ever looking so ordinary as to be anonymous, only careful study revealing the watchful intelligence in his brown eyes.

'Well, let's recap. Russia is somehow still fighting on despite being driven far to the east'– 'not surprising when you consider the alternative', muttered Geoffrey – 'and we've managed to keep Finland out of the fighting by threatening to attack them from Norway. This has helped keep Murmansk and Archangel available, despite the best efforts of the Germans to isolate them – of course the Russian defence has been helped by the winter and by support from some of our forces – which is just as well as the convoys from our ports and from America, via the North Cape or Vladivostok, are basically what's keeping the Russians going.' Don paused, his demeanour taking on what his friends privately called his 'professor' look, and sipped some more brandy. 'We're sending them the best equipment we can: the latest versions of the Brigands and Herefords, the new Churchill tank with the seventeen-pounder high-velocity gun and so on. As long as they can hang on, we can retain the initiative because Hitler will have no time or resources for any other adventures. So the ball is in our court; what do we do next?' He looked enquiringly around the table.

'Do what we did in your time,' offered Harold, 'launch an invasion of Italy from North Africa.'

Don grimaced. 'That's Churchill's favourite theme. Partly because he's obsessed with achieving something worthwhile in the Mediterranean, partly because he's worried about the risk of an invasion of France and determined to avoid the sort of losses we suffered on the Western Front in the last war.'

That seems a reasonable concern to me,' commented Geoffrey, 'and assuming that we somehow manage to get the Americans on board at some point, an assault in the Mediterranean would have the advantage of giving their green troops some battle experience before throwing them across the Channel. So why not plan for that?'

'Let me guess,' said Peter with a small smile. 'Avoiding a diversion of effort, is that it?'

Don nodded. 'Partly. The fighting in Italy absorbed a tremendous amount of resources and dragged on for years.'

'But the Schwerpunkt theory only holds true if you are able to concentrate your forces,' argued Charles. 'While the Battle of the Atlantic is still undecided there is a practical limit to the forces which can be gathered and sustained in Britain. We need almost all of the shipping capacity just to keep the country going. There's also a limit to the effort we can make in the Far East, simply because of the distances involved and the amount of shipping that it would tie up. So we might as well deploy the surplus elsewhere, where they can do some damage to our enemies and distract Hitler from his assault on Russia.'

'What are our other options?' Mary asked. 'It seems to me that either we just sit tight and rely on bombing or we divert more forces to Russia to engage the Germans directly. With Norway in our hands, the journey isn't as hazardous as the terrible Arctic convoys Don's told us about and they would arrive at a friendly port and not have to fight their way ashore.'

'Whatever we do, we're faced with the logistics problem,' Don said. 'The sea lanes are like pipes which limit the flow of men and material along them, the size of the pipe depending on the shipping available – and of course the efforts of the Germans in blocking the pipe. Fighting a campaign anywhere in the world means not just delivering masses of men and equipment but being prepared to keep them supplied indefinitely. That takes such a huge shipping effort that we have to judge very carefully how we can make best use of the resources. Unfortunately, there is no simple right answer.'

'It seems fairly obvious to me,' declared Peter. 'We have the means in Bomber Command to bring the war home to Germany in a way that nothing else can. We can really hurt them directly, and they have to divert fighter squadrons from Russia to counter our bombers, not to mention all the effort they are having to put into flak batteries and the like. And we can do this at a risk and cost which is very low in comparison with an invasion.'

'But that kills innocent civilians, women and children,' Mary objected. 'How can that be justified?'

'That isn't the main purpose, but in any case, are there any such things as non-combatants when a whole nation is at war?' countered

Peter. 'The work those civilians are doing is supporting the war economy which is keeping Germany fighting. Drive them out of the cities through the fear of bombing and you badly damage Germany's war effort.'

Don nodded. 'I don't like it either, but that's the argument that's won the day so far. For the time being, at least, bombing it will be.'

'Alles nach Bär! Alles nach Bär!' The urgent voice of the fighter controller crackled in the headphones. The Oberstleutnant acknowledged briefly and banked the big Heinkel onto a new course. 'It's Berlin,' he told his crewman. He thought back to the control centre again, where the staff would have at last sorted out the main raid from the various decoys which had been dropping Düppel to confuse the big Freya surveillance radars. The local fighter control would now be taking over, the Fighter Control Officer hunched over the horizontal glass-topped Seeburg table, on which the locations of various radar targets were indicated with points of light. The radars were accurate enough to guide the Nachtjägers to within three hundred metres of the target, well within the range of their on-board detection systems.

The voices of other pilots came thick and fast over the Reichsjägerwelle, the fighter broadcast frequency, as their pilots all set course for the capital. The hunt was on!

The Flight Lieutenant in the Pathfinder Mosquito was concerned. The preceding weather plane had warned of continuous cloud cover over Berlin; the bombers would not be able to see the target. The Pathfinders would have to use sky markers to indicate the target to the following bombers, and that was never as accurate.

He ran through the figures in his head. The Mosquito was equipped with a comprehensive array of navigational aids as well as the big Target Indicator flare which occupied the remainder of the bomb bay. The Oboe radio navigation system was the most precise of them, able to locate them to an accuracy of 150 yards which was plenty good enough for blind bombing. Unfortunately it had a maximum range of 250 miles from Britain at a height of 30,000 ft, which was not good enough to reach Berlin. On a trip like this, it could only be used as an aid to dropping route-marking flares, which would reassure the following bomber stream that they were on course. In theory, they all had their own navigation aids but the electronic devices were notoriously unreliable.

Gee was the other radio navigation system carried by the Pathfinders. It had a much longer range, at least in theory, and a transmitter in Norway helped to extend the system, but the accuracy of only 6 miles was not good enough for blind bombing. In any case the Heinrich jamming stations were powerful enough to swamp the Gee transmissions as they approached Germany, so it was of limited use.

The final aid was the new lightweight H2S ground-mapping radar set, which had only recently been miniaturised sufficiently to be carried by the Mosquito. This was also carried by many of the bombers, but Berlin was a notoriously difficult radar target; it was just too big and dispersed. Even when the aid worked properly, the available accuracy was only to within one or two miles, not good enough to hit the target factory. They would have to go down and find it the hard way. He glanced at the navigator, squashed into the cramped seat beside him, studying the radar image.

'How far are we from the target?'

'About ten miles.'

'Stand by to drop Target Indicator.'

'Standing by.'

'We must concentrate our efforts in both production and organisation. Otherwise we will never have the resources we need.' Speer was being as firm as ever, relentlessly drilling home his main theme, but Herrman was not sure he would succeed this time.

'But, my Führer,' reasoned Himmler, 'it really is better to allow privately-owned industries to manage their own affairs. Everyone knows that management by government is inherently inefficient.'

Just as almost everybody knows, thought Herrman, that Himmler was trying to ensure that the SS took over as many key industries as possible in order to give themselves a private source of supply, away from the interference of the government. In this argument he had the acquiescence of the other Nazi warlords, who were all competing to extend their power bases by controlling as much of the economy as possible. Speer had an uphill task ahead of him.

'I'm not talking about trying to manage the businesses. I'm talking about coordinating their efforts in order to ensure that the right materials are being produced in the right quantities. To achieve that, we must obtain central planning control while decentralising management responsibility.' Speer leaned forward, trying to communicate his vision. 'If we establish a Main Committee for each type of production – for example weapons – and Main Rings of factories concerned with the appropriate raw materials and intermediate products, such as alloy steels, we can ensure a continuity of planning from iron ore to gun.'

Göring, who for once had joined forces with Himmler in an attempt to stave off the threat from Speer, took a different tack. 'Who will decide what is made? Who will control development and production? That is the responsibility of the individual services who must know what is best for their needs.'

'The problem with the present system is that the services state their needs without any interest in, or knowledge of, how they may be met. They might ask for things which are simply impossible to make. Under my system, the Wehrmacht will still formulate their requirements and be responsible for approving the finished product, but the development and production will be the responsibility of industry, in consultation with the military of course.'

Himmler returned to the attack. 'And how exactly would this centralised organisation cope with the sort of bombing raids our industry is facing now?'

Göring stirred, uncomfortable with this line of argument. The failure of his beloved Luftwaffe to live up to his prewar boasts that no enemy bombs would fall on Germany was a sore point.

'We will decentralise production as well as management. Manufacture elements of a weapon in many different places and only bring them together for final assembly. We are already doing this with the new submarines; it minimises the amount of time they spend in the dockyards, vulnerable to bombing.'

'But that would only make your system vulnerable to disruptions in the transport network. Hit the railways and it all grinds to a halt.'

Göring interrupted, steering the discussion onto safer ground. 'But what about our people? If all of our efforts are concentrated on producing munitions, what will be for sale in the shops? What kind of life will our women and children have?'

A lot better than they would get if Stalin's armies roll through Germany again, thought Herrman, but he knew better than to take on Göring and Himmler, who then produced his trump card. 'Why, our friend here would have our womenfolk working in factories instead of looking after their husbands and children!'

Hitler's emphasis on preserving normal family life was well known. Up to now he had listened to the arguments in silence, but he suddenly turned to Herrman. 'What does my policy adviser think of all this?'

Herrman felt his heart sink and his bowels clench with dread. He fought down a desperate need for a drink and tried to compose his thoughts, to walk the tightrope between letting Germany continue on its disastrous course and earning the bitter enmity of the Nazi warlords. 'Of course,' he temporised, 'the Minister of Munitions is correct that we should ensure that our war production is as efficient as possible, but we must not forget the importance of preserving family life and the well-being of our people.'

Hitler grunted in what sounded like approval, then dismissed them without giving his views. Outside, Speer hung back to talk to Herrman.

'I understand you advise our Führer about general policy. Do you think he will accept the need for the policies I described?'

Herrman was wryly amused at the opportunity to show his omniscence. 'You'll get most of it,' he predicted, 'Göring can't really be bothered with anything as mundane as industry, but you won't beat Himmler.'

Speer walked thoughtfully beside him, obviously choosing his words, unsure of Herrman's exact status and influence. 'We are beginning to get real problems with manpower. Too many Germans have been conscripted, and the impressed workers that Todt use are of relatively little value. We must mobilise our economy for all-out war, in the same way that the Russians and even the British have done.'

'Just how much damage to production are the RAF raids doing?'

Speer shrugged. 'Not as much as you might think. Machine tools are extremely hard to damage. We find factories blown apart and burnt out, but most of the machinery still intact, so we can get back to work again quite quickly. The main problem is when the workers lose their homes or are scared away. And Himmler was correct about the transport issue, of course. If the railway system is disrupted, we have real problems.'

Herrman was curious to get to know this able organiser, of whom he had read so much in his previous existence. 'Is the Luftwaffe not getting on top of the problem?'

Speer shrugged again. 'I think their priorities are wrong. Before the war they took the view that bombers could not do much damage. If they tried to fly low and straight to hit the target, the Flak would get them. If they flew higher or tried to weave to avoid the Flak, they wouldn't hit the target. Away from the target area, the fighters would get them. If they tried to bomb at night, our new Freya radars would spot them, and and Würzburg radars could control night-fighters as well as Flak.' He sighed. 'Experience has shown that it isn't as simple as that, of course. The bombers swamp our night-fighter control system by streaming through the Kammhuber Line in such concentrated formations that fighters only have time to be zeroed onto a few of them. Then there are the countermeasures to our radar which often leave us fighting blind. Also, there aren't enough fighters. For an air force, the Luftwaffe places a surprising amount of reliance on their Flak defence, in order to disrupt the bombers over the target. Yet statistics prove that night-fighters are two to three times more effective than Flak, in terms of the resources involved. Even if we had the fighters, we would have problems with finding enough pilots. Not enough are being trained, and they are not being rotated or promoted to the staff so the lessons they are learning are not being passed upwards.'

'What are the production bottlenecks you are experiencing?'

Speer sighed again. 'There is a constant competition for resources – for Flak, fighters, bombers, U-boats, tanks and radar. This leads to a shortage of some raw materials, such as aluminium and wolfram. Too much aluminium goes into Flak shell fuzes, and there is a great demand for wolfram for Hartkernmunition,' he said, referring to the tungsten-cored armour-piercing shot which had dramatically improved the performance of anti-tank guns. 'Also, it's difficult to get the production balance right between offensive and defensive weapons. Our Führer is very concerned to take the offensive at every opportunity, so he is keen on bombers and these new pilotless missiles. The problem is that each heavy bomber costs many times as much as a fighter, and the V-weapons are taking a huge development effort. Then there is radar. Our electronics resources are being focused more on radio navigation systems than radar, because they help the bombers. We're also having to make a major effort to catch up with the new centimetre-wave technology, which has real potential in guiding anti-aircraft missiles.' He turned to Herrman, clearly keen to persuade him. 'If we don't put more effort into defence, we may lose the capability to make the offensive weapons our Führer wants.'

I know, thought Herrman, I know that all too well.

'We have a Kurier for you.' The Fighter Control Officer's calm voice had an edge of triumph. The Oberstleutnant knew that the Naxos and Korfu systems used by ground stations would have been on the alert to get a bearing on any transmissions from the Rotterdamgerät (H2S) carried by the bombers. When they were close enough, his Heinkel's own Naxos-Z system would pick them up. He listened carefully to the coordinates and adjusted his course. It was probably a

Mosquito Zeremonienmeister, guiding in the other bombers. The Pathfinders were fast, but they were on a converging course, and closing in. His headphones crackled again. Berlin was covered by cloud, but it was thin enough for the Leichentuch tactic. He edged the straining Heinkel to a still greater height. They would not need to use the 'Schräge Musik' guns tonight.

Suddenly, the ground appeared to glow pale grey. The Oberstleutnant grinned wolfishly. The Leichentuch was working! The defenders of Berlin had turned their searchlights onto the base of the layer of cloud blanketing the great city, illuminating it to create a glowing background against which aircraft could easily be spotted from above; a tactic ghoulishly known to the nightfighters as the "shroud".

There! Just crossing ahead and below! The slender, fleeting shape of a Mosquito speeding on its way to the target. The Oberstleutnant threw the Heinkel into a shallow, curving dive, the note of the big twelve-cylinder Daimler-Benz DB 603 engines rising painfully up the scale as the Nachtjäger accelerated.

'Ente in sight!', he yelled.

'Machen Sie Pauke-Pauke,' the ground controller shouted. The Oberstleutnant hardly heard the excited instructions of his radar operator. He needed no such guidance now. The British plane slowly drifted across the Revi sight, slipping into the centre as the Oberstleutnant pressed the firing button. The big MK 103 cannon roared into life, the Minengeschoss shells speeding towards the target at nearly nine hundred metres per second. They carried no tracers, so as not to blind the pilot or alert the target, but the flashes of hits around the centre of the Mosquito were clearly visible. It seemed to stagger in the air, panels flying free, then suddenly a large, streamlined object fell from the British plane, plummeting down towards the glowing clouds. A second later, the Mosquito broke up, torn apart by the Heinkel's devastating firepower. There were no parachutes. As the pieces of the sleek little bomber tumbled gracelessly to Earth, the Oberstleutnant shouted in triumph to the fighter controller, then turned his aircraft back into a climb to await the arrival of the bomber stream. Below him, bright colour bloomed.

'If we do have to bomb, at least we should try to pick those targets which will do real strategic damage rather than just terrorising the population.' Mary argued.

'We do,' countered Peter, 'but they have a tendency to be surrounded by the houses of their workers. And with the best will in the world, despite all of these advanced tactics and navigational aids Don's been talking about for years, not every bomb will find its target. There will be some collateral damage.'

'What about those synthetic oil plants? They seem to have been the best targets the last time around.'

'Unfortunately those are less significant at the moment. Germany has captured extensive oil fields as a result of their successes in the east.' Charles, who had been sitting quietly in a corner of the room almost lost in a large leather armchair, made a rare contribution. Having gained their attention, he went on. 'Lord Cherwell's paper has a certain appeal to our leader.'

Don groaned. 'That man is the bugbear of my life. Lindemann is totally insufferable. Everything the critics said about him in my time has proved to be true. But try as I might, I can't prise him away from Winston. He thinks he's a wonderfully imaginative scientist, and they've known each other for a long time.'

'What paper is this?' Enquired Geoffrey.

'He has argued that Bomber Command should be obliterating cities in order to end the war by making people homeless and destroying the national morale. He has also vigorously opposed the production of long-range aircraft for Coastal Command – he wants our whole production capacity diverted to bombers. He just doesn't understand the role of our anti-submarine aircraft in defending our convoys. He thinks that just because they don't sink many submarines they're wasting their time. The fact that they keep the U-boats away from the convoys by keeping them submerged won't enter his head. Nothing enters his head except his own ideas – he doesn't recognise anyone else's.'

'You must admit he has a point, though,' observed Peter. 'In more ways than one. Thanks to your influence, Coastal Command now has as many long-range aircraft as Bomber Command, but while the bombers can demonstrate the massive damage they're inflicting on the enemy, all the maritime reconnaissance planes have to show for their efforts is a patch of oil every now and then, where a U-boat might or might not have been destroyed. That doesn't give our propagandists much to go on. Stirring battles over the Reich, now, that's much more exciting.'

'And not just for domestic morale,' commented Charles. 'We have to convince the rest of the world that we're still fighting a war. Not just the Soviets, although they need all the encouragement we can give them, but the Americans as well. They're still generally not interested in getting more involved in Europe. There's a strong isolationist streak there, and the argument about keeping American sons from dying in foreign wars has a lot of appeal. Even the ones who appreciate the need to stop the Nazis want to focus on Japan as a revenge for Pearl Harbor before they even think about the possibility of war with Germany, and that includes some of their most influential military leaders, such as Admiral King. We've got to keep the fact that we're still fighting a war in the minds of the American public, and the bombing campaign is the best way of doing it.'

'Nonetheless, sooner or later an invasion there must be,' said Don. 'Otherwise there are just two possibilities. Either Hitler completes his conquest of the Soviet Union, at which point he can invade us with overwhelming force at his leisure, or Russia survives, recovers and eventually manages to beat Germany, in which case we will be faced with an entirely communist Europe. We have to intervene at some point, and not just by sending in bombers.'

'The trick is to pick the right moment,' mused Harold. 'One which offers the least risk to our forces.'

Don grimaced. 'Not so easy. You could argue that now would be a good time, while the bulk of German forces are engaged far to the east. But without the Americans it would be very risky. Of course, if the Russians give up then an invasion becomes impossible – Hitler will be far too strong. The only chance will be if the Russians start forcing the Germans back and weakening them. In those circumstances, the longer we wait before invading, the weaker the Germans will be and the better the chance of success. But the longer we wait, the further Stalin's troops will get into Europe, and we'll end up with the Cold War all over again, only this time we might not be lucky enough to avoid a nuclear war.'

'Which does, of course, raise another option,' Charles said quietly, breaking the gloomy silence. 'With the information you were able to provide, massive resources are being put into nuclear research. According to progress reports, we should have the first atom bomb late next year. I seem to recall you saying that the USA reckoned that using the bomb to end the war in your time saved them an estimated million casualties which they otherwise would have incurred in invading Japan. The same calculation could apply in Europe.'

Don shuddered. 'I don't even like to think about that. Atom bombs dropped in Europe! That isn't what I've been struggling to achieve.'

'We might not have much option. After all, Hitler has your equivalent to advise him. Germany's research in your time was way off target. That might not be the case now. Who knows how close they are to their own atom bomb? We're doing our best to find out, but their security is tight.'

'One thing's for sure,' said Harold, 'despite all of the problems, our army and navy are steadily building up and Stalin is demanding that we find somewhere to use them in order to take the pressure off him. Churchill hates seeing them idle, as well. He thinks it suggests that we're not trying hard enough. Something's going to happen, sooner or later.'

The mother listened anxiously to the news as Berlin radio gave a running commentary of the progress of the approaching British bombers. All of the most obvious targets on the coast and in the Ruhr had already been passed, and it was beginning to look as if they were heading for Berlin. Still, she consoled herself, Berlin was a huge city covering hundreds of square kilometres. It had been bombed before and she had never even been aware of it. They would probably be all right, but to be on the safe side, would spend the night in the basement. She went to look for her daughter, who she found awake in her room, peering out of the window.

Outside, the night was carved up by the probing searchlights, which cast huge circles of light on the base of the clouds far above. She could see and hear nothing of any attack, but decided it was time to leave anyway. She gently took her daughter by the shoulders to pull her away from the window, looking down at her with a smile. Suddenly, her young face was illuminated by an unearthly reddish glow. 'Look, Mama!' She cried, 'the lights! Look at the Christbaüme!'

The Christmas tree, she thought numbly. Time froze. The mother looked at her daughter's radiant face then, with a tumbling fall of dread, lifted her eyes to the sky. Her breath was punched from her body in a scream of utter horror and despair, as the coloured flares of the Target Indicator fell gently to earth, all around them.

The crew of the modified Avro Manchester sat in virtual darkness relieved only by the faint glow of the instruments. They had been hard at work since crossing the coast, and the tension was palpable. They were not only defenceless, but they could not even attack. Theirs was an ECM – electronic counter-measures – plane which was packed with instruments of deceit to mislead, confuse, misdirect and jam the German defences.

Flying just ahead of the bomber stream, they had covered the approach by dropping 'Window' – strips of aluminium foil a foot long and just over half an inch wide – to blanket the defence radars. Two thousand strips were contained in a bundle and one bundle was remotely ejected from the aircraft every minute. As the bombers approached, they activated 'Carpet': an electronic jammer transmitting on the same frequency as the German radars.

Not only the radar was attacked. The 'Tinsel' device broadcast noise on the fighter control radio channels which were constantly monitored to catch shifts in frequency. As an alternative, from time to time the ECM planes carried a German-speaking crewman who tuned in to the fighter channel to mimic their broadcasts in the hope of leading the defenders astray.

Despite all of these measures, the German defences succeeded every night in locating and destroying several of their tormentors. And the favourite targets of the night-fighters seemed to be the ECM planes whose task required them to transmit at high power across many frequencies: a beacon to any defenders who could penetrate their veils of confusion and secrecy.

The Heinkel droned through the night; the Oberstleutnant's headphones and vision were alive with the confused sounds and sights of the battle: shouted commands of the FCO trying to penetrate the jamming, occasional responses from the other Nachtjäger pilots, once a flare of light a dozen kilometers away as an aircraft went down – whose he could not say.

Far below, he knew the radar operators would be struggling to defeat the jamming; picking out the aircraft at the edge of the bomber stream, coaxing the new Würz-Laus switch on the Würzburg radar to highlight the moving targets from the clouds of slowly falling Düppel.

Meanwhile, his crew had their own tasks. His radio operator muttered to himself as he struggled with the counter-measures, trying to trap and locate the transmissions from the elusive Eloka plane.

'We have another Kurier for you!' The FCO's voice broke through, gave quick directions. The Heinkel turned sharply, forcing the crew into their seats. As their speeding fighter banked steeply onto the new heading, they could see patches of brighter light glowing and fading through the Leichentuch. Bombs were falling.

'T.I. visible, straight ahead.'
'Navigator to skipper. Three minutes to go.'

'OK. Keep alert everyone.' A long period of tense silence. The voice of the replacement Master Bomber could be heard, calmly directing the incoming Manchesters, trying to minimise the 'creep-back' as the terrified bomb-aimers dropped their bombs a few seconds early in their attempt to get away as quickly as possible from the killing zone over Berlin.

'Hello bomb-aimer. Bomb doors open.'

'OK. A little to the left – steady – steady – bombs going – bombs gone.' The plane lurched upwards as ten thousand pounds of destruction plunged from the bomb bay: the drum-shaped 4,000 lb 'cookie' surrounded by a swarm of tiny incendiaries. The crew waited, the tension was almost unbearable.

'OK, photoflash gone off'. Relieved of his duty to prove that the bombs had been dropped over the target, the pilot instantly banked and accelerated the Manchester to clear the target area, to get away from the deadly, glowing clouds.

'Boozer warning!' The voice was urgent. Their electronic defences had picked up the trace of a radar pulse; they were being hunted. The crew stared frantically from every observation port, eyes straining to spot the incoming night-fighter. Above them the stars gleamed, cold and unwinking in the cold, high air. Behind and above the bomber, some of the stars flickered, briefly.

'Fighter! Dead astern, high' the observer screamed. The Manchester suddenly lurched, throwing the crew into stomach-churning chaos, as the pilot slammed the port throttles wide open and the starboard closed, kicked the rudder pedals and hauled desperately on the control column. The huge plane corkscrewed violently away, dropping like a stone, as the shadow of Death swept overhead. All throttles fully open, the bomber recovered and strained for height and distance, desperate to get away from the revealing, glowing clouds. No-one spoke for a long time.

The drone of the engines was soporific, providing almost the only sensory input as the aircraft drifted through the dark of the night. The crew struggled between trance and tension, the taste of fear like iron in their mouths. They had been cruising steadily, interminably, slowly approaching their destination. They listened to the brief exchanges on the radio as damaged bombers fought to make it back to base. The navigator sat hunched over his instruments, calculating distance to run, time to the nearest airfield.

'Damaged plane making emergency landing ahead. Airfield landing lights will be on briefly.' The pilot acknowledged the radio operator's report and maintained his course. A few minutes later, a row of dim lights gleamed ahead and to port. The pilot banked the aircraft, turning to line up with the lights. Ahead, a dark shape momentarily obscured the lights as the damaged bomber went in ahead of them. The pilot lined up carefully behind it until he could make out its shape, then flicked on the illumination to the gunsight. A moment later, the four Mauser MG 151/20 cannon in the belly of the Junkers Ju 188 roared into the night, their shells sparkling as they exploded all over the stricken Manchester. The bomber flew steadily for a few seconds, then fire blossomed from one of the engines. For a little longer it flew on as the Junkers hammered it, then slowly, wearily, a wing dropped and the plane gracefully slid downwards until an eruption of fire ended its fall.

The German intruder raced away from the burning wreckage, from the avenging British night-fighters who also cruised the dark like hungry predators in an endless, nerve-racking contest of electronics, skill and luck.

The fire chief gazed wearily at the rubble which filled the streets, and which was covered with a grey shroud of ash. They had been able to do nothing about the firestorm. The massive bombs dropped first had crushed the water supply to the fire hoses as well as blowing the roofs off all the buildings, opening them up for the incendiaries which followed. The intensity of the fire had sucked in air from the surrounding area at gale force, fanning the flames further. Only when there was nothing left to burn did the flames die down sufficiently for the hard-pressed fire-fighters to tackle. Now they picked their way through the ruins, peering through the gloom caused by the vast cloud of smoke hanging over the area.

One of his men called from the ruins of a nearby building. The tone of voice told him all he needed to know. He walked over resignedly. The building had once been an apartment block, but was now an empty shell.

'Down there,' the fireman said grimly, indicating some steps leading into a basement. The fire chief switched on his torch and clambered down. There was little structural damage; the building had burned but had not been hit by high explosive.

In the basement, he shone the torch over the huddled bodies. It was the usual story. The firestorm had sucked all of the oxygen out of the air, leaving its victims nothing to breathe. His arm drooped, the torch beam sliding down to illuminate the face of a young woman. In her arms was the body of a young girl. He stared at them for a moment and wondered what had happened to the world. Then he turned and headed back up the stairs. There was plenty to do, in trying to help the living. There was always plenty to do.

**Summer 1942**

The Kapitan conned his Type X carefully into its assigned berth in one of the massive U-boat pens at the Lorient base. As he watched his crew and the shore party tying up the vessel, he was surprised to see a senior intelligence officer standing by the berth, evidently waiting to see him. The officer stepped on board as soon as the gangplank was in place and climbed up to the conning tower. The Kapitan briefly spoke to his crew members who promptly vacated the tower.

'You will be receiving my report shortly,' the Kapitan said with mild curiosity. 'The mission was executed as planned.'

The officer grimaced. 'Oh, yes, and don't we know it. That ship you sank was carrying nine hundred young women; American nurses who had volunteered to help care for the victims of the German bombing raids on England. Hardly any survived.'

The Kapitan was shaken. 'That's not what we were told!' He protested. 'There was supposed to be some important cargo or people on board!'

'I know, but this time the xB-Dienst got it wrong, and badly. The Americans are screaming for revenge. It's not impossible that we might end up at war with them over this.' As if on cue, the wailing sound of air-raid sirens permeated through the open gates of the pen. The gates began to close. The two men looked at each other in amazement, a single thought in their minds: an air attack, in daylight?

Konrad Herrman sat in silence, shocked by the news Stadler had just given him. 'The Americans bombed Lorient?' he asked, still trying to absorb the enormity of what had happened.

'They did indeed. It seems that they flew three squadrons of B-17s from America to a base in England and launched their attack from there, escorted by British long-range fighters. They didn't cause much damage and they lost several planes, but that's not really the point. Dönitz threatened to resign if he couldn't take the war to the Americans, but he needn't have bothered; Hitler was as furious as he was. So there you have it. Despite your best efforts, Hitler has just declared war on the United States of America.'

Herrman put his head in his hands. 'Then God save us all!'

**Autumn 1942**

'Now the Americans are with us, we must invade Europe soon – otherwise it will be too late!' Harold Johnson was unusually emphatic, his face creased with intensity. 'The Russians haven't just got their backs to the wall, they're practically plastered onto it!'

'So Molotov said, with some emphasis, on his recent visit,' added Charles, 'what's more the Americans are already putting pressure onto us to do something as soon as possible; not to mention the Canadians, whose troops have been hanging around here for ages.'

'But where in Europe?' countered Geoffrey. 'The Germans are still terribly strong in France and more experienced than our troops. Even under equal conditions, a defender has a much better chance than an attacker, given the advantage of firing from cover, over known ground prepared with defensive positions, minefields and barbed wire. You need about three times as many attackers as defenders to make up for that. Then consider the disadvantage of launching a seaborne attack and keeping it supplied from the sea thereafter. We would need immense local superiority to stand any chance of survival, let alone winning.'

'There's no doubt that we have to land somewhere or the Russians are finished,' interposed Charles. 'Furthermore, since the US has launched their massive transport effort with high-speed liners, their troop levels are building up too. Everybody wants action.'

'But to launch an invasion which failed would be worse than not trying at all. Far better to knock off some of the softer targets first, like Italy or even southern France. That would give us the opportunity to practise our landing techniques and give the unseasoned American troops a taste of battle.'

Don snorted. 'You've been listening to Alan Brooke. To attack away from the key objective is just a waste of resources. To land in Italy would divert so many landing craft, aircraft, men and equipment that it would put back any invasion of France by a year. It would also allow the Germans to study our techniques and tailor their defences accordingly. And it wouldn't be any soft touch, either; nobody is better than the German soldier in mounting a dogged defence against the odds, and the mountainous terrain of Italy would suit them perfectly.

Sooner or later, everyone knows that we will have to land in northern France. The only question is when; it mustn't be too soon – we must be well prepared for it – but there shouldn't be any undue delay either.'

Peter Morgan frowned. 'There's still a lot to be done to wear them down with our bombing attacks. They're showing no signs of weakening yet.'

'Nor will they. You're forgetting what I told you years ago. You can't bomb people into submission. Thank God I managed to keep Harris out of the Bomber Command job, otherwise the task of refocusing them onto strategic targets would have been that much harder. All you RAF types want to do is prove that you can win the war on your own. Well, you can't.'

'We could if we had the atomic bomb,' Peter remarked softly.

Don groaned. 'God help us all if that is ever used.'

'Getting a bit religious, aren't we?' Mary teased lightly. 'The last I heard, we were some way off that.'

'What, the bomb or religion?' Charles sardonic, as usual.

'Let's look at this objectively,' argued Don. 'At the moment the Wehrmacht is at full stretch fighting in Russia. The lines of supply from Germany are so long that it takes a major effort just to keep them going. What's more, partisan resistance activity is so vigorous along much of the lines that a whole army is being tied up in protecting them. Trying to shift any substantial portion of their army back to France would pose immense logistical problems. And we know that if they tried that, the Russians would counter-attack in support of our landing, helping to pin the German troops in the East. Despite their commitments in the East, the Germans assume that we will invade at some point, but they're probably still expecting 1944. If we attack in 1943, we'll catch them with their defences unprepared.'

Geoffrey looked dubious. 'Maybe. But their armoured strength is essentially unbeaten. Furthermore, they have a habit of returning armoured divisions to France for rest, re-equipment and training. Granted that most of their occupation troops are second rate, they still have some extremely dangerous units amongst them. And consider the problem from our viewpoint. We still have limited shipping capacity for landing troops and equipment on the beach – the main constraint – and the US troops in particular are very green, with no combat experience. It would be a terrible risk.'

Don was adamant. 'For the Russians to lose, and leave us and the Norwegians isolated in Europe, would be an even bigger risk. The size of the forces we are talking about in the West are a small fraction of those engaged in the East. With Russia beaten, Hitler would be able to turn his full force against us. We must stop that from happening, at almost any cost.'

'The main problem wouldn't be landing as such. We can pick our spot, with the advantage of surprise, and will almost certainly get ashore. The problem will be staying there once the Germans get their counter-attacks organised. We will need to maintain a massive supply effort across the Channel just to keep the army supplied.'

'I wouldn't take the landing quite so much for granted.' Don was in lecture mode again. 'Don't forget what was learned in my time…'

Howard grinned. 'We know. Accurate intelligence; realistic training; advanced saturation bombing of transport nodes and troop concentrations; intensive naval bombardment in support of the landings; air superiority maintained over the battlefield; tanks to support the first wave of troops; and the need to land away from harbours, which will be too well defended.' This was variously greeted with laughs, cheers and applause, and Don grinned wryly. 'Well, I'm glad someone's been listening. Let's hope the planners have as well.'

Charles sighed. 'Well, we'll soon find out. Churchill will be meeting Roosevelt soon.'

Don looked up, interested. 'Oh? Where?'

'Anywhere but Casablanca!' They all groaned. 'One of these days,' said Geoffrey, 'we'll do exactly what was done before; then that will really fool them!'

Mary was pensive. 'What decisions are they likely to take?'

'Depends who they choose to listen to. My betting is on an invasion in the later spring or early summer of next year.'

'Several months away. In that case, we'll just have to hope that the Russians can hold out until we land.'

Peter grinned wryly. 'If not, it won't be for want of trying.'

'Target zone in sight. Lots of smoke about. We'll approach from upwind – it'll give us a better chance of seeing what we're shooting at. Keep a sharp eye out for bogeys.'

The Flight Sergeant acknowledged his Squadron Leader and banked his aircraft to follow the rest of the formation. The big Herefords skimmed low over the flat north Russian plain, the gleam of the Severnaya River was visible to port. Above them cruised the protective umbrella of Brigands. Ahead of them, battle raged.

His headphones crackled with a three-way conversation between his Squadron Leader, the observer in the little Auster flitting above the scene, and the Forward Air Controller in the thick of the fighting. The Canadian armoured unit had disembarked at Archangelsk only three weeks before and had immediately been rushed to the front to block the Wehrmacht's determined thrust northwards. If the Germans succeeded in their aim to cut the Allied supply line before the harsh winter set in, resistance in this area would almost certainly collapse.

'Red flares going up mark our front line. Attack the formations due south. One pass with rockets. Circle to starboard. Repeat with guns, as often as you can.'

The squadron acknowledged and settled into their attack run, spreading slightly as each pilot selected his target. The Flight Sergeant checked the armament selector switch, adjusted the reflector sight and armed the guns. He eased the throttles open, the sound of the twin Hercules engines rising to a howl as the speed built up. The view to either side of straight ahead was a blur; directly in front of him the unmistakable shapes of armoured vehicles and running men suddenly snapped into focus. He thumbed the firing switch and a salvo of sixteen rockets flowed in a rapid stream from the underwing launchers. He hauled the Hereford up and to the right as the ground in front of him erupted in smoke and flame. The shape of a tank turret suddenly emerged, somersaulting slowly as it flew through the air. Then he was clear and circling round, memorising where other tanks had been, watching out for the other aircraft in his formation. He flicked the armament switch and settled down to the second run, aiming a short distance from his previous target. More movement ahead as men ran for cover. He thumbed the firing button and the six Vickers-Brownings blared, their tracer bullets walking across a field towards the enemy. Just before they reached the tanks, he pressed the second button and the plane shook at the deep hammering of the twin 40 mm cannon, lightweight Bofors guns firing super-velocity, tungsten-cored ammunition. The tracers streaked towards the tanks, the flash of impact clearly visible. He dragged the plane round again and felt it judder. Flak! He scarcely noticed the roar of his dorsal turret gunner returning fire as he kicked the rudder controls and pulled the Hereford into a violent corkscrew, going right to the deck to escape the gunners. Suddenly he was clear, skimming the ground, no sign of battle. Instruments looked OK, controls felt OK. He had a brief word with his gunner then returned to the fray. His CO had left him in no doubt: the Germans had to be stopped.

The Meteor engine roared as the massive Churchill tank lumbered forwards, the squealing tracks crushing the concealing undergrowth with the weight of forty tons. The long barrel of the high-velocity, seventeen-pounder gun quested as if sniffing the air for a scent of the enemy. The tank crawled slowly past a wrecked Humber, the crater of a hollow-charge warhead clearly visible on the side of the turret.

The Sergeant peered through the episcopes which gave him a restricted view all round the Churchill. He hated fighting 'buttoned down', but the German snipers were too close and very good, as several of his fellow commanders could have testified had they still been able to. He strained his eyes to see ahead, perversely cursing the dust and smoke thrown up by the Herefords' devastating attack. Movement caught his eye two hundred yards away and his gunner was firing the co-ax Browning even as he gave the order.

'Load HE!' He heard the clang as the long round was slammed into the breech. 'Fire!' The tank rocked as the main armament fired, a concussion of sound which was felt rather than heard. At that range the trajectory was flat, the explosion of the shell almost instantaneous. The Sergeant paused, waiting. Nothing moved. He flicked the transmit switch on the R/T, spoke briefly to his troop commander.

A few minutes later he noticed stealthy movement around him as the infantry moved forward with bayonets fixed to their Besals, the 'winklepickers' whose job it was to seek out any lurking Panzerfaust men, to protect the precious tanks just as the tanks protected the infantry when the enemy armour rolled.

Later still the Churchill grumbled forwards again, a massive, sleek shadow in the haze, tracks crumbling the burnt earth as the tank manoeuvred through the blackened ruins.

'Götterdämmerung,' muttered the Sergeant, who in a previous existence had enjoyed more intellectual pursuits.

'What was that, Sarge?'

'Never mind,' he said drily, 'just swearing.' As the tank rumbled on, he surveyed the devastated landscape, strewn with the wreckage of the German Panzer Regiment. This time they had been lucky. Next time, the Luftwaffe might be there first.

The Intelligence Corps Captain walked beside the Wing Commander as they inspected the aircraft. Many of the Herefords bore the scars of small-arms fire, of no great consequence given their comprehensive armouring. The large hole in the tail fin of one of them was a different matter.

'Looks like the work of the new thirty millimetre flak gun,' the Captain commented. 'Uses the same weapon as the MK one-oh-three aircraft cannon, in a powered twin mounting. Total rate of fire of over eight hundred rounds per minute. Not nice.'

The Wing Commander grunted sourly. Three of his aircraft had failed to return from the last mission. Ground fire around the German units was intense and a new danger was emerging. 'The Brigand pilots reported mixing it with some of those new jets we were warned about.'

The Captain looked up in interest. 'Really? How did they get on?'

'The survivors did quite well. Kept low and kept turning. Gave the jets the least chance to use their superior speed. One of them even claimed a possible.'

'The survivors?'

'Four of them didn't make it back.'

The Captain whistled thoughtfully.

The Wing Commander continued. 'The Focke-Wulf 190s aren't too bad: the Brigand is a close match for them. These new jets need dealing with in a different way.

The Captain nodded. 'We have some ideas about that.' He nodded at the sleek form of a Reaper parked under camouflage netting to one side of the airfield. 'Those PR boys have located their base. Not too difficult, they need better runways than the prop jobs, and the jet exhausts leave scorch marks. These jets are very vulnerable on take off and landing; their only real asset is top speed. We're organising a little surprise for them the next time they prepare for a mission. Some fighter Reapers will be waiting for them, right over their airfield.'

The Wing Commander smiled grimly. 'That will be much appreciated. How's the ground fighting going?'

'We're holding them, just about. We have one Canadian and two British armoured divisions in place now with more on the way. Only just in time. The Russians really didn't want to accept our help – they just wanted us to send them the equipment. The fact that they agreed at last shows the desperate straits Stalin is in. It isn't a comfortable thought, but what happens here could well decide the outcome of the whole war.'

**Winter 1942-43**

'Sorry I'm late, had a last minute briefing.' Charles took off his coat, shaking off the snow which had been falling all morning, swirling in the fitful wind around the grey canyons of Whitehall. He rubbed his hands together, eyes briefly scanning the room until they located the refreshments. 'Any tea left? It's a little fresh out there.'

'Tell all,' commanded Mary as she poured a cup, 'how went the summit?'

Charles prolonged the moment while he savoured the tea, warming his hands on the cup while he mischievously enjoying their impatient curiosity. He seemed in an unusually good mood. 'Most interesting, I gather. Much of it consisted of a battle between the military men, but it wasn't just us and them – there was some infighting among the Americans.' He settled down into a chair next to the clanking radiator. 'It went pretty much as Don predicted: Admiral King and General MacArthur wanted to focus on Japan, but if it had to be Europe, their navy preferred the Med. Spaatz was there for their Air Force; he didn't think any invasion was necessary – just more bombing. But General Marshall was worried about US forces being 'locked up' in the Med if Germany marched through Spain to seize Gibraltar, so he favoured a landing in Northern France. And, what's more, he was supported by Roosevelt.'

'Did Brooke behave himself?' Don's expression was wry. The Chief of the Imperial General Staff's aversion to the gamble of a cross-Channel invasion was well-known.

'Pretty well. Churchill is still emotionally attached to Mediterranean adventures, but he's taken on board your lessons, however reluctantly. He's also genuinely alarmed that Russia might fold at any moment. God only knows how they've managed to hang on for so long.'

'So, what do we have to deal with then?'

Charles grinned at Mary. 'Quite a detailed programme, actually. Winnie wants us to slog through it, then he'll join us this evening for a full discussion.' Mock groans echoed round the room.

'Not another all-nighter!' They settled down to listen.

Hours later, Churchill arrived in his usual expansive mood and settled in his chair, accompanied by his post-prandial brandy and cigar. 'Very well then, give me your summary!'

Don cleared his throat and commenced. 'First and foremost, the logistics issue. The primary concern is the impact of the U-boats on trans-Atlantic shipping. We need about thirty million tons of cargo to arrive in Britain each year just to keep us going. We also need to ensure that we, or rather the Americans, are building more merchant ships than we are losing. On top of that, we need considerable extra capacity to bring over all the equipment and supplies needed by the American element of the invasion force. Until the past few months, we have only just about been breaking even. More recently, we have begun to edge ahead of the game. We have virtually continuous air patrols over the convoys, except in the very worst weather, long-range patrol planes also covering the routes the U-boats take to and from France, and more destroyers assigned to form hunter-killer groups operating around the convoys. In conjunction with the new higher-frequency radar which can pick up their schnorkels, as long as the sea isn't too rough, plus better intelligence from Enigma decrypts, we are enjoying increasing success in taking out the electroboats before they can damage the convoys. That battle isn't won yet, but we can just about meet the shipping demands. 'Repeated bombing of the U-boat assembly yards in Germany is cutting down on the number of new electroboats being completed, as well,' interjected Peter, 'and so is the patrolling of the routes they have to take to get from Germany to France.'

Churchill nodded. 'And the secondary concern?'

'The number of landing craft we need to transport the invasion force to France. That's the other blockage in the pipeline. It's particularly a problem because the French beaches we're looking at have a very shallow gradient, so ordinary ships would run aground while still a long way offshore. We need plenty of vessels which can carry heavy loads while having a very shallow draft. These are now in production, and we should have enough by next summer to land five divisions in the first wave.'

'So far so good. What comes next on your list?'

'Men and equipment. We are reasonably well off for both, this time. The rapid conquest of North Africa has meant that we don't need to keep large forces tied up in the Med'. He raised his hand to forestall a comment from Churchill – 'I'll come on to that – although our success in throwing back the initial Japanese invasion of Burma and Malaya has ironically meant that we're more heavily engaged there. Still, the Aussies, Kiwis and Indians are doing much of that fighting, which takes a lot of the pressure off. More serious is the diversion of some our best armoured divisions to Russia. Still, given the limited numbers we can carry across to France, we will have enough troops and equipment for the invasion.'

Mary smothered a smile at Don's confident handling of the formidable Prime Minister. He was a very different man from the displaced and bewildered person she had met eight years before.

'Our equipment is now first rate. Of course, the German kit is better than in my time too, but we had more room for improvement. The new

Churchill Two tank, with thicker armour and the seventeen-pounder gun 'necked out' to a thirty-five pounder, is fully the match of the Panzer Four 'Panther'. The American equipment is generally OK but I'm worried about their tanks.'

Churchill nodded. 'We took the opportunity to reinforce the message about the consequences if they sent the Sherman into Northern Europe against the Panther tanks. They weren't at all happy because a heavier tank causes shipping problems, but they understood the argument that quality rather than quantity is of paramount importance, especially in an amphibious landing when quantity is so limited, so they've put a top-priority programme in place to field a new heavy tank and have reserved production of their new ninety-millimetre ack-ack gun for it.'

Don nodded. 'Good. That leaves us to consider where, when, and the diversionary programme. We've undertaken a thorough review of the landing sites, but the outcome is the same as in my time; no great surprise there, as the geography hasn't changed.'

'Go on. I'd be interested in hearing your conclusions as this was briefly discussed at the summit.'

His friends grinned surreptitiously as Don shifted even more obviously into lecturer mode and started ticking off points on his fingers.

'First, the landing zone must be within reach of fighter cover from England. This limits us to a zone between Belgium in the east and the Cotentin Peninsula in the west. It's also important to have some airfields not far away for us to seize, so we can forward-base some squadrons there as quickly as possible. Next, we must land on beaches large enough to allow the huge volume of continuous unloading which will be going on until we can seize enough port capacity – which although it's a top priority won't be easy as we know the Germans will destroy the facilities of any port they are in danger of losing. Those beaches must also be sheltered from the worst of the weather – which can be pretty savage, and was in my time – and must not be too heavily defended by overlooking gun batteries, and there must be easy ways of getting off the beaches and on to the road network. Basically, we've got to ensure that we can maintain our build-up of forces at a faster rate than the Germans can reinforce theirs.'

Peter cleared his throat. 'There's another element to that, of course. The RAF will be doing its utmost to prevent any reinforcements getting there, both by engaging them on the move with tactical units and by hitting the main transportation centres with strategic forces.'

Churchill nodded slowly. 'So the logic still takes us to Normandy, then?'

'Yes, it's not ideal but it's the best compromise. The beaches are good, Cherbourg is reasonably close and is convenient for dealing with shipping direct from America. But there's a lot of marshy ground behind some of the beaches, especially in the west, and we know that the Germans will flood the lower-lying areas. The obvious alternative is the Pas-de-Calais as it's only twenty miles or so from Dover and would provide a much more direct route into Germany, but the beaches are exposed and have few exits, it's strongly defended, and the ports in the area are inadequate. We could try the Seine area in between the Pas-de-Calais and Normandy, but it would mean clearing both banks of the river before we could use Le Havre and Rouen. This would mean a double operation, and the two halves couldn't be mutually supporting given the width of the Seine estuary. That takes us inevitably to the sector around Caen and the Cotentin Peninsula, although we would have to expand from there fairly rapidly as even Cherbourg wouldn't be enough by itself to meet our shipping needs.'

'Belgium – or Denmark even, from Norway?'

'The beaches are inadequate in Belgium and they're strongly defended. Denmark is of course an entirely new possibility to me, but I think we should include it in our diversionary programme. If the Germans are certain where we're going to land, they will, without any doubt, be able to concentrate their forces to push us back into the Channel. They have over forty divisions in France, and we can put five across in the first wave, with another five shortly afterwards. We need to sow as much uncertainty in their minds as possible, not just concerning where in Northern France we're going to land but also the prospect of landings in Southern France, Sicily, and now Denmark too. We will need to commit some quite significant resources to confusing them, including actual raids in several different locations.'

Churchill nodded soberly. 'This will be very much a throw of the dice, with a lot depending on it. From our viewpoint, it would be much better to delay the invasion until Germany has been so weakened by bombing and the battle with Russia, that there would be little opposition to a landing. Sadly, we can't afford to wait that long: Russia's situation has been critical for months, and it's touch and go whether or not they can hang on, even with the support. Even so, I'm very worried, very worried indeed, especially after your graphic description of all of the things that went wrong in your time. In this case, to try and fail would be infinitely worse than not trying.'

'We do have some ideas for reducing the problems the Allies experienced in my time, which we'll go into later.'

Churchill raised an eyebrow and enquired, with a touch of irony, 'have you decided on the date yet?'

Don wasn't falling for that one. 'Well sir, that will of course be a matter for yourself and the President. However, bearing in mind the importance of avoiding stormy weather, the need for a high tidal range to make it easier for the landing craft to get on and off the beaches, and the usefulness of a full moon to aid the night-time airborne attacks, that gives us three possible target dates: the twentieth of April, the nineteenth of May or the eighteenth of June. The first date could be too vulnerable to spring gales, the last will give us little time to expand the invasion area before the end of summer, so that leads us to the nineteenth of May next year, give or take a few days.'

Churchill nodded. 'That confirms the views of the more orthodox bodies. Now let's have another brandy and talk about these ideas you have…'

It was, indeed, a very long night.

## Spring 1943

### U.S. JOINS BATTLE OF GERMANY; NON-STOP AIR WAR PLEDGED

Don glanced at the headlines and passed over a penny for the newspaper. After almost a year of preparation, the Americans were in action at last. The picture on the front page showed a squadron of B-17s, bristling fiercely with multiple gun turrets. Much good will it do you, he thought, when the Me 262s get amongst you. At least they couldn't say they hadn't been warned. He walked on, feeling saddened.

He might have been surprised to learn that the Americans had heeded some at least of the dire warnings and predictions that the British had been so keen to make. The crews certainly felt confident enough as the huge formations gradually coalesced in the clear morning air. Each wing of fifty-four aircraft formed one immense defensive system, consisting of three eighteen-aircraft combat boxes stacked one above the other. Each box consisted of three squadrons in staggered formation. The entire battle formation was over a mile wide, half a mile deep and six hundred yards long. Any enemy fighters attempting to attack would face the concentrated fire of scores of heavy machine guns, whichever way they came. Six miles behind came the next combat wing, then the next. One hundred and sixty aircraft headed for north Germany, screened from above by an equal number of the new Merlin-engined P-51 Mustang long-range fighters and some supporting squadrons of RAF Reapers, whose apprehensive pilots in no way shared the enthusiasm of their inexperienced allies.

The B-17s bore little resemblance to the sleek Manchesters other than in the number of engines, and could not match their speed, altitude and bombload performance. But then, they were designed for a different purpose. While the British bombers fought in darkness, relying on concealment and speed for their survival, the big, tough, Boeings went in under the glare of the sun, challenging the enemy to come, returning fire with fire.

'You have to balance the rights and wrongs of the situation. So a few thousand German civilians get too close to our primary targets for their own good. What's that against the millions being slaughtered in Russia? And the millions more who'll be killed if we don't stop the Nazis as soon as possible?' Peter was defending his beloved RAF, as usual.

Inevitably, it was Mary who rose to the bait. 'Just because the Nazis are committing horrible crimes, that doesn't make it right for us to follow suit. What are we fighting this war for anyway, if not to preserve decent values?'

'Mary, if we fight this war with our gloves on when the enemy is wearing knuckledusters we're likely to lose, and that'd do far more damage to our "decent values" than anything we could think up. Besides,' added Don, looking somewhat uncomfortable to be arguing against his wife, 'it's not just good for our public's morale to see us hitting back, it's essential to reassure the Russians that we're doing our best.'

'I know, I know, we've been through all that before. But as far as public morale is concerned, you should see the results of the latest survey. The strongest supporters of bombing live miles away from the action. Our people still living in the blitzed cities are much more reluctant to visit the same fate on the Germans.'

'However you look at it,' commented Peter, 'it's working. We know that German industry is being turned upside down to disperse itself across the country, on top of which an increasing percentage of their research and production is being diverted to anti-aircraft measures. What Bomber Command has achieved is being added to by the American Eighth Air Force, because now the Luftwaffe is having to bring back their day fighters as well'.

'What's more, Hitler's determination to strike back means that still more effort is being put into reprisal attacks against England,' murmured Charles, as usual appearing to enjoy the heated debate. 'Which ever way you look at it, we're taking some pressure off the Russians.'

'Furthermore,' Peter added, 'our decrypts show that we're succeeding in undermining the Lufwaffe's defences altogether. They're already fully stretched and beginning to skimp on their training. Every time the Americans send in a daylight attack they down a few more of the Luftwaffe pilots. And every replacement will be less experienced, so will be an easier target the next time round. It doesn't even matter if we bomb nothing, just by forcing the Luftwaffe to attack the bombers, we can wear them out in months.'

Mary cast a look of exasperated appeal to Don, who shifted uncomfortably in his seat. 'I'm afraid he's right. With our Empire Air Training Scheme we're assured a constant stream of well-trained pilots from abroad, more than we can use, actually, and our American friends are doing much the same. The only problem is the new German jets. We have them as well, of course, but they don't have the range to accompany the bombers deep into Germany.'

Peter nodded. 'Correct. Those Me 262s gave us a real scare at first, but they seem to be tricky and difficult to handle – they're losing a lot of pilots to accidents. And we've got their bases pinned down. They're easy enough to kill when they're low and slow. Not much fun when they get among the Fortresses, though.'

The Gruppe Kommandeur sat in the cockpit, the familiar trickle of tension running through him. He heard laughter far away, near the accommodation blocks, where the off-duty staff were relaxing, and shivered slightly despite the warmth. The Gefechsstand had ordered Sitzbereitschaft – cockpit readiness – over an hour ago, and still no word. The Americans would be coming, all right, he had no doubt of that; the only question was exactly where and when. The Me 262 had a limited range, so it was important to hold them on the ground for as long as possible.

Far above, the fast Fw 187 Fühlungshalter – master fighters – would be hunting the bomber formations, not to attack but to follow, radio their locations and report on the weather. Once battle was joined they would report the results of the attacks, giving the commanders on the ground a constant appreciation of the progress of the battle. That is, if they managed to avoid the attention of the escorts, the Kommandeur thought grimly.

He tried to relax, stretching as much as he could, tensing and relaxing each muscle group in turn. Fighting he never minded, but this waiting...

He tried to distract himself by running a mental checklist over his aircraft. First, the guns. The four three-centimetre Rheinmetall-Borsig MK 108 'pneumatic hammers', two with eighty rounds each, two with a hundred, each capable of firing at ten rounds per second. Eight seconds of firing with all four guns, another two seconds with two guns, provided that the ammunition belts weren't broken by any violent manoeuvres as they so often were. The muzzle velocity was low at only five hundred metres per second, but the jet's attack speed added another two hundred to that, and the Minengeschoss shells were devastating. The techs had calculated that only three or four hits were necessary to bring down one of the American bombers, compared with fifteen or twenty hits from the two-centimetre guns. They had gone on to calculate that only about two percent of shots hit their target, so only one-fifty to two hundred three-centimetre rounds needed to be carried for each kill, instead of nearly a thousand two-centimetre. He smiled wryly. Those were average figures. Anyone in this crack Gruppe unable to do a lot better than that would soon find himself on other duties.

Then there were the engines. The young face of the Kommandeur creased slightly. They were a brilliant design, no doubt about it, but he had heard from a Junkers engineer that a shortage of nickel and chromium had resulted in inferior alloys being used, which severely restricted the reliable life of the jets. It was also important to avoid making violent throttle changes, which could lead to flame-outs. He consciously relaxed again. Either they would last through the sortie or they wouldn't. There was nothing he could do to affect that, so there was no point in worrying.

He put his mind into happier channels. Now those new guided missiles they were testing, they would really make a difference...

The alarm sounded a few seconds later.

The bomb-aimer peered down through the nose of the B-17. A scatter of individual clouds and below that, a continuous thin haze, the ground invisible. He sighed in frustration. The magnificent Norden bombsight on which so many hopes had been placed would be no good, as usual. The Air Force had not properly appreciated that not everywhere enjoyed weather like California's. Still, as he wasn't the lead bomber that wasn't his responsibility. His job was simply to drop the bombs when the leader did. In ideal conditions the entire combat wing would drop its load to an accuracy of a few hundred yards, but if the leader was depending on the H2X bombing radar they would stand no more chance of hitting the target than the RAF's night bombers under similar conditions.

He looked around at the rest of the formation, and grimaced. Contrails streamed from the engines, like giant white arrows pointing at the aircraft. Once the defending fighters got above the cloud, they would have no trouble finding them. Higher still were the escorts; not that they did much escorting, he reflected, mulling over the arguments over tactics. All the fighters did was chase the German fighters, leaving the bombers to deal with any which got through. He could understand the argument for that, but it still would have been mighty comforting to have the 'little friends' around them.

Five kilometres behind the bombers and two thousand metres above them, the Kommandeur assessed the situation. His aircraft and the other three of his Schwarm had been accurately placed by their ground control radar, helped by the lurking Fühlungshalter. Focke-Wulf 190s of their neighbouring Geschwader had covered their take-offs, engaging the attacking Allied fighters so the jets could climb safely away. Considerable cost and effort had been expended to place them exactly where they were. Now it was up to them. He gave a brief command and the long attack dive commenced.

Now he felt no nervousness, only a fierce concentration as the bomber formation steadily expanded in his field of view. His gaze flicked between the instruments and the gunsight. Eight-sixty, eight-eighty, nine hundred kilometres per hour! The jet streaked through the fighter cover, dived underneath the bombers which suddenly seemed to rush backwards past him, then he pulled up and shed speed rapidly to give time to aim. The huge shape of a B-17 filled the gunsight as the aircraft vibrated to the hammer of the cannon. One second, two, then the starboard inner radial exploded into flame, propeller spinning crazily away. Eighty rounds fired, a detached part of his mind thought, that was better than two percent! He banked onto another target, saw the ball turret swivel to point towards him, fired again, a raking shot as he swept past. No time to assess damage, time to ram the throttles open and climb away from the bombers. The Messerchmitt suddenly juddered and slewed to one side, an engine streaming smoke, as the defending Mustang plunged almost vertically past him. The Kommandeur cursed and turned the crippled plane away. Get lower, lose speed, bail out, he thought mechanically. And hope I can persuade the locals I'm not an American bomber pilot before they do anything rash.

The Unteroffizier surveyed his crew with satisfaction, all poised in their allotted places around the FlaK. The Kanonier 1, whose job was to lay the gun in azimuth, K2 who set the elevation, K3 who loaded the gun and K4, 5, 6 who passed the ammunition. He looked around the platform of the huge concrete FlaK tower, raised high above the city in order to give an unrestricted field of fire. His gun and the other three of the battery were grouped around the Kommandogerät 36 director, which still relied on optical height and range setting in view of the intense jamming of the radar directors by the attacking Eloka aircraft.

The guns were the new 11 cm FlaK 43, developed from the 10.5 cm FlaK 39 by boring out the rifled barrel to create a smoothbored cannon designed to take the long, fin-stabilised Peenemünde Pfeilgeschoss arrow shells. These were not only fired at a much higher velocity of around 1,200 metres per second, but because of their shape did not slow down as quickly so reached the altitude of the bombers much sooner, greatly assisting accurate shooting.

The techs had been right about the fuzes, he thought. At first, the idea of using contact instead of time fuzes had seemed like madness, but as the techs pointed out, even the beautifully engineered clockwork fuzes were only accurate to half a percent. This meant that the vast majority of shells were bursting too high or low to do any damage, and in any case had to explode very close to the B-17s in order to bring them down. It was more effective to rely on direct hits, especially as this enabled smaller shells to be used which could be fired at much higher velocity. There had been some talk of tiny radar fuzes which would explode shells only when they were close enough to damage the target, but these were apparently all being reserved for the new anti-aircraft missiles just entering production.

The Unteroffizier looked hopefully at the sky. The cloud seemed to be clearing. Just a bit more and the oncoming bombers would get a warm reception!

The P-51 pilot was simmering with frustration. His magnificent Mustang, as the British who had ordered their development called them, was as far as he was concerned the best prop-engined fighter in the sky: fast, agile, hard-hitting and with tremendous range granted by the wonderful Packard-built Merlin engine and the lightweight underwing drop-tanks. He should have had mastery over anything the Luftwaffe could put up – but that was before those damned jets appeared. He had only managed to get one of the new planes in his gunsight and all he could achieve was one brief, long-range burst before the Messerschmitt sped away.

Still, his instructions were clear: stay with the bombers until well away from the target area, then as soon as the defending fighters had gone, go down and attack ground targets. 'Shoot up anything that moves,' his CO had said. 'You never know what it might be adding to the Nazi war effort.'

The P-51 planed down through the thin layer of cloud, emerging over a rural landscape. Well ahead, the pilot could see movement – vehicles on a road.

He eased the controls, lining up with the road, watching the vehicles as they seemed to rush towards him. The shape of a bus sank into the gunsight and he pressed the firing button, the Mustang juddering as the six fifties hammered in response. Seventy heavy machine gun bullets per second ripped up the road behind the bus, then tore through it. The pilot was vaguely aware of the bus swerving and turning over, bodies spilling from it, then the second vehicle was in his sights – a tanker! The bullets tore through it, then the incendiaries took effect with a devastating explosion. The P-51 bucked violently in the blast, then was knocked sideways. He had been hit – some debris had smashed into the plane! The pilot climbed hard, anxiously scanning gauges. Ominously, the oil pressure reading was falling rapidly – a glance in the mirror showed a plume of white smoke. It was instantly clear that he wasn't going to make it back.

The pilot nursed the plane carefully, turning to head back to the border. The engine note roughened, rattled in a final effort, then abruptly stopped. The sudden silence was chilling. The pilot hastily pulled back the cockpit canopy, undid his straps and heaved himself out as the plane began its final dive. He tumbled for a few seconds, then gasped in relief as the parachute opened.

He looked around as the swinging motion reduced, and uneasily saw that his turn had taken him close to where the vehicles he had strafed still burned. As he approached the ground a small crowd of people converged on him. He landed with the approved roll, unclipped the harness, then rapidly raised his arms as he heard the angry voices. Arms seized him, fists punched. He was dragged rapidly over the field, frozen with panic at the hostility burning from the people. He suddenly stopped and the crowd parted. He was in front of the bus. His burst of fire had riddling it like a colander. Bodies sprawled in the wreckage, lay beside the road. They seemed surprisingly small. The crowd forced him closer, their unintelligible voices a scream of accusation and hatred. Children, he thought numbly. They were all children.

'I didn't know!' He yelled. 'I didn't know!' He was still yelling as they dragged him to the roadside tree. His own parachute harness was suddenly produced and roughly knotted around his neck. He kicked out desperately as his feet left the ground. As he swayed above them, his last sight was of a sea of faces filled with bitter fury and contempt. I really didn't know, he thought, and died.

'They won't be able to keep that up for much longer.' Peter's voice was sombre as the Oversight Committee clustered round the table, studying the latest reports from the Eighth Air Force. The number of B-17s shot down in the last three raids had reached an alarming fifteen per cent. The escort fighters were almost powerless in keeping the new Messerschmitt jets away from the bomber formations and were taking losses from defending fighters as they tried to attack the jets near their bases. In cloudy weather the bombing was relatively ineffective, in clearer skies the FlaK defences were formidable.

'This is the report that really bothers me,' Peter said, pushing forward a summary of the sighting reports from the crews of several bombers on the last raid. Large rockets had been seen streaking up towards the formations. The ECM planes had apparently had some success in disrupting the control system, but three bombers had been brought down by rockets exploding nearby.

'They only appear to be radio command guided at present,' commented Don, 'but they're bound to be working on radar guidance, probably with a choice of frequencies to get around the jamming. Once they perfect that, we're in real trouble, not just in clear weather but at night and in bad weather, too.'

The gloom was palpable. Don walked slowly over to the huge map of Europe and central Asia on the wall. The vast area occupied by the Germans was marked out in tape, the only defiance on land being shown by the Russians, pushed far to the east, with the support of British and Canadian troops in the north.

'It seems to be stalemate everywhere,' he said. 'The Germans can't beat the Russians into submission, but are holding them. We can't beat the U-boats, but we're holding them. Germany is suffering from the bombing raids, but not enough. We are preparing for an invasion but worried sick about the risk; Germany is still so strong in armour and aircraft. It can't go on like this. Sooner or later, something's got to give. We can't delay the invasion for much longer.'

Charles watched them leaving the room, mulling over the information he had acquired just before the meeting and relieved that he had decided not to pass it onto the others, especially Don and Mary. The codebreakers had managed to crack the German naval codes in use a few months ago and were catching up with the backlog of decrypts. One of the messages had been brought to his attention. It seemed that someone had arranged for the xB-Dienst to know the course of the ill-fated ship carrying the American nurses, but had given them completely wrong information about what the ship was carrying. Charles was torn by a mixture of disgust at the cold-blooded slaughter of the young women, and professional admiration of the effectiveness of the intelligence trap which had brought the USA into the European war. He nodded thoughtfully. That particular decrypt would be destroyed.

# CHAPTER 9 - SLEDGEHAMMER

**Spring 1943**

The night was moonless, the sea heard more than seen, gentle waves surging lazily up the beach before withdrawing with a faint hiss. A different pattern of splashes disturbed the rhythm; starlight gleamed from shiny black rubber. The frogman crouched in the water, scanning the shore with eyes and ears at full alert. A lick of wind cooled the exposed parts of his skin, brought with it the smell of tobacco, a quick laugh. He focused, spotted the red glow. The men were stationary, talking quietly.

He waited for a few minutes until the glow suddenly curved its ballistic arc towards the beach and the voices receded. He moved forward, paused to scrape up some samples of sand, carefully sealed them away along with the notes he had already made about the beach obstacles and mines lying in wait for any invasion force.

The frogman came to where the men had stood among the dunes, followed their faint trail as much by touch as sight until a horizontal oblong of light flared briefly ahead, illuminated from behind by light spilling from an opened internal door. He stopped, reviewing the image of the oblong imprinted on his mind. It had been interrupted by a metallic gleam, humped at the back, straight at the front but with a regular pattern, which he recognised as ventilation holes in a barrel casing. An MG 42 machine gun, commanding the beach from its pill-box.

The frogman retreated silently, making no attempt to disguise his footprints leading back into the sea. With any luck they would be found in the morning, along with many others at different places along the coast of north-west Europe, all part of the scheme to keep the Germans off-balance, guessing where the blow would fall. He swam smoothly out to the kayak where his comrade waited to take him back to the small Norwegian submarine, lying in wait off the coast of Denmark.

The tent city at Kew Gardens seemed an incongruous place to house the headquarters of SHAEF, the Supreme Headquarters of the Allied Expeditionary Force charged with invading Europe. The choice was due to fall on Bushey Park near Hampton Court, but Don had hastily advised against this, in case his opposite number remembered the significance of that location. The Oversight Committee had been allocated a large house backing onto the Gardens, with room for them all to stay while they performed a suitably disguised role as a 'hush-hush' intelligence evaluation unit. On a pleasantly warm and sunny spring afternoon, Don, Mary and Charles relaxed in deckchairs and savoured their cups of Earl Grey while Hope gurgled happily in a playpen.

'So far so good,' Don murmured.

Charles picked up the undertone of anxiety and raised an eyebrow. 'What particular item is troubling you this time?'

A sigh. 'Nothing specific. It's just that so much can go wrong.'

'Never mind,' Charles responded lazily, 'in this kind of business all you can do is prepare as well as possible until it has passed beyond your ability to influence. An enterprise as great as this slowly gathers its own momentum. First the big decisions – when and where – become set in stone, then all the smaller ones – how and who – are worked out, each one being set in its place. The closer we get to D-day, the harder it becomes to make any changes at all, other than adjusting the landing time by a few hours.'

'He's right,' Mary chipped in, 'there really is little or nothing any of us can do now to make any difference. We have to trust to the military to carry it out; all we can do is pray.'

'I know, I know. The trouble is that there are so many different factors, there's always something that I might not have said, or communicated clearly enough, which might make a difference; save a few lives, avoid a problem. Getting the equipment right is the simple part; the biggest uncertainty is with the things I can't see. Did I really impress on them sufficiently strongly the need for naval gunfire support officers in the first wave ashore to direct the shooting, or the communication systems between the army and the tactical fighters in support? Not to mention a sufficient quantity of wireless sets with the airborne troops – the lack of those caused some real problems. These kind of things make a huge difference, but I can't know if they'll happen properly until, well, until they happen!'

The other two grinned a shade wearily. 'You've been bothering everyone you can get your hands on about everything you can think of for months.' Mary said gently. She brightened up. 'Just run through what has gone right. You won over Churchill, against the wishes of Sir Alan Brooke,' – 'and nearly all of the Imperial General Staff,' interjected Charles drily – 'to agree with the Americans, forget about the Mediterranean and launch a direct attack on northern Europe, otherwise it would have been 1944 before we could put together enough landing ships, men and equipment to invade France.'

'Well, I only hope that was the right decision. The opposition had some powerful arguments. The Americans are untried in battle, the German army unbroken, the Luftwaffe damaged but not yet crippled by the fighting over Germany. It's a terrible risk.'

'But nearly all of the German Army is far to the east in Russia, too far to be brought back to France in anything less than weeks if not months. And our forces are much better equipped than they were in your time. Thanks to you, we know what has to be done and we know how to do it.'

'You forget, the Germans know how we did it, too. And they still have the best army in the world. Did I mention that they consistently inflicted casualties at a rate fifty percent higher than they sustained them?' (Patient nods.) 'We will need better equipment and tactics just to survive.'

Mary was undeterred. 'Then you managed to get Churchill to dissuade Roosevelt from making his 'unconditional surrender' statement, in order to leave the German opposition to the Nazis some hope. You said how much harder they fought because they had nothing to lose.'

Charles grinned. 'Yes, I rather enjoyed that saying of theirs you remembered; "we might as well enjoy the war, because the peace will be terrible!"'

Mary continued firmly, 'you were quite right to argue against the invasion of Italy. It's no threat to us and a liability to the Germans. We would just have lost tens of thousands of men in a long war there, to achieve nothing. We must focus our resources where it matters.'

'Schwerpunkt!' Charles nodded approvingly.

'And don't forget the benefits the invasion will bring, in neutralising those U-boat bases and airfields in France. That will make a huge difference to the Battle of the Atlantic. Then there were the casualties. All those hundreds of thousands of European civilians who will die if the war goes on for another year, among them, over half a million Jews.'

'Well, the major decisions are taken now,' Charles pointed out reassuringly. 'Eisenhower is in charge, with Alexander leading the armies and Montgomery in charge of planning. The best team, I think you said? You've even managed to get Churchill to insist on including the Fighting French in the invasion force.'

Don grimaced in recollection. 'Yes, the Americans really don't like de Gaulle.'

'Anyway, with the continuing delays being reported in perfecting an atom bomb, we really don't have much choice. Just as well that we can see no signs of German progress in that direction either.' Charles rose and stretched in the sunshine. 'Come on, we have another briefing meeting this evening. Let's catch up with the latest.'

The Arado 234B-1 reconnaissance jet streaked over the coast of southern England at seven hundred kilometres per hour and eleven thousand metres altitude, cameras whirring steadily. The pilot had been given explicit instructions following several similar runs. There were some areas along the Hampshire coast which the Luftwaffe wanted a closer look at; some interesting shapes barely visible under camouflage netting, possibly a large formation of armoured vehicles being prepared for the expected invasion. The dockyards were also of interest. So far, there was no sign of the giant concrete structures the pilot had been briefed to expect – just lots of shipping. For some reason these structures, which according to Intelligence were apparently known by the curious name of 'Mulberries', were important in answering the key question: how ready were the Allies? Would the invasion be this year or next?

The pilot kept his eyes on the ground – he had been warned that the British had introduced a similar anti-aircraft missile to the type operated by the Luftwaffe. Not surprisingly, they seemed to be concentrated around the ports where they had taken a heavy toll in the recent bomber raids.

The pilot reached the end of the run, then turned and began a smooth descent to gain a closer view of the camouflaged area. The speed slowly built up to eight hundred kilometres per hour then eased back as the little jet steadied at six thousand metres. The ground unrolled beneath him rapidly. He checked the plane's course then set the cameras rolling again. A brief flash of light in the mirror caught the pilot's eye; for moment he stared in disbelief and dismay at the sight of a plane – closing on him! Then the nose of the chasing plane flickered with fire and the Arado began a frantic evasion routine, the pilot concentrating too hard on getting away to use his fixed, rearward-firing cannon.

The Major watched the gradual fall of the remains of the plane, one wing tumbling by itself, the black cross clearly visible at it approached the ground. He turned away from the funeral pyre to look at the camouflage netting stretched behind him. Underneath, carefully just visible, were the plywood models of tanks. Hardly a proper war, he thought, but at least this secret would be kept a little longer.

The Flight-Lieutenant climbed out of the Hawker Typhoon, gave a thumbs-up to his ground crew. 'One down – I got the jet!' He called out, to be greeted by cheers and applause. He looked back at the little plane, still officially on the secret list. It still looked strange to his eyes, sitting straight on its tricycle undercarriage, the slim, pointed nose, now streaked with gunsmoke, naked of any propeller, the side intakes above the swept-back wing, the jet exhaust under the tail. Had he known it, the Hawker bore a remarkable resemblance to a certain RAF advanced jet trainer from Don's previous life ('we know you can't help us with the technical details,' Peter had said, 'but even an idea of what sort of layouts worked well would help. We're really in the dark over how to begin!').

'How were the guns?' the armourer wanted to know.

'Faultless!' The new Molins Hispanos were capable of a thousand rounds per minute, and four of them nestled under the nose of the plane. 'The poor chap never knew what hit him!'

The underground command post was brutally functional like all of its kind. I could be almost anywhere, Herrman thought wearily. It was odd to think that, for the first time in his life, he was in France. What on earth was the typically overdramatic name they gave to this one? Oh yes, FHQ Wolfsschlucht 2, located at Margival, near Soissons. At least Hitler's generals had the sense to pick more congenial accommodation: von Rundstedt, the C-in-C Army Group West, was installed in a castle at Saint-Germaine, while Rommel's Army Group B HQ was at La Roche-Guyon, the chateau of the Ducs de la Roche.

Herrman dragged his attention back to General Jodl, the Chief of Staff to the head of the OKW, the Oberkommando der Wehrmacht, or joint defence staff. As usual, the capable Jodl was doing the briefing while his ineffectual superior, Keitel, sat and listened.

'We still have no clear idea about Allied intentions, but the build-up of forces in southern England and Norway is obvious. Unfortunately there has also been much activity in North Africa and an invasion of Sicily, or even Italy or southern France, cannot be entirely ruled out. We have been warned about the British predilection for 'disinformation' in constructing decoy aircraft, tanks and even landing vessels, and in generating false radio traffic, and while no definite information has been gathered from England or Norway, we have intelligence reports from Africa which suggest that much of the activity there might be false. Furthermore, to use Norway as a jumping-off point for a major invasion would be very risky for them: so close to Germany, the advantage would be with us. After careful consideration, we have concluded that an invasion of northern France is the most likely eventuality, and it might come very soon. This causes us certain obvious problems. As we know, OB West has sixty divisions available, among them twelve Panzer divisions. However, they are of very variable quality. The Seventh Army, responsible for the Cotentin peninsula and the Channel coast, has fifteen infantry divisions but ten of them are bodenständige.'

Herrman searched his memory for a moment before recalling that these comprised very young, very old or unfit soldiers and were essentially static, with no vehicles.

'The Fifteenth Army which holds the Kanalkueste to the east is stronger as this is felt to be the most vulnerable area. Reinforcing these from the Eastern Front will not be easy. Our current front line is deep inside Russia and, although we have been improving and extending the railway system, it would still take a considerable period of time to move any significant armoured forces back to France. However, our practice of delivering new armoured vehicles to northern France, and manning them with experienced divisions rotated out of line for rest and retraining, means that we have a core of highly capable and mobile units to buttress the armies. The problem we have is in identifying the landing place or places and the best means of deploying our defences to counter them. I will now hand over to General Rommel, who has been touring the north coast and checking the defences.'

Herrman began to pay more attention. He liked Rommel, a tough, no-nonsense but fair-minded professional, and had urged Hitler to appoint him to this post. His energetic, hands-on style of leadership was a useful complement to von Rundstedt's cool, intellectual approach. Rommel had not, this time, had the opportunity to make his mark in North Africa, but instead he had distinguished himself in Greece, which still, so far, represented Germany's only defeat of a British army.

Rommel swept his gaze around the room, over the impassive Hitler and the core of the general staff. 'The fixed defences are in place, although we badly need some more radar sets to cover the Channel. All feasible landing beaches are mined and protected by obstacles to destroy, or at least greatly hinder, landing barges. They are also covered by protected machine-gun posts. Every mile of the coast is covered by artillery positions, either well camouflaged or heavily protected against counter-battery fire. However, this will not be enough to prevent an invasion. When the Allies come, they will come in great force, with massive air and naval support. Despite their intensive counter-intelligence activities, we have received reports of special vehicles they have developed to deal with our defences.'

Herrman smiled inwardly. He doubted that Rommel would be aware of the source of those reports.

'They have the huge advantage of being able to choose the time and place of their attack. We do not know if they will take the shortest route to Pas-de-Calais, or will land further west on the coast of Normandy. We know that the best time to defeat a landing is immediately, before a beachhead has been established, but we do not have enough forces to ensure that all of these possibilities are adequately covered. We will need four things in place if we are to defeat them: fighter aircraft to prevent their bombers from disrupting our defences, bombers to attack their landing ships by day, U-boote and S-boote to attack them by night. And, above all, strong Panzer forces to smash their initial landings before they can establish themselves.'

Von Rundstedt stirred and Rommel paused to look at his superior officer, knowing what was coming.

'The question is how best to deploy the Panzers. In my opinion they should be held back in reserve, ready to move forward in great force as soon as we can identify the actual landing place. If we keep them forwards, close to the beaches, they must necessarily be spread thinly and it will be much more difficult to pull them into large formations at the landing place.'

Rommel nodded respectfully. 'Normally, I would entirely agree. Our problem is twofold. First, it is better to deliver an instant response when the invaders are most vulnerable. Even a small Panzer unit could wreak havoc on the initial stages of a landing, whereas calling up reserves would inevitably delay a response. Secondly, our fighter strength is at a premium, given the necessity to counter the American bomber attacks on Germany, and might not be able to protect against the swarms of Allied fighter-bombers we can expect. We understand that they have been intensively practising ground-attack techniques and this could cause us serious problems in moving our troops from their reserve areas. On balance, I think that deploying them in small units on the coast would provide our best opportunity to defeat the invasion.'

Herrman awaited Hitler's response with interest. He had of course provided a comprehensive briefing on what had actually happened on 'his' D-day: von Rundstedt had won Hitler's support then and most of the Panzers had been held back, only to find that they were seriously delayed in setting off because Hitler had insisted that they could only move on his orders and no-one wished to wake him from sleep to obtain permission. Once they did move, their progress was severely hampered by fighter-bomber attacks, together with sabotage of roads and railways by the Resistance.

Hitler nodded thoughtfully. 'It is a difficult decision. The Panzers' main strength is in concentrated attack. I have decided on a compromise. Those Panzer units which are completing training and would normally be heading east soon will be distributed under local control. However, the units which are re-equipping and training will be held back under von Rundstedt's command.'

Herrman concealed a grimace. The need for a clear chain of command, with all defences under one commander, was intellectually recognised by Hitler, but the man was constitutionally incapable of trusting any one man with an important task. Even the organisation of the OKW was confused; it was supposed to be the senior military body, with the OKH – the Army command – subordinated to it, but in practice Hitler treated them as equal. He just had to hope that von Rundstedt responded quickly when Rommel needed those units. Still, although a bit messy, the solution was better than in his time. Now it was a question of wait and see.

'Now,' Hitler declaimed, leaning forward, his eyes gleaming with the enthusiasm he showed when concocting his often unrealistic strategies, 'I want further strengthening of the defences. Concentrate first on the harbours – the Allies will need to seize some quickly if they are to continue to supply their force. Then I agree to the focus on the beaches of the Kanalkueste, which I feel is the most likely target this time. I know that Pas-de-Calais would not be such an easy target for them, but our new V-weapons are being launched from there so they will want to neutralise it as soon as possible.'

The meeting went on long into the evening.

The cyclist pedalled slowly along the coast road, the traditional baguette in the front basket announcing his early-morning visit to the baker. He was not as young as he had been and the slight upward slope caused him to pant for breath. Near the top he paused to recover, taking out a handkerchief to mop his brow. He glanced around unobtrusively before setting off again to coast gently down towards the stream. The night had been disturbed by the rumbling roar of powerful engines and he was anxious to discover what this portended. Over the stream was a small open copse. Something bulky, hard-edged and metallic gleamed among the trees.

A soldier, assault rifle slung casually over a shoulder, suddenly stepped out into the road and demanded his papers in appalling French. The cyclist was well-prepared; a local farmer, he had permission to live in the area. The German checked the papers, passed them back and waved him on. The cyclist pedalled steadily home, planning the message he would need to smuggle to his comrade who held the radio transmitter. He had recognised the uniform insignia, and was sure that the Allies would be very interested to learn of the presence of a Waffen-SS Panzer unit on the Normandy coast!

Geoffrey Taylor accepted another slice of cake and settled back in the armchair.

'How is central London faring these days?'

'Pretty well, Mary. I think the Luftwaffe's attention is elsewhere. These new 'buzz-bombs' are the biggest nuisance, but our new Typhoon jets can easily catch and destroy them.'

'All well at Grosvenor Square?' Don enquired. Geoffrey had been seconded to liaise with ETOUSA, the European Theatre of Operations USA.

'You can feel the excitement. New faces all the time and a real buzz about the place. About a hundred and fifty thousand troops a month are arriving now; they're packing them into high-speed liners to avoid the U-boats, twelve thousand at a time. Half of southern England must be under canvas by now.'

'Do you get to listen to any Londoners?' Mary asked, 'what are they saying now?'

'Oh, there's a lot of talk. They all know there's going to be an invasion, of course. They've noticed that a lot of commuter train services have been stopped so they can be switched to military transportation. Some people have relatives on the coast and are grumbling because they can't get to them; the coastline has been virtually sealed off to civilians, in view of all the training exercises as well as troop build-ups. Basically, the people are just holding their collective breath, waiting for the day.'

'No problems, with all those American troops about?'

Geoffrey grimaced. 'Some. Unfortunately, all the money and fine presents they bring are dazzling some of the London ladies and their menfolk aren't too happy about it. The sooner the invasion happens, the better for Anglo-American relations. Still, it's interesting to hear so much unfamiliar music around London. Glenn Miller, Tommy Dorsey, Benny Goodman, Artie Shaw – it's almost like being in the USA!'

Despite the years of preparation, Harold Johnson felt a frisson of excitement as he entered the Georgian building of Southwick House near Portsmouth, the base for Operation Neptune: the naval operation for crossing the Channel. He hoped briefly that the Germans didn't know about this one; it was one of the few places that Don had forgotten about, and by the time he remembered it had been used in this role before, the planners were well ensconced and unwilling to move. It was now the HQ for the Supreme Allied Command and accordingly surrounded by massed batteries of AA guns as well as nearby night and day fighter squadrons on permanent alert.

He slipped into the back of the room being used for the briefing, his role as usual to listen and report back to Don, to check for anything which might sound alarm bells. The audience was full of fairly senior officers of all branches and several nationalities. Harold judged that they were staff officers belonging to various units, there to hear about the overall grand plan so they could begin to fill in the details of their own units' part in the action.

The speaker, a young and brisk naval intelligence officer of surprisingly high rank, first ran through all of the material gathered prewar: the maps and photos used to prepare models and the huge D-day wall map behind him. This information had been kept up-to-date by aerial reconnaissance and a steady trickle of information from the French Resistance movement, aided by Fighting French agents flown in at night, in hazardous operations. More recently, coastal defences and beach conditions had been plotted by frogmen making secretive visits all round the coastline.

'The Germans will be well aware we're coming but, I sincerely hope, they still don't know where, let alone when.' No-one laughed: this was too serious. 'There is a good case for heading straight for the Pas-de-Calais. It's by far the shortest crossing so it maximises the chance of achieving surprise and minimises the exposure of the ships to attack. Unfortunately, it's also probably the most heavily defended stretch of coastline in the world. We have accordingly decided on Normandy. The landings will be distributed over a wide front, with sectors allocated to the British, Americans, Canadians and the Fighting French. We have preferred dates, depending on the moon and the times of the tides, but will reserve final judgment until we can check the weather. We have ships and aircraft out in the Atlantic doing nothing but providing us with weather reports. Ideally, we would like to capture a port as quickly as possible and use that to land most of the troops and supplies. This would be particularly convenient in the case of Cherbourg, as American troops could land there directly from the USA. Unfortunately, our intelligence appreciation has revealed that the major ports are so heavily defended that they will take a considerable time to subdue, and by that time they will probably have had all of their dock facilities destroyed anyway. So we will have to rely on beach landings. We did consider building special floating harbours which could be sunk in position, but again this idea was rejected as too cumbersome and inflexible. Instead, we will be relying on direct beach landings, sinking blockships offshore to protect from the worst of the weather and constructing piers to speed offloading from those ships not designed for beaching. We have calculated that we have a sufficient margin of shipping not just to deliver the initial assault, but also to keep the supplies coming.' The officer paused to sip from a glass of water. 'Of course, the Germans have been busy preparing a warm reception. We know that they have installed mines and beach obstacles on a liberal scale anywhere they think we might land, as well as covering the beaches with strong points, backed up by both fixed and mobile artillery and, we now hear, some Panzer units distributed along the coast. They have also flooded as many as possible of the low-lying drained areas, particularly the river valleys around Caen and the Cotentin Peninsula. This will not only make conventional landings very difficult in those areas, but also hazardous for our paratroops who would be at risk of drowning on landing. Despite this, these flooded areas have a key part to play in our plan, as you will hear.'

The intelligence officer went on to outline the plan of attack. There was a long, tense pause after he had finished, as the gathered staff officers absorbed the plan, turned it over in their minds to see if it felt right, then began to work out the implications for their units. Some hands began to rise. The officer nodded at one.

'What about diversionary attacks? Are we landing anywhere else at the same time – Denmark, Italy or southern France, for instance?'

'We're going to some lengths to keep the Germans guessing about that one. More to the point, Stalin will be launching a major offensive before D-day with all of his remaining reserves. The German forces in the east will be thoroughly pinned down by the time we land.'

Harold noted with wry amusement that the intelligence officer had neatly avoided answering the question. These staff officers didn't need to know about the plans for other areas, so they weren't being told. He reflected on the wide range of elaborate deception plans, particularly focused on the Pas-de-Calais, which Don had insisted on calling Operation Overlord. 'Too obvious,' the others had groaned, 'Your opposite number would never fall for that! It's just as bad as calling the main operation Sledgehammer – he's bound to remember that was the name of a plan for a 1942 raid on France.' Still, some of the plans were rather more than just deceptions.

As the questions petered out, the naval officer called for attention. This was obviously the bit where he was planning to send them off in a state of optimism, tempered by a note of caution; oh hell, Harold silently berated himself, I've been to too many of these!

'In total, we have well over two million men gathered for the attack; that's over thirty divisions, with a very high proportion of them armoured or mechanised. We will be launching our attack with ten divisions, half in the first wave, half already afloat and waiting to follow on. The Germans are spread thinly along the coast, so when we land it will be with overwhelming force.' He paused for effect. 'The important thing to remember is this: a successful landing is obviously absolutely crucial, but nevertheless the landing will be the easiest part. Everything has been planned and there is an excellent chance of the plan working smoothly. The moment the landing has taken place, the uncertainties of war begin to take effect. We do not know exactly how the Germans will respond, but it will be violently. The difficult part will be to deal with their counter-attacks and press on with the exploitation phase of our attack while keeping our troops supplied with materials, food and fuel.'

And replacements for the casualties, thought Harold, there will be plenty of them.

A fine drizzle was drifting down as Harold left the building. He turned up his collar and walked down the driveway to the waiting car, the moisture beading on his face, trickling down his cheeks. I hope that's not an omen, he thought. There will be tears enough before this is over. For a moment he paused, visualising the immensity of what they were about to do. Millions of men, countless weapons, all poised to throw themselves across the water at a fierce and unrelenting enemy. He shuddered; the risks were appalling and even success would demand a high price. He walked more slowly, feeling suddenly depressed. So much could go wrong; there was so much still to do!

**Early Summer 1943**

The USAAC pilot tried to ignore the constant howling of the wind through the numerous holes in the B-25's fuselage. At least, he thought, it had blown away the smell of high-explosive from the cannon shells which had detonated inside his plane. One of the gunners had not survived the onslaught from the Me 262 jet but the rest of his crew was surprisingly unhurt. He pondered once again the brutal randomness of war; the sheer chance which meant that one man lived while the man next to him died, like some decimation lottery. Still, it looked as if the rest of the crew were going to make it back from this one. The shadow of a 'little friend' flickered briefly across the canopy, the P-51 keeping close watch on its battered charge as it struggled wearily across the Channel.

The raid had been risky from the start. The target, as so often these days, was a railway junction and marshalling yard, a key point on a supply route from Germany into France. Of course, the Germans knew it was a key point as well, so it was surrounded by the predictable layers of flak. The P-47 boys had gone in first as usual, shooting up every flak gun they could find, but the bigger guns were protected by smaller ones and he guessed that more than one of the tough fighter-bombers would have fallen prey to the deadly quad 20 mm or twin 30 mm cannon. Despite their efforts, the bomb run had been nerve-jangling, the deadly flare of the big, high-velocity tracer shells flashing just past the plane several times. Art, his young new bombardier, had kept his nerve and planted the bombs squarely over the target and the pilot had thankfully hauled the big Mitchell round, careful to keep station with the rest of his formation, and headed for home. They were just beginning to relax when the jet bounced them in one fast, raking pass, 30 mm cannon shells hammering the bomber for a terrifying fraction of a second before the plane disappeared, barely glimpsed as it sped away from the defending fighters.

Now all the pilot could do was wait and watch the gauges, hoping that nothing vital had been hit and they would make it back to base. He thought for a moment about what else had been going on over the deadly skies of Europe. He knew from his friends in other units that the Allied pressure on the Luftwaffe was relentless. Some units specialised in knocking out bridges with guided bombs – a nerve-racking task to hold the plane steady through the eruption of flak, while the bombardier steered the bomb home – and others hit radar stations or bombed the ports harbouring the deadly U-boats and E-boats, but the most dangerous task was taking the battle to the enemy. He grimaced as recalled the graphic description of one visiting pilot who had – understandably – been consuming more alcohol than was good for him.

The P-47s had gone in first to hit the fighter bases, aiming to knock out as many jets as possible before they could get off the ground. The Luftwaffe was intolerant of such enterprise so there was the usual barrage of flak. Then the medium and heavy bombers went in – it hardly mattered what the target was – they were there as bait. As the jets climbed to attack, they were met by diving P-51 escort fighters, pilots frantically calculating distances, angles and relative speeds in the hope that when they pulled up onto the tails of the jets they would, for a few seconds, be able to hold them in their gunsights. As the jets approached the bombers, other escorts hurled themselves into their path, desperate to distract them if not shoot them down. Some did not survive. The four MK 108 cannon carried by the Me 262 were not good dog-fighting weapons – their muzzle velocity was too low – but any fighter unlucky enough to occupy the same airspace as a burst from those weapons would simply disintegrate.

The air battle was soon over, the jets heading for home as their fuel ran low. As they shaped up to land at low speed, they were at their most vulnerable and more Allied fighters swooped on them, battling through the defending Fw 190s sent up specifically to guard against this tactic.

The war against the Luftwaffe was one of grinding attrition, the pilot reflected. Both sides were taking heavy losses. He knew that ultimately the Allies would win this particular battle – America was producing so many planes and training so many pilots that Germany would run out of both long before them – but that was of little comfort to the crews, many of them just teenagers, who went out day after day, knowing that each time they went out, the odds were stacked more heavily against them.

A green patchwork quilt slowly materialised below him, the landscape blooming with the life of early summer. They would make it back, this time.

The guard wrapped his coat more tightly around him, silently cursing the strong, cool, north-easterly breeze. The unseasonably hot weekend they had just enjoyed make the change in the weather all the less welcome. He stared gloomily out over the sea. From his elevated position, the choppy surface broke the reflection of the full moon into shimmering fragments. No sign of the invading armada, he thought sarcastically. However, he knew better than to deviate from the orders of his commanding officer so he stayed at his post, trying not to think of his comrades sound asleep in the comfort of their bunker.

He turned around and glared back at the spider's web of the radar dish gleaming in the moonlight, feeling suddenly vulnerable. He had heard the gossip that many of the gun batteries along the coast were dummies, left as decoys while the real guns were moved back. His own position was too good to leave, commanding as it did the approaches to a vulnerable stretch of coastline. He looked around again, feeling uneasy. Not long before, Allied aircraft had cruised invisibly past not far away. He had heard no bombs and the FlaK batteries had held their fire, not wanting to reveal their positions until it really mattered. Now the night was still again.

The guard stomped his feet and marched around a little to warm up, slinging the heavy weight of the StG.40 onto his other shoulder for a change. He tried not to keep looking at the luminous hands on his watch as they crawled interminably towards the time when he would be relieved.

He heard a quiet quacking noise in the dark and looked towards it, puzzled. What was a duck doing up here, making a noise at this time of night? The noise came again and he walked slowly towards it, pleased for even the most trivial diversion to relieve his boredom. Perhaps he could capture a prize for tomorrow's dinner.

The sergeant watched him coming, put down his 'Duck, Bakelite' which the SAS paratroopers used to locate each other, and waited. As the guard approached, a dark form rose up behind him, there was a brief gleam of steel, then only one man stood. The small team, who had practised for months the skill of landing their steerable black-silk parachutes precisely onto a target lit only by moonlight, moved swiftly into co-ordinated action. The charges were placed at critical points around the radar station. The team melted back into the night. They would be long gone by the time the explosives detonated.

The pilot gazed through the windscreen of the glider at the tow-rope pointing towards the vague shape of the Albemarle transport ahead of him. For now, he had little to do but wait until the tow-plane's crew advised him that they were close enough to the target for him to cast off. Then, he would need to steer the big Horsa down to the landing ground, to deliver its cargo of two dozen troops and their equipment where it was needed. He thought for a moment about the paratroop planes which had preceded them, and wondered how they had got on. One of his friends had the job of dropping dummy parachutists away from the landing zones, designed to let loose with a barrage of fireworks to simulate gunfire as soon as they hit the ground. He smiled at the thought of the panic among the German commanders as they received frantic messages about paratroop landings scattered halfway across Europe.

Landing by glider was better, the pilot reflected, as the troops all landed together and were immediately ready to fight as a unit instead of spending minutes, or even hours, just locating each other. But some targets had no suitable landing grounds, so parachutes were the only way of getting the troops to them with the silence needed for surprise. At least, there was no excuse for not finding the right landing place, as all of the transports had been fitted as a rush job (as if someone had only just remembered it, he thought) with the highly accurate Oboe navigation system normally used for blind bombing.

While he waited for the signal, he focused for the hundredth time on reviewing the reconnaissance photographs of his destination: the narrow strip of land between the Orne River and the Canal de Caen. And most particularly, the appearance of the vital road which crossed both waterways via the two bridges which were to be seized and held by his men and those in the other five gliders somewhere in the night around him.

The signal flashed in the cockpit and the pilot pulled the lever to release the tow. Minutes later, the moonlight gleaming on the twin waterways led him in to a precise landing by the Pegasus Bridge over the canal, or more precisely a controlled crash as the glider ploughed through the vegetation. The heavily-armed troops poured out of the Horsa as three others landed in quick succession, another two landing by the Orne Bridge at Ranville. Speed and surprise were their main weapons against the garrison defending the bridge. The first that most of the sleeping German soldiers knew of the attack was when grenades went off in their dugouts, followed by a burst of Solen fire.

The officer rallied his men after the brief but savage battle was over. Now the problem would to be hold the bridges until reinforcements could arrive, the long way.

The lieutenant looked down from the bridge onto the landing craft's open well, conscious of the discomfort of the troops as the vessel moved uneasily, idling slowly through the lively sea, waiting for the signal to move into position and head towards the coast, still many miles away. It could have been worse, he thought. Not much more than a week ago there had been a full gale in the Channel; it had blown for three days, the worst May gale in forty years. The planners must have been having kittens, he reflected. After the unusually hot weekend which had followed, Monday had been cool, clear and sunny and everything seemed perfect. Then the strong wind had started to blow, pushing the bulky, shallow-draft vessel away from its intended course, much to the disgust of the helmsman who had been forced to keep a close eye on the position. The choppy sea had not made the American troops any happier, either. They had been uncomfortable enough as it was in their stiff uniforms, chemically impregnated against mustard gas, which felt constantly damp and gave off a sour odour. Even their boots had been impregnated with special grease to make them impervious to gas. The lieutenant glanced at this watch. It was past midnight. Wednesday the nineteenth of May had just begun.

The Gefreiter looked gloomily over the barrel of his Hotchkiss machine gun at the indistinct greyness of sea and sky. Dawn was just breaking. The wind was chill against his face and he snuggled more deeply into his greatcoat. Rumours of an imminent Allied invasion were building up to fever pitch but he was relatively unconcerned. He was guarding a strip of sand dunes, planted with coarse grass, which separated the beach from the newly flooded lowlands behind him. The La Barquette locks near Carentan had been operated to allow the River Douve, and its tributary the Merderet, to flood a wide area crossed only by a few causeways. Anyone foolish enough to land on his beach would find themselves with a long swim before reaching dry land, or would have a long and hard fight to use one of the few causeways!

He turned his head, trying to locate a far-off murmur of sound which gradually penetrated his consciousness. It sounded like distant aeroplane engines. He scanned the sky, reluctant to sound an alarm until he could identify the source. The noise built steadily and the hairs on the back of his neck began to stand up as he raised his binoculars for a systematic sweep. Where were these planes? They should be silhouetted against the sky by now – it sounded like a whole air fleet! The air was vibrating with the intensity of the noise and the Gefreiter felt panic rising in his breast. He dropped his binoculars then gaped in astonishment at the clouds of spray speeding towards him. Huge machines, skimming over the water faster than any ship, hurled themselves at the beach. He dropped flat as one charged straight at him, went over him in a violent blast of noise, wind and sand! Trembling, he slowly straightened and looked up. The sea was clear again. He looked round and saw the clouds of spray rapidly diminishing as the incredible craft sped across the flooded land. Eventually, he remembered the field telephone.

The commander of the hovercraft chuckled briefly at the memory of the white, astounded face of the soldier they had flown over, then concentrated on keeping to his course. He had seen a score of times the cine film, made by a reconnaissance Reaper which had flown this route at low level, and it was playing in his mind now as he checked the few landmarks in this flooded land. He looked to either side and behind, to check that the other eleven craft in this group were still echeloned with him, for all the world like a flight of massive geese finding trouble in taking off. He looked ahead again, spotted the church steeple he was waiting for, crowning higher land ahead. They were approaching dry land.

The commander began to slow the hectic pace and the scream of the Merlin engines, hastily stripped from decommissioned Spitfires as the plane was retired from service, slowly reduced, the big propellers above and behind him winding down. This craft had no brakes and he needed to locate his target with precision. The broad straight road which paralleled this part of the river valley came into view and he slowly manoeuvred the giant craft into position, nose close to the road, then cut the engines. The hovercraft settled ponderously, like an elephant lying down. A quick glance showed the rest of his flotilla to each side.

A ramp dropped just below the cockpit and with a snarl of its powerful engine, the Churchill tank lumbered out of the bowels of the craft and onto the road, its massive gun barrel questing menacingly. To either side, other vehicles disembarked. The hovercraft could carry one Churchill or two of the smaller Comet AA tanks or Covenanter APCs. With the benefit of much practice, the small armoured formation assembled itself in the correct order: four Churchills first, followed by two Comets, then eight Covenanters, two more Comets and the last two Churchills.

The commander watched the small but powerful formation rumble off towards its first objective. It might not look much, but he knew that this scene was being repeated in many places. Some hovercraft were carrying reconnaissance units with armoured cars (they could carry eight of the heavy ones, sixteen of the light) and a screen was being thrown around the whole landing area. The heavy armoured units had various roles: some were to seize key communications nodes, others moved outwards, ready to block reinforcements, while still others headed inwards, towards the coast, preparing to take the German defences in the rear.

As the armoured unit disappeared into the early morning, the commander signalled to the other hovercraft and the big fans began to spin up. They would be very busy shuttling to and fro for as long as they could, bringing up reinforcements and supplies. He sighed grimly. The advantage of surprise having been played, the other trips would not be so easy.

Elsewhere along the Normandy coastline, German soldiers awakened to another strange sound; a throbbing, clattering noise filled the air and they looked up into the dawn light to see large helicopters skimming low over the coast. The helicopters each carried a section of Royal Marine Commandos, laden with weapons and supplies, who had taken off from Merchant Aircraft Carriers only a few miles offshore. Their pilots homed in on the beacons thoughtfully placed by Special Boat Service units parachuted in the night before, and neatly dropped their troops precisely where they were wanted.

The sky was now light enough to see clearly and the defenders gaped at the panorama revealed to them just off the coast. Row upon row of ships filled their vision. Every telephone along the coast was picked up. Just inland, the old farmer stopped searching and grunted with satisfaction as he held up a loop of wire. He fumbled for his pliers for a moment, then carefully snipped through the wire. He climbed back on his bike and laboriously pedalled on. There should be some more telephone wires, a little further on.

The pilot of the Hereford II pulled the plane out of its shallow dive and steadied its course as the French coast grew rapidly before him. Columns of smoke rose where the fighter-bombers had dropped napalm on the local flak defences. The squat, square shape of the massive reinforced concrete casemate moved smoothly into the centre of the gunsight, the central dot tracking up towards the barrel of the coastal gun poking out of the wide, black aperture. He thumbed the firing button and a stream of 0.5 inch incendiary-tracer rounds streaked towards the target. They kicked up the sand in front of the casemate and walked up the concrete in flickers of fire. The pilot thumbed the other button and the Bofors 57 mm gun thumped into life, sending a mixture of high-explosive shells and armour-piercing shot around and through the aperture at a rate of two per second. A violent puff of smoke burst from the aperture just before the pilot had to haul the big plane upwards to clear the casemate. He grinned with satisfaction – at least one of his shots had hit a vulnerable spot! He turned the plane to watch the other members of his unit tracking steadily in to attack the other casemates of the battery, then turned for home. A quick reloading session, then there would be plenty of other targets beckoning.

The turret of the Churchill II rang like a massive gong, leaving the crew momentarily stunned by the violence of the shock. The Second Lieutenant in command, his head out of the turret, checked briefly to make sure that the crew were OK and the tank intact, its well-sloped, four inch thick armour no more than gouged by the glancing strike of the German projectile. He returned to scanning the land ahead with the 6x30 binoculars, focusing with difficulty as the tank lurched for the cover of the hedge-topped bank ahead and accelerated down the lane, its Meteor engine roaring. A brief flash flickered in his vision just before a distant copse disappeared from view and this time the commander felt the air blast accompanying the deafening bang as the supersonic shell just cleared the top of the tank.

'Follow the lane,' he ordered, then switched to the inter-tank net to direct the next tank behind to engage the copse with HE. He heard the thump of the big four-inch gun as it lobbed a low-velocity 35-pound HESH shell at the wood. If it was a PaK that was engaging them, the shells would really distract them. If it was a tank, then a direct hit was unlikely but the attack would keep their heads under armour.

The lane went past the copse at a distance of about half a mile, the steep banks on each side, so typical of this bocage country, shielding the tank from view. When he judged they were side-on to the enemy's position, the lieutenant ordered the driver to slow down, engage the lowest gear and turn towards the bank. He traversed the turret to one side to keep the long gun barrel out of the way as the Churchill rammed the bank, then slowly pushed through it, sawing from side to side so that the serrated 'Rhino' attachment on the front of the hull could dig through the bank. After a minute, the tank burst through into the field. The commander, binoculars to his eyes, rapidly traversed the turret to the front. It should be... there! The land dipped to a shallow valley before rising to the copse, giving a clear view across the intervening hedgerows. The squat profile of a Panther tank was intermittently visible through the smoke and flames now pouring from the copse.

'Load AP! Gunner, fire when ready!'

The Churchill rocked under the violent kick of the powerful gun, the tracer of the APDS shot a brief streak as the projectile covered the distance in half a second. There was a pause, then the Panzer's turret suddenly lifted into the air in a flash of flame. The sound of the detonation arrived a couple of seconds later.

The lieutenant grinned with relief as his crew cheered. The new 45 ton Panzer IV Ausf.B 'Panther II', armed with a high-velocity 88 mm L/71 gun, was a formidable opponent but had most of its armour protection on the frontal arc. His own tank was at least as well protected and had the benefit of the tungsten-cored AP shot which the Germans could not use because of a shortage of tungsten. He reversed the tank back into the lane, then waited for the rest of his troop to join him. They still had a couple of miles to go to their destination on the shore.

From the little Auster, bouncing through the disturbed air near the coast, the view revealed by the dawning light was spectacular. The invasion fleet was laid out below them. The observer had been told that nearly seven thousand vessels were involved, in more than fifty separate convoys, and he could well believe it. The minesweepers were closest to the shore, carrying out their unglamorous but vital and hazardous work to clear the way for the landing ships. Behind them came destroyers, ready to protect them from attack. Next came the huge variety of landing craft, most loaded with troops, tanks, guns and supplies, some fitted with rockets – the LCT (R) – or guns for shore bombardment (LCG) or, for AA defence (LCF), a few festooned with radar and wireless aerials for their fighter direction role. MAC ships further out were a hive of activity as the peculiar-looking new helicopters shuttled to and fro, transporting Marines and supplies. Moored parallel to the coast were the big ships, battleships and cruisers, guns ready to herald the frontal assault, surrounded by AA frigates. Around the perimeter of the fleet loitered more destroyers and sloops, providing a screen against submarines. The ships all moved very slowly, careful to keep their speed below four knots in order to avoid triggering the 'Oyster' pressure mines which reportedly littered the sea bed. No safe way of sweeping these had yet been devised.

High above him, the protective umbrella circled. Further out were the P-51s and the Reapers. Right overhead were the new Typhoon jets, burdened with the biggest auxiliary fuel tanks they could carry, but still forced by their short range to come and go in a regular shuttle.

The observer checked his watch and called 'here we go' to the pilot, just as the big ships erupted with fire. The long flashes from their guns were followed by billowing smoke, almost obscuring the shock waves sweeping across the surface of the sea as the battleships opened fire. *Rodney* and *Nelson* were down there, the observer knew, lobbing their one-ton shells many miles inland. They were joined by older British battleships and some American ones as well. By comparison, the fire from the cruisers passed almost without notice.

As the barrage of fire continued, the invasion force started its crawl towards the shore. First to hit the beach were the Tritons, amphibious armoured tracked carriers launched from a couple of miles offshore. Some of these were fitted with old Cromwell turrets with 25-pounder guns for suppressing enemy defences, others carried Marine Commandos which they planned to deposit just inland from the beach danger zone, to protect the armoured vehicles against Panzerfaust-armed defenders. The LCTs went next, some carrying three heavy tanks, other a larger number of smaller vehicles. Waiting further back were the bigger ships which would not approach until the shore had been secured: the LSTs, which could carry fifty tanks across oceans, and the LCI infantry carriers. As the Auster circled, the observers saw more flame and smoke erupting close to the shore as the LCT (R) vessels reached close enough to let loose their terrifying stream of over a thousand rockets, fired in just half a minute. The shoreline had by now disappeared under a pall of smoke as the first landing craft crept in. Some smoke was laid deliberately to confuse defending gunners, but much was simply the result of the devastating bombardment.

The LCT slowed as it ploughed into the beach, the ramp quickly being dropped into the shallow water. As the Churchill roared forward, a rattle of machine-gun strikes echoed through the vehicle. The commander did not need to glance at his map to know the location of the Widerstandsnester, or resistance nest; he had memorised the carefully plotted positions days before, wondering about who had collected this information and the risks that had been taken. The turret swung smoothly round and the commander peered into the periscope. Just... there! The tank's HESH shell slammed into the German bunker, flattening into a cake of HE before the base fuze detonated, the shock wave blasting the bunker's inner layer of concrete through the interior. The machine gun stopped firing.

As the Churchill growled up the beach, passing a wrecked Triton, the commander could see other armoured vehicles pouring ashore; among the first were some of Hobart's 'funnies', specialist Flails: modified Centaurs whose rotating chains thumped the sand to detonate the anti-tank mines which littered the beach. Behind them came many Covenanters, carrying their cargoes of hand-picked infantry past the deadly beach and into the interior, their task to reinforce the Triton-mounted first wave and penetrate further inland to suppress all local resistance as quickly as possible. Some of the Comet AA tanks were there too, not just to defend against aircraft but also to turn their 20 mm Polstens onto any suitable ground targets.

The Churchill lurched to a halt as it approached the crest of the low dunes behind the beach. This point was most likely to be covered by a second line of PaK guns, whose reported locations were still being pounded by the ships offshore. While waiting for the rest of his troop, the commander opened his hatch and peered behind him. The growing light revealed a remarkable scene, the water covered with ships and craft of all sizes as far as he could see. Great gouts of flame and smoke periodically came from the battleships in the distance. Closer to shore, the water around the teeming craft erupted in splashes of all sizes as the surviving defenders fought back. The noise was a continuous, mind-numbing, battering of machine gun and cannon fire punctuated by the blasts of explosions and the strange, express-train roar of heavy shells speeding overhead. The commander spotted three LCTs which had not made it ashore, victims of artillery shells or Teller mines attached to beach obstacles; they lay at odd angles, burning, and one suddenly tilted over and sank as he watched. On the beach itself lay a Churchill, a track torn off by a mine. So far, though, casualties seemed to be light; the bulk of the invasion force was getting ashore as planned.

The members of the Oversight Committee clustered tensely around the big table in the living room, now covered with maps and situation reports. A junior Intelligence Officer kept popping in and out, bringing fresh reports. Most attention, though, was focused on the first reconnaissance photographs which had begun to trickle in. One showed an extensive area of marshland, water streaked with broad, parallel lines of foam from the hovercraft. One line ended short of the land, the craft obscured by smoke. Evidently, some of the defenders had reacted quickly.

The vast array of craft and larger ships was revealed in panoramic views. Their neat arrangement was disturbed in several places as smoking, damaged ships were hauled out of station. Some had run over Oyster mines too quickly, others been hit by those coastal artillery batteries which had so far resisted suppression by airborne troops, air attack or naval gunfire. Overall, though, the big gamble appeared to be paying off.

'So far so good,' muttered Don. 'No sign of the Luftwaffe yet.'

'They'll be there,' said Peter quietly. 'We know they've been training with their new jet bombers and we think they have some new anti-ship missiles as well. They've been holding them well back, out of trouble, but they can't pass up this chance.'

Mary had been scanning one of the reports. 'The armoured units landed by hovercraft have met little resistance; that tactic seems to have been a complete surprise – it was definitely worth switching the landing grounds around to give the British forces a crack at the Cotentin Peninsula. Key points along the Route Nationale 13 to Cherbourg, at Carentan, St Mère-Église and Montebourg, have already been secured. And the beaches to the east of the Vire, with the restricted exits, were taken from the rear. They're now just waiting for the reinforcements from the beaches before moving on Cherbourg.'

Don felt a shiver of goosebumps. He remembered the terrible slaughter at Omaha Beach as the American V Corps landed head-on into strong defences, and the smaller but equally ferocious and bloody struggles over the causeways leading from Utah.

Geoffrey grunted. 'There have been some losses in local tank battles, though. Those Panzers are waking up. It's a close match between the Churchill Two and the Panther, but the APDS shot should give our boys the edge. A bigger problem will be the number of those PaK eighty-eights they have. Our tanks will have to stay on the offensive, which means driving into the sights of their guns. We tried to plot the positions of the PaK units but of course they'll be moving into different locations now, the first our boys are likely to know about them is when they open fire.'

'How are the Americans doing?' asked Don.

Geoffrey looked up from the papers he had been studying. 'Not bad. They've taken some losses but are getting ashore. We'll just have to wait and see how the new Pershing tank acquits itself though – the cavalry have had little time to get it ready.'

Charles picked up another paper. 'The coasts of Europe are being blanketed by 'Window' to confuse the radar stations which we didn't attack, every wireless communication station we could identify has been bombed or jammed and the decoy raids have all gone in on schedule. Let's hope those units don't get carried away by success and forget they have to pull back before their supplies run out.'

'What's the latest weather forecast look like?' This had been the object of more than usually obsessive study over the past few weeks, nearly leading to collective heart failure during the savage storm which had only ended at the beginning of the previous week.

'Looks good,' said Mary, 'calm seas still being forecast for the next few days.'

'Any reports of German reinforcements being brought up?' Don asked.

'Not yet,' Charles responded, 'I expect they're still trying to sort out the decoys from the real invasion. That shouldn't take them long, though, then we can expect to see the first organised resistance.'

'Every hour counts,' muttered Don. 'A successful landing is only the first step. Sustaining the invasion will be a long, hard, grind.'

'Radar contact; hostile planes approaching!' The Commander turned to the indicated direction, binoculars reflexively sweeping the sky even though he knew that it would be some time before the bogeys were within visual range. Most of the day had passed, so far with little Luftwaffe activity; a few Arado 234 recce jets, some of which had succeeded in evading the watchful Typhoons. The LCT, not the most glamorous of warships, had been heavily modified to act as a fighter direction ship, a task betrayed by the massive radar aerials. A new Allied IFF system was being tried for the first time in action, and it was working well in distinguishing the hostile aircraft from the swarm of Allied planes overhead.

The Commander was expecting trouble. By now, the Germans should have identified the main invasion force and readied their first strike. A stream of information was relayed to him from the Control Centre: several aircraft, coming fast from the east. The outer screen of Reapers had already been vectored on to them, but it was clear they would only have a fleeting chance of interception, on a hazardous collision course; the attackers were obviously jets, travelling too fast to be caught in a tail chase. The P-51s would do no better; only the Typhoons could match their speed.

The Control Centre was dark and stuffy, the controllers' attention fixed on the green dots and lines on the radar screens. The Commander looked over their shoulders, noted that there were only nine aircraft, still ten miles away. A Reaper, identified by its IFF return, approached the first jet head-on. The two blips merged, then broke up into many small pieces. He winced; the Reaper pilot had misjudged his attack, kept firing his guns for a fraction of a second too long. The eight survivors came on. Typhoons were now closing with them. This should be interesting, he thought.

Suddenly the green blips of the attackers multiplied as each split into two. A missile launch, this far out? He was puzzled: the bombers could not hope to control their missiles with any accuracy at such a range. His puzzlement increased when half the blips – obviously the bombers – suddenly turned through 180 degrees and retraced their course before the Typhoons could reach them. What was going on? He went back on deck, and after a few moments' searching spotted the missiles by the flares of light from their rocket motors. They came on through an intensifying barrage of AAA fire from every ship within range, but most of the fire fell behind, the directors unable to compensate for the high speed of the missiles.

A sudden brilliant flash in the sky signalled a lucky hit, but seven missiles came on. The Lieutenant-Commander watched, fascinated, as each missile's course diverged and they began to dive towards the invasion fleet. They were huge, he saw now, with stub wings and rounded noses. Rounded? The horrible truth suddenly dawned: those were radomes – the missiles were radar guided! He swore suddenly as they plunged unerringly towards their targets and vanished from view almost simultaneously. He held his breath, then groaned quietly as a seven massive explosions ripped through the fleet, billowing clouds of red-tinged smoke rapidly towering overhead. Seven vessels had been hit, and badly by the look of it. He turned back to the Control Centre. The Typhoons would have to be reinforced, he decided. Some should be stationed further out so they could reach the missile carriers before they could launch. Others would be held close in and ordered to intercept the missiles – if they could. This invasion was suddenly beginning to look costly, he reflected. He just had to hope that the Germans didn't have too many of those missiles.

The burning ships provided convenient beacons in the night sky as the S-boote crept slowly forward, anxious to make no noise or wash which might be detected by the escorts lurking around the teeming shipping lanes. The Kapitänleutnant had only a few of the fast torpedo boats in his Flotilla, after days and nights of intensive bombing of their Cherbourg base, but each was carrying two torpedoes in their tubes with two more reloads, set for shallow running to ensure that they did not pass beneath the shallow-draft LCTs.

The Flotilla had approached from the land, hoping to confuse the radar on the defending ships, but were now entering the danger area. The silhouettes of ships were visible against the glowing sky and the Kapitänleutnant assessed their size and calculated the range. About three thousand metres. Suddenly, a searchlight speared out nearby, swept over the sea, passed over, swung back and caught one of the Flotilla. The Kapitänleutnant screamed an order and the S-boot surged forward as the supercharged diesels roared. To either side he could see the other four boats leaving plumes of spray as they raced towards the targets. Two and a half thousand metres, he thought – nearly there. Behind them, the destroyer which had spotted them was turning to give chase, but could not hope to catch the 40-knot boats; they were not called Schnellboote for nothing! Guns flashed and the feared thumping of the 57mm Bofors pursued them. The boats snaked and swerved to throw off the aim but pressed on, ever closer.

Two thousand metres! He checked his line on the nearest ship and gave the order. The two torpedoes lanced forward into the night but the Kapitänleutnant did not stay to watch their course; his boat heeled round in a tight curve and headed for the masking protection of the shore. Behind him, one of his Flotilla flashed into flame and shuddered to a halt. No time to stop – the Royal Navy would have to pick up any survivors. The S-boote turned again onto a reverse parallel course with the destroyer, slowed to a crawl. The crew held their breath. Suddenly, booming explosions reverberated across the sea and two – no, three – ships staggered under the impact of the torpedo strikes.

Half an hour later, the remaining S-boote slowly accelerated away from the battleground back to their base, their task completed. Their low silhouettes and the proximity of the land had enabled them to escape. As they steadied on a course back to Cherbourg, the Kapitänleutnant began to relax, and congratulated himself on a difficult task, well executed. It was almost his last thought. He stared at his huge shadow, suddenly projected onto the sea in front of him, and just had time to realise that they had not escaped, after all, before the torrent of cannon and machine gun fire from the radar and Leigh-light equipped Hereford tore his boat to pieces.

The Kapitän of the U-boot saw the flames thought his periscope and grimaced as he guessed their source. It had been hard enough reaching this point, given the tremendous efforts made by the Allies to stop them. Constant bombing of their pens by the massive 'earthquake' radio-controlled 5,000 kg bombs, nightly minelaying by the RAF in the approach channels to their bases, intensive day-and-night anti-submarine patrols by warships and aircraft; the pressure was never-ending. This was especially bad over the past few weeks, with the Allies determined to block any U-Boote trying to interfere with the invasion. Even the small and sophisticated new Type XI coastal submarines like his own, equipped with Schnorkels as well as powerful motors and massive batteries for high underwater speed and endurance, were frequently trapped and sunk. He turned back to focus on the burning ships on the horizon. One attack, then out – if he was lucky.

The Panzer Lehr Division Major grappled to control his impatience and frustration as his tank company had to pause yet again to clear away a tangle of vehicles and trees chopped down to block the roadways. There would be an accounting, he thought grimly, with these 'Free French of the Interior' once the invasion had been thrown back into the sea. Once the bulk of the blockage had been shifted he waved on his tanks, the Panthers grinding they way over and through, clearing the path for the support vehicles following on behind. The Major sat back as his command car roared forward once again, checking his map and calculating distances and times.

It had taken most of the day for OKW to sort out all of the information flowing in about heavy raids on Italy, Denmark, Southern France and the Pas-de-Calais, and identify the Normandy invasion as the real thing. Late in the afternoon, von Rundstedt had ordered his reserve Panzer units into action. They had made good progress through the night but dawn had broken and they still had thirty kilometers to go to reach the nearest of the landing sites. He gritted his teeth; the Allies had had a virtually uninterrupted twenty-four hours to consolidate their landings. The small tank units spread along the coastline had proved no match for the quantity of armour the Allies had been able to put ashore; the huge 'hovercraft' had proved a most unwelcome surprise, bypassing immediately many defences which it had been calculated could hold out for days.

He looked back and grimaced at the long plume of dust thrown up by the churning tracks of the Panzers, then he looked round at the sky. They would not have long to wait, he knew.

Ten minutes later, as they were passing through an apparently deserted village, the first deadly shapes appeared over the rooftops, resolving rapidly into the expected formation of fighter-bombers. The USAAF P-47s paused for a moment to line up then swept in, wing guns blazing. His driver hauled the vulnerable command car off the road and down a side street, seeking cover. Behind them, the usual chaos of battle; the roaring of tank and aircraft engines, the rapid tearing noise of the planes' guns, the deeper hammering of the automatic FlaK, the explosions as bombs and rockets detonated, shock waves sweeping through the streets, blowing in windows and doors and shaking the command car.

The attack lasted for only a few minutes, although it seemed much longer. The command car gingerly nosed back into the main street. At first the Major could see little through the smoke and flames. As the fresh breeze cleared the air, he saw wrecked houses on either side of the road, one tank blown sideways by a close bomb hit. Then hatches started popping open on the other tanks as the crews emerged to check the damage. A quick roll call showed only the one tank lost to a bomb; it would take more than heavy machine guns to penetrate a Panzer IV's armour. Furthermore, the crews of the armoured Flakpanzers, with twin 30 mm MK 103 cannon, claimed two aircraft destroyed. His satisfaction was soon diminished, however, as news came from the rear of his column. Fuel tankers and other unarmoured support vehicles had been massively hit. The Major ordered the Panzers forward again with a heavier heart. He had his tanks, all right, but little chance of refuelling or rearming them. They had enough for one battle, then would have to pull back or abandon their vehicles. Still, they had no choice but to go on; the invasion must be thrown back!

The landing beaches were the site of intense but organised activity. The construction of complex artificial harbours had been rejected in favour of building more landing ships, capable of depositing their cargoes directly onto the beach. A steady shuttle of these built up piles of supplies, which an ant-like procession of vehicles moved to storage areas further inland. Each landing zone had some partial protection from the worst of the weather provided by a screen of 'Corncob' blockships forming curved 'Gooseberry' breakwaters. Within the sheltered area were some Lobnitz floating pontoons – 'Whales' – which provided pierheads for conventional ships to disembark their troops and supplies. The landing grounds provided diffuse radar returns so had so far proved difficult targets for the big German long-range guided missiles, and several concentric rings of light and medium AA guns on flak pontoons moored by the Gooseberries deterred a closer approach. However, the topmasts of several ships indicting the position of wrecks further out to sea provided a silent demonstration of the hazards of approaching the coasts.

Inland, the Allied consolidation of the beachhead was progressing more or less to plan. Companies and regiments were being formed up (with some adjustment for the gaps left by the men and cargoes which had failed to make it) and moved out to join the steadily-moving front line, an ill-defined area disputed by groups of infantry and the occasional small armoured units; the bocage was not a country suited to the evolution of major formations. The Allied High Command was hopeful that Caen and Cherbourg would fall into their hands with little delay.

Lt General Karl-Wilhelm von Schlieben, the commander of Fortress Cherbourg, glared down from his considerable 1.9 metre height at his subordinates, his expression grim. He let them stew for a few moments before speaking, reflecting that most of them had grown too soft on the comforts of static garrison duty in this hospitable land. He had been astonished but grateful to be hauled unceremoniously away from the Eastern Front, where he had expected to stay for some months before reassignment. His feeling of gratitude did not last long. In just four days since the Allied landing, the powerful British armoured forces, supported by the ever-present fighter-bombers, had smashed through his weak garrison divisions, leaving the remains to be mopped up by the infantry units following on behind. They were now probing his defence perimeter, less than ten kilometres from the city. Meanwhile the remote coastal batteries had been knocked out by pinpoint bombing raids using those massive, concrete-piercing guided bombs, while the immediate defences of the port were being heavily shelled by battleships. His position was hopeless, he knew, but his orders were clear: Hitler had ordered the defending troops to fight to the last bullet to give time for port facilities to be demolished. It was highly unlikely that this could be achieved.

His officers shuffled uncomfortably. Time for them to receive their orders. One thing he was sure of: they would not like them.

The clean roar of the Hercules engines was music to the ears of the ground crews tending the new Brigands. The RAF corporal studied them in satisfaction as they lined-up for takeoff. The planes were bristling with sixteen rockets, eight double-stacked under each wing, waiting their turn to be called up to the 'cab rank', ready to pounce on the slightest sign of resistance at the request of the Forward Air Controllers riding with the leading army units or patrolling the skies in AOP Austers. The tempo had been intense and unrelenting for four days now, the Allies desperate to keep the Germans reeling, giving them no time to organize a defence line before they were through it and hitting them again. Very much like the Blitzkrieg which led to the fall of France in 1940, their Squadron Leader had said, only this time the Germans were on the receiving end.

As the roar rose to a howl and the fighter-bombers accelerated along the makeshift runway hacked rapidly out of the ground by engineers, the corporal cursed the swirling dust for the thousandth time. It got everywhere, considerably multiplying the maintenance required for guns and engines. And into the food and drink as well, he thought glumly.

Three days later the first Allied troops stood on top of the Forte du Roule, on a steep cliff overlooking Cherbourg. The massively constructed fortress, which had proved such an obstacle to the Allies in Don's time, had been hit by a succession of super-heavy, radio-controlled, armour-piercing bombs and now stood cratered and derelict, a straggle of traumatised survivors being led away. From this vantage point the soldiers looked down on the great port city, the view obscured by the smoke from many fires. Much of the firepower of the Allied fleet had been focused on capturing Cherbourg as quickly as possible and a new weapon was being tried; proximity-fuzed shrapnel shells which burst over the targets, showering them with high-velocity steel balls. These were flaying the German units trying to carry out their demolition orders, without significantly damaging the port facilities. Small-arms fire could be heard in the distance where infantry units were working their way into the city in a race against time to seize the port intact.

One week after the invasion, the American tank crews were still learning the foibles of their new Pershing heavy tanks and the best way of dealing with them. Their confidence had been rising steadily following some hard-fought victories against the Panther tanks, with few casualties suffered in return. The main problem was the need for constant maintenance to keep the under-developed vehicles on the road.

A smell of coffee drifted across the laager as the tankers awoke, crawling from underneath the tarpaulins stretched from the side of their vehicles, cursing at the attentions of the mosquitoes which seemed immune to the deterrent creams.

The lieutenant grinned wryly at his men, whom he had got to know very well in a week of hard fighting.

'OK, listen up. This morning we're moving in support of an attack to encircle Caen from the east. We expect the Krauts will be kind enough to present us with lots of targets, since there's a Panzer Division known to be in the area. We will have Thunderbolts on immediate call, as usual.'

The Feldwebel peered through the grass stalks fringing the ditch at the line of vehicles some 300 metres away. His men to either side of him were, he knew, almost invisible under their camouflage of netting and vegetation; certainly enough to fool the observation planes which had been cruising overhead, looking for PaK guns. The Feldwebel had much experience of the Eastern Front and had chosen the ambush with care; the distant road was, for once, exposed to the side instead of being obscured by banks and hedges. The view was perfect.

He grunted in satisfaction as the lead Pershing jerked to a halt. Its commander had spotted the line of badly-filled holes which crossed the road and instantly identified them as mines. In fact, there were no mines there but the ruse was having the desired effect, as the following vehicles bunched up behind the lead tank and stopped. Perfect!

'Los!' He shouted, and the men beside him pressed their firing buttons. Like a covey of rocket-propelled game birds, the missiles roared into the air, wires trailing behind them. Their trajectories gradually dropped, then steadied as they were gathered into the sights and steering commenced. The Feldwebel held his breath and watched, fascinated, as the dots of fire streaked towards the unsuspecting vehicles. The road suddenly flashed into flame and smoke as the hollow-charge warheads struck home. An orderly queue of tanks was transformed in a few seconds into chaos as vehicles burned and exploded. The Feldwebel grinned in satisfaction and signalled his men to retreat rapidly along their pre-arranged route. The ditch would shortly be a very unhealthy place to be.

To the south-west of Caen a Canadian artillery battery was awaiting the order to commence firing in support of the planned envelopment of the town. Despite the usual breakfast grumbling about the boiled Compo tea, made from heavily chlorinated water, and the boring Compo rations, the men felt the tension coiling inside them as they waited to hear from their Forward Observation Officer located at an Observation Point overlooking the planned battlefield.

They had moved into their pre-planned location with some difficulty only the night before, the light of the waning moon unable to help much through the overcast sky. Now they were still, with no vehicle movement permitted; signs reading 'dust means death!' had been erected; their German opposite numbers would be alert for any signs of a target.

The FOO scanned the distant fields from his location within the roof of an old barn. After checking his bulky radio, he had spent much of the night positioning sandbags around his OP. Nothing was moving in the distance, but he could hear the roar of engines from just behind him as the Churchills rumbled forwards preceded by a screen of infantry, now cast much wider to counter the threat of the new guided anti-tank missiles. Dust rose from the tanks and as expected it wasn't long before the first 'Moaning Minnies' came in; the wailing mortar shells causing the troops to drop flat before their detonations erupted around the area. The FOO regarded the blasts with professional interest; they were not big enough to come from the biggest of the Nebelwerfer, so were probably from the 15 cm version, which had a range of just over 7,000 yards; well within reach of his 25-pounder troop. He scanned the horizon more intently, searching for signs of activity. In the distance, dust was rising.

The observer in the Auster looked through his binoculars and whistled through his teeth. 'Looks like an entire Panzer Division is on the move – must be trying to stop us from surrounding Caen. He switched on his microphone to send a warning, but died even as he drew breath to speak.

The pilot of the Fw 190 led his Schwarm away from the tumbling wreckage of the observation plane, climbing back up to their station. The Army had planned a major battle around Caen, and the Luftwaffe had promised full support. The Allies were about to face their first major challenge.

The roaring of powerful engines and the clanking and squealing of tracks was a constant background din which the Standartenführer had learned to tune out of his consciousness. He peered through the dust, constantly aware of the risk of air attack. At least, he thought grimly, any plane which attacked him would have one of the new Flakpanzers to worry about; he turned to check that the vehicle was keeping station behind him, its two 3 cm MK 103 cannon mounted one on each side of the squat turret. Not that the fighter-bombers were much of a threat, he reflected – news from the battlefront had indicated that their rockets and bombs were too inaccurate to hit a tank, except by unlucky chance, while their 2 cm cannon and machine guns posed no threat to the thick armour. He looked with satisfaction at the massive barrel of the new high-velocity 8,8 cm L/71 gun which, along with thicker armour, distinguished the Ausf.B version of his Panther. The 2d SS Panzer Division 'Das Reich' had just finished working-up with the new vehicles and after a frustratingly slow journey towards the battlefield he was looking forwards to coming to grips with the enemy around Caen.

The bombardier in the Mosquito picked up the flare on the tail of the 2,000 pound medium-case bomb as it dropped clear of his aircraft, and nudged the joystick to ensure that it was responding to his control. The thin line of the road far below him disappeared under the long, narrow dust haze which represented the position of the armoured column, but he was only concerned with the point of the column. The other planes in this attack had been briefed to drop their bombs in a line, working back along the column. He grinned as the bomb obediently moved a fraction sideways at his command to line up precisely with the road. In a few seconds time, that Panzer division would be receiving the shock of its life.

The succession of massive detonations seemed to go on forever, the violent shock-wave from each of the instantaneously-fuzed bombs stunning the senses and tumbling vehicles too close to the explosions, while the shards of steel from the bomb casings sliced through the column. The Standartenführer's tank wasn't hit, but he was so stunned that he could barely hang on to the hatch ring; his ears rang like a bell and blood poured from his nose. Recovering slightly, he looked around him. Most of the armoured vehicles seemed to have survived, but the whole column had ground to a halt. He could see men wandering around outside their vehicles in shock, others slumped on the ground. He was too deafened to hear the roar of the Brigands as they dived in a steep line, releasing their rocket projectiles in rippling salvoes before following up with their cannon. The smaller RP explosions were hardly noticeable after the big bombs, but after the strafing run yet more of the lightly-armoured vehicles were hit. He clenched his teeth grimly and shook his head to clear it; it was essential that they pressed on! He never saw the Hereford IIs as they came in from behind, their 57 mm guns firing tungsten-cored ammunition which accurately punched through the rear armour of tank after tank. Some Fw 190s raced in too late, distracted by the aggressively-handled Brigands. Only disorganised remnants of 'Das Reich' would survive to reach the Caen battlefield.

Thirty miles away, the Canadian artillery battery was a hive of desperate activity as the gunners strove to keep up with the demands of the FOO. The day had started early with a Time-on-Target shoot at a 'Mike' target – all twenty-four guns of the regiment synchronizing their fire in order to land all the shells on the target at the same instant for maximum effect. Orders followed steadily throughout the morning with barely a pause, the quieter periods between more intense efforts being filled with harassing fire, with each of four guns of the troop firing in turn at prescribed intervals. Then orders for a concentrated effort would come from the radio operator linked to the FOO; 'Hello Foxtrot, I have an Uncle target for you.' All seventy-two guns of the Division would shift their aim to a specified grid point. 'Fire for effect, intense fire, scale ten.' The guns would fire ten rounds in two minutes, then stop and await the next command. Sometimes, the barrels of the 25-pounders became so hot that they started to glow, and a bucket chain was set up to the nearest stream, to pour water down the barrels. At other times, the gunners almost collapsed with exhaustion, ears ringing with the noise of their fire, arms aching from the effort of humping the twenty-five pound shells. Whenever possible, they took cover in the slit trenches by the guns; their position had been identified by some of the dreaded 'eighty-eights' whose supersonic-velocity time-fuzed shells gave no warning – they just exploded overhead, showering the area with fragments, instantly followed by the metallic, yowling screech of their noise catching up with them. Despite the heat generated by their efforts, the gunners all wore helmets and many had body armour; fabric-covered, moulded pieces of dense plastic, made of separate pieces dangling on shoulder straps. They knew nothing of their targets, saw no enemy except for an occasional glimpse of the intense air battle raging overhead. Their world was their guns, and they fought them until they dropped.

Over the whole of Normandy, the fighting on air, land and sea was intense. But Caen was the focus; in the skies over the old town, the Luftwaffe tussled with the RAF and USAAF, each simultaneously trying to attack the enemy's land forces while defending their own from such attacks. Piston engines and turbines competed in a strange battle of generations; and the combats did not always go the way of the fast new jets. Offshore, battleships and cruisers loosed salvo after salvo of massive shells at the behest of their airborne observers, tormenting the German troops, while fighters circled anxiously, ready to pounce on attempts to launch the new radar-guided missiles against them. On land, the Germans had the benefit of numbers, but the effectiveness of their formations was patchy in terms of quality and equipment. The battle raged furiously, both sides locked in desperate determination. It was as if each soldier knew that the future of the war, and of the postwar world, was being decided here – and now.

## CHAPTER 10 - GÖTTERDÄMMERUNG

**Summer 1943**

The mood in von Rundstedt's HQ was grim. Rommel was slumped in a chair, grey with exhaustion, his clothing creased and covered with dust. He had been touring the front in his usual fashion, racing from one crisis to another in his staff car, heedless of the danger from the prowling Jabos which had almost shot him off the road twice already.

'Cherbourg has fallen, and they have surrounded Caen.' Von Rundstedt's voice was bleak.

Rommel nodded wearily. 'They have paid heavily for it, but they can afford it. We have damaged but not broken their supply lines from England, and they are receiving reinforcements faster than we can transfer them to the area.'

'The Führer will be furious. What explanations do you have?'

Rommel shrugged. 'Many small matters, adding up to one big defeat. Too many of our divisions were of poor quality – the best troops were always being weeded out to send East. Then we couldn't get the good Panzer divisions there in time. First, the Allies bombed all of the bridges and rail junctions, aided by the partisans blowing up whatever they could. Then their Jabos constantly harassed the units whenever they tried to move.'

'This was predicted, so the Luftwaffe transferred many fighter Geschwader from Germany; why could they not deal with them?'

Rommel snorted. 'Few of them were effective. They were used to flying missions under the control of a sophisticated radar-directed home defence system. Many of them were unable to find the French airfields when they tried to transfer and crash-landed all over the place. Many more were hit by Jabos as they landed. Most of the rest were like fishes out of water without being told exactly where to fly and what to attack. They should have transferred units from Russia, they would have been better suited.'

'Even so, you cannot deny that we had far larger forces.'

'I know,' Rommel sighed, 'but they had the concentration of strength where they needed it, aided by that damned naval gunfire. The troops did their best, and are still holding Caen, but we have lost the initiative. We no longer stand any chance of pushing them back.'

'What next?'

'They seem to be content to leave Caen encircled while fresh formations are moving up to carry their advance further. When can we expect reinforcements from the East?'

Von Rundstedt grimaced. 'That's another problem. Russia has launched a heavy counter-attack, alongside the British forces there. Given the scale of their successive defeats it is amazing that they could pull together the necessary resources, but they seem to have a limitless supply of men and materials.'

'And space' agreed Rommel sourly.

'The partisans also seem to have been coordinated and probably reinforced by air, as they have stepped up their attacks on the supply lines. Furthermore, it seems that some British heavy bombers transferred to northern Russia and carried out precision attacks on bridges and other key points of the railway network. So we can't expect much help to reach us in the near future.'

Rommel got up abruptly and started pacing around the room. 'I must go and see Hitler. Now is the time to reach an agreement with the British and Americans, while we are still strong. They have nothing in common with Russia, except that they are all fighting us. If we can reach an honourable treaty with them, we can deal with the Russians. The longer we wait, the weaker our bargaining position will be.'

Von Rundstedt raised an aristocratic eyebrow. 'You know the Führer's position on that – he likes his generals to concentrate on fighting while he deals with policy and strategy.'

'I know. But if matters continue on their present course, there is a strong chance that Germany will eventually be defeated. That must not happen. He has to see reason.'

Von Rundstedt regarded his younger and rather impetuous colleague thoughtfully. 'In that case, I can only wish you good luck.'

The bottle of champagne was a rare extravagance, carefully hoarded for just such a moment. The Oversights, as Mary had taken to calling them, sprawled in the garden of their base at Kew, relaxing in the warm afternoon sunshine.

'Isn't this a bit premature?' Harold was the pessimistic one, as usual. He had been badly shaken by the loss of several fine ships to the radar-directed missiles.

'Taking all things into consideration,' drawled Charles, savouring the wine with a connoisseur's air, 'I think we are justified a modest celebration.'

'If only through pure relief,' added Don drily. The past few weeks had seen him in particular under intense strain as the crucial events unfolded across the Channel.

Mary nodded. 'Let's tick off the reasons. First and foremost, the biggest gamble of the war has paid off. We are firmly ensconced on the Continent, with acceptable losses, have seized a major port which the Germans hadn't had much time to damage, have beaten the German Army in a standup fight around Caen and are now advancing further into France. What's more, the Free French have landed in southern France, just as the Germans were pulling their forces out to send them north, and are holding on. The Russians are still, amazingly, fighting back with our support, so the Germans are on the defensive across the board. And all the time, our bombers are hitting their supply lines and key industrial plants, especially those concerned with fuel and other chemicals. Furthermore, the crippling of the Japanese navy stopped their advance very quickly and the Americans and our Commonwealth forces are now making steady progress against them. That will take a while longer but the outcome is inevitable. The war will be won, and much earlier and at far less cost than in Don's time.'

'Let's hope so. But the Germans are far from finished yet. They are also stronger than they were in my time, and Hitler will not contemplate defeat or negotiation. Now is the time when we need to get rid of him; up to now his faulty judgment has helped us, but now his stubbornness will just prolong the war and add to the cost, both human and economic.' He turned to Charles, 'more in your department, I think.'

Charles nodded, suddenly thoughtful. 'It was hard work getting anyone interested in offering support to the Schwartz Kapelle,' he said, adopting the Gestapo's name for the German resistance movement against Hitler. 'There was a general feeling that they stood no chance of success, and anyway who wants to deal with a bunch of traitors?'

Don leaned forward intently. 'This really is vital now; we have to let them know that we will negotiate an honourable peace if they get rid of Hitler.'

'Unfortunately, their idea of what constitutes honourable is rather different from ours. Our intermediaries have told us that the plotters expect Germany to retain many of her territorial gains, including Austria, Danzig – reconnected to Germany, of course – and the German-speaking part of Czechoslovakia. They feel that Germany's military successes have earned them that much, at least. And neither

Winnie nor Roosevelt will contemplate that; it was hard enough to get them to consider anything less than unconditional surrender.'

'But just think of the alternative: a Europe in ruins, divided by an iron curtain for almost half a century, with the East suffering under Russian oppression. Is that what they want to see? Some sort of deal has to be struck, or all of this will have been for nothing!'

For once, Konrad Herrman would have agreed entirely with his British opponent. He sat alone, but for his rapidly-emptying bottle of schnapps, in his small flat in Berlin, contemplating the nightmares ahead. It was still possible for Russia to be beaten, but with the attention of the Wehrmacht divided between them and the steadily advancing Allied forces in France, the chance was receding daily. He felt useless and hopeless. He thought of Stefan again, and silently began to cry.

Much later, he left his flat and stumbled into the warmth of early evening, trying to clear his head. He gave no attention to where he was walking, but his feet led him to a small park not far away, where he often sat to enjoy the sunshine. At this time, there were still many others walking about, enjoying the summer weather. This part of Berlin had not been bombed, and there was nothing to indicate that the country had been at war for four years, except that the grass of the park had been replaced with vegetable plots. He trudged along the path, heedless of the others around him. A man jostled him from behind and he stepped aside in some irritation, but the man said nothing and walked away quickly. Herrman retraced his steps to his flat, but when he put his hand in his jacket pocket for the key, he also found a folded piece of paper.

Once in his flat, he locked the door and unfolded the paper. On it was written a brief note:

'You are being watched wherever you go, but we need to speak with you privately. Please go tomorrow lunchtime to the restaurant by the park.'

Puzzled, he tore up the paper and flushed it down the toilet. Whatever this was about, he didn't want to leave any evidence which might be regarded as involving him in anything illegal. He had no intention of visiting the restaurant.

The next morning it was cloudy and colder, a fitful wind rattling the windows. He listened to the morning news. As usual, the message was upbeat, about successes on the battlefield and acts of bravery. Herrman made a wry note that the successes and actions were all local, against a wider picture of the Wehrmacht being forced back onto the defensive. One item suddenly caught his attention: the RAF had bombed Leipzig last night. His home city, where he had enjoyed the only period of happiness in his life, bringing up his young son. Without knowing why, he put on his jacket, went out and started walking aimlessly. Without planning to, he found that his steps once again took him to the park. He looked irresolutely at the restaurant then, with an irritated shrug, he walked in. He wondered briefly what his unseen SD escort would do: follow him in, or wait outside?

Rabbit featured prominently on the menu, as usual. These 'balcony pigs' were a popular source of meat and widely kept, as more traditional meats were in short supply. Herrman could of course have eaten whatever he wished, but he often liked to share the simpler food of the local people, gaining some comfort from proximity to their ordinary lives, a stark contrast to the entourage around Hitler. In a fit of frugality he ordered escalope of kohlrabi with potatoes and awaited events. His meal arrived, as tasteless as he had feared, and was dutifully eaten. Afterwards, he lit a cigarette and waited. Nothing happened, so he headed towards the toilet at the rear of the restaurant, feeling that he had wasted his time. As he came out, a man was waiting to come in. He spoke in an urgent murmur.

'Please go through the kitchen and out of the door at the back – we will distract your escort.'

To his own surprise, Herrman found himself walking through the kitchen, ignoring the puzzled looks of the staff, and out to the street. An official-looking car was waiting, its engine running. The door opened and he stepped in. There was a man in the back as well as the driver; he looked vaguely familiar.

'Good afternoon, Professor Herrman. I trust you enjoyed your lunch?'

Herrman just looked at him in silence, feeling weirdly detached from events, as if he were sitting back and watching himself in the same way as he watched others.

'We have met before,' the man said, 'my name is Hans Oster. There are some friends I would like you to meet.'

The car drove to a house in a quiet suburb in an area with which Herrman was unfamiliar. Inside, the walls were panelled with dark wood, the room he was shown into was filled with well-stuffed armchairs. The windows were small and closed, revealing a glimpse of a small garden. The air was filled with tobacco smoke. Several men in civilian clothes stood up as he walked in, and Oster made introductions:

'Field Marshal von Witzleben, General Beck, General Major Speidel, Herr Goerdeler and Herr Popitz.'

Herrman suddenly remembered who Oster was: a Brigadier General and the Head of the Central Division of Military Intelligence under Admiral Canaris. At the same instant, his increasingly erratic memory clicked into place and he realized what he was facing; the core of the German opposition to Hitler. Carl Goerdeler, he knew, was a former mayor of Leipzig, Johannes Popitz a former Prussian Minister of Finance. Speidel he had met before; he was Rommel's Chief of Staff, and Herrman remembered the curious looks he had received from him in the past. The others were traditional German officers who despised Hitler – 'the corporal', they called him – and his National Socialist Party.

'We know more about you than you might imagine,' continued Oster once they had sat down with some coffee, delivered by a silent young man whose bearing indicated a soldier. 'It is difficult to keep secrets for so many years without some people being indiscreet, allowing us to put together the pieces. You have an interesting history.'

Herrman received this in silence, his feeling of detachment still present.

'I think you will know who we are, or rather what we represent,' Oster continued. 'We are opposed to this war and most of all to Hitler and his Nazis. We want to see an honourable end to the war, before more damage is done. It is not in the interests of Germany that it should continue. We have reason to believe that you might share our views.' He paused and waited.

Herrman stirred himself, realizing that it was impossible to remain detached, that this was real, this was here and now. He spoke without considering his words. 'You are entirely correct. The war must stop as soon as possible. Otherwise the consequences for Germany will be terrible – absolutely terrible.' He felt the sudden relaxation of tension in the room and realized that the others had had been holding their breath, awaiting his response. They had taken a considerable risk, he realized, placing their future in his hands.

'So,' Oster breathed, 'the question is, what can we do about it?'

Speidel grunted. 'Rommel has been to see Hitler; he argued the case for negotiating with the British and Americans as strongly as he could. There was a blazing row. Hitler has dismissed him as disloyal and ordered him home.'

Oster turned again to Herrman. 'You are in a unique position – he listens to you like no other. What can you do to help? How can we stop this tragedy?'

'I have tried. I have warned him about so many things, but somehow events…' He found it impossible to continue, his chest constricting.

'We have had some indirect contact with the Allies,' Oster continued, 'not too encouraging so far, but at least they are listening and responding. They will not contemplate a peace with Hitler, but we think that there is a good chance that they would negotiate with us if he and his Nazi associates were no longer in command.'

Herrman's memory flicked back in time. 'That may be possible, especially if my – opponent – has encouraged them to listen. He cannot want the war to end with half of Europe under Russian control either. It will not be easy, however. They will not want to see Germany gaining anything from this war. But, believe me, even returning entirely to our nineteen-thirty-eight borders would be infinitely preferable to the alternative we are now faced with.'

The others were silent; severely shocked, Herrman realised. They had not been aware of the starkness of the choice before them.

'Then the sooner we act, the better.' Von Witzleben spoke for the first time. 'We must save what we can, while we can.'

After the meeting, Herrman was returned to a street close to his flat. He walked home in deep thought, not noticing his SD minder – stationed outside his apartment building – who had been in a state close to nervous collapse. After the altercation outside the restaurant in which he had somehow become involved, Herrman had vanished for several hours. Then SD man had been torn between reporting his disappearance and waiting in the hope that he would turn up. Now he wasn't sure what to do. If he reported the absence, he would risk severe punishment for losing his charge. On the other hand, if no-one had noticed… he decided to keep quiet and thankfully awaited his relief.

Hitler was in a bad temper at the start of the meeting, which only became worse as Herrman tried to push his arguments.

'I will NOT contemplate such a craven course of action!' He shouted, the veins on his forehead standing out. 'We have our V-weapons pounding London. We have our jet fighters hammering their bombers and we have jet bombers under test which will be uncatchable! We carry on fighting until we win!' He paced angrily around the room. 'First Rommel and now you! Am I surrounded by defeatists?'

Herrman felt his sense of hopelessness returning. It seemed so obvious to him that now was the right time to deal with the Allies, to retain as much as possible of their gains, above all to keep the Russians and their army far away from the borders of Germany. But once with Hitler, he realised that such logic stood no chance. He bowed his head, and fell silent.

Far to the east, Field Marshal von Manstein regarded the map and considered his options. The Russian attack had been held, at some cost. The two armies had fought themselves to a stalemate of exhaustion and an uneasy truce reigned as they regathered themselves and repaired the damage to their forces. Neither would be in a position to launch another attack for a while. He considered the northern sector and grimaced. The British and Canadian forces there were small in number but very well equipped, highly mobile and well-led. He had tried several times to trap them into a standing fight, hoping to wear them down with strength of numbers, but each time he had found that Russians had taken their positions, ready to die as long as they could take some Germans with them, while the British withdrew and regrouped to plan their next point of attack.

He checked the schedules for reinforcements; they had been reducing sharply as resources were diverted following the Allied landings in France. Furthermore, of those sent to him a proportion was always lost on the way or delayed by damage to the railway. He was faced with the dilemma of whether to keep his strength focused on the front line but running short of supplies, or to use ever more of his forces in protecting the supply lines, several thousands of kilometres long.

He walked away from the map and looked out of his window at the city of Perm. It was most easterly of the Russian cities he had captured. As he contemplated the barrier of the Ural Mountains drawn across his path just to the east, behind which his opponents rebuilt their strength, he forced himself to admit, for the first time, that the German Army was never going to cross them.

Churchill glowered, clearly displeased. Don gathered his determination and ploughed on.

'I know how you feel about leaving the Germans with anything, but believe me, the alternative will be much worse. If we carry on fighting until they give up, well, that isn't going to happen as long as Hitler is in charge. He will fight on to the end. Apart from the devastation that will bring to Germany, it will also cause thousands of unnecessary casualties among our own troops and airmen. And it will inevitably result in Stalin recovering his authority and his territory, and achieving communist dominance over Eastern Europe. You surely cannot want that to happen!'

'Doctor Erlang, I am well aware of the points you raise, but there are other issues at stake here. The President does not wish to deal with the Germans, and does not see Stalin as the threat that you do. Of course, I accept your word entirely about what he is like, but it is not easy for me to move Roosevelt. He is very sure of himself. Then there are the political aspects in both our countries. Can we really leave Germany as strong as it was before the war, if not more so, after fighting them for so many years and at such cost? The public would never understand.'

'They might if Hitler was overthrown, if the Nazis lost power.'

'That is a couple of very large 'ifs'. The opposition you refer to is small and powerless by comparison with the Nazi machine. I cannot see them standing any chance of staging a revolt. They would have no popular support, and the Gestapo would crush them.'

'That would depend on what they did, and how much of the army they could swing behind them. In their hearts, the German officer class must know that they cannot win this war, that its prolongation would just lead to more German defeats and suffering. And they have never had any respect for Hitler. We know that some senior and influential officers are behind this scheme.'

'Including Rommel?'

'No, whatever his disagreements over strategy, Rommel will almost certainly remain personally loyal for as long as Hitler is in power. Of course, if he were overthrown it could be a different matter.'

Churchill pondered for a while. Then he came to a decision. 'Very well, I will talk to Roosevelt and Stalin about considering an approach from Germany for peace; but only after Hitler is no longer in power.'

'That's it, then. We have hope dangled in front of us, only to see it snatched away again.'

No-one disagreed with Oster's summary. The secret meetings Herrman had continued to hold with the plotters had see-sawed in mood over the past weeks. First there was despair that Hitler was refusing to listen to reason. Then a cautious optimism that signals had been received via diplomatic channels that the Allies might be prepared to negotiate – but hopes had just been dashed again when it was made clear that they would not consider any talks while Hitler and the Nazi Party were in power.

'We cannot just sit here and do nothing, knowing what we do about the fate which awaits Germany.' Carl Goerdeler was depressed but determined. 'We must at least make preparations – get as many senior Army officers as we can on our side; plan the moves we would need to make to take over.'

'We have already done much of that. However, there is a limit; the more people we contact, the more certain it is that our activities will come to the attention of the RSHA,' von Witzleben warned.

'I know that, but time is running out. The Russians and their Allies continue to pin most our army down in the east, while in the West our forces are steadily being pushed out of France. It will soon be too late for Germany.'

Oster was thoughtful. 'If the Americans and the British are willing to negotiate, they may be willing to help us. If we can tell them where Hitler is at a given moment, one Mosquito raid should solve the problem.'

'Too risky. He moves around at short notice. And if the first attempt failed, we would never get another chance.'

Speidel was right, Herrman thought; that would not work. He looked at his empty glass of schnapps, and at the inviting bottle, then carefully and firmly put the glass down. 'We must try another way,' Herrman said. I have an idea...'

## Autumn 1943

Stadler looked concerned as he accompanied Herrman to the meeting room at the Eagle's Nest. 'I hope you know what you're doing,' he remarked, 'the Führer doesn't like such requests for meetings, particularly with all of the senior hierarchy present. It isn't like you to be so dramatic, or mysterious.'

'What I have to say is very important, and it concerns all of them. It is a message they must listen to, for the future of Germany.' Herrman felt surprisingly calm, his constant sense of detachment sustaining him.

'Very well, but I should warn you that Hitler is not as fond of you as he was. He is increasingly short-tempered these days. You had better choose your words with great care!'

In the room, Herrman looked around the faces staring at him with varying degrees of interest, curiosity and suspicion; Göring, Himmler, Goebbels, all there. Hitler glowered. 'Well, what is it?'

'Something I have remembered – well, not remembered exactly just pieced together from scraps of memory. I think it could make all the difference. It concerns a place near the Eastern Front line, not far from Perm.' He walked over to the large wall map showing all of Europe and the USSR, a red line marking the current position of the battle front. 'It's easier to show you what I'm talking about.' The Nazis walked with varying degrees of reluctance over to the map. Herrman turned to face them, waited until they were gathered round. He was acutely conscious of the view through the window behind them, autumn sunshine outside fading into a beautiful haze in the distance, the mountains looming on the horizon. He slipped a hand into his waistcoat pocket.

'Well?' Hitler said.

'Stefan,' said Herrman, and closed the circuit on the bomb which lined his waistcoat.

Stadler picked himself off the floor, covered with plaster from the ceiling, ears ringing from the blast. He looked through the wrecked doorway into the meeting room, gaping in shocked disbelief at the bloody shambles within. For once in his life, he had no idea what to do.

'It's as you predicted,' Charles reported, 'Goerdeler is the acting Chancellor, von Witzleben has assumed command of Wehrmacht. The plotters were prepared, of course, and moved very fast to seize control of communications before the Nazis woke up to the fact that they weren't going to get any more orders from on high, ever.'

Don nodded, 'It was a stroke of genius to declare Hitler's death the result of a plot within the Nazi Party and to declare martial law. By the time the Nazis began to recover from the shocks, the army was in full control.'

'How many senior Nazis have they arrested?' Mary enquired.

'Not too many; it seems that an awful lot were killed "resisting arrest". Anyway, the Germans are still fighting on all fronts but Goerdeler has asked for an armistice pending peace talks. Winnie seems to have pulled it off; Roosevelt and Stalin have agreed.'

'Sounds like a long and difficult period ahead.'

'Maybe not so hard. It seems that your opponent managed to talk some sense into the new German leadership before he died, just as you did to Churchill. The outline of a probable agreement is already taking shape. Basically, Germany will revert to its nineteen-thirty-eight borders with a few minor adjustments here and there to resolve outstanding problems. And Russia will be kept back within its border – as part of the deal, German troops will remain to keep order in the former Soviet states until they can be replaced by the Western Allies, pending free elections there. The Allies are guaranteeing their independence.'

'I'm surprised Stalin agreed to that.'

'He didn't have much option. The alternative would have been for Britain and the USA to sign a separate peace treaty, allowing Germany to concentrate on Russia.'

'Would we have done that?'

'I don't know, but Stalin was evidently convinced – probably because he would have done so in our position. Anyway, his forces were close to collapse; he really had very little bargaining power. He must be relieved still to be in charge of Russia.'

'So what happens next?'

Mary laughed. 'Next comes a walk in Kew Gardens. I just want to enjoy kicking the leaves around, now that all the tents have gone!'

## Spring 1944

Don and Mary walked slowly up the hill, enjoying the crisp and cold Alpine air, Hope chatting happily between them. It had snowed during the past week, and the mountains dazzled in the thin sunshine. The buildings had been demolished; not because of the bomb damage, but to eradicate all sign of those who had once lived here. There was one exception, added at Don's request. They walked over the level platform which marked the site of the building to a point in the centre, where a small gravestone poked above the thin covering of snow. The inscription was brief:

Professor Konrad Herrman.
Died 15 September 1943.
He gave his life so that others might live.

Don stood for a few moments before the grave, his eyes unexpectedly welling with tears. He thought back to the world they had both left far behind in the future, of the hopes and fears they had brought with them to the past. He had met Stadler, had heard much about what drove his fellow time traveller, of his growing despair.

'You made it right, in the end,' he whispered, 'you made it happen.'

Then he turned and, hand in hand with his wife and daughter, walked down towards the new world they had made between them.

# ANNEX 1: PRINCIPAL CHARACTERS

## HISTORICAL

| | |
|---|---|
| Ludwig Beck | German General, member of German resistance to Hitler |
| Walter von Brauchitsch | German Field Marshal and Army C-in-C |
| Alan Brooke | Field Marshal, Chief of General Staff |
| Neville Chamberlain | British politician, Prime Minister 1937-40 |
| Claire Chennault | American Colonel in charge of "Flying Tigers" |
| Winston Churchill | British politician, First Lord of the Admiralty and Prime Minister 1940+ |
| Karl Dönitz | German Admiral, C-in-C U-boats |
| Nikolas von Falkenhorst | German General in command of Operation Weserübung, the invasion of Norway |
| Mitsuo Fuchida | Commander, Imperial Japanese Navy |
| Eberhard Godt | German Käpitan, Dönitz' Chief of Staff |
| Joseph Goebbels | German Minister of Propaganda |
| Carl Goerdeler | leader of German opposition to Hitler |
| Hermann Göring | German Nazi, Reichsmarshall of the Luftwaffe |
| Lord Halifax | British politician, Foreign Secretary 1938-40 |
| Heinrich Himmler | German Nazi, Reichsführer-SS |
| Adolf Hitler | German Führer, head of the Nazi Party |
| Alfried Jodl | German General |
| Wilhelm Keitel | German Field Marshal |
| Ernest King | USN Admiral, Chief of Naval Operations |

| | |
|---|---|
| Gustav Kleikamp | Käpitan zur See, Captain of the "Schleswig-Holstein" |
| Takeo Kurita | Rear Admiral of the Imperial Japanese Navy |
| F L Lindemann | Lord Cherwell, Churchill's scientific adviser |
| Birger Ljungberg | Norwegian Colonel, Defence Minister in 1940 |
| Douglas MacArthur | American General, in charge of defence of Philippines |
| Erich von Manstein | German Field Marshal |
| George Marshall | US General, Army Chief of Staff |
| Joannis Metaxas | Greek General, dictator of Greece 1936-41 |
| Chuichi Nagumo | Vice-Admiral, Imperial Japanese Navy, in charge of Pearl Harbour attack |
| Johan Nygaardsvold | Norwegian politician, Prime Minister in 1940 |
| Richard O'Connor | British General, commanding in North Africa |
| Omori | Rear Admiral, Imperial Japanese Navy |
| Hans Oster | Major General, second-in-command of Abwehr |
| Jisaburo Ozawa | Vice-Admiral, Imperial Japanese Navy |
| Kim Philby | British intelligence officer, a double-agent for the USSR |
| Johannes Popitz | member of German resistance to Hitler |
| Erich Raeder | German, Grossadmiral of the Kriegsmarine |
| Erwin Rommel | German General / Field Marshal |
| Franklin D Roosevelt | US President |
| Gerd von Rundstedt | German Field Marshal |

| | |
|---|---|
| Karl-Wilhelm von Schlieben | German Lt General, defender of Cherbourg |
| Ivan Simson | Brigadier, Royal Engineers |
| Ubaldo Soddu | Italian General in command of invasion of Greece |
| Carl Spaatz | USAAF General i/c strategic bombing |
| Albert Speer | German Minister of Munitions |
| Hans Speidel | German General, Rommel's Chief of Staff, and member of German resistance to Hitler |
| Josip Stalin | Dictator of the USSR |
| Henry Tizard | British scientist, Chairman of the Aeronautical Research Committee and the Committee for the Scientific Survey of Air Defence, Rector of Imperial College, London |
| Archibald Wavell | British General/Field Marshal |
| Erwin von Witzleben | German Field Marshal, member of German resistance to Hitler |
| Isoroku Yamamoto | Admiral, Commander in Chief, Imperial Japanese Navy |

## FICTIONAL

| | |
|---|---|
| Mary Baker | British, assistant to Don Erlang |
| Blackett | British Squadron Leader in Coastal Command Intelligence |
| "Chairman" | civil servant chairing the Oversight Committee |
| "Creamed Curls" | RAF representative on Oversight Committee |
| "Diplomat" | Foreign Officer representative on Oversight Committee |
| Charles Dunning | British civil servant employed in the security services |

| | |
|---|---|
| "Elderly Cigar" | civil servant on Oversight Committee |
| Don Erlang | British historian transported from 2004 to 1934 |
| David Helmsford | British Naval Intelligence officer |
| Konrad Herrman | German historian transported from 2004 to 1934 |
| Harold Johnson | British Naval Intelligence officer |
| "Military Man" | Army representative on Oversight Committee |
| Peter Morgan | British RAF Intelligence officer |
| "Ruddy Face" | Navy representative on the Oversight Committee |
| Kurt Stadler | German SD officer |
| Swinton | British Captain in Naval Intelligence |
| Geoffrey Taylor | British Army Intelligence officer |

# ANNEX 2: GLOSSARY OF TERMS AND EQUIPMENT

The equipment mentioned in this book and listed here falls into three categories:

1. Historically accurate - shown in plain text
2. Historically accurate but for minor changes or earlier availability – *[alterations described in square brackets and italics]*
3. Substantially different from historical equipment which may have had a similar name – ***shown in bold italics [with comments in square brackets]***

## British Terms

| | |
|---|---|
| AA | Anti-Aircraft (artillery) |
| ack-ack | slang for AA |
| AEW | Aircraft Early Warning; an aircraft carrying radar to detect the approach of other aircraft *[not introduced until after WW2]* |
| Aldis lamp | naval lamp with shuttering, used for sending Morse code signals |
| AP | Armour Piercing |
| APC | Armoured Personnel Carrier *[not in wide use until after WW2]* |
| APDS | high-performance anti-tank ammunition (Armour Piercing Discarding Sabot) *[available 1940 instead of 1944]* |
| archie | slang for AA fire |
| ARV | Armoured Recovery Vehicle |
| Asdic | submarine detection equipment using echo-location (Allied Submarine Detection Investigation Committee) |
| ASV | air-to-surface vessel; radar carried by aircraft to detect ships |

| | |
|---|---|
| *Besal* | *compact self-loading .303 inch rifle using the bullpup layout [the historical Besal was an LMG, designed as a Bren alternative]* |
| Blackshirts | members of the British Union of Fascists, led by Oswald Mosley |
| boffin | slang term for scientist |
| Bofors | Swedish gun manufacturer |
| Bren Gun | adaptation of a Czech light machine gun to fire the .303 inch cartridge (from BRno and ENfield) |
| Browning | adaptation of an American machine gun to fire the .303 inch cartridge |
| canister | artillery or tank shell holding a large quantity of steel balls, for short-range defence |
| *Cavalier* | *self-propelled anti-tank gun mounting a 17-pounder gun on a Crusader chassis [the historical Cavalier was a tank]* |
| *Centaur* | *armoured recovery vehicle based on the Crusader tank [the historical Centaur was an unsuccessful prototype tank]* |
| *Churchill* | *40-45 ton battle tank with 17 pdr or 35 pdr gun [the historical Churchill was an entirely different tank]* |
| centimetric radar | high-frequency radar capable of great precision at short range |
| *Colt* | *self-loading pistol in 9x25 calibre (based on the M1911A1)* |
| *Comet* | *anti-aircraft tank mounting twin 20mm Oerlikon or Polsten cannon, based on the Crusader [the historical Comet was a tank]* |
| *Conqueror* | *self-propelled artillery gun mounting a 62 pdr gun on a Crusader chassis [the historical Conqueror was a 1950s heavy tank]* |
| Corncob | programme of blockships used to protect D-day landing beaches |

| | |
|---|---|
| *corvette* | *fast anti-submarine and anti-aircraft escort warship of 1,500 tons, armed with 4 inch, 40 mm and 20 mm guns and Squid AS mortar [historically used to describe a class of smaller and less capable escorts]* |
| *Covenanter* | *armoured personnel carrier and command car based on the Crusader tank chassis [the historical Covenanter was an unsuccessful prototype tank]* |
| *Cromwell* | *Crusader assault tank equipped with a 25-pdr gun in the turret and fitted with thicker armour [the historical Cromwell was a medium tank]* |
| *Crusader* | *18-20 ton four-man tank and the basis for a range of other armoured fighting vehicles. MkI with 2 pdr gun, MkII with 6 pdr, MkIII with 14 pdr [the historical Crusader was an early, unsuccessful tank which saw service in North Africa]* |
| Crystal Palace | huge steel and glass hall erected for the 1851 Great Exhibition |
| Dingo | light 4x4 armoured car built by Daimler |
| E-boat | Enemy boat: Allied term for German S-boot (*q.v.*) |
| EW | electronic warfare; confusing or jamming enemy radar and communications systems |
| Eyeties | slang term for Italians |
| FAC | Forward Air Controller; an officer based with ground troops who gives instructions to supporting aircraft |
| Foxer | noise-making device towed behind a ship to confuse acoustic torpedoes |
| Free French | French who remained at war with Germany, in defiance of the Vichy Government. Also known as the Fighting French |

| | |
|---|---|
| *frigate* | *warship of c.4,000 tons, armed with eight 4.7" dual-purpose guns, Bofors, Squid and torpedoes [historically this term was applied to much smaller escort vessels]* |
| Gee | radio navigation system, used by bombers |
| gen | slang term for information |
| GNAT | German Naval Acoustic Torpedo: British term for Zaunkönig (*q.v.*) |
| Gooseberries | breakwaters to protect D-day landing beaches, made from Corncobs (*q.v.*) |
| H2S | ground-mapping radar used by bombers |
| HE (1) | High Explosive |
| HE (2) | Hydrophone Effect; the sound of ship propellers detected by means of an underwater microphone |
| *HEDS* | *(High Explosive Discarding Sabot) high-performance anti-aircraft ammunition* |
| Hercules | aero engine built by Bristol |
| HESH | High Explosive Squash Head: a type of HE shell *[available earlier]* |
| HF/DF | high-frequency direction finding; used to locate radio sources, particularly by the RN |
| Hispano | French 20 mm aircraft cannon adopted by the RAF (HS-404) |
| huff-duff | slang for HF/DF |
| *Humber* | *6x6 armoured car, capable of taking the same turrets as the Crusader tank [the historical Humber was a 4x4 design]* |
| hydrophone | microphone designed for use underwater; used to detect the sound of propellers at a distance |
| IFF | Identification Friend or Foe: an electrical device fitted to aircraft which responds to radar signals with a coded signal to indicate that an aircraft is friendly |

| | |
|---|---|
| IRA | Irish Republican Army: an organisation dedicated to joining (British) Northern Ireland to the (independent and neutral) Irish Republic |
| Lee Enfield No.4 | standard bolt-action infantry rifle made during WW2 *[not built]* |
| Leigh light | powerful searchlight carried by British anti-submarine aircraft |
| London Naval Treaty | agreement between naval powers to restrict the size and number of warships to be built *[modification made to permit the use of 15 inch rather than 14 inch battleship guns]* |
| MAC ship | Merchant Aircraft Carrier: a bulk carrier (grain or oil) fitted with a flight deck (and sometimes a small hangar) *[available in 1940 rather than later in the war]* |
| Master Bomber | Commander of a bombing raid, who circled around the target observing where the bombs were falling and giving instructions to the incoming bomber crews; a role which could be combined with that of Pathfinder *[developed in 1940 instead of later in the war]* |
| Merlin | aero engine designed by Rolls Royce |
| MG | Machine Gun |
| MGB | Motor Gun Boat |
| ***Molins Hispano*** | ***Hispano cannon modified to fire at 1,000 rpm instead of 600 [this was developed, but not put into production]*** |
| MTB | Motor Torpedo Boat |
| OB convoys | outbound, ie from the British Isles |
| Oboe | very accurate radio navigation system, used by bombers *[developed much earlier in the war]* |
| Oerlikon | Swiss 20 mm AA gun |
| ***Osprey*** | ***air-launched, semi-active radar guided anti-ship missile*** |

| | |
|---|---|
| Pathfinder | Bomber carrying flares to mark the target for following bomber crews. Usually had particularly skilled navigators or advanced navigation aids *[implemented much earlier in the war]* |
| pdr | pounder: a measure of the size of a gun based on the nominal weight of its shell |
| *PIAT* | *shoulder-fired recoilless anti-tank gun (from Projector, Infantry, Anti-Tank) [the historical PIAT was not recoilless, had a lower performance and was available later]* |
| Polsten | 20 mm AA cannon: a simplified version of the Oerlikon |
| RT | Radio telephone |
| SAS | Special Air Service: specialist troops |
| SBS | Special Boat Section or Squadron: specialist Marine troops |
| Schmeisser | incorrect British name for the MP 38 sub-machine gun, chambered for the 9x19 mm cartridge. |
| Serrate | an airborne receiver which picked up signals from German night-fighters' radar |
| SHAEF | Supreme Headquarters of the Allied Expeditionary Force |
| *Sledgehammer* | *operation to invade N France [historically, the name was used for a planned raid on France which did not take place]* |
| *Solen* | *British submachine gun in 9x25 mm calibre (from SOLothurn and ENfield) [based on the Solothurn S1-100 SMG]* |
| sonobuoys | disposable buoys containing hydrophones and radios; dropped by aircraft and used to track submarines |
| Spandau | incorrect British name for the MG 34 and MG 42: general purpose belt-fed machine guns |

| | |
|---|---|
| | chambered for the 7.92x57 mm cartridge and notable for very high rates of fire. |
| SPATG | self-propelled anti-tank gun |
| SPG | Self-propelled gun |
| Squid | three-barrel anti-submarine mortar *[available for the start of the war]* |
| TBS | Talk Between Ships: a short-range radio |
| Treaty of Locarno | 1925 pact confirming the frontiers between Germany, France and Belgium, and the demilitarized zone of the Rhineland |
| Treaty of Versailles | 1919 agreement which ended the Great War |
| *Triton* | *amphibious armoured tracked carrier, some with gun turrets* |
| U-boat | German submarine (Unterseeboot – under sea boat) |
| Vichy Government | responsible for the part of France which Germany left unoccupied by its troops after the invasion |
| Vickers MG | standard medium machine gun throughout WW2 |
| *Vickers-Browning* | *British heavy machine gun: an adaptation of the Browning MG to take the Vickers .5 inch cartridge [curiously, the IJA did exactly that to produce the 12.7 mm Ho103 aircraft gun]* |
| VT fuze | "variable time" (proximity) fuze for AA shells |
| Washington Naval Treaty | 1922 agreement limiting the size of navies and the types of ships in them |
| Window | code word for strips of aluminium foil dropped by aircraft in order to confuse enemy radar |

**British Weapon Calibres:**

| | |
|---|---|
| 2 pdr | tank/anti-tank gun *[modified to use Bofors 40mm ammunition]* |

| | |
|---|---|
| 6 pdr | tank/anti-tank gun *[modified to use Bofors 57mm ammunition]* |
| 17 pdr | tank/anti-tank gun, 76.2 mm calibre |
| 25 pdr | artillery field gun, 88 mm calibre |
| *14 pdr* | **tank gun using a cartridge based on the 6 pdr case necked out to 76.2 mm *[equivalent to historical 75 mm, but with longer case designed for APDS]*** |
| *35 pdr* | **tank gun based on the 17 pdr case necked out to 102 mm calibre, designed for APDS** |
| *62 pdr* | **medium artillery gun firing the same 4.7 inch/120 mm shells as naval guns *[used instead of 4.5 and 5.5 inch guns]*** |
| .303 inch | rifle and machine-gun cartridge (7.7x56R mm) |
| .5 inch Vickers | heavy machine gun cartridge (12.7x81mm) |
| *3 inch* | **AA gun, using the same ammunition as the 17 pdr tank/anti-tank gun *[used instead of 3.7 inch gun]*** |
| 4 inch | naval dual-purpose gun |
| 4.7 inch | naval dual-purpose gun *[L/50 gun with 62 lb shells standardised instead of earlier 4.7 inch L/45 and later 4.5 inch guns]* |
| 7.5 inch | *[coast defence gun, taken from Cavendish class cruisers]* |
| 9.2 inch | coast defence gun |
| 15 inch | naval gun; battleship main armament |
| 16 inch | naval gun; main armament of battleships *HMS Rodney* and *Nelson* |
| 9mm Mauser Export | pistol and submachine gun cartridge (9x25 mm) **[adopted for Solen SMG and Colt pistols]** |
| 40mm Bofors | army and naval AA gun *[adopted earlier and more widely used]* |

| | |
|---|---|
| 57mm Bofors | Swedish automatic anti-aircraft gun *[historically not developed until after 1945]* |

**British Aircraft**

| | |
|---|---|
| *Albemarle* | *STOL/rough field tactical transport designed by Armstrong Whitworth with two Hercules engines, capacious fuselage with rear ramp between twin booms [historical Albemarle was an unsuccessful medium bomber]* |
| Auster | light observation aircraft |
| *Beaufighter* | *British single-Hercules-engined single seat naval fighter-bomber built by Bristol [the historical Beaufighter was a twin-engined strike fighter]* |
| *Beaufort* | *British two/three seat single engined naval torpedo/dive bomber and anti-submarine/reconnaissance aircraft, built by Bristol [the historical Beaufort was a twin-engined torpedo bomber]* |
| *Brigand* | *British fighter bomber designed by Bristol, a version of the Beaufighter without naval equipment but with extra armour [the historical Brigand was a postwar twin-engined light bomber]* |
| Blenheim | twin-engined light bomber and night-fighter designed by Bristol |
| *Hampden* | *British twin-Hercules-engined day and torpedo bomber built by Handley Page [the historical Hampden was a less powerful and versatile aircraft]* |
| *Hereford* | *version of Hampden equipped for ground attack, with twin 40mm (Mk.1) or single 57mm (Mk.2) Bofors guns [historical Hereford was a version of the Hampden with different engines)* |
| Horsa | troop-carrying glider |
| Hurricane | single engined single-seat fighter designed by Hawker *[replaced by Brigand after 1940]* |

| | |
|---|---|
| *Manchester* | *four-Merlin-engined high-altitude high-speed unarmed heavy bomber, designed by Avro [the historical aircraft was an unsuccessful twin-engined precursor to the Lancaster]* |
| Mosquito | high speed twin-engined bomber/night-fighter designed by de Havilland *[developed earlier and used more extensively]* |
| *Reaper* | *twin-Merlin-engined single-seat long range fighter and reconnaissance aircraft, built by Gloster* |
| Spitfire | single engined single-seat fighter designed by Supermarine *[earlier improvements to engine power and armament]* |
| Stringbag | nickname for Swordfish |
| Sunderland | four-engined maritime reconnaissance flying boat designed by Short Bros of Belfast *[design modified to use Bristol Hercules engines, with a longer fuselage and wings]* |
| Swordfish | Obsolete naval single-engined biplane torpedo/bomber/anti-submarine aircraft, designed by Fairey |
| *Typhoon* | *single-seat jet fighter [the historical Typhoon was a piston-engined fighter-bomber]* |
| *Warwick* | *very long range, heavy maritime reconnaissance bomber with four Hercules engines [the historical Warwick had two Centaurus engines]* |
| Wellington | twin-engined medium bomber designed by Vickers |
| Whitley | twin-engined medium bomber designed by Armstrong Whitworth |

**British & Commonwealth Ships**

| | |
|---|---|
| *Anson* | *battleship of the King George V class* |
| *Ark Royal* | *nameship of 25,000 ton aircraft carrier class [the historical class did not have angled decks]* |

| | |
|---|---|
| *Atherstone* | *Hunt class corvette [the historical Atherstone was a Hunt class destroyer]* |
| Australia | Australian heavy cruiser |
| Barham | battleship, Queen Elizabeth class |
| Berwick | heavy cruiser |
| Canberra | Australian heavy cruiser |
| Cornwall | heavy cruiser |
| Courageous | aircraft carrier, adapted from a WW1 battlecruiser |
| *Dido* | *4,000 ton frigate with eight 4.7 inch guns [the historical Dido was a 5,500 ton light cruiser with 5.25 inch guns]* |
| Eagle | aircraft carrier, adapted from an incomplete WWI battleship |
| *Frobisher* | *light aircraft carrier [converted from the historical heavy cruiser]* |
| Furious | aircraft carrier, adapted from a WW1 battlecruiser |
| Glasgow | light cruiser |
| *Hawkins* | *light aircraft carrier [converted from the historical heavy cruiser]* |
| Hood | battlecruiser *[extensively modernised before WW2]* |
| *Illustrious* | *aircraft carrier of the Ark Royal class [the historical Illustrious class differed from the Ark Royal in having an armoured deck and a smaller hangar capacity]* |
| *Inflexible* | *aircraft carrier of the Ark Royal class* |
| *Invincible* | *aircraft carrier of the Ark Royal class* |
| Jervis | destroyer |
| *King George V* | *nameship of 35,000 ton battleship class ("KGVs"), built around four older 15 inch* |

| | |
|---|---|
| | turrets *[the historical ships had new 14 inch armament and were available later]* |
| Kingston | destroyer |
| Malaya | battleship, Queen Elizabeth class |
| ***Manchester*** | ***10,000 ton light aircraft carrier based on cruiser hull [the historical Manchester was completed as a cruiser]*** |
| Nelson | battleship, sistership to *Rodney* |
| Newcastle | light cruiser |
| ***Prince of Wales*** | ***battleship of the King George V class*** |
| Queen Elizabeth | battleship, WW1 vintage |
| Renown | battlecruiser, sistership to *Repulse* |
| Repulse | battlecruiser, sistership to *Renown [modernised before WW2]* |
| Rodney | battleship, sistership to *Nelson* |
| Seawolf | S class submarine |
| Sheffield | cruiser |
| Talisman | T-class submarine |
| Tribune | T-class submarine |
| Valiant | battleship, Queen Elizabeth class |
| ***Vindictive*** | ***light aircraft carrier [converted from the historical heavy cruiser]*** |
| Warspite | battleship, Queen Elizabeth class |
| Queen Mary | British passenger liner |
| **German Terms** | |
| Abwehr | military intelligence and counter-intelligence organisation |
| Barbarossa | code name for invasion of Soviet Union |
| Befehlshaber der U-boote | U-boats Commander (Admiral Dönitz's title) |

| | |
|---|---|
| Blitzkrieg | "lightning war"; the principle of a sudden, overwhelming attack using mechanized forces in conjunction with air support |
| bodenständige | an adjective describing a fortress (stationary) army unit |
| Christbäume | Christmas tree; name given by Germans to RAF Target Indicator flare |
| Düppel | term for Window (*q.v.*) |
| Einsatzgruppen | SS extermination squads |
| Elektroboot | submarine with high underwater speed and endurance |
| Eloka | Elektronische Kampfmassnahmen: electronic countermeasures |
| Enigma | Encoding machine |
| Ente | Duck: fighter controllers' slang for a target |
| Fall Gelb | code name for the attack on France and the Benelux countries ("case yellow") |
| Fallschirmjäger | paratroops |
| FAT | pattern-running torpedo (Feder-Apparat Torpedo), aka G7a |
| Feldwebel | Sergeant |
| FHQ | Führerhauptquartier (*q.v.*) |
| Flak | abbreviation (informally adopted by the British) of Fliegerabwehrkanone; anti-aircraft gun |
| Flak 38 | 2cm automatic anti-aircraft cannon (also available in four-barrelled Flakvierling) |
| Flakpanzer | AA tank |
| Flakvisier | sighting system for anti-aircraft guns |
| Fliegerführer Atlantik | Luftwaffe commander of maritime aviation over the Atlantic |
| Fliegerkorps | air corps, typically with 300–750 aircraft |

| | |
|---|---|
| Freya | air defence radar |
| Fühlungshalter | master fighter; fighter pilot who guided attacks on Allied bombers |
| Führer | leader: title given to Hitler |
| Führerhauptquartier | (FHQ): Hitler's headquarters (there were several) |
| Führersonderzug | Hitler's special train |
| G7a | submarine torpedo |
| Gebirgsjäger | mountain troops (translation: mountain hunters) |
| Gefechsstand | command post |
| Gefreiter | Army rank, equivalent to lance-corporal |
| Geleitzugschlact | travelling convoy battle |
| Generalleutnant | Lieutenant-General |
| Generalmajor | Major-General |
| Geschwader | Luftwaffe unit equivalent to a wing (90 planes) |
| Gruppe | Luftwaffe unit equivalent to squadron |
| Gruppe Kommandeur | Group Commander; Luftwaffe rank |
| Hartkernmunition | hard (tungsten) cored AP projectile |
| Hauptman | rank equivalent to Army captain or flight-lieutenant |
| Heinrich | radio jamming, used against Gee |
| Horchdienst | radio "eavesdropping" service |
| Hornisse | SPATG using the 8,8cm AA gun in an armoured box on the Panzer III chassis. |
| Jagdpanzer | "hunting tank": a model of heavy SPATG |
| Kammhuber Line | a line of defences against night bombers |
| Kampfgeschwader | bomber unit |
| Kanalkueste | part of Channel coast between Normandy and Pas-de-Calais |
| Kanonier | gunner |

| | |
|---|---|
| Kapitän | Captain, German navy |
| Kapitänleutnant | First Lieutenant, German navy |
| Kesselschlacht | cauldron battle: one in which the enemy is surrounded |
| Kommandogerät 36 | Flak director |
| Korfu | used to detect H2S transmissions |
| Korvettenkäpitan | naval rank equivalent to Lieutenant-Commander |
| Kriegsherr | term for the Führer |
| Kriegsmarine | German Navy |
| Kurier | target (used by fighter controllers) |
| Lagebesprechung | Hitler's daily conferences to discuss the military situation |
| Leichentuch | shroud – anti-bomber tactic of using searchlights to illuminate clouds from below to reveal bombers flying above them |
| Leutnant | equivalent to second lieutenant |
| Luger | service pistol, the first to use the 9x19mm Parabellum cartridge |
| Luftwaffe | German air force |
| Luftwaffehelferin | female Luftwaffe staff |
| "Machen Sie Pauke" | order to attack (informal term used by fighter controllers) |
| Marder | self-propelled anti-tank gun (the specification varied) |
| Marine-Kurier | naval radio system sending compressed messages in short bursts to minimise the risk of detection |
| Mauser Kar 98 | standard bolt-action infantry rifle firing the 7.92x57 mm cartridge. |
| Metox | radar warning receiver; not sensitive to centimetric radar (see Naxos) |

| | |
|---|---|
| MG 131 | aircraft heavy machine gun, 13 mm calibre (Rheinmetall-Borsig) *[available earlier]* |
| MG 151/20 | aircraft cannon, 2 cm calibre, designed by Mauser |
| MK 103 | large, high-velocity aircraft and anti-aircraft cannon, 3 cm calibre (Rheinmetall-Borsig) *[available earlier]* |
| MK 108 | compact, low-velocity, fast-firing 3 cm aircraft cannon (Rheinmetall-Borsig) *[available earlier]* |
| M-Geschoss | Minengeschoss or mine shell; light weight and high capacity |
| Nachtjäger | night-fighter |
| Nachtjagdgeschwader | night-fighter unit |
| Naxos | radar warning receiver; sensitive to centimetric radar (see Metox) |
| Naxos-Z | airborne version of Naxos |
| Nebelwerfer | mortar |
| Obergruppenführer | Waffen SS rank equivalent to General |
| Oberleutnant | equivalent to first lieutenant |
| Oberst | equivalent to colonel |
| Oberstleutnant | equivalent to Lieutenant Colonel |
| OKH | High Command of the German Army (Oberkommando des Heeres) |
| OKL | High Command of the German Air Force (Oberkommando der Luftwaffe) |
| OKM | High Command of the German Navy (Oberkommando der Marine) |
| OKW | High Command of the German armed forces (Oberkommando der Wehrmacht) |
| Panzer | shortened form of Panzerkampfwagen (*q.v.*) |
| Panzeraufklärungsabteilung | armoured reconnaissance unit |

| | |
|---|---|
| Panzerbefehlswagen | armoured command vehicle |
| Panzerfaust | shoulder-fired recoilless anti-tank weapon |
| Panzergrenadiers | troops accompanying armoured units |
| Panzergruppe | armoured group |
| Panzerjäger | anti-tank self-propelled gun (translation: tank hunter) |
| Panzerkampfwagen | tank (translation: armoured battle vehicle) |
| Panzerspähwagen | armoured car |
| Panzertransportwagen | armoured transport |
| Peenemunde | research centre for rockets and projectiles |
| " Pfielgeschoss | arrow shell – long-range sub-calibre HE artillery shell |
| Personenkraftwagen | armoured personnel carrier |
| Pioneeren | pioneers – military engineers |
| Pz | abbreviation of PzKpfw (*q.v.*) |
| PzKpfw | abbreviation of Panzerkampfwagen (*q.v.*) |
| PzKpfw II | light tank |
| *PzKpfw III* | *25-30 ton battle tank with 5 cm L/60 gun (7,5 cm L/45 in later versions) [similar to the historical PzKpfw III but with thicker sloped armour and introduced instead of the historical PzKpfwIII and IV]* |
| *PzKpfw IV* | *(Panther) 40-45 ton battle tank armed with 88mm L/56 gun; Ausf.B with 88mm L/71 and extra armour [similar to the historical PzKpfwVI Panther. The historical PzKpfw IV was an earlier 25 ton tank]* |
| Reichsjägerwelle | fighter broadcast frequency |
| Rheinmetall-Borsig | armaments firm, designers of MG 131, MK 103, MK 108 |
| Rotterdamgerät | term for British H2S |

| | |
|---|---|
| RSHA | Reichssicherheitshauptamt: Reich Central Security Office |
| Rudeltaktik | tactic of attacking convoys with groups of submarines (known as "wolf packs" by the British) |
| SA | Nazi private army (Sturmabteilung: Storm Detachment) |
| S-boot | (plural S-boote): Schnellboot (fast boat) = MTB |
| Scharführer | Waffen SS rank equivalent to Sergeant |
| Schnorkel | retractable air tube enabling submarines to run their diesel engines underwater |
| Schräge Musik | "jazz or oblique music": used to describe upward-firing aircraft guns employed in attacking bombers at night |
| Schwarm | a formation of four fighter aircraft |
| Schwartz Kapelle | "Black Orchestra": Gestapo name for German resistance movement |
| Schwerpunkt | "heavy point": the main focus of effort of a military attack |
| SD | Sicherheitsdienst = Security Service: the intelligence branch of the SS |
| SdKfz 221 | 4-ton, 4-wheel armoured car, with 7.92 mm MG |
| Sichelschnitt | sickle: used to describe the curving line of attack towards the Channel ports |
| Sitzbereitschaft | cockpit readiness |
| SS | Schutzstaffeln: elite guard of Nazi Party |
| Standartenführer | Waffen-SS Colonel |
| *StG.40* | *automatic assault rifle designed around the 7.92mm Kurz (7.9x33mm) cartridge [identical to the historical StG.44 but available four years earlier]* |

| | |
|---|---|
| Stuka | term for a dive-bomber (Sturzkampfflugzeug) which became particularly associated with the Ju 87 |
| Sturmbannführer | Waffen SS rank, equivalent to Major |
| T5 | see Zaunkönig |
| Truppenwetterdienst | military weather forecasting service |
| Typhoon | code word for operation to seize Moscow |
| Untermenschen | subhumans (literally, underpeople): Nazi term for Slavs |
| Unteroffizier | army rank equivalent to Corporal |
| Waffen SS | military wing of the SS |
| Walther P38 | standard service semi-automatic pistol chambered for 9x19 mm Parabellum cartridge. |
| Walter turbine | experimental submarine propulsion system |
| Wehrmacht | armed forces (translation: defence power) |
| Weserübung | code name for the invasion of Denmark and Norway |
| Wolfram | tungsten |
| Wolfsschanze | "wolf's lair": code for the Rastenburg FHQ, East Prussia (aka Sperrkreis I) |
| Wolfsschlucht | "wolf's glen": code for the Brûly-de-Pêche FHQ, Belgium |
| Wolfsschlucht 2 | FHQ located at Margival, near Soissons, France |
| Würzburg | fighter and gun direction radar |
| Würz-Laus | feature which allows Würzburg to distinguish moving objects |
| Y-Gerät | radio navigation system for aircraft |
| xB-dienst | special section of Naval Intelligence concerned with code-breaking |
| X-Gerät | radio guidance system used for bomber navigation |

| | |
|---|---|
| Y-Gerät | radio guidance system used for bomber navigation |
| Zaunkönig | naval acoustic torpedo (sound king); also known as T5 |
| Zeremonienmeister | Master Bomber |

## German Weapon Calibres

| | |
|---|---|
| 7.92 mm | rifle and machine-gun cartridge (7.92x57 mm) |
| 7.92 mm Kurz | short cartridge of lower power for assault rifle (7.92x33 mm) |
| 9 mm Luger | pistol and submachine gun cartridge (9x19 mm) |
| 2 cm Flak 38 | light automatic AA weapon (20x138 mm) |
| 3,7 cm Flak 18 | medium automatic AA weapon (37x263 mm) |
| 5 cm Pak 38 | L/60 anti-tank gun (Tank version known as KwK 38) *[introduced earlier in place of 3.7 cm guns]* |
| *7,5 cm Pak 40* | L/45 anti-tank gun *(Tank version known as KwK 40) [both guns modified to use the same ammunition: historically they were different]* |
| 8,8 cm Flak 18 | L/56 anti-aircraft gun also used as an anti-tank and field gun. Tank version is KwK 36. |
| 8,8 cm Pak 43 | L/71 high-velocity anti-tank gun |
| 10,5 cm Flak 39 | high-velocity AA gun |
| *11cm Flak 43* | *smoothbore heavy AA gun firing fin-stabilised HE shells* |

## German Aircraft

| | |
|---|---|
| Arado 234 | twin-jet reconnaissance bomber *[in service from 1942].* |
| Bf 109 | single-engined, single-seat fighter, designed by Messerschmitt |
| Dornier 217 | twin-engined bomber |
| *Dornier 317* | *German four-engined heavy bomber [the historical Do 317 was an experimental twin-engined bomber]* |

| | |
|---|---|
| Fieseler Storch | Army co-operation and spotter |
| Focke-Wulf 187 | twin-engined single seat fighter *[historically only experimental; put into production with more powerful DB engines]* |
| Focke-Wulf 190 | single-engined single-seat fighter |
| **Heinkel He 177** | **German four-engined heavy bomber *[the historical He 177 had two double engines driving two propellors]*** |
| Heinkel He 219 | twin-engined night-fighter *[developed much earlier]* |
| Junkers Ju 52 | three-engined military transport |
| Junkers Ju 87 | single-engined two-seat dive bomber (Stuka) |
| Junkers Ju 88 | twin-engined multi-role warplane *[in service earlier]* |
| Junkers Ju 188 | refined version of the above *[in service earlier]* |
| Me 262 | Messerschmitt jet fighter *[in service earlier]* |

**German Warships**

| | |
|---|---|
| Admiral Graf Spee | German Panzerschiff: "pocket battleship" |
| Admiral Scheer | German Panzerschiff: "pocket battleship" |
| Gneisenau | German battlecruiser *[not built]* |
| Leipzig | German light cruiser |
| Lützow | German Panzerschiff: "pocket battleship" |
| Nurnberg | German light cruiser |
| Scharnhorst | German battlecruiser *[not built]* |
| Schleswig-Holstein | German battleship of pre-Great War vintage |
| Type VII | German U-boat, conventional type |
| ***Type X*** | ***German Elektroboot [the same as the historical Type XXI, but available in 1940 instead of 1945]*** |

| | |
|---|---|
| *Type XI* | *coastal version of Elektroboot [the same as the historical Type XXIII, also available years earlier]* |
| *Type XII* | *German supply submarine [the same as the historical Type XIV]* |
| U240 | Type VIIC U-boat |
| U470 | Type X Elektroboot |

## Other Nations' Terms

| | |
|---|---|
| Allison | US aero-engine firm |
| Betasom | Italian submarine unit based at Bordeaux |
| Capitano di Corvetta | Italian naval rank equivalent to Lieutenant Commander |
| Co-Prosperity Sphere | The area of SE Asia which Japan planned to bring under its control |
| H2X | American version of H2S |
| Hotchkiss | French MG used by German occupation troops in France (and also by the UK) |
| IJA | Imperial Japanese Army |
| IJN | Imperial Japanese Navy |
| Il Duce | Italian term for Mussolini, their leader |
| Katyusha | Soviet artillery rocket |
| KV-1 | Soviet heavy tank |
| Lochagos | Greek Army rank, equivalent to captain |
| Marine Nationale | French Navy |
| Maroszek | Polish anti-tank rifle |
| MAS craft | Italian light torpedo boats |
| Norden bombsight | American daylight bombsight |
| Pershing | US heavy tank with 90 mm gun *[in service earlier]* |
| Regia Aeronautica | Italian Air Force |

| | |
|---|---|
| Regia Navale | Italian Navy |
| Rodina | Russian: "Motherland" |
| sonar | American term for Asdic (SOund NAvigation and Ranging) |
| Stavka | Soviet High Command |
| T26 | Soviet light tank |
| T34 | Soviet medium tank |
| TNHP 38 | Czech light tank, used by Germans |
| USAAC | United States Army Air Corps (to which USAAF crew belonged) |
| USAAF | United States Army Air Force |
| USN | United States Navy |
| 0.5 inch Browning | American heavy machine gun (12.7 x 99 mm cartridge) |
| 1.1 inch | USN automatic AA gun (28 x 199 mm cartridge) |
| 5 inch | USN dual-purpose gun (anti-ship + anti-aircraft) |

**Other Nations' Aircraft**

| | |
|---|---|
| Aichi D3A | Japanese dive bomber |
| Aichi E13A | Japanese seaplane |
| B-17 | "Flying Fortress" USAAF heavy bomber |
| B-25 | "Mitchell" USAAF medium bomber |
| Mitsubishi A6M | IJN single-engined, single-seat fighter ("Zero") |
| Mitsubishi G3M | IJN twin-engined bomber |
| Mitsubishi G4M | IJN twin-engined bomber |
| Mustang | see P-51 |
| Nakajima B5N | IJN single-engined bomber |
| P-36 | USAAF single-engined, single-seat fighter |
| P-40 | USAAF single-engined, single-seat fighter, |

| | |
|---|---|
| P-47 | USAAF single-engined, single-seat fighter |
| P-51 | USAAF single-engined, single-seat fighter |
| PZL P11 | Polish single-engined single-seat fighter aircraft |
| Thunderbolt | see P-47 |

**Other Nations' Ships**

| | |
|---|---|
| Abukuma | IJN light cruiser |
| Akagi | IJN aircraft carrier |
| Anderson | USN destroyer, Sims class |
| Arizona | USN battleship |
| California | USN battleship |
| Chikuma | IJN heavy cruiser |
| Chokai | IJN heavy cruiser |
| De Ruyter | Dutch cruiser |
| Dunkerque | French battlecruiser, sistership to *Strasbourg* |
| Haruna | IJN battleship |
| Hiei | IJN Kongo-class battlecruiser |
| I-57 | IJN submarine |
| Ise | IJN battleship |
| Java | Dutch cruiser |
| Kaga | IJN carrier |
| Kirishima | IJN Kongo-class battlecruiser |
| Kongo | IJN battlecruiser |
| Littorio | Italian battleship |
| Marconi | class of Italian submarines |
| Mogami | IJN light cruiser |
| Musashi | IJN super-battleship, Yamato class |
| Mutsu | IJN battleship (sister to *Nagato*) |
| Nagato | IJN battleship (sister to *Mutsu*) |
| Pennsylvania | USN battleship |
| Ryoja Maru | Japanese troopship |
| Shokaku | IJN carrier |
| Soryu | IJN carrier |

| | |
|---|---|
| Strasbourg | French battlecruiser, sistership to *Dunkerque* |
| Tone | IJN heavy cruiser |
| Vittorio Veneto | Italian battleship, Littorio class |
| West Virginia | USN battleship |
| Yamato | IJN 70,000 ton super-battleship |
| Zuikako | IJN carrier |

# AFTERWORD

This book is a story written around a whole series of 'what ifs?'. The initial premise, that anyone from the present could wake up seventy years earlier, is obviously fantasy of the purest sort, but the remainder of the speculation is intended to be as realistic as the author's knowledge of World War 2 can make it.

What if the UK avoided giving that guarantee to Poland, which led to the declaration of war on Germany in 1939, which led to most of the British Army being based in France in 1940 – from which they later had to be evacuated via Dunkirk at great cost – which in turn meant that the forces the UK could send to Norway were inadequate?

What if the UK had used the few years before the war to prepare for it in a much more accurately focused manner, with improvements to inter-service cooperation in general and amphibious warfare capabilities in particular? Might this (along with the suggestion above) have resulted in the Germans being thrown out of Norway in 1940, rather than the British? If so, this would not only have enormously reduced the risk of the Arctic convoys to Russia, but would also have allowed the British to intervene directly in the fighting in northern Russia. It might also have allowed the British to defeat the Italians in North Africa before the Germans (in the form of Rommel and his Afrika Korps) came to their rescue, thereby avoiding years of expensive warfare before North Africa was finally secured.

What if the British had avoided the 1940 clash with the French fleet in Oran but had worked to recruit the French colonies to the Free French, to join the Allied cause instead? That also could have helped in securing North Africa quickly.

What if the UK had prepared more effectively for the Japanese invasion of Malaya and Singapore and provided the defences with adequate modern equipment? This would have been much more feasible if the fighting in North African ended quickly. Could the loss of these colonies have been avoided and the three and a half years of fighting in the Pacific been much shortened?

What if the Allies had focused on the invasion of Northern France rather than diverting so much military effort into the invasions of Sicily and Italy? Could D-day have happened a year earlier, and would it have succeeded against a stronger Wehrmacht?

What if the Allies did take seriously the German conspirators against Hitler, and avoided the 'unconditional surrender' demand which reportedly discouraged the opposition to Hitler and considerably toughened the resolve of the Wehrmacht to carry on fighting until the last?

There are also, of course, many matters of a more technical nature; changes which could have led to a great improvement in the capability of the Allied armed forces within the same overall level of resources and without requiring huge breakthroughs in technology (all of the proposals in the book were either developed shortly after the suggested dates, or would have been technically feasible at the time).

What if the British, who started and finished the war with some tanks of good quality but signally failed to produce anything to compete with the Panzers in between, had developed a coherent programme for a family of armoured fighting vehicle? This would include the armament for them, making earlier use of APDS technology (being developed by the French before World War 2).

What if the RAF was partly deflected from its obsession with strategic bombing and made instead to focus more on the tactical support role as well as maritime patrol? This would have resulted in earlier development of fighter-bombers and armoured twin-engined attack planes (the Brigand and Hereford in the book) as well as more long-range MP aircraft (the Warwick – rather different in the book from the historical plane).

What if the RAF had developed electronic navigation aids and other techniques for accurate night bombing at the start of the war, instead of close to the end, enabling them to attack precision targets rather than whole cities?

What if the RAF bomber fleet had focused on high-speed, unarmed strategic bombers (the Mosquito and a fictional scaled-up version in the 'Avro Manchester') instead of the relatively slow, armed heavy bombers?

What if the RAF had a long-range fighter available from the start, enabling bomber escorts to be provided as well as, for instance, interceptions over Norway? The designs were there on paper, but not implemented.

What if radar had generally been developed at an accelerated rate and used more widely, for example in airborne early warning systems?

And especially the centimetric radar able to detect submarines – and even schnorkels – with precision.

What if guided bombs and missiles had been developed and used earlier, instead of having only a minor effect on the war (and that almost entirely in German service)?

What if the Fleet Air Arm and RAF Coastal Command were provided with adequate numbers of modern aircraft (the Beaufighter, Beaufort and Warwick in the book), instead of being last in the queue for competitive planes for much of the war? This could easily have been afforded by switching production more quickly away from obsolete or obsolescent types such as the Fairy Battle, Boulton Paul Defiant, Bristol Blenheim, Hawker Hurricane (once the Battle of Britain was over) and most of the historical bombers and naval aircraft which were of little combat value and had no development potential.

What if the RN's aircraft carriers, given the benefit of more and better aircraft, had been designed for rapid handling of larger quantities of aircraft like the USN and IJN designs? The Invincibles would have lost their armoured decks, but gained in hangar capacity and the effectiveness of their aircraft complement. Angled flight decks (not actually introduced until the 1950s) would have assisted with this since they made it possible to fly off and recover planes at the same time. The book also assumes the conversion of the big old Hawkins class cruisers to light carriers suitable for accompanying cruiser forces, and the construction of some of the wartime six-inch gun cruisers as light carriers.

What if Merchant Aircraft Carriers (MAC ships) had enabled continuous air cover for convoys from the start of the war, instead of only being introduced relatively late?

What if the Royal Navy prepared more thoroughly for the submarine threat, with earlier development of the 'Squid' forward-firing mortars and their associated specialist Asdic, together with the development of a class of fast AS 'corvettes' (similar to the historical 'Hunt' class) which were built in large number, partly by limiting the number of (more expensive) fleet destroyers? Airborne AS weapons were also poor at the start of the war, and the faster development of high-resolution radar, Leigh lights, airborne depth charges and homing torpedoes would have been of great assistance.

What if the RN took the aircraft threat more seriously from the start and acquired more effective AA capability instead of being woefully ill-equipped for much of the war? This could have involved the general use of the 4 inch AA twin mounting in destroyers rather than 4.7 inch guns in low-angle mountings intended for surface engagements. The book also proposes the replacement of the rather disappointing, slow-firing 5.25 inch DP armament, used in new battleships and the historical Dido class light cruisers, with lighter and faster-firing 4.7 inch guns in twin DP mountings. In consequence, the Dido class would have become smaller and less expensive 'frigates'. More rapid acquisition of the 40 mm Bofors guns, plus encouraging Bofors to accelerate the development of their 57 mm automatic AA gun, are also proposed.

What if the RN economised considerably with the design and production of the new King George V class battleships by reusing existing 15 inch guns and turrets (by far the most costly and time-consuming element of a battleship to manufacture) instead of developing new 14 inch armament which proved extremely troublesome in service? This could have freed up resources to carry out the planned, but never implemented, upgrades to the battlecruisers *Hood* and *Repulse*, as could a decision not to modernise the old QE class battleships.

These are the simple 'what ifs'. The complex ones are concerned with Germany having equivalent foresight, and the British knowing that the Germans knew...

Germany did of course make many mistakes in World War 2, the most serious (as with Japan) being to start it! However, as the story emphasises, the key strategic errors may have been very difficult to avoid as they were tied up with the ideology and psychology of the Nazis in general and Adolf Hitler in particular.

One major German error was to allow the British Army to escape from Dunkirk by relying on the Luftwaffe to prevent this, instead of instructing the German Army to go in and capture them. However, this does not arise in this book as the British Army was kept out of France.

Leaving the UK undefeated while attacking the Soviet Union created a two front war for Germany, which ultimately led to its defeat. However, expansion to the east was always Hitler's aim; he had no particular quarrel with the UK and would (at least initially) have preferred a negotiated peace. If he believed that he had the strength to conquer the USSR and that its defeat would force the UK to negotiate (as it probably would have done), it is difficult to imagine him refraining from attack.

Hitler's second major strategic error was to reject the welcome from many of the people of Russia's subject states, who initially saw the Germans as rescuers from Stalin's oppression. Had he recruited them to his aid, he would not only have secured willing allies but also dramatically shortened the length of his Eastern Front supply lines which ran through hostile territory. However, the ingrained Nazi contempt for the Slavic people prevented this.

His third major mistake was to declare war on the USA in December 1941 when he did not have to; however, the USA was already fighting an undeclared war against the German U-boats as well as keeping the UK and the USSR supplied with vital materials and equipment, so it is hard to see how open warfare could have been avoided for very long. If it had been, the outcome of the war would have been difficult to predict.

On the more technical side, the U-boat was historically Germany's most effective weapon against the UK and it is suggested that the very expensive and strategically rather pointless heavy cruisers, battlecruisers and battleships could have been deleted in the interests of boosting U-boat development and production (although the earlier Panzerschiffe – 'pocket battleships' – and light cruisers would have been already built). However, the historical Type VII and IX submarines were primitive by comparison with the Elektroboote (actually, the Type XXI and the coastal Type XXIII, designated Types X and XI respectively in the book) which were just entering service at the end of the war. There was no technical reason why these could not have been developed much earlier. Had that happened in reality, together with earlier development of the advanced pattern-running and homing torpedoes, they could well have brought the UK starving to the negotiating table. However, in this book their effects are more or less balanced by the earlier development of RN anti-submarine technology, the MAC ships and the much more extensive deployment of long-range maritime patrol aircraft; aided of course by the retention of the British bases in the Republic of Ireland which historically were given up in 1938.

The Luftwaffe has also been criticised for focusing almost entirely on supporting army operations rather than developing a strategic bombing role (the opposite criticism to that of the RAF!) This meant that their bombers were mostly small, with limited range and bombloads, and they relied for long-range maritime patrol (important for providing convoy information to U-boats) almost entirely on small numbers of a converted airliner. A bomber/MP fleet more balanced around heavy four-engined types as well as medium twins (based on the excellent Ju 88 and its derivatives) could have served them better.

It is assumed that both the UK and Germany could have developed jet aircraft earlier if sufficient official encouragement – and resources – had been provided, but it seems doubtful that these could have had a significant effect on the outcome of the conflict as they would, to some extent, have balanced each other out.

It is also assumed that with appropriate direction the more powerful aircraft guns, like the 13 mm MG 131 and 30 mm MK 103 and MK 108, could have been introduced earlier, as could Flak developments like the 30 mm guns, smooth-bored large-calibre weapons, and guided surface-to-air missiles.

In terms of Army equipment the suggested German tank development is simplified, with one tank replacing the historical PzKpfw. III and IV (designated PzKpfw III in the book), and one larger tank, capable of mounting either version of the 88mm gun (and designated PzKpfw IV 'Panther'), replacing the actual PzKpfw. V (Panther), IV (Tiger) and 'King Tiger'.

In small arms, the late-war StG.44 was the first of the modern line of assault rifles firing cartridges intermediate in power between the pistol rounds used in SMGs and the full-power rifle/MG rounds. This concept was being explored before World War 2 and the first prototypes were actually produced in 1942, so development could have been brought forward to produce the 'StG.40' in the book.

Finally, there is one area of author's licence which I employed for obvious narrative reasons: it was Hitler's normal practice to meet his senior Nazi commanders individually rather than collectively as portrayed in the book.

Anthony G Williams

October 2004

Printed in the United Kingdom
by Lightning Source UK Ltd.
134175UK00001BA/174/A